THE

FIFTEENTH
ARTICLE

Gloria

So wonderful to know you! He is God of our yesterdays, todays, and tomorrows Linda R

ENDORSEMENTS

The Fifteenth Article is a sobering look at a future every American should pray never comes to pass.

—**Jeff Gerke**, freelance editor

The Fifteenth Article is an incredibly sophisticated thought-experiment about what our future may look like if we continue the path we currently walk. With a sophisticated imagining of a dystopian American government, Rondeau weaves a tale of deep intrigue and suspense. Fans of dystopian sci-fi will want to add this to their "to-read" list.

—**Aaron D. Gansky**, award-winning author of *The Hand of Adonai Series, The Bargain, Who is Harrison Sawyer,* and *Heart's Song: A Modern-Day Rock Romance.*

"*The Fifteenth Article* is chilling prophecy about today's culture. Its characters face deadly choices—both thrilling and challenging its readers."

—**R. E. J. Burke**, author of the *Raising Up Pharaoh* epic.

Get ready for an interesting, to say the least, and thrilling ride—make that read—when you pick Rondeau's latest novel! Carrying you through, from page to page, you'll be captured by the action and the skill of her writing. Rondeau never fails to create a setting that is alluring, and this one is no different, set in a futuristic world and new government. The tension in waiting to find out who will prevail will keep you perched straight up. I have no qualms in recommending this book to all lovers of fast-paced, political thrillers. Well done, Linda Rondeau!

—**Carole Brown**, author of the Amazon bestselling book *The Redemption of Caralynne Hayman*

This book takes the reader on a ride into the future when there is one world order and Christians have to decide whether they will stay true to their faith or suffer the consequences. The author certainly puts the reader right into the midst of all that is going on. A wonderful cast of characters that sometimes are hard to know if they can be trusted or not and a story line with lots of surprises and twists and turns kept me thoroughly engrossed from the first page to the end.

—**Ann Ellison**, author

Linda Rondeau's new book is a near-future tale of twisted morality and technology that begins with a clutch to the throat and won't let go, even after the last page.

—**Lisa Lickel**, author of *Meander Scar*

The author shows clear imagination, and the story is definitely an interesting read.

—**Ian Miller**, author

The author has evidently given much consideration and context to the present trends and circumstances that threaten such societies: the "Balkanization" or further fragmentation of the Americas and other areas of the globe; pandemic viruses and cataclysmic natural events; centralized regimes and tyrannical rule; euthanasia and population control; mass-media programming and propaganda; conflicts and war … five stars!

—**H. Kirk Rainer**, author

In *The Fifteenth Article*, Linda Rondeau creates a story world I want to explore and characters I want to know. Rondeau addresses controversial issues our world faces now and will face in the future. She crafts a story worth reading.

—**T. Tarver**, author of *Dark Eyes, Deep Eyes*

A futuristic fast-paced tale, *The Fifteenth Article*, will keep you on the edge of your seat. Rondeau knows how to grip the human heart.

—**Alice J. Wisler**, author of *Rain Song, Still Life in Shadows*, and three other novels.

A sweeping drama! Rondeau skillfully creates a realistic society on the brink of revolution in the not-too-distant future. Hope, fear, love, faith—the passions of her complex characters draw you into their intricate political intrigue until their causes become your causes.

—**Suzanne Hartmann**, author of *Peril*, the first in the *Fast Track Thriller* series

THE
FIFTEENTH
ARTICLE

LINDA WOOD RONDEAU

Elk Lake
PUBLISHING, INC.
PLYMOUTH, MASSACHUSETTS

Linda Rondeau

Cover Design: Jeff Gifford
Graphic Design: Cheryl L. Childers
Editors: Cristel Phelps, Deb Haggerty
Published in Association with The Seymour Agency

PUBLISHED BY: Elk Lake Publishing, Inc., 35 Dogwood Dr., Plymouth, MA 02360

Library Cataloging Data
Names: Rondeau, Linda Wood (Linda Wood Rondeau)
The Fifteenth Article / Linda Wood Rondeau
422 p. 23cm × 15cm (9in × 6 in.)
Description: Elk Lake Publishing, Inc. e-book edition | Elk Lake Publishing, Inc. POD paperback edition | Elk Lake Publishing, Inc. Trade paperback edition | Elk Lake Publishing, Inc. 2017.
Identifiers: ISBN-13: 978-1-946638-39-7 (e-book) | 978-1-946638-40-3 (POD) | 978-1-946638-41-0 (trade)
Key Words: Future; revolution; dystopian; thriller; one world order; prophecy; social experiment.

LCCN: 2017951347 Fiction

DEDICATION

To Steve-
My favorite history enthusiast and my best friend in life.
No matter what our future brings, I know together we will weather
any storm.

ACKNOWLEDGMENTS

No literary work is one person's effort. This book is no exception. To list everyone who encouraged me would be a book unto itself.

Special thanks to my patient and supportive husband, Steve, and to my children, who have never doubted this book would eventually come to life.

Many thanks to my agent, Julie Gwinn, and to Elk Lake Publishing, Inc. for their belief in this work.

Thanks also to my many writing friends and critique partners.

Perhaps the greatest respect and thanks must be given to our American founding fathers. Their commitment and vision for a free society was perhaps the greatest inspiration for the writing of this work. *The Fifteenth Article* is inspired by the American colonists 'thirst for life, liberty, and the pursuit of happiness.'

"In the beginning of the contest with G. Britain, when we were sensible of danger, we had daily prayers in this room for the Divine protection. Our prayers, Sir, were heard, and they were graciously answered ... And have we now forgotten this powerful friend? Or do we imagine that we no longer need His assistance? I have lived, Sir, for a long time, and the longer I live the more convincing proof I see of this truth, that God governs in the affairs of men. And if a sparrow cannot fall to the ground without His notice, how then can an empire rise without His aid? We have been assured, Sir, in the sacred writings, that 'Except the Lord build the house, they labor in vain that build it.' I firmly believe this, and I also believe that without His concurring aid we shall proceed in this political building no better than the builders of Babel."

—Benjamin Franklin's 1787 "Speech to the Convention for Forming a Constitution for the United States"

AUTHOR'S NOTE

The writing of our nation's earliest documents, the Declaration of Independence and the Constitution, were not the writings of one individual. Many of these ideas were adopted from the influence of an earlier work, the Declaration of Rights drafted by Virginia visionaries such as George Mason and Patrick Henry, who penned the original fifteenth article:

—Article XV of the Virginia Declaration of Rights

"That no free government, or the blessings of liberty, can be preserved to any people but by a firm adherence to justice, moderation, temperance, frugality, and virtue, and by frequent recurrence to fundamental principles."

—Patrick Henry, May 1776

PROLOGUE
Eternal Pathways Euthanasia Services/America Prime

A small box—but a large inheritance.

Governor Devereux handed the gift to his Second, a man esteemed as much a friend as an honest politician. Fared held the case close to his heart—a heart Devereux had learned to trust over the many years they'd been friends.

Tears streaked Fared's cheeks. "Is there no other way?"

Devereux found comfort in those tears. At least, someone in America Prime besides his daughter would mourn him. If only Congress had passed the mantle to this man instead of Edwin Rowlands, a reptilian of the worst order.

He welcomed comfort, especially by this dear friend. Devereux whispered a prayer for courage, strength to follow the Maker's plan in these troubled times. "This is my choice, my friend. I give my life freely. Please don't grieve for me." He pulled the Arabian hulk into an embrace and whispered in his ear. "Keep this gift safe. The fate of the world may very well depend upon this box."

He released his grasp and clapped Fared twice on the shoulders. "I have also left you my Renoir. Promise me you'll safeguard the painting."

Fared's face portrayed a shroud of compassion, a symbolic burial cloth, a pittance of formality to a meaningless ritual, an offering gravely appreciated. Rowlands might have been given the office, but Fared carried the burden.

The caretaker motioned all was ready. Was he? With one last breath for courage wrought from the direst of necessities, Devereux walked into Chamber Nine.

CHAPTER ONE
Sector Four/New Edinburgh

Bridget Cavanaugh sniffed the air like a deer before the fatal shot.

Plasma bursts splintered the door seconds before the Interprovincial Equalization Authority stormed the domicile, their faces hid behind visor-hinged helmets. Someone had tipped them off.

"IEA! On the floor. Now!"

Ian darted in front of her, a reckless attempt to protect. A white stream ripped the air, and he fell to the floor. If only she'd told him about the baby ... maybe he'd have been more cautious. Blood oozed from his side—a bad wound—very bad. She fought the urge to rush to him, to kiss his brow and join him among the martyred. There was an unborn life she must shield, just as Ian had tried to protect her.

The female officer pointed her weapon chest high as she shouted orders toward her partner. "Perez, check your target's pulse. If he's not dead, neutralize him. We can't take a chance he'll get feisty again."

Bridget forced her tears behind a façade of calm—a skill learned from IEA days—while Perez placed a large thumb on Ian's wrist then pricked his neck with a hypo. "Should keep him under control."

Bridget glanced toward Ian, the hypo a mixed blessing—though the sedative might slow the bleeding, he'd be of no help. She calculated the chances for escape. Slim was better than none. They'd been trained for such a raid in tangent. Ian's wound was most likely mortal. Should she attempt an escape on her own? No. As long as he breathed, she'd not leave her baby's father behind.

She focused her gaze on the officers to find something to exploit. Only one button sat over Perez's globe insignia, a common rank, whereas the female officer's uniform showed two, a team leader.

The woman officer nodded toward the table. "Perez, over there."

A familiar quality edged her voice … from a previous encounter, perhaps. When? For Bridget, the past was a haze, only her life with Ian worth remembering.

Perez recorded the requisite evidence image of the smuggled books. With one short plasma burst, charred debris filled the air like volcanic ash.

Bridget scanned the full height of the female, two inches taller than her partner. The woman sidled up next to him and stroked his back. "Nice work."

Something else about the woman echoed in Bridget's distant memory. Her walk. Like a lioness about to pounce. Yes, of course, Angelina Bartelli.

Perez swung in Bridget's direction then poised his question to his superior. "Want me to neutralize her, too?"

Bartelli lifted her visor and confirmed her identity, her hot breath an insult as she leaned in near Bridget's ear. "What do you think, Cavanaugh? Are you going to cooperate?"

Say nothing.

A deeper fear than neutralization consumed her—Da might be implicated. If the IEA proved the Highland governor's daughter and her intimate belonged to the Resistance, Congress would not hesitate to authorize a province-wide purge. Since Da's position was already shaky, the scandal would topple him for sure.

"Nothing to say in your defense?"

"You fired at a Citizen without warning, Bartelli. Typical."

"Careful, Bridget, or I might let Perez have at you."

"I have not resisted."

"Perez, didn't you see this target pull a blade when I shot McCormick?"

Perez lifted his visor and snapped his head in her direction. His brown face twitched as he leered toward his target. "Say, the word, Bartelli."

"I suppose we'd better not damage the goods. Governor Cavanaugh would be outraged."

"What?"

"Don't you recognize our governor's daughter?"

He holstered his weapon. "Now you tell me."

Bartelli patted Ian's cheek. "As for our immobilized friend, the governor would probably look the other way if we finished him off. An act of mercy. I doubt he'll live to see morning."

"Da knows about this raid?"

"Don't be so naïve, Bridget. He signed the warrant himself."

"On what grounds?"

"Conspiracy."

Da would have no part of this. Either the warrant was forged, or Da had been forced to act.

Bartelli placed her foot under Ian's arm. "Perez, help me raise this lump so I can begin the arrest protocols."

Perez raised Ian to a stand and propped him against the wall. He moaned; perhaps the hypo hadn't been strong enough. If she and Ian were to escape, she'd have to act quickly.

She remembered an impulsive Officer Bartelli, a new recruit assigned to Bridget's IEA team—she hoped as hot-headed now as she was then. Bartelli's temper was the Achilles heel upon which Bridget could depend. She hazarded a puny laugh. "Go on. Terminate us. The Reformation won't be stopped by our deaths. Bring us down, and more will rise to take our places. Your lover boy, Jimmy Kinnear, said the same thing the day he defected."

As if scripted, Bartelli clapped an open hand across Bridget's cheek. "Enough!"

Bridget positioned her body so the next baited slap would be in full view of the scanner. "So, you still love your darlin' Jimmy? Why didn't you defect with him?"

The jibe worked. Bartelli's complexion turned to crimson. "Don't be ridiculous. That was four years ago. Jimmy's a traitor—like you."

"Jimmy fights for truth."

Bartelli punched Bridget's jaw with her P-74. Nausea threatened her composure. At least the abuse had been caught by the monitor. Hope rose.

After retrieving a micro from her pouch, Bartelli clicked a sequence of codes. By the sound of her entries, Bartelli had never changed her permissions. The scantily clad EVE, the Mainframe's external virtual educator, projected. "Officer Bartelli, how may I assist you?"

"Arrest Protocols."

EVE minimized and the visor-helmeted icon, ADAM, projected. Bridget sneered. "Quite the pair, don't you think, Bartelli?"

"A necessary evil."

"They're holographic robots who dictate every move you make. The IEA is as controlled as the whole of Citizenry."

"Not control, Bridget ... order. You never could accept the concept of order. Why you quit the IEA. Too bad. You could have become the next Chief of the Highland Precinct."

She squared her shoulders while ADAM continued citing article subsections and legal statutes. "Ian McCormick, you have been found guilty of treason against the Constitutional Government ..."

Ian slumped. Perez jabbed his target in the stomach then pulled him back up against the wall. "Stay awake, you fool."

Bridget steeled herself to prepare for life without Ian, a fate worse than death. To what cause would she align herself then? The Reformation Party, Ian's cover for his resistance work, had been his passion, not hers; his mantra, "Let every man choose his own path." She had served as Ian's partner for the thrill, not the mission. What did she care for the preservation of antiquities? Smuggling artifacts to the Treasure Keepers defied the Constitutional Government. That was Bridget Cavanaugh's mission—to bring down all of Da's enemies.

Angelina minimized ADAM as she shouted at Ian's prone form. "Do you understand these charges?"

He chose discreet silence.

Obscenities flowed from Angelina's inner rage. Bridget recalled the tactic, to incite rather than subdue targets, an excuse to terminate on the spot. Processing a dead target was much less tedious—a simple click of a button, a complete delete of a life once lived, obliterated by a blip on a screen.

Bartelli lifted Ian's chin with the tip of her P-74. "I asked you if you understood the charges against you?"

He rolled to face Bridget, then shot her his secret smile, a signal he understood her plan. He met Bartelli's sneer with one of his own. In full view of the scanner, she smashed a purloined porcelain statue of St. Peter against the wall. The shards landed inches from Ian's head. "Well, Mr. McCormick, indication is immaterial. Carlos … I mean Officer Perez … will verify."

Bartelli turned toward Bridget and re-sequenced ADAM, who then spouted out the new set of arrest protocols. "Bridget Cavanaugh, you have been found guilty of conspiracy."

"The name is Bridget McCormick."

Bartelli snorted.

ADAM's hologram hiccupped before he scanned Bridget from head to toe. "Subject's identity confirmed." He beeped and chimed through the remaining protocols. When finished, Bartelli minimized him. "Bridget Cavanaugh, do you understand these charges?"

Silence, her best defense.

Bartelli put her thumbprint on the projected arrest document then hit FILE. "Doesn't matter—your guilt has already been established." She stuffed the micro into her satchel and repositioned her P-74. "Perez, wipe the blood, remove the scanner, and let's take these two to booking, so we can log out for the night." She winked. "Maybe find more enjoyable things to do."

Bridget stole a quick, deep breath. "Not so fast, Perez. Haven't you forgotten something, Officer Bartelli?"

"Do you think I'm incompetent?"

Bridget turned a welted face directly into the scanner. "It's all on record. How you shot an unarmed target without warning … the physical abuse … your unprofessional conduct with your partner.

Or did you forget you have to submit the target's domicile security images along with the arrest history—including our wee chat about Jimmy Kinnear?"

"I don't—"

Perez glanced toward the scanners. "You crossed the line, Bartelli. These two aren't worth losing our careers over. Let's blast the domicile scanner and say they escaped."

Bartelli paled with awareness. "It's too late to stop the dump into the Mainframe even if we did destroy it."

Bridget wet her lips. "If you let us go, we can fix that detail."

"Shut up, Bridget, before I decorate the walls with your brain matter. I should have known you'd pull a stunt like this."

Ian moaned his proposal. "We ... have insiders ... can alter both our scanner and ADAM's feed. Or ... didn't you notice his hiccup? Our sources ... already know... what you did."

"Why am I not surprised?" Bartelli holstered her P-74. "All right. I'll give you an hour's head start. Then I'll report you as fugitives. I'll say you must have been warned, and we found the domicile on fire when we arrived. You'd better make sure the Mainframe is doctored to corroborate our story, or you'll be terminated before you leave the sector."

As Bridget moved to Ian's side, he mouthed his devotion. "I love you, Mrs. McCormick."

Bartelli cackled. "You know, of course, every IEA officer in the province will be looking for you. You won't get far, Mr. Reformist."

Ian shrugged his shoulders. "Perhaps not."

"Perez, ignite. Bridget, your time starts now."

CHAPTER TWO
Denver Hub/Western America Outworld

Jacob disengaged his son's reconstructed solar micro. "Amelia, it's only a matter of time now. Only a matter of time." He shoved the micro to the other side of the table aware of her scowl. "I know, I know. I should put all this in the Maker's hand and quit fuming. I can't help it—I'm frightened. Not just for us. For the whole Network. Sometimes, I think we should never have defected."

Amelia lifted her apron and tucked the cleaning cloth into the waistband of her pantaloons. "You, my dear husband, worry far too much. Aren't you happy here?"

"Mark my words. If there is an ounce of truth to Michael Grafton's editorial, our new governor will have us all terminated in one sweep."

"He can't. Not even a governor is above the law, though no doubt he'll bend procedures as far as he can to suit his purposes."

"Rowlands hungers for power. You wait. He'll find a way to do us in. Our farms … that's what he wants, even if he annihilates the entire Network."

A man was supposed to provide for his family, give his wife nice things and a decent home. At least, that's what he'd promised Amelia the night he proposed. Twenty-two years later, and the best he could offer was a sod house with the same stick table he'd built after Benjamin's birth.

Jacob worked his jaw as he contemplated his lot. For Amelia's sake, he'd pretend to possess some confidence in the Maker. "Of course, I didn't get to read the entire article. The feed went dead. Third time today. I don't dare risk another hack."

Amelia set a plate of scrambled eggs in front of him. "The Network has come so far in the last ten years. Remember how hard life was when we first came here? How disorganized the outworld was? Didn't you say that Devereux considered the Network as a viable alternative state? Your dream of an independent territory is within view, Husband. Until then, at least we have plenty to eat."

He flicked off a sandworm. "If you don't mind the flavoring."

"Shush now and eat your eggs. I had to throw out the bread. Too moldy."

Mold, she calls it. Poppycock. "Why don't you call the thing what the thing is?"

"Bacteria infestation embarrasses me. I was once a medical professional. Perhaps, if I cleaned better—"

"You're sick, woman. Don't blame yourself. We're both too old to keep up with all this scrubbing … especially in this heat. Worsens every year." He glanced out the front porthole. "There was a time when evergreens covered these mountains instead of thin moss. If I only had lumber, I'd build you a proper house with good ventilation. One that didn't have to be scrubbed every day."

The same lame promise he'd made for the past twenty-two years. Why she stayed with him he'd never know, nor did he fully understand why she wouldn't agree to go back to America Prime. He shouldn't have preached on the street or riled the University by teaching an illegal religion class. Then maybe they'd have stayed in the City, enjoyed the comfort their status provided. He'd been selfish in his zeal and never gave a thought how the consequences would impact his pregnant wife. She deserved more than bacteria-laden bread, sandworms, and outworld heat.

She tweaked his cheek. "I made a vow all those years ago, 'Withersoever thou goest.' The promise still stands."

"Someday, we'll have as nice a house as Kyle Skinner. Maybe even Thomas Muldoon's. Can't match Davu's place, though. You'll have a stove instead of an ancient hearth. We'll have a sun converter to power a washing machine … and inside plumbing. No more outdoor privy for the mayor's wife. We'll have centralized air purification. You'll be toasty warm in the winter and as comfortable in the summer as a desert cactus—a house so modern even a Citizen would be envious."

"Jacob, you're fantasizing again." Amelia squeezed his hand. "You and Benjamin are all I need."

Amelia always saw through his charade, yet caressed his ego with her love. Jacob took a bite of eggs with the fork he'd whittled yesterday then shoved the plate toward Amelia. She ate less than a gnat these days. "Share this with me."

She shook her head.

His bones creaked with every step as he headed toward the kitchen cabinet. He took out a chipped china plate, flicked off another sandworm then lumbered back to the table where he scraped half the eggs onto the second plate. "No arguments. You need your strength."

Her brown eyes sparkled for a few seconds. "Fine, but I'm not hungry."

Jacob brushed a third sandworm from the table. "The desert winds carry more and more of these critters every year. The house is infested. I swear I felt one in bed last night."

"Thomas Muldoon has designed traps to be placed around the perimeter. Soon they'll be a bygone nuisance."

"In the meantime, I'll try to scrounge up a sealed container or two in the next hunt." Even he sensed the futility of his promises, such commodities as rare a find in the hunts as fresh fruit in the desert. "Or, I'll strike a bargain with Davu."

Amelia stiffened. "You'll do no such thing. Davu will demand blood in return. I'd rather do without than go to that gouger. The sandworms are harmless as long as they're not ingested. Our outworld doesn't have half the health concerns as the Sierra Province. The dust mites carry so many diseases the list fills a micro disk."

"I'll whittle us another fork tonight after we get back from the mayors' conclave. That's something I know I can produce."

"Good. I'd rather not eat with my hands like the Nomads do." She took a meager bite of her eggs. "I'll ask Mai Katakoa for a bin. She found more than she needed in the last hunt, and she owes me a favor for the house call I made when her youngest had Rat Bite fever."

Jacob took his last nibble. Normally, he'd lean back against the chair and rub his satisfied tummy. Nothing was normal about today. Nor would there ever be another normal day in the Network, not with Rowlands as governor.

"Jacob, are you sure all this worry isn't because of the mayors' conclave?"

"Thomas Muldoon thinks I worry far too much over Rowlands' appointment."

"How would that change anything? The Network has had its best crop yield ever. Soon we will be in a position to work out a trade agreement with other provinces. Any wise politician will see the benefit of a trade agreement."

"That's what Thomas says. He believes our best days are ahead."

"You disagree?"

Jacob leaned back against the chair. If not for the conclave and his brother's expected visit, he'd find a corner and nap. "The mayors are blind. They can't see that our freedoms are mere illusions. Devereux understood the economic benefit of the Network's independence. Rowlands sees our growth as a threat to a unified world government. He's worried other outworlds will follow our example."

Amelia brought the dishes to the galvanized tub, pushed down on the pressurized air pump and rinsed them off. "What I wouldn't give for an automatic dishwasher like in the old days. My mother and I sang hymns while we cleaned up the kitchen."

Jacob enveloped this beautiful woman, the love of his life, in his arms. "Well, you and I can sing while the coffee perks."

"You? You can't carry a tune."

"The Good Book says to make a joyful noise to the Lord."

"Well, then, when you sing, I expect the Maker is quite pleased."

Amelia broke free of Jacob's embrace. "I've got chores to do, and besides, Ahmed should be here soon."

Jacob stoked the fire in the hearth. "Looks like we're nearly out of kindling. Not much winter season left, though. These chilly mornings and blistering afternoons should blend into one sweltering day soon enough. Thomas Muldoon and I will have the air purification system installed by then. I promise."

He remembered his boyhood springs when the first crocus spirited Father into a gardening frenzy. Every April, Ambassador Goodayle played the gardener as he whistled with his labors. When the lilacs bloomed, the ambassador perfumed the house with bouquets. Jacob was seven when their last lilac bush died soon after the Great Tsunamis that catapulted the world into the second Dark Age.

Amelia took out her scrubbing rag from under her apron and stepped toward the table. The effort induced another coughing spell.

Please, God. Not cancer. He kissed her hand, roughened from years of gathering eggs and spreading hay for the goats, evidence of his failure as a husband. "Next hunt, I'll find lotions and perfumes. I can't do much about the dishwasher, though. If Benjamin returns before then, we'll bargain for tools and some material. Then he and I will build you a new house. You'll see."

Amelia tucked loose, gray strands into the rolled bun that graced the nape of her neck. "I don't need a new house. Scented soap would be nice, though."

Jacob took the rag from Amelia's hand and washed the table. "I'm certain Davu can find some for you."

She bristled.

"Okay. I won't go to Davu. I promise."

"The next hunt will be lucrative, Jacob. If not, the Maker will send you more students to tutor. We need nothing Davu has to offer."

"If Benjamin doesn't return, I'm afraid I'll be useless in the hunt. The nimble get first pick. An old fool like me has to glean from what's left behind."

Amelia's eyes filled with tears. "Benjamin will be released. Ahmed promised."

Seemed Ahmed kept his promises to his sister-in-law far better than her husband. Jealousy was indeed a sin, perhaps made worse when the object of such vain emotion was one's brother. "Speaking of Ahmed, he should be here soon. I offered to meet him at the landing pad. He insisted on having one of Davu's men transport him to our hut, probably an excuse to sample their newest transport line."

"The Series 456?"

"Ahmed said only America Prime's Diamond Transport Company and Davu's Transport Services own them under exclusive contracts ... not even President Schumann has one yet."

"And you didn't insist? You don't fool me for a minute. You want to see the transport for yourself."

"I heard the Series 456 can travel three times faster than a hovercraft, certainly far superior to outworld rovers. Just think. We could reach the Border Community in less than an hour." Loud bangs on the metallic door shook the hut. "There's the devil now."

"Shh. You shouldn't say such things. Not even in jest."

Jacob nuzzled her cheek. "I love you, my dearest wife. I wouldn't last a day if you left me here alone."

She surrendered a quick kiss. "Now, don't keep Ahmed waiting."

Jacob strained to slide the thick iron door open. Despite his valiant effort, his puny strength only budged the panel a few inches, barely enough room for Jacob to wedge through let alone an overweight dignitary. Jacob spat on his hands, and Amelia came to his aid. While they pushed, Ahmed assisted from outside. The panel finally inched forward enough, and Ahmed squeezed through.

Jacob stuck his head outside. "Where is it?"

Ahmed chortled.

Jacob loved many things about his brother. Not his laugh, a burr to even the deaf. Although Amelia, enamored with her one-time suitor, often said his boisterous hee-haws were as contagious as the fever. Jacob silently scolded himself. He shouldn't be so critical of Ahmed. After all, Amelia chose intelligence over ambition, and

Ahmed married the vainer of the sisters. Despite poverty, Jacob was the luckier man.

"I thought you might want to see it. I apologize. My driver sped off as soon as my feet hit the dirt."

Amelia rubbed Jacob's back. "There'll be other opportunities."

Ahmed removed his shermagh, shook off the dust and rubbed his balding head. "The driver told me Davu plans on expanding his fleet. Although, I'll wager the luxury transports will spike all the fees considerably."

Jacob nodded. "What did the huckster charge this time?"

"Two rams. Do you know what I have to go through to get one, let alone two, not to mention the difficulties in transporting a live animal? Sub-city herders are reluctant to part with any livestock. I nearly emptied my accounts."

An exaggeration to be sure. Only the privileged few, even in America Prime, could afford to purchase first generation sheep—ewe or ram. Amelia placed the coffee urn onto a burner on the stone stove. "So Davu would gouge even the Second Governor?"

"Without hesitation. I wish the government would allow you people to bank. Coins are so much easier to transport. Much more pleasant for the nose, too."

Their shared laughter eased Jacob's anxious spirit. He mourned his youth, when he and Ahmed pretended to be pirates, put a mast on Father's canoe, and dreamed of conquests—those days of innocence before the rivers fouled and polluted the soil.

Ahmed hiked up his dishdasha and sat. Jacob lowered his eyes at his brother's costume, attire Devereux overlooked—likely viewed as far too rebellious by Ahmed's new superior. "When are you going to stop thumbing your nose at the law? One of these days, you'll find yourself a guest in that fine prison you designed."

He laughed again. "City women say the Arab traditional dress becomes me. Seems ladies swarm to the rebel spirit."

"Forever the womanizer, I see."

"Devereux liked my dress preferences."

"Even though ethnic clothing has been banned for over a decade?"

"Why change so convenient a magnet? I'm meeting Rowlands later this morning. We'll soon discover his level of tolerance as well as my future with his administration if indeed I have one. He's likely to relegate me to an office in Sector Ten if he doesn't place me on his assassination list."

"Your choice of garments will be the least of your differences with Rowlands." Jacob slapped Ahmed with an affectionate tap to his shoulders. "You are a clever organizer, and your popularity with the masses will be an asset. Better Rowlands keeps you under his thumb than sets you free to be a thorn in his side. You would make a formidable adversary, especially a martyred one."

A raucous cough made both their heads turn and Jacob rushed to Amelia's side. "Sit. Please."

"I'll have plenty of rest when I die. For now, there's too much to be done." She turned in a huff and retrieved a wrapped sleeve of goat cheese from the cupboard. "The coffee has perked. Now, do the honor of serving our guest. The animals need to be fed, too." She gave Ahmed a nod of acknowledgment. "Always good to see you."

Jacob followed her movement until she vanished from his sight. He loathed himself to see her live like this—humility one thing, destitution quite another. Shouldn't a mayor be more affluent, even if he was elected because no one else wanted the job? He poured the brew into two cups and handed one to Ahmed. "Amelia's cough is much worse. She needs medicine."

"I'll see if I can finagle some for you."

"I don't want you to do anything illegal. If you're arrested and imprisoned, the Network will fare poorly without our ambassador."

"I have ways and means, Jacob. You let me worry about the legalities. Okay?"

Jacob sliced the goat cheese into three pieces, certain to give his guest the largest—he was the Second Governor after all—then set a piece aside for Amelia. "My wife is particularly fond of goat cheese, yet never serves herself any."

Ahmed chewed off a large chunk. "Excellent, as always. You married a good cook, Jacob."

Would he be willing to trade the best of America Prime for a day without Amelia? No … not even an hour. "The Maker has blessed me in many ways."

"Do you need more coffee?"

"We have enough. Davu negotiated a trade agreement with the Congo Province. We had a surplus harvest last fall."

"Not a wise move, brother. Trading without government approval is certain to start a ripple in Congress."

Outworlders had defected for freedom. Why shouldn't they have the right to trade on their own behalf? Would they willingly surrender their values for United Earth's promised protection? Why couldn't his compatriots see that a formal declaration of independence was the only certain way to preserve their freedoms? "Ahmed, we'll pay one way or another. If Congress doesn't tax the coffee with a higher tithe of our crops, then Davu will exact his own brand of usury for negotiating the agreement."

Ahmed's belly laugh filled the hut. "If outworlders could buy and sell, Davu would be the richest man in the world."

"Davu has no qualms about scraping the last breadcrumb from his under-the-table deals, although his cleverness has decreased our dependence upon charity hunts and his economics have provided many of us with luxuries we only dreamed possible."

Ahmed tapped the table. "Like furniture?"

"This table's still in good shape ... a fine work of craftsmanship, I might add. Granted, your crushed stone furniture isn't riddled with sandworms. This table serves my family well."

"I remember the day we made this table ... the day Benjamin was born. Hard to believe that was nearly twenty-one years ago."

Jacob felt no shame for his tears. Ahmed was Jacob's friend as well as a brother. "What if Benjamin never comes back? It's been two months with no word as to his welfare."

"I'm sure he's fine. Relatives are not allowed to visit ... not even Second Governors. I do have my sources, however. The last report I received, Benjamin was still alive."

"Congress should have promoted you instead of giving the governorship to Rowlands. Might have been better if Devereux waited for the assassin's blast. Then you'd have taken over until the next election."

"Charles believed he followed the Maker's plan. Though I respect his beliefs, as far as I can see, the Maker deserted this planet years ago. Devereux was a good man and a devoted friend. He asked me not to retire ... to keep my post. I said I would."

Ahmed took a sip of his coffee. "Glad Amelia made this. Yours is lethal."

"One of the few things we agree on, brother."

Ahmed's brows drooped in contemplation as he spoke. "And as for Benjamin, that's why I've come this morning. Before Devereux died, he signed Benjamin's pardon. Not even Rowlands can reverse the decision without alienating the Humanitarian Party, and he needs their support. If all goes well, Benjamin will be home by sunset."

Jacob rushed to the door and shouted into the wind. "Amelia, come inside. Great news! Benjamin is coming home!"

He grabbed a bottle of fermented grape juice, found two pewter cups and poured the excuse for wine. "Let's do this right." They clinked their cups together in celebration.

Ahmed leaned toward Jacob, his voice a near whisper as if the walls had ears. "I hear the Denver Hub alone has taken on five new defectors this week. Congress is wary of the Network's growth rate—even the Humanitarians. You can expect some swift and severe legislation in days to come. Legislation I may be powerless to stop."

Did Ahmed believe he could straddle the fence forever? "Ahmed, you're more than our ambassador. Most Network outworlders consider you a friend. Rowlands doesn't appreciate our values as Devereux did. The time will come when you must decide whose side you're on. The Good Book tells us that no man can serve two masters."

"Don't preach to me, Jacob. Your father crammed Scripture down my throat, too. Leave provincial politics to me. Worry about your own house."

Ahmed might as well have called Jacob the failure he was, dependent on his brother for everything except the air he breathed. Was there nothing of Jacob Goodayle's life worthy of comment in a history book? Was he doomed to die a misfit in both worlds?

"Well, brother, you should know as of last week, the Network has named me Mayor of the Colorado Community. So, I guess politics do concern me after all."

"What happened to Greif Henson?"

"The fever took him. His Second stepped down. A shame that one man's misfortune often gives rise to another's opportunity."

"Seems outworld leaders don't live any longer than the Constitutional Government's."

A warning? A true statement nonetheless.

"Ahmed. I will say an extra prayer for you today."

"Be sure you do so in secret. The government is aware your so-called meetings are a cover-up for religious services. You're risking an IEA sweep."

"When I first came here, the original Accord gave the outworlds autonomy as long as we held no formal religious assembly. Supposedly, the Constitutional Government grandfathered the defector's rights when they revised the Accord. How can they undo what was guaranteed?"

"Laws are open to interpretation according to who's in power. The Accord had no Constitution. Perhaps why the system failed."

"Still, the Accord did bring us out of the ashes left by our own folly."

Ahmed sighed. "Before she died, my mother predicted a time of great global turbulence. I wish she'd been wrong."

"I remember your mother. A beautiful woman. She always wore a caftan, though she was a Christ follower, a pure rebellious spirit."

Ahmed stood. "To her undoing. I have to go. I do not want to be late for my meeting with our new governor."

Amelia darted through the door. "Husband, don't give me false hope." She turned toward Ahmed. "Our Benjamin is coming home?"

"He'll be home in time for supper."

She planted a wet kiss on Ahmed's cheek. Must she be so demonstrative toward a man not her husband? Ahmed might deserve her gratitude, certainly not her devotion.

A cloud of dust whooshed into the hut through the open door. "My transport." Ahmed raised his hands to his lips and backed out, half prone. No end to his affectations.

Jacob followed Ahmed outside and circled the transport. So sleek, the bubbled compartments were barely noticeable. "So, this is the Series 456."

Ahmed climbed into the passenger seat. "She's a beauty. Big enough for a fat man like me to ride comfortably, with plenty of leg room, too."

The transport lifted to a hover position, then zoomed out of sight before Jacob could blink. He returned to the hut as a gust of wind upended the furniture and extinguished the solitary lamp. He'd been robust in his youth, an athlete as much as a scholar. Now the slightest drudgery drained him.

"Come, Amelia. Maybe if the two of us push hard enough, we can close this wall of resistance." They strained against the panel until the lock clicked.

Amelia wobbled as she righted a toppled chair, her bark worse than any before. "Sit." When her cough subsided, Jacob embraced her. "Once Benjamin returns, I'll ask him and Thomas to install insulated windows. Ventilated air should help you breathe easier."

Amelia waved Jacob's good intentions away. "I'll not have the house full of peepholes. If I need fresh air, I'll go outside."

"Very well." He went to the mantel over the fireplace and opened the decorative matchbox Benjamin had given him last Christmas, a rusted domino tin he'd found during a hunt and repainted. Jacob struck a match against the stove and relit the lantern. "I'm afraid for Ahmed."

"Why? What has he done, now?"

"Most believe Rowlands practically pushed Devereux into the Euthanasia Chamber. Ahmed should have accepted retirement rather than force Rowlands to keep him on. How can Ahmed balance his integrity on the back of Rowlands' scaly skin? If only government officials were permitted to defect. He'd be an asset here and a lot safer."

Amelia grunted as she pushed down on the pump. "See if you can get this thing to give out more than a few drops at a time. Washing these few dishes will take me all day. And now I'll have to scrub the furniture."

Perspiration formed on Jacob's brow as he worked the pump until a tiny drizzle trickled into a basin. "What a life."

He glared at the door as he grabbed his goat-hide cap from the rack. Did he have enough strength to deal with the monster one more time today? "Leave your worries for the moment. We'll fight the well when we get back from the conclave. We should leave now or we'll be late."

Amelia wrapped a lace shawl around her shoulders, one Benjamin had found for her on his first hunt. She never left the house without it. They pushed together until the panel broke free from the latch and slid open. Once outside, they heaved one more time to secure the lock. Amelia tipped to one side from the exertion, and Jacob caught her before she fell. When Benjamin returned, father and son would install an impregnable remote-controlled door—like Thomas Muldoon's.

Jacob programed the auto-control for the designated coordinates. Soon, the hovercraft lurched into motion and barreled toward Network headquarters outside the Denver Hub. He prided himself on his invention. Though small, barely enough room for two, he'd built this transport from parts he'd found in the hunts. Undoubtedly, the only mechanical success he could credit to his name—his design faster and more maneuverable than the standard outworld hovercraft, even those in America Prime. Thomas Muldoon said he'd like to make blueprints from Jacob's model and build a fleet for the Network. Alas, like the cook's never-to-be-repeated recipe, the bubble model proved an aberration.

Amelia rested her head on Jacob's shoulder. "I can't wait to see Benjamin again. He's been away so long."

"Only two months. To a mother, I suppose, a lifetime." He pulled her into an embrace and drained the well of his passion against her lips.

"Your kiss spelled hunger, though not for intimacy. What is it?"

She seemed to know his thoughts before he did. "I was prepared to repatriate to win Benjamin's release. I'm a scholar, not a farmer, and I remember how soft these hands were when we wed. Think of it, Amelia. All the medicine you need. The controlled air would cure your cough in no time." He tugged at her hemp pantaloons. "Even Adam and Eve had better clothes."

Amelia wriggled from his embrace. "I'll not hear such talk. You know my condition is beyond help ... even in America Prime. Besides, my place is by my husband, the Mayor of Colorado."

He searched her eyes and found the peace that always steadied him in these times of profound doubt. Adoration flowed from her lips to his. Then she pulled back and wiped the mist from her eyes. "I'll not listen anymore to regrets. We have plenty to eat. And if the well dries up, we'll drink berry juices and bathe in the river."

Something gray hazed the horizon. He switched to manual control then slowed to a hover position while he examined the dashboard scanners. "Network headquarters is on fire again."

CHAPTER THREE
Sector One/America Prime/Provincial Headquarters

Edwin Rowlands paced the length of his new private office, the largest of the hundred within Headquarters. Father would advocate a confrontation of this magnitude be within the confines of privacy. No chance of wrong ears overhearing a threat hidden in masked congeniality. However, the Governor's mansion screamed to be remodeled whereas this office merely whimpered for a facelift, and the remodeling in his mansion might cause too much distraction from this very important session. He'd need his wits to go one-on-one with Ahmed Fared.

The buzzer signaled the skirmish had begun, and he'd determined to get the better of the Indomitable Arab, so-nicknamed by adoring fans. Edwin checked the security viewers. If nothing else, Fared was punctual though unwise to present himself dressed in ethnic garb. This man was either extremely brazen or an absolute fool. The man knew any reference to specific nationality was illegal, a law Fared himself had pledged to uphold. His choice of fashion only proved him to be the hypocrite Edwin suspected.

He activated the voice-over on the monitor. "Enter."

Father said to let a foe stand in awkwardness before you acknowledged his presence. Wise counsel, except that Fared showed no sign of uneasiness, his only movement, a glance at his timepiece, his calm equal to Edwin's. Would this prove to be nothing more than a stalemate?

As hoped, Fared was first to break the silence. "You wished to see me, Governor Rowlands?"

Edwin moved a stack of papers from his desk to a side table then offered a handshake. Fared offered none in return. Edwin motioned toward a chair in front of his desk. "Take a seat, Mr. Fared."

Rather than sit, he merely glanced toward the assigned chair.

So, the game begins. "I chose my private office for this meeting since my den is in disarray. I've scheduled the government complex for remodeling next week. Do you wish any changes to your rooms?"

"No. I'm quite satisfied with the current décor."

"I did take a quick peek while you were out this morning. I admire your taste in art. Especially the Renoir. Intriguing."

"A gift from Governor Devereux."

Fared's tone dripped rebellion. What a legacy Devereux left—a motley, undisciplined staff with a disgruntled Arab at the helm, as annoying a man as walked the earth at all accounts—except for his Renoir, a property worth envy.

The Articles of Constitution were short-sighted as to the longevity of Seconds. Once the Preservation Act became the Fifteenth Article, he'd then propose an amendment that would limit a Second's tenure, as well as suggest the mandatory retirement of a Second when a First's office became vacated. No newly elected leader should be saddled with a Second as disagreeable as this Bedouin.

As the laws currently stood, Edwin had only two options to rid himself of an unwanted Second. Terminate Fared with a P-74 blast to the head or manipulate a forced walk into Eternal Pathways, as Devereux had done. Fared's popularity with the Citizenry, however, negated either option now.

Edwin, again, pointed toward the chair. "We can speak freely. I took my internal scanners off-line. You should know my expectations from the onset. Agreed?"

Fared finally sat. "Agreed. Clear expectations are the basis of any good working relationship."

Edwin circled the desk as he studied Fared's mound of flesh. What charm did such an obese man possess to obtain so amorous a following, especially among the female Citizenry?

"First on the agenda. This pretense must end."

"I'm not sure I understand, Governor."

"This Arab farce. I've studied your dossier. You were born here in America Prime, at the time still called Colorado Springs."

Edwin uncrossed his arms and projected Fared's biography through the micro. "This masquerade of yours smacks of sedition. The late governor might have looked the other way. I will not."

Father believed an adversary should be circled like prey. Edwin stood to full height and strode the circumference of Fared's chair. "From this biographical summary, I see you are the product of a rebellious heritage. Mother … Hadiya, murdered by Islamic Militia. Your father … Mohammed Ahmed … incarcerated after he refused to relocate. You were then adopted by a Christian family. If I'm not mistaken, your adoptive brother, Jacob Goodayle, defected twenty-one years ago and currently serves as a Network mayor to the Colorado Community."

Fared leaned back. "A man is more than the sum of his childhood influences." He presented his implant. "I have sworn my allegiance to the Constitutional Government. Regardless of my brother's opinions, or my parents' martyrdom—"

"Treason."

"The term is irrelevant, Governor Rowlands. I still believe in the vision of one world, one people, one government. I will serve you as faithfully as I served Governor Devereux."

Edwin minimized Fared's dossier. "Don't waste your rhetoric on me. According to these records, your fetish for Arab garb began after Goodayle's defection. Even Devereux warned you to stop." Edwin thrust a finger into Fared's chest. "Make no mistake. I will arrange your assassination at the first sign you are no longer useful to me. Are we clear?"

Fared smiled as he pushed Edwin's finger aside. "Absolutely."

Father had never counseled on how to subdue this kind of mockery. Perhaps Constable Becker could find some excuse to arrest Fared as a traitor and be done with the matter. However, Father did warn not to be hasty in the elimination of an enemy. Sometimes a foe can be a leader's biggest asset. "Glad we understand one another. Now, about your brother—should I be concerned about his new position?"

"When Devereux appointed me, I was given free rein as to my involvement with the Network. I don't need to remind you, my tenure as ambassador is for life. I have an obligation to inform the Governor of Network business. I expect you will uphold my dual contract as Ambassador and Second Governor. This much I can assure you. If loyalties come into conflict, my primary responsibility is to the Constitutional Government."

Goodayle was the least influential of the mayors, a pauper who barely kept his family fed. No need to rush to remove his influence. For the moment, he'd respect Fared's position on the matter. "Agreed."

Fared leaned forward. "Anything else, Governor?"

Though he seethed inwardly, Edwin forced an exterior aloofness. "My sources tell me you visited the Network this morning. I'd like an update."

"I'll tell you all you need to know. First, though, my nephew is due to be released today per Governor Devereux's signature, his last official act before his euthanasia."

"Young Goodayle was caught inside America Prime. Outworlders are forbidden access to the City or sub-city. Hardly a minor offense."

"He's just a boy, Governor. Believe me, espionage was the last thing on his mind. More likely his curiosity trumped his good judgment. What man has not committed a foolish act in his youth?"

A pointed question. "True. There is much I'd like to forget from my boyhood days."

"EVE?"

"Among other things. ADAM was Father's invention. However, I must take full credit for the harlot. She'll haunt me all my days, I fear."

"As for Benjamin? If you release him, your generosity will go a long way toward appeasing the Humanitarian Party."

"Very well. I understand you want to personally escort him."

Fared hesitated then nodded. "And I have your word no harm will come to the boy or me either?"

Edwin put his thumbprint on Benjamin's release order then handed the disc to Fared. "Give this to Warden Barnes." He sat on the edge of the desk. "Now on to other matters. Have you read my proposed Preservation Act as I asked?"

Father said to study a man's physical response rather than his words. Fared raised an eyebrow, a clear indicator of his disapproval. No matter. He, Edwin Rowlands, was the governor, not Ahmed Fared.

"Yes, I have. I don't think—"

"I didn't ask for your opinion, Mr. Fared. I do expect your cooperation in its implementation once the regulations become law. The offer of repatriation still holds, particularly for the Network. I can't guarantee for how long. If these people don't comply, President Schumann will be forced to take action against them. No one wants bloodshed."

Fared's pallor whitened. "Is there no other way?"

"I understand how distasteful these measures must seem to you. The Network's disregard for the Constitutional Government can no longer be tolerated. Congress must dissolve the former agreements. The Accord is dead and so is any prior legislation. Constitutional law must be extended to the outworlds as well as the cities or world order will be undermined."

"I'm sure negotiations can be made to avoid civil war."

"Besides exceeding allowable populations, some inhabitants, even leaders, hold religious services in their homes. If the IEA's information is accurate, your brother has advocated the construction of a school. Such acts smell of Separatist ideology and will not be tolerated by my administration."

"The Network has shown coexistence is of benefit for both the outworld and the City. We must not throw out the pearls in our quest to dominate."

"You don't believe your brother favors secession?"

"What my brother advocates or doesn't is immaterial. He is only one of many mayors. He does not have their support."

"That may be so at this time. However, if his sphere of influence spreads, he could become a threat to what you term beneficial coexistence. Besides the Network's threats, Kinnear's Revolutionary Army advocates a military coup. If either faction secedes, what then? The world will be plunged into chaos. My Preservation Act will revoke the right of defection and reclassify dissension, past and present, as treason."

"Governor, a charge of treason strips the accused of their rights. Only a presidential pardon can commute execution. Do you really want that kind of bloodbath on your hands?"

Edwin examined Fared's whitened pallor. "You see the dilemma, then." Perhaps now, his adversary would listen to reason. "As the Network's Ambassador, I expect you to make repatriation more agreeable than continued autonomy."

"I have a suggestion."

Of course, you, do. "Let's hear it."

"Bring all outworld leaders into the City for a conference. Offer an olive branch. Listen to their objections and build a bridge to peace."

"I don't negotiate with defectors. Neither will President Schumann."

"Please, Governor. Hear me out." Fared leaned further in, his face taut with intention. "Defectors were not expected to survive, let alone build a society as the Network has miraculously done. As we learned from the Schism, parallel societies eventually encroach upon one another. If we blend the societies, both will benefit."

"In other words, you propose we extend our boundaries." A plausible idea, however, not without risks. "Certainly, you don't suggest thugs and rebels be treated as equals or be granted representation without repatriation."

"If we pursue a hard line and yet offer nothing, we risk war. Network resources are far more valuable than their tithe. If residents remain on their land and become Citizens, everyone benefits. You will be heralded as a savior instead of a butcher. Surely amendments can be made to satisfy both the outworlds and the Citizenry."

Edwin circled his desk and sat. Cavanaugh and the Humanitarians had fought hard against the Preservation Act. Fared's proposals might win over the necessary votes to get the measure passed by Congress.

Father's ghost breathed caution into Edwin's soul. "Compromise often proves deadly." Advice Edwin could not lightly disregard. Yet, some compromise might be mandatory if the vision for total world order was to be realized. "There is merit to your suggestion. We'll talk more after you've escorted Benjamin Goodayle home."

Fared's version would not muster, of course. A tweak and bend here and there might at the least bring the factions into line. Threats existed within the City walls as well, the growing Reformation movement included.

Time for the clincher. "You know, Fared, President Schumann won't live another six months. Cancer has spread to his liver and lungs. He's asked me if I would consider nomination as his replacement. He also states his Second plans to retire when Schumann's post is vacated."

Fared glared.

"Let's be honest. We don't like each other. That said, I do admire how your mind works. If I am elected President, I may consider you as my Second, despite our differences."

"I'll give the matter some thought."

"One more consideration. Media coverage has managed to hack classified intelligence, not to mention their gross misrepresentation of my proposed Preservation Act. They paint me as a monster, when I only seek to do what is best for all concerned, particularly Western America. They fuel the various factions against me."

"You want me to silence the journalists?"

"I'll handle Excelsior Media. You take care of the others. Understood?"

"Understood."

Edwin circled Fared one last time then sat behind the desk. "That will be all."

He backed out the door with an Arabian bow, likely a final act of defiance. The man should know better than to test his superior's resolve on the matter.

Edwin allowed himself a moment to bask in the possibilities his Second's ideas generated. Amnesty. He didn't much care for the word—dispensation a better term. Defectors would have no viable alternative. Surely their freedoms would not be worth dying for—a futile death at that. No way could any outworld, not even the Network, survive an all-out civil war. As Schumann's successor, he would force quick passage of the Preservation Act. History would hail him as a messiah.

Now would be a good time to lure the governors, except for Cavanaugh, to the Australian retreat—before Congress convened next week. A few nights of wine and playmates and the governors would agree to anything.

CHAPTER FOUR
Sector Ten/New Edinburgh

Bridget helped Ian sit while she stood against what was left of a stone tenement, and sighed as a waif ran past them. The child stopped. "You got any food?"

Bridget shook her head. The child, perhaps six or seven, her growth most likely stunted from lack of nutrition, shrugged her shoulders and took off. Before she conceived, these poor children had not crossed her mind. This child's image seared on Bridget's heart. If she survived this ordeal, she'd find a way to bring relief to the innocents.

They had dodged scanners all night, stealing transports and by-passing the known patrol points. Through gasps and moans, he'd led the way through Sector Ten until his strength failed. "We will … rendezvous with Resistance leaders … escort us into the badlands … Kinnear's territory."

During her IEA days, she'd learned how to carbonize implants to make them mute, and Ian's insiders had managed to disable the night glows to give them the cover of darkness. A Humanitarian had helped them with a transport. Unfortunately, the fuel cell gave out in Sector Nine. They'd finally breached Sector Ten, the area Citizens called The Forlorn District. Yet, the next mile might as well be a thousand. They were too late. The City was rising with the dawn's haze. Impossible to reach Rendezvous Point now without being spotted, and no doubt Bartelli made good her threat to report Bridget and Ian as fugitives.

A few seconds' respite to plan the next critical minute.

From their location, Bridget saw the factory meme dormitory, once the proud Holyrood House. She remembered how Da lamented over the plight of Sector Ten residents, primarily relocated Nomads too sick or too old to contribute to society, labeled undesirables. No reputable Citizen would venture into Sector Ten, the abyss of human refuse.

How she wished she'd paid more attention in school, her focus on clothes and parties rather than history lessons, except for Mum's stories of the Royal Mile. So sad that now the poor rummaged where Kings and Queens once feasted.

How did the government think these desperate souls existed on the once-a-week rations dumped onto city streets? No wonder so many Nomads starved within their first year of relocation while waiting to be assigned productive work and affordable housing.

Ian must have sensed her sorrow as she gazed upon the squalor. "Every curse ... holds hidden blessings," he said. "The conditions ... keep IEA away."

True. Law required a certain number of officers patrol the streets surrounding the meme dormitories, although patrols depended more on scanners and were comprised of mostly rookies or officers nearing retirement. Thankfully, most could be bribed.

"Da brought me here once before I joined the IEA. He told me he had given the Highland delegation proposal after proposal to improve conditions. Sadly, the Humanitarian Party seemed too weak to garner enough votes. Think of it, Ian. If the Reformists and Humanitarians joined forces, their influence would change the world."

"Different goals ... Bridget. Tell me ... did your da ever say ... why ... he's soft ... on the Revolutionary Army?"

Thoughts of Da brought a smile. "He believes the wee bit of sabotage Jimmy Kinnear does is more than compensated by his larger service to the poor."

"Makes sense."

"Da knows which side his political bread is buttered on. Oh, he conducts an occasional arrest to keep his critics at bay. I don't think he meant for you to be hurt. Da's a good man."

"I know ... Bridget ... I hold your father ... no ill will. I brought my end upon myself."

Ian's eyes fluttered.

"Stay with me, Ian. We'll find Jimmy soon, and maybe he can get you a doctor."

He smirked. "We can hope. Bridget ... don't give up ... Sector Ten ... many old buildings."

Of course. Scanners couldn't penetrate the old, coarse brick and limestone. If not for Ian's injury, they could snake their way through the old tenements indefinitely.

"We'll keep moving." Bridget risked a glance toward the intersection. One armed female officer. "I'll figure out a way to distract her then we'll make a run for it."

"You ... mean ... hobble. Leave me... Bridget. You ... can ... make it. We both ... know ... I'm as ... good as ... dead."

"We go together or not all."

Ian scooped up a piece of old brick, squeezed Bridget's hand around it and nodded.

"Haven't played pitch ball since primary school. I'd rather die while trying to make a break than wait here for the end." She tossed the brick away from the tenements. The officer turned, lowered her P-74 and advanced toward the thud.

"Now!"

They scurried, and Ian stumbled. As Bridget helped him back up, the officer turned in their direction.

"Halt." A hail of plasma bursts flew over their heads. Warning shots. The next volley would be deadly.

Bridget risked a backward glance just as an errant factory meme, most likely a fugitive from the dormitory, flailed his arms at the officer. Perhaps he'd suffered a breakdown. As they were considered valuable property, an officer would be discharged if he destroyed a meme without profound justification.

Bridget took advantage of the distraction and dragged Ian toward the row of tenements. They were met by a white-haired African woman. "Follow me." The woman spoke with a slight French accent. A Nomad? "Gerard, the meme, will keep the officer engaged until I'm able to hide you. We must hurry."

Her sympathetic eyes beamed with concern. "We know who you are. Why you are here."

"Can you help us?"

She nodded. "My name is Felicia LeCroix. I will explain more when you are safe."

Felicia's brown face glowed, much like the angels Bridget had seen in Grandmother Cavanaugh's white-leathered Bible, the keepsake she rescued from her moldy basement and smuggled to the Treasure Keepers.

In the growing daylight, Ian seemed more a ghost than a man. "Bridget ... trust ... friends. Will ... contact Jimmy."

"Hurry, Monsieur McCormick." Reaching into her pocket, Felicia pulled out a high-intensity, short-distanced flashlight, IEA issue. "This way."

Once beyond the intersection, they ducked into an alleyway between tenements. "My flat connects to a secret chamber used by Mary Queen of Scots as a sequestered chapel. Only a few of us know of its existence. You'll be safe there."

"Us?"

"Oui. I am part of the Revolutionary Army. So is Gerard."

"Where did you come from?"

"The North African Province."

"I didn't think anyone survived the sand storms."

"Yes. The land is uninhabitable. The government has conducted many roundups. They brought me here ten years ago."

Bridget grunted. "You were better off in Africa."

"Perhaps the Maker has found more use for me here."

Bridget blushed with shame. How could anyone emanate such hope in this squalor?

"My flat is too far underground for scanners."

"The dungeons? No one survives there."

"We do."

Ian groaned as he collapsed. "Leave ... me."

Bridget pulled on Ian's collar and spat her determination. "Get up or I'll drag you."

Ian screamed with pain as Bridget and Felicia helped him to a stand. "It's not far. Try hard Monsieur McCormick."

Bridget gulped back the tears. "Felicia, you stay on the other side of him. Maybe between the two of us we can keep him upright the rest of the way."

When they reached the last flight of stairs, Felicia shone her flashlight on a series of narrow metal doors. "My flat," she said as she opened the portal on the far right and helped them inside a one-room domicile, sparsely furnished with a single table, cot, desk, and chair. A marble ledge topped an antique hearth, a fixture as out of place in this dank, dark reality as a gas-powered vehicle on the thoroughfare.

Felicia lifted a large statue of President Schumann, pressed a buzzer and a narrow portion of the wall next to the mantle lifted to reveal another spiral staircase, this time ascending about two flights. She motioned to follow.

Ian's weight crushed against her, each step a test of endurance.

Felicia shone her flashlight into a large open chamber. A kneeling rail rested along the side wall underneath a wooden crucifix, the room a mausoleum to a persecuted queen. "There's a canopy bed along the right wall. Be careful. I fear these structures will not hold up much longer. The ceilings could cave at any moment."

The air reeked from mildew deposits. Bridget crossed the room to the bed, then eased Ian onto the mattress. She gagged on the resulting puff of dust, more from thirst than the stench. Something furry brushed her ankle. She clenched her teeth and stifled a scream as Felicia raised a silhouetted hand in warning, then moved stealthily about the chamber while the flashlight's beams danced to her busyness. She drew out candles from a stand in the middle of the room, inserted four of them into the candelabra then placed the rest to the side along with a supply of matches. "After you are settled, I will go to Rendezvous Point. These candles should last until I am able to return. And perhaps bring back a doctor, food, and supplies."

Images of the Scottish Catholic queen who hid her prayers from an irate English conqueror played in Bridget's mind like a micro-projection. Felicia lifted a canvas portrait of the famous visionary, Jacques Fontaine, the man who united a fractured world and formed the Accord.

Bridget recalled how often Da quoted Fontaine's wisdom. If only Da were here now, she'd tell him how much she regretted her rebellion. Though hated, the Reformation Party was not illegal. If she and Ian had not used their political connections as a front to smuggle banned artifacts to the Treasure Keepers, Da would not have been forced to arrest them.

He'd been a far better father to her than she a daughter to him. Whenever she experienced a nightmare, Da would cradle her and hum her favorite lullaby. If only he could sing to her now. For the moment, the Maker had brought her comfort in the form of an ancient African woman. Bridget squeezed Felicia's hands in gratitude. "Thank you for your kindness."

"There is strength in this room. I come here often to pray. Though we may not all agree with the tenets of her faith, we must respect how she defied a monarch to worship as she thought best." Felicia pointed to a curtained section. "There is a privy there. I apologize for the primitive conditions. These old buildings have no sanitation systems."

"We'll make do." Tears escaped, and she forced them aside. No time for sorrow. She must be strong for all their sakes. "We don't want to put anyone else in danger. You have risked too much already."

"Mademoiselle, whatever the Maker requires, there is joy in the doing. Don't be troubled on my account." Felicia brushed fallen debris from the furniture.

Bridget moved to Ian's side—his breaths, more shallow. "Ian, I need to examine your wound."

"May I help, Mademoiselle? Years ago, I was a doctor."

Ian nodded his approval.

Bridget removed his torn shirt and gasped at the putrid puss seeping from the gash.

"Monsieur McCormick, you must rest," Felicia said, her eyes wet with concern.

He managed a smile through his groans, his lips blue and dry. "Only if … you call … me Ian. My… wife's name is … Bridget. If you … address her … as Mademoiselle again … she'll cuff … you … on the head."

"You have performed the ceremony, then?"

Bridget kissed Ian's hand. "Ian and I found an old priest, ordained before the Accord. He married us in a private ceremony behind a brick wall. At least, we have united in the eye of the Maker if not the law."

Felicia stepped back as a smile escaped. "Ian and Bridget, then. I will be back soon, I promise." As she moved toward the steps, she motioned for Bridget to follow, then took hold of her hands. "Your husband's condition is grave. For now, all we can do is make him comfortable and put him into the Maker's care."

Grief won out.

"Does Ian know about the baby?"

"How did—"

"A woman can sense things a man cannot. You should tell him while I'm gone."

"You don't think Ian will last until you get back?"

"His wound is badly infected. Only the Maker knows how long. The only way in or out is through my flat. I will secure the panel when I leave."

Bridget glanced toward Ian who had fallen unconscious then watched in helplessness as her angel disappeared into the darkness.

CHAPTER FIVE
Sector Two/America Prime

Michael Grafton stormed through the halls of the Excelsior Media Building. A tornado of emotion, she slammed the door to her office. How dare the government—Edwin—shut her down. She clicked the intercom. "Barry, get me Governor Rowlands' office. Now!"

Barry's smile, a rare quality found in current meme generations, normally soothed her anxiety. His sense of humor often added bouillon to a flavorless life. Not today. "Very well, Mistress Grafton. Do you wish to use your personal hail or Excelsior Media's? The codes are different."

"Whatever makes him respond the fastest."

"Then I'll use the Excelsior hail."

"Send me the feed as soon as he's online."

"Yes, Mistress Grafton."

She drummed impatient fingers against her desk. This intended broadcast would have made Grandfather Grafton proud. There must be some way to circumvent Edwin's censorship. What if she used his feed? She punched in a numerical sequence then hit, SEND.

EVE projected. "You have entered an invalid code for this function."

"Explain."

"No further information is available."

Michael pounded her desk then minimized the obnoxious icon—Edwin's design, the manufactured essence of an adolescent mind. A chime intruded upon her anger, and Barry's image projected. "Governor Rowlands is online. He is about to leave for the Oceanic Province where he'll convene an emergency session of the governors. He wanted me to let you know he's in a hurry."

"Edwin's always in a hurry. So, an emergency session held at the resort?"

"Do you still wish to speak to Governor Rowlands?"

"Oh, very much so. Patch the hail into my private viewer."

Edwin's image projected into her office, his face taut with evident displeasure. "Michael, must you always project my image? I'm requesting EVE to block this application from now on."

"From even your intimate?"

"You know I can't tolerate people gawking at my likeness."

"You project others."

"A political device, my dear."

"Edwin, don't block your projections." She stroked his holographic cheek. "They are all I have of you anymore." The nearest they came to intimacy these days.

"I see Barry's up to his usual disrespect. Wasting my time with a joke he heard from one of your reporters. Then, after a long descriptive set up, he forgot the punch line. I thought his generation was supposed to be funny. When are you going to euthanize him, Michael? I swear he shows more and more signs of dementia every day. He's dangerous."

"Ridiculous. Barry's about as dangerous as a stuffed toy. He's like the brother I never had. I can't bear to put him down."

"Then send him to one of the Humanitarian storage facilities for outmoded memes. Their maintenance fees are reasonable."

"And let him rot like an old bucket?"

"He's a machine, Michael. He has no soul."

"You don't believe anyone has a soul, Edwin."

"Humans outlive memes, and that is why we are superior and their masters."

This conversation was pointless—a useless, winded debate with a man she could never outthink. "Grandfather Grafton believed every meme, man or woman, has a soul with a direct link to the Maker. They are flesh, aren't they?"

"Let Barry join Hiram in the great beyond where they can debate the matter with their precious Maker. Since when did you become religious?"

"I'm not. Barry's future is my decision, not yours. I say he stays right where he is—my assistant."

"Why did you hail me? I'm very busy."

"Busy or preoccupied?" Edwin's preoccupations had become more numerous and younger as the years progressed. The last preoccupation was Greta from the Alpine province, a seventeen-year-old who could pass for thirty.

"You're more woman than I can handle, Michael. Why would I want to be unfaithful?"

"Don't get off the subject, Edwin."

No matter how many or in what variety, Edwin's lusts were insatiable, the reason she refused more intimates into their mix.

Even the max would not be enough for him—more people to be unfaithful to.

"Barry mentioned a retreat?"

"For political reasons, Michael. I promise to give you an exclusive on the story when I return."

He purposefully distracted her with false promises, like a witch with poisonous fruit. Why? "You blocked my editorial, 'The Pitfalls of Repatriation.' I want the article back. Citizens have a right to fair and balanced reviews of government policy. No matter how much perfume you put on the presentation, the truth is your so-called Preservation Act stinks."

"Stinks? Not a very nice word."

"Truthfully descriptive, though."

"I'm making amendments, Michael—amendments to favor both the Constitutional Government and the outworlds. You'll see. Until then, I don't want any more publicity." His broad smile proved to be a weapon for which she had no defense.

"Michael, be a good girl and leave government to the politicians. I'm sure there are other stories for you to focus on. My sources tell me The Council of Business Management has approved the construction of a new textile factory in Sector Four. The agreement will provide a hundred jobs or more."

"Little help to Sector Ten when those positions most likely will be filled by memes. Cheaper than paid labor."

"I struck a deal with the company. I approved the project on the condition of a blended workforce, a fifty-fifty ratio of meme and humans. At least twenty percent of those human workers must be drawn from Sector Ten."

"No doubt that will win points with the Humanitarian Party."

"How well you know me. There is another story Excelsior might like to print."

"Nothing you say can change my opinion about the Preservation Act. The Citizenry has a right to know the ramifications if the law is passed."

"What would you say if I told you I've figured out a humane way to end our troubles with the Network?"

"I'm listening."

"If they repatriate, all will be forgiven. America Prime will welcome them back with open arms."

A trap. Edwin never compromised. "Defectors have accepted the harsh conditions for the right to worship, though without assembly, a modified freedom granted by the Accord's Resolution. And you want to take even this privilege away, make defection a treasonous act?"

"And does your fair and balanced report include the fact defections in America Prime are on the rise? If the Network continues to grow, they might separate, and if they separate one people, one world, one government will disappear!"

"The numbers don't disturb you, Edwin. You wouldn't care if the defections came from Sector Ten. You are more troubled because the outworld attracts the elite—the philosophers, scientists, teachers, and engineers—the brightest and the best who look for what they cannot find in America Prime."

"What's that?"

"Individuality."

"This individuality, as you call it, is religious dogma—and a dangerous concept. Humanity's preservation depends upon the government's supremacy over the fantasies of men."

"Save your rhetoric for the masses, Edwin. Your silver tongue has no effect on me."

She admired Network ingenuity ... the ability to hack the newsfeeds despite the IEA's enhanced security measures, how they always managed to stay one step ahead of the monitors, why she risked the illegal feeds into the outworlds. "Some say the crusade to end religion is a religion of its own."

"Control of the masses by the few is the only certainty to peace. I'd give you permission to quote me if you didn't twist my words to make me look like a monster. Is that what you think of me now? Have you no love left for me at all?"

Was there? She didn't love him as she once did ... as when they signed their familial contract—young lovers who fought to shape a new world from the ruins of the old. Success had drained Edwin of passion, filled him with delusions, stolen his heart and turned him into a hollow automaton.

"Edwin, release my feed."

"Ouch, Michael. I hear a threat underneath those words. Or what?"

"I'll dissolve our familial contract."

"Now don't be rash, my dear."

His image froze—the transmission paused, no doubt while he found a corner of the room in which to pout before he resumed their conversation. Excelsior Media was her last defense against Edwin's dominance. His need for power had nothing to do with money. He had wealth of his own, probably the wealthiest man in America Prime and certainly among the most wealthy in United Earth. Rather, he possessed a psychotic need to control the world as much as he tried to control her. He owned every media enterprise except Excelsior—the one broken link in his chain to dictatorship. Let him brood.

While controversy sold media, Michael avoided taking a personal stance. Journalists were supposed to be neutral, weren't they? Truth lived on both sides of a debate. Although, lately, there had been little to debate. Edwin seemed incapable of rational thought, and his constant barrage of cancerous determination eroded her resistance to his incurable need to dominate. If only she could match Grandfather's moral integrity.

"Edwin? Are you still there?"

His projection remained frozen.

Her thoughts wandered to the early years of their union. How much Edwin had reminded her of Grandfather Grafton. Edwin campaigned for a stronger Constitution as much as Grandfather protested against a global government. Why hadn't she seen the beast beneath the beauty? Edwin craved power even more than he craved women. He would play the political chess game until he'd made himself a god.

How could she fight a deity? Her continued opposition would certainly lead to imprisonment—worse yet, exile to the remotest province. Nor would he be above the assassination of an intimate.

The micro beeped, and Edwin's projection reanimated. "I'm sorry, Michael. I received another hail requiring my attention. Now, what's this silly nonsense about dissolving our familial contract?"

"I'm serious, Edwin. If you don't release my feed, I will do it."

"Don't be so dramatic. You should know by now, theatrics will not change my mind."

She knew him—his petulance and manipulations. And he knew her as well. No doubt his words were intended to unsettle, throw her off guard. He probably anticipated this call and had rehearsed his response. What Edwin didn't know was how she played him too. "How am I supposed to keep this business afloat with all your intrusions?"

"You can always sell Excelsior to me?"

"No. You'll never own Excelsior. Not even after I die."

"Very well, keep your hobby. Citizens don't want their happy lives disrupted by your unsubstantiated dribble. Your grandfather riled a lot of people with his gibberish—why he was forced to resign from The Washington Post. No wonder he was assassinated."

His threats had little power against her resolve.

"Truth is not dribble. Reform only takes a spark, Edwin. Once upon a time, you were that spark."

Edwin's projection wore a reddened face. She'd struck a nerve, and he speared her in return. "You'll never be the journalist Hiram Grafton was."

No. She'd never come close.

"If you continue to oppose me, I will not be able to guarantee the safety of your informers."

Did she dare risk the lives of her sources? His projection softened, his voice cooed. "Michael, if you will rethink this rebellion … when I get back, we'll add a nursery." She had predicted his response almost verbatim. "Dearest, we don't want to bring a child into this uncertainty, do we? The Network is growing day by day and threatens the very principles by which the Constitutional Government was founded. We've struggled for more than twenty years to lay this incredible foundation for future generations."

"Not we, Edwin. You. This is not the government I fought for. Only history will determine whether the Network is a threat or a stepping stone."

How cruel of Edwin to bribe her with the one thing she wanted above all else. A year from now, she'd pass the allowable age limit to give birth. Nightmares visited her. In the dream, Marauders snatched her child away. "The world has always been in flux, Edwin, yet humanity perseveres. I don't want to wait any longer. If you'll agree to a child now, I promise not to defy you again. Just give me this one story."

Edwin smiled in victory. "I'll be back in two days. Wear the red chemise I bought you on my last trip to Oceania. I'll bring the ambiance."

She raised her hand to her lips and blew his projection a kiss. "And you'll release my codes, now?"

When Edwin's image disappeared, EVE prompted the reinstatement codes.

Michael touched SEND. "Done."

CHAPTER SIX
Network Headquarters/Western America

Jacob Goodayle picked up his rake and sifted through the charred remains of the manse. Sparks flew as metal scraped metal. He stooped down and whisked off the ashes covering the shrapnel left from an exploded canister.

"Thomas, what do you make of this?" He handed over the evidence. "Kyle said he thought he heard an explosion before the flames started. He and the family were out tending the animals when they heard the noise. Good thing no one was inside. They'd have been killed for sure."

Thomas rolled the cylindrical device in his hands. "Low impact … like the one used to level Sean Finn's barn. This device, though, is too advanced for the Marauders. They'd have used manure." Thomas rubbed his hand on the exterior casing. "These materials can only be found in America Prime."

"Why?" Jacob asked. "What's behind these attacks?"

"Disruption. If you want my honest opinion, the Constitutional Government's out to make the hair on our arms stand up so we'll all repatriate, and the Network will fall apart. There's so few of us, the loss of even one family is felt."

Lennie Legacy sidled up beside them, pitchfork in hand. "Another bomb, hey? Who's planting them, I'd like ta know?"

Thomas handed Lennie the canister, and he sniffed the exposed burned wiring. "Jacob, I think Thomas is right. Don't look nothin' like the Marauders would use. Their style's more like make a small blast, hit, pillage, and run. They don't set fires, neither. No sense to it. Why burn up food and goods?"

Jacob resumed sifting. "Maybe the Mayors' Council should recommend an investigation. What do you think, Lennie?"

"I thinks there's a traitor among us, is what I thinks."

Jacob scanned the horizon. Between Colorado's Denver Hub and the Cheyenne Hub of the Wyoming Community, defectors and natural-born outworlders alike had reclaimed the land. Some fields had been planted already and more needed plowing. "So far, not many have decided to repatriate. If more move back to American Prime than defect, we could face a collapse. The larger we grow, the more labor we need to sustain our growth. If the crops fail, we can't pay our tithe."

Thomas looked up toward the reserve silos. "I'll volunteer to head up a team to investigate these bombings. We need this harvest, Jacob. Davu predicts the government's going to raise our tithe again this year."

Lennie sneered. "Ain't nobody got the inside track to Congress like Davu."

Thomas placed debris in piles, ferreting out anything salvageable. "What will Kyle and Caroline do now, Jacob? Did they say?"

"They have food stored in the barn. The nights are too cold yet to sleep there." Jacob's rake hit a cabinet buried under charred cross beams, still in one piece. As he tugged on one of the beams, a sharp pain radiated across his chest.

Lennie patted his shoulder. "Best let us younger lads do the liftin'."

"I'm fine. Just indigestion. Probably the goat cheese I had earlier."

"Your gills are pretty gray there, Jacob."

He pried the cabinet doors open. Maybe the Maker worked a miracle and saved a keepsake or two. When Jacob defected, he surrendered everything, even his clothes to the government, driven into the outworld naked and impoverished. He ached for Kyle's losses as he sifted through the charred hymnals that once belonged to Kyle's grandfather.

Thomas took the canister to Kyle, and Lennie left to help rake where the meeting room had been. Alone, Jacob mused about life's quandaries. Network society had few uses for a philosopher, and Amelia chided him for daydreaming when he should be feeding the chickens. Solitude was his best friend, and one who seldom paid a visit these days.

He wondered if, in some way, the government's attacks might be a source of increased unity rather than friction. In recent years, the Network had become more cohesive than ever. Fire, intended or not, was a dire threat to the hubs, and an out-of-control conflagration could level a hub in a matter of days. Yet, the fear of fire unified them. When the alarm sounded, every man, woman, and child fought the blaze, the entire hub—a team of firefighters. Even the Nomads descended from their mountain tents to assist.

With advanced technologies, fire-proofed materials and genetically enhanced memes trained in fire-fighting techniques, fires posed little to no threat in America Prime, except for Sector Ten, where the old wooden and brick structures were left to burn out on their own.

Jacob planned to propose a training program for firefighters—a station in every hub, not limited to putting out fires. They would educate residents in prevention strategies as well. Education was the key to any viable society—why he believed a school was paramount.

He tingled with the possibilities. Sometimes blessings came from disaster. Unfortunately, few shared his optimism. Fear, a far more corrosive emotion, ran rampant these days. Education always made the best weapon against fear.

Jacob picked up a shard and drew deep breaths to quiet the chest pain. Kyle's prize dinnerware. He'd given Davu half his goat herd in exchange for these gold-etched porcelain dishes. Just last week, Caroline hosted a state dinner for the mayors and their families.

"To show off the new dinnerware, I suspect," Amelia had said.

Lord, forgive my petty jealousy. Although my hut may be small and made of sod, I have a comfortable bed to sleep in tonight and my Amelia to share it with. I am blessed.

Kyle raised his hand as if to summon all who remained. "Caroline, Peter, and I are moved by your kindness. Please, you've done enough. I don't want the Marauders to take advantage of your absence. Go back and protect what is yours. The Maker will provide for us. We are alive. We're thankful for that."

Thomas Muldoon stepped forward. "Chairman Skinner, we'll have the manse rebuilt in no time. I can't guarantee it'll be as big as the first one. However, I know for a fact it'll be better than Mayor Goodayle's."

The laughter uprooted a flock of ravens. Jacob pointed his rake at Thomas. "Careful, friend. Don't go bragging, now. Doesn't the Good Book say the least shall be first?"

"In that case, Jacob, you'll be at the head of the line."

Thomas never missed an opportunity to poke fun at Jacob's humble hut. Yet, a better friend could never be found. Still, Jacob's cheeks burned with the reminder of his ineptitude. He had spent his life in pursuit of knowledge. Amelia would have fared better with a carpenter or an engineer like Thomas, not a dreamer like Jacob. Why she stayed with a man of meager means, stood by his visions, he'd never know. He only knew he dreaded a life without her.

Flashes of their wedding day danced through his heart like images in Mother's old digital photo viewer. Amelia's white pantaloons and lace over-blouse flapped in the wind. Purple florets adorned her dark braids. He wore a gold-buttoned, silken vest. They met by Lover's Bridge and exchanged vows presided over by the Reverend Sylvester Hodges, Father's boyhood minister, and one of the few clergy who survived the Schism.

His heart ached to see the end of marriage, replaced by a nondescript institution called a Familial Contract, the ultimate result of humankind's inability to define marriage.

"Jacob?"

Kyle's presence stole Jacob's attention away from his private thoughts. He set down his rake then gripped Kyle's shoulder. "My hut might be the joke of every hub, but you're still welcome to stay with us until a new manse is built."

Kyle grasped Jacob's hand in a firm handshake. "Walk with me, Jacob."

None of Kyle's walks had ever been short. They walked for nearly a mile, and Kyle had yet to speak. Jacob conjured up his own soup of contemplations, privileged to shadow this man who had found him and Amelia shivering and naked along the eastern perimeter of the outworld. At that time, only ten families formed a hub of protection within a hostile and what most deemed inhabitable land. Kyle took them in, fed and clothed them, and taught them how to farm.

Whatever Kyle asked of Jacob, he would find the means to do.

When the men reached the edge of the first fields, Kyle stopped, took off his cap, and stared at it. Most often Kyle looked a man right in the eyes when he asked a favor. "I appreciate all you've done for us today, including your offer of shelter. Not necessary."

"Where will you go? You shouldn't stay in the barn. Peter's a frail boy. He'd get pneumonia for sure."

Kyle cleared his throat. "I'm going to repatriate."

No. Not Kyle. Not a man who had envisioned a system of interlocked hubs that would form communities and those communities to be weaved into a network of settlements, eclectic communities where tolerance reigned and people worshiped as they pleased.

Some Network members, children of Nomads and outworld born, repatriated out of curiosity or disillusionment. Some branded defectors, tired of the hardships, bribed their way back into the domed cities.

Kyle Skinner was not the kind of man to repatriate because of a bomb. Something else, something more desperate had prompted this decision.

"Why?" Jacob asked. "We'll rebuild the manse, bigger and better." He jabbed Kyle in the ribs. "A veritable Taj Mahal, outworld style."

Kyle smiled. "You always raise my spirits, Jacob. Your special gift. We can't all be carpenters."

"Are you avoiding my question?"

"No." Kyle's chest heaved. "I don't expect anyone to understand."

"If you enlighten me, I'll try."

Tears streaked Kyle's sooty face. "Peter is dying. He has leukemia."

"I'm so sorry. I would take the disease on myself to spare Peter. When did you discover this?"

"We've known for about a month, now. Ahmed has smuggled in medicine. Peter needs an operation, a simple procedure in America Prime. Unavailable to outworlders."

No parent should have to watch a child die, especially if a cure was available and within reach. If Benjamin had been so cursed, Jacob would repatriate, even be tempted to buy transfusions or cloned body parts from meme medical farms. "I don't blame you, Kyle. I've considered the prospect myself, for Amelia's sake. She refuses."

"America Prime offers life for my son. How can I deny him that?"

"You're willing to buy memes?"

"No. I wouldn't sacrifice my beliefs. We don't need a meme. The operation can be done with my tissue. No meme will die so my son can live."

Jacob put his hand on Kyle's shoulder. "I admire your integrity."

"Thank you for the good thoughts, Jacob."

"When would you go? Who will lead the Network?"

Kyle put his hat back on, his tug, a proclamation. "I've sent messengers to convene the Council of Mayors in two hours."

"My son Benjamin will arrive early this evening. Ahmed will be with him. I have no way of sending him a message that I'll be late."

"I need you there, Jacob. Ahmed will wait for you. I plan to resign tonight and name you for my replacement."

Jacob smiled, aware of his answer before he asked. "Me? And not Davu, your Second?"

Kyle snorted. "I'm thankful our bylaws don't require me to pass the mantle to the Second Chairman. Davu is a smart man. He doesn't have your heart. We'll hold elections, and I'm sure the mayors will go with my recommendation."

"I'm not worthy, Kyle. I'm a poor politician. I was named head delegate for the Denver Hub because no one else wanted the job. I became Mayor of the Colorado Community the same way. I'm sure there are others more capable and willing to serve, and if Rowlands passes his Preservation Act, you'll need a warrior for a chairman, not a philosopher."

"I expected your resistance." Kyle gripped Jacob's shoulder. "You, my friend, are a Moses, reluctant to the core. I see a different future than despair."

"I only hope your confidence in me is not misplaced. If I'm elected, I'll serve, though I can never replace you."

Kyle gestured toward the trail, and Jacob fell into rhythm with his friend's long strides, the silence an opportunity to brood. Who would have thought that Jacob Goodayle would ever be Chairman? How could he possibly lead in these times, a man who could barely keep a roof over his wife's head? One thing was certain—if he were Chairman, the Goodayle Family would have a new house—one Amelia could not refuse.

CHAPTER SEVEN
Penal Colony/America Prime

The guard strained to read Ahmed's insignia.

With an agitated swish of his palm, he flashed his implant under the guard's nose. "Is this proof enough, Mr. I-Don't-Care-What-Your-Name-Is?"

"Officer Hamilton, sir." He returned the disc then tipped his cap as if this do-over of civility would assuage Ahmed's anger. "My apologies, Mr. Fared. I see Warden Barnes has released the prisoner in question to your custody. You don't resemble your images on the security files."

Ahmed forced a grin. "Apology accepted. I decided to shed the beard along with the dishdasha and the shermagh … see what standard dress feels like and scratch a five-o'clock shadow. Although I find this government-issue suit, though contemporary, is far less comfortable."

"I understand."

"I doubt you truly do. Now, may I see my charge?"

Officer Hamilton exited, and Ahmed waited alone in the marbled lounge. A residual scent, perhaps left by some perfumed advocate, made his nose itch. Drat the scanners … always watching, the privy the only place where a man could abandon civilization and play the animal. Should he suffer the itch or risk the embarrassment to scratch his nose? He looked for a privy sign, saw none, sat and brooded over the losses technological advancement had placed on the human experience, thankful, at least that scanners were finally outlawed in the privy. He laughed when he recalled the headlines: Citizens Outraged by Privy Scanners. They really believed their outcries had influence.

Leave them to their delusions.

Nor did the public ever truly know the motivation behind the scanner reform. That riding on the waves of public opinion, the then delegate Rowlands spearheaded the revision of scanner law after he was caught by Devereux in an unquestionable act of intimacy with another delegate's fifteen-year-old daughter. Nor did the public know that Rowlands' flip-flop on Devereux's sanitation project for Sector Ten was managed in exchange for Devereux's silence. And Rowlands assumed his lapse of judgment would remain buried since the only witnesses, Devereux and the girl, were both dead.

Ahmed had questioned Devereux's willingness to ignore Rowlands' behavior. "Such is the way of politics, my friend. Leverage should be weighed carefully. The Good Book warns against trying to separate the tares and the wheat. We must tread carefully when we seek to root out corruption for sometimes change creates more harm than good. Never fear. Rowlands will have his day in court, if not on Earth, then at the Maker's hand. His justice is more terrible than any imagination of mankind."

All well and good for Devereux. His choice to be a Christ follower brought him to Eternal Pathways and robbed the Constitutional Government of the best leader the times had to offer. Rowlands beguiled the innocent, a wannabe monarch who twisted the dreams of nobler men, an ignoramus who gave no deference to anyone else, including his intimate. What idiocy brought men like this to rule over the righteous, to prosper when good men starved?

Benjamin emerged, a shackled, tall, thin pole next to Officer Hamilton's abbreviated form. Ahmed grabbed his nephew from three feet away and pulled him into an embrace. "Good to see you, my boy."

"Uncle Ahmed? I hardly recognized you. What happened to your beard?"

"Gone. Our new governor was very persuasive. Besides, the shermagh made my head itch." Ahmed twirled on the tips of his toes. "Don't you think the new look becomes me?"

"You're too funny. Pops says you can make a dead man laugh."

"I seriously doubt I possess so magical a power."

"Your power got me out of prison."

Ahmed gazed at Benjamin's sallow features. If only the detention committee would agree to the reforms Ahmed had presented at last meeting. The current practice to withhold food as a means of control seemed ridiculous. A starved prisoner would not survive the torturous inquisition procedures. Seemed the committee was made up of nitwits and he was the sole voice of reason.

He glowered at the midget of a guard. "Release him, Officer Hamilton. Now."

"Yes, Mr. Fared."

Hamilton clipped the restraint, and Benjamin rubbed his gangly arms.

"Come, my boy. Your mother has butchered the proverbial calf in honor of your return."

"Did Pops finally barter with Davu for cattle?"

"No. I spoke metaphorically. Your mother's roasted goose tastes far better than tender sirloin."

"I'll take your word for it, Uncle Ahmed. I've never had first generation beef."

"A guard will transport us via tram to Defector's Gate in the sub-city. Davu's air shuttle will meet us at the landing pad on the rim of the sub-city then take us to the Denver Hub where your father will meet us with the bubble craft."

Officer Hamilton pointed to an escalator. "The tram to the sub-city is this way."

Benjamin fell silent, so unlike the boy who'd argue politics the whole night long. By the time they reached the IEA tram, Benjamin had said no more than six words. Maybe his tongue would loosen once they were outside America Prime.

Officer Hamilton never lowered his P-74 and followed closely behind. No matter. Benjamin was alive, and Ahmed would be willing to hurl his three hundred pounds through burning hoops to keep him that way. "You know, Benjamin, before I came to live with your father's family, we traveled by fossil-fueled vehicles. Very slow, though. A trip from old Washington, DC to the former San Diego took three days."

"Yeah, well, Network hovercrafts might be faster than the old motor cars. Even Pops' supercharged transport is a snail compared to the Series 456. I've heard they're as fast as a plasma burst."

Finally, a spark of interest. "My biological father bought the last Cadillac off the assembly line the day before the ban on fossil-fueled cars, though he knew the government would eventually confiscate it."

Benjamin fell silent once more. Might as well give the boy his space for the moment. Amelia would not stand for his withdrawal—and she could wring a soliloquy from a mute.

Officer Hamilton keyed a command, and a tram zipped into the loading platform. Once onboard, he keyed another command while Ahmed and Benjamin secured their safety harnesses. Gravity shock waves were more severe in IEA tunnels than in the public transportation thoroughfares. Ahmed leaned back and closed his eyes. Within five minutes, the tram decelerated then came to an abrupt halt at a checkpoint. Officer Hamilton detached his safety harness and stood. "This is as far as I go, Mr. Fared. Another guard with Level Ten clearance will escort you to the sub-city portal. Protocol, you know."

Protocol indeed. There were no protocols where Benjamin was concerned. The few outworld inmates who survived imprisonment were indoctrinated and repatriated. Rowlands probably invented the weighty procedures to annoy his Second.

Hamilton handed the disk to an armed female officer, tipped his hat toward his charges and left. The officer slipped the disk into her micro for verification. Ahmed's image projected, and her right eyebrow slanted as she compared the old file to his newly shaven face.

"You don't resemble your image, sir."

"So I've been told."

"I'll need to scan your implant."

When he returned to provincial headquarters, he'd create a new official image and be done with this inconvenience. Ahmed waved his implant over the officer's micro, and ADAM projected. "Identity confirmed."

"Sorry, sir. I hope you understand I was only following procedures."

"Procedures I voted for. You needn't apologize."

The officer pointed in a westerly direction. "This way."

If not for her stern jaw, she'd be pretty enough … olive skin … probably Arabian.

Ahmed and Benjamin followed her to a readied sonar rover, a model specially designed for IEA sub-city underground transport—a metallic, windowless, round bubble. Until now, he'd never ridden in one. She programmed the coordinates and engaged the engine. "Will you be staying the night in the Network, Mr. Fared?"

"I expect to stay at least overnight. Care to join me?" Ahmed winked.

A blush heightened her rosy cheeks.

"What is your name, my dear?"

"Sonya Riyad."

"From Old Kabul?"

"Yes, Mr. Fared. My surname was changed because of the Uniformity Act."

Rowlands would uniform sex if he could. "My father dropped most of the ancestral customs when he served as an ambassador before my birth, although he surnamed me after his given name. All those Arab identifiers were too complicated, in my opinion. In the old days, a mother became short-winded calling her child to dinner."

She laughed, and her soft coo enticed him.

"How long have you been an officer?"

"I graduated from the academy five years ago, and from security advanced training last year. This is my first security post."

Benjamin scowled. "Must you be so obvious, Uncle Ahmed? I'd like to get home to my mother's cooking. I haven't eaten in two weeks."

"Not much further."

Sonya steered toward an exit ramp, then parked by the gate, a defector's final stop before being expelled naked into the outworld. Thankfully, he and Benjamin would not have to shed every bit of protection. Once through the gate, they'd have to walk through a mile of brambles before they reached the clearing to meet Davu's shuttle. Some said the path through the bush was strewn with skeletons, most likely a myth to deter potential defectors.

Sonya led them into the portal's promenade than walked back toward a steel buttress. Ahmed waited for something ... anything to indicate they had not been led into a trap. The ground shook, and a nine-foot section of wall lifted. Detection scanners lined the whole of the promenade with blips and beeps sufficient to scare the dead. As they reached the end of the tunnel, fresh air greeted them.

His obesity caused few problems in the City since transportation was readily available. This walk winded him. Perhaps a signal he should consider a weight loss regime or undergo a surgical procedure. He had no excuse being overweight in America Prime. Yet, the ladies flocked to a corpulent man.

They reached the pad thirty minutes before Davu's shuttle was due to arrive. Opportunity, perhaps, to loosen Benjamin's tongue as to what troubled him. "No more scanners from this point on, Benjamin. I sense your lip must be bitten off by now."

"I have a favor to ask."

"I am your servant."

"Don't say that yet. You're not going to like what I have to ask you. Neither will Pops."

"Go on."

Benjamin's shoulders heaved. "You know I will reach Accountability on Friday?"

"Yes. Your father has already spread the word."

"No need for a party. I've decided to repatriate."

"You're right. Your father will not be pleased. Why would you want to do this? Did prison rob you of your wits?"

Benjamin's hesitancy was as transparent as a woman's sheer over-blouse.

"Out with it. It's a girl, isn't it?"

"Why do you say that?"

"Because I was once a young man. The scented women of America Prime smell much better than outworld girls, even those of the Network. Am I right?"

"Her name is Christine. Christine Devereux."

Ahmed laughed, partially to hide his concern and partially because the very thought amused him. "The late governor's daughter?"

"Yes."

Benjamin faced far more danger in America Prime than he might realize. "And does Christine share these feelings?"

"I think so. I met her during the Holiday Hunt. She was one of the Humanitarians who stacked the goods outside the southern sub-city wall. She gave me the matchbox tin I painted for Pops, and we talked for a while. She's the reason I've been sneaking into America Prime. When I heard her father was in trouble, I tried to meet her at her estate, and I got caught. I lied. Said I'd broken into the City for food. Before I was arrested, we talked about a familial contract. I love her."

Ahmed drew his nephew into a large bear hug. "Ah. Love will drive a man where reason will not go. My Anna affected me that way. Perhaps if we'd stayed together, I would be a man of valor today."

"You're too hard on yourself, Uncle Ahmed. You're the bravest man I've ever known."

Ahmed laughed. "Benjamin, my boy, bravery is one step shy of foolishness—passion and emotion are reserved for the young, and I passed my prime a long time ago."

"I don't believe you."

Young eyes like Benjamin's saw only black and white with little room for compromise. Older men dwelled in the gray of life. The day would soon come, however, when desperate winds would push every man, woman, and child to one side or the other. "I'll help you break the news to your father. And I will pledge to keep an eye on you. Fair enough?"

"I knew you wouldn't let me down, Uncle Ahmed."

Davu's shuttle driver landed on time. When the hatch opened, Benjamin pushed Ahmed into the hold. The indignities of these infernal small shuttles … designed for the rail thin, not the hefty. Another ten minutes and they'd join Jacob at the hub's landing pad. A better arrangement for father and son, still Ahmed would have liked another ride on a Series 456. At least, he would be blessed with a peaceful evening.

Nights were the best part of the Network. Children played ring toss while mothers grouped to swap clothing or patch torn garments. When he strolled along the trailed perimeter, he often came across a makeshift band where young people danced a jig to homemade piccolos, flutes, organs, and guitars. Or some might gather at a neighbor's home where they'd sing the hymns of old, passed down by memory from generation to generation. Jacob always gave Ahmed a sign before contraband Bibles and hymn books were handed out. If they weren't seen, Ahmed would not have to report the hub for illegal assembly.

When they deplaned, Ahmed gave Davu's pilot a bag of black market drugs as payment. Benjamin scoured the horizon. "It's too quiet. Where is everyone?"

"I hadn't told you, Benjamin. My sources reported the Network manse burned to the ground this morning. I thought people would have returned to their homes by now. If there's a meeting, you can be sure your father's in the thick of it."

Benjamin shook his head. "What caused it?"

"My sources think the fire was started by an incendiary device."

"You mean like a bomb? This was not the work of Marauders."

"No."

"Then who? Certainly not the Nomads. They've managed to coexist with the Network both inside our boundaries and out."

Benjamin might as well learn now that politics was the devil's tool chest. "I suspect this is sabotage by government agents."

"Why? We pay our tithes. Why can't the Constitutional Government leave us alone?"

"There are those who believe the Network has become too strong and want to see its collapse."

"And you support this?"

Ahmed sighed. "Of course not. These men don't realize how their attacks only serve to strengthen the Network. Outside conflict tends to force a community to reexamine their values. When people recommit to what unifies them, the community strengthens."

"The Constitutional Government fears our common purpose?"

"One of many reasons the government wants to disrupt the Network."

Benjamin scowled. "What's there to be afraid of? There are so few of us. One raid by the IEA could wipe out an entire community in minutes. See, Uncle Ahmed? That's why I want to repatriate. Be a government worker like you. Make a change from the inside."

Ahmed swung his right arm over the man-child's shoulder. "My dear boy. You are too eager to be the righter of wrongs. Leave politics to the stooped and aged. A young buck like you should be about mischief, not bent on reform."

Benjamin's eyes pleaded. "A rebellion by the Network would only lead to massacre—something no one wants, including the Constitutional Government. Pops and I disagree on that point. The Constitutional Government has many weaknesses to be sure. However, civil war is not the solution. Most in the Network prefer a return to the principles of the Accord. We resent the government's intrusion into our private lives. Christine says Citizens have to get permission just to have a baby."

A philosopher like his father, Benjamin's idealism, his cry for freedom, had become the mantra of the Network's young. "Evil has always masqueraded as benevolent. In this age, he wears the face of Edwin Rowlands. His passion for his pseudo-utopia makes him even more dangerous. He sees himself as a political messiah, determined to spread his skewered religion. He'll oppose any law above the government."

"Then you see why I want to repatriate, to change things from the inside out?"

Ahmed tousled Benjamin's hair, and he shirked away in manly objection. "You think far too much for a boy your age."

"Will you help me?"

"I'll try. Chances are your father will probably never speak to me again." A hum, followed by a thickening dust cloud, clued Jacob's arrival. "Good. Here comes your father. I was beginning to worry."

They stepped to the side of the clearing as the hovercraft decelerated and parked. A soot-smeared man emerged. "Is that you, Ahmed? Benjamin?"

"Pops?"

How he envied Jacob. A man should have something of himself to pass on—a legacy—one of flesh and bone and not a blip on a history disk, easily manipulated and misrepresented. What would those living after him say about Ahmed Fared? Some might speak well of him—how he tried to bridge two worlds grown apart. If the truth were known, he rather liked being a prince in both.

Jacob peered in Ahmed's direction. "I see you finally decided to camouflage yourself among the denizens of America Prime?"

"Rowlands idea, not mine. I had to scramble to find a size to fit me." He gave Jacob two pats on the shoulders. "Is everyone well? I heard about the fire."

"We're a little weary, although the manse is lost. We'll build another, of course. And most of the mayors are determined the new manse will be bigger and more modern." Jacob motioned toward Benjamin. "Come, your mother won't rest until she smothers you with kisses and fills your belly with goose and potatoes. She sent me on ahead while she prepared dinner. She wants to try out the new solar speed cooker Esther Muldoon gave her in payment for the house calls when her baby had pneumonia. After dinner, we'll plan your party."

Ahmed caught Benjamin's downcast glance. "Don't rush the boy, Jacob. He needs rest. Take your son home and let him bathe off the day. Then the two of you can start fresh in the morning. That's what your father would have said."

Jacob's hearty laughs never failed to bridge any distance between them. "Good advice. I hope you'll stay the night, Ahmed. I've news to share."

As the transport sped toward Jacob's hut, the ills of America Prime escaped Ahmed's thoughts. A deeper concern pressed on his heart. "How is Amelia this evening?"

"She's exhausted most of the time. However, Benjamin's return has energized her spirits. Ironic. My wife has dedicated her life to the study of herbs and their healing properties. Her knowledge has brought many outworlders back from the brink of death. Yet, there's not a single plant in United Earth that can help her."

Benjamin turned his attention to his father. "Is Mother going to die?"

"We have to trust in the Maker's will."

"Mother's faith is strong. It's you she worries about."

Jacob decelerated and parked the hovercraft next to the hut. Amelia barreled out the open door and engulfed her son as if a lifetime had separated them. "The Maker be praised. He's brought you back to us!"

Benjamin finally smiled. "The Maker had a little help from Uncle Ahmed."

"Thank you, Ahmed. You're too kind to us."

The evening winds had picked up and flapped against the door as the party scrambled into the hut. Benjamin pushed the door closed with little effort, even in his weakened condition. Oh, to be young again and have the strength of a bull.

Amelia finished the meal preparations while Jacob lit the solitary lamp over the table. "What a frightful wind."

"Pops, where are the Skinners going to stay while the manse is being built? The nights are too cold to stay in their barn, especially with Peter's poor health."

"The family is staying at Thomas Muldoon's place until they are able to go to America Prime. Kyle has decided to repatriate."

Of all Network residents who might join the Citizenry, Ahmed had never suspected Kyle Skinner. "Interesting turn of events. I hope he's not going to end up in Sector Ten."

"Caroline has an uncle in Sector Four who will sponsor them. They'll need an advocate. Will you vouch for them, Ahmed?"

"Why would Kyle Skinner want to repatriate?"

"His boy, Peter, has leukemia."

"I'll see what I can do." What father would not give his own life for his child? "Kyle Skinner is an honorable man, and honorable men struggle to remain so in America Prime. A sponsor will certainly expedite the process. Otherwise, Peter would die before the paperwork is completed. However, Kyle is a Christ follower. He'll need to be discreet. Given his former Network position, the IEA will target him for surveillance. If he starts preaching, he'll be terminated before he even gets his implant."

Amelia carried in a tray loaded with plates, a pot of potatoes, and roasted goose. "Enough sad talk. Husband, tell Ahmed the news. Or were you waiting until he took his first bite so he'd choke on your good fortune?"

Jacob shrugged his shoulders as he sat. "Ahmed has sources. He probably already knows."

"What secrets are you keeping from me, brother?"

"You're looking at the new Network Chairman. They elected me not more than an hour ago. The sun sets upon a new era in our outworld."

Shouldn't a brother buzz with pride over such news? Maybe … if the brother were not risking a P-74 burst to the head. Didn't Jacob understand he still lived only because of negotiated protection? His climb in Network leadership endangered them both. "If I were a man who prayed, I'd put you at the top of my list. Instead, I'll simply offer my condolences."

"Coming from you, brother, praise enough."

Conversation happily drifted from Kyle's unfortunate circumstances to the yet unpublished Festival plans. "Rowlands assures me he will enter negotiations with an open mind. America Prime will offer amnesty to anyone who repatriates during the Festival. A good compromise, Jacob—good enough to avoid catastrophe."

"I'm sure many will take the bait." Jacob tilted his head in Benjamin's direction. "You've been too quiet, son."

Now was not the time for Benjamin to spill his plans to repatriate. News like this was better digested after desert. "Let him be, Jacob. He's probably too tired for conversation. Right, Benjamin?"

"Yeah. I'm pretty tired."

Amelia put lettuce leaves in a bowl and set the dish next to the potatoes and goose. "Everything's ready."

Jacob stretched out his hands and gazed toward heaven. "Thank you, Our Provider, for this meal and for the miracle of our returned son."

Ahmed remained silent while Benjamin and Amelia said, "Amen."

Jacob passed out plates. "Well, Mrs. Goodayle. You'll soon have the house I always promised. Thomas says the new manse will be raised by next month. Your husband has made something of himself after all."

Amelia tweaked his cheek, as he set a plate for her.

"Sit."

Ahmed smiled at Amelia's motherly attention over Benjamin. In some ways, she was much like his Anna, both intelligent and beautiful, but Anna was vain and selfish. Jacob had married the kinder sister.

Ahmed's thoughts drifted to the miracle of the Network. A few years had brought remarkable improvements. Outworlders conquered the inhospitable land, and now the forgotten had become the feared.

These next few weeks would cause even the most apathetic to make hard choices and test the character of the most devout. How would history measure those choices—his, in particular? Would the truth of his climb be revealed? He rose, not from personal conviction, but rather from selfish ambition? How painful to look inside one's self and see his own shallowness. Yet, perhaps the Maker permitted his success for a nobler purpose. For the first time in his adult life, he gave more than a minute's thought to a power greater than Ahmed Fared.

CHAPTER EIGHT
Sector Ten/New Edinburgh

Bridget kissed Ian's cold lips. Without so much as a whimper, he'd slipped into eternity while she slept. At least his suffering was over. She could only hope he'd find out about the baby from the angels who ushered him into his reward.

The last few days blurred her thoughts. Yesterday afternoon, Bridget and Ian had joked how the morrow would find them on the shuttle to America Prime, had waved their travel documents into the air then put them on the table while they enjoyed one last romantic supper. She was about to tell him about the baby. She planned to excuse herself into the bedroom and bring out the quilt she made from the scraps of Mum's garments. "Wouldn't this be a great present for a wee son, Ian," she would have said. He would have hugged her and held her hands as they laughed on the shuttle trip to Western America where Ian planned to occupy a senior delegate seat won by the Reformation Party.

Such was the stuff of dreams, and they'd come so close to all they'd hoped for. This was to be their last mission—to smuggle a gold-embossed crucifix into Western America where operatives would then secrete the treasure to the Sierra Province. What had given them away? Had she been so excited about the baby, she'd been careless? Or perhaps the doctor thought Bridget's hefty bribe insufficient and reported her illegal pregnancy, a conception before final government approval.

Perhaps in heaven, all things would be revealed, and Ian would gain a perch in the highest realms to watch his son grow. Aye, she'd have a lad, and he'd have brown eyes like hers and curly blonde hair like his da. A mum sensed these things.

She had been born into a prominent family, as Ian had been. What future awaited her unborn? The image of the waif she'd seen earlier revisited. Was this what the future held for her child? Would he be forced to eke out a bare existence in the badlands of the Artic Province, the offspring of an outlaw? She bristled against whatever design the Maker had put upon her. Why go on? Why not simply lie down next to Ian and wait for the end?

Although too early for quickening, she felt a movement within as if her baby screamed he wanted to live. Even if you have to dodge scanners the whole of your life? Not if there were a way to prevent it. No son of Ian McCormick or grandson of Bryan Cavanaugh should be forced to die of malnourishment.

Ian often spoke of the Network in Western America, how they assembled and had plenty to eat. Each hub had a water system, a method of education, and even a government of sorts, albeit illegal. He'd hoped to glean a modus operandi by observation of the Network, bring the knowledge back to the Highland Province, transform the disorganized outworlds to a thriving subculture, and blend that society into provincial life. Wouldn't reform be a better option than revolution? What would happen to the fledgling political movement without its charismatic leader?

Her hope, like Old Scotland's, lay dead in her arms. Her child's and her future mapped with uncertainty—alone and unprotected. Would a radical group kill her on the spot or take her hostage and demand a ransom from Da? Ian McCormick had been the hero of the Highland outworlds, not Bridget Cavanaugh.

She forced her thoughts from death to life.

She must beg for Da's forgiveness and trust in his gentleness. How pleased he'd be to learn he'd be a grandfather. Perhaps then he'd forgive her, and the baby could be raised in the same loving home as she'd known. If she signed an Affidavit of Contrition, claimed Ian forced her into helping the Treasure Keepers, Da could restore her status as a free Citizen. She would retake the Oath of Allegiance, forget the Reformation Party and work for Da and the Humanitarians.

Of course, they'd be watched closely, her sudden repentance highly suspicious. Risky, true enough. Ian had taught her how to live a secret life as a rebel and serve the government at the same time. Aye … a return to her father's home was the best of all her options. When Felicia returned, Bridget would thank her for her kindness, bury Ian, and then bribe an officer to bring her home.

Where was Felicia? What time was it? Gauging by Ian's stiffened corpse, more than half a day had passed. Bridget lit the last candle stub. Death's stench, laced with human excrement, sucked the breath from her. She should leave now and find an officer—beg for mercy. If she could break the panel, perhaps she could escape. She searched the chamber, and found nothing heavier than the mattress, now Ian's coffin. She slid to the floor in a useless heap and let loose her grief.

A sound like scraping metal brought her from the abyss of sorrow.

The panel opened.

Bridget leaped to her feet with hope. Felicia had not abandoned her. Through the glare of the flashlight, Bridget made out the form of an IEA agent, a P-74 raised, a target beam hot on her chest. She had wanted to join Ian. So be it.

The figure removed his helmet. In the dim light, his smile still made a heart thump, handsome a man as ever there was. At least she'd thought so until she met Ian McCormick. "Well, as I live and breathe, Jimmy Kinnear in the flesh."

Jimmy put a finger to his lips then handed her a canteen. She only managed two gulps before he pulled the precious water from her grasp."

"Jimmy, where's Felicia?"

"Dead. Gerard, too."

"How did you know—"

Jimmy knelt at Ian's side, as one who surrendered respect to one greater than himself. He faced Bridget, speaking in hushed tones. "I'm sorry I didn't get here in time. Ian's death saddens all who fight in the name of freedom."

The tears Bridget thought spent flowed afresh. "Jimmy, what do I do now?"

Gray streaked his hair, and his once pudgy face, taut with years of rebellion, set off his firm chin. "You're coming with me."

"No. No more causes. I want to see Da. You know about the baby?"

Jimmy nodded. "Felicia told me before she died."

"What happened?"

"She contacted us about your escape and Ian's injuries. While attempting a rescue, we ran into a nest of agents at the intersection. Nemo Savakis' team."

"I remember him. They called him Dog-headed Savakis."

"Dog-headed is being polite. One of my soldiers killed an officer. Savakis had me in his sights. Felicia threw herself in front of me—foolish woman thinking my life mattered more than hers. Gerard and I tried to hold them off. There were too many. He sacrificed himself for me, too. I doubled back, stole the dead officer's gear and uniform, and here I am."

Bridget ached for the losses. Ian, Felicia, and Gerard. For what? For artifacts, paintings, pieces of paper and a weak hope of future freedom to speak their thoughts without fear. "I'm sorry about Felicia. She'd be alive if she hadn't tried to help us."

"Don't blame yourself. Blame the times we live in. We have to fight or the government will swallow what humanity we have left."

"You can fight, Jimmy. Like Ian, you have the heart for causes. I'm simply a pregnant woman who went where her man led."

"You do him honor if you take up his gauntlet."

The one thing she would not do. "Reformation was Ian's dream. Not mine. I helped him because I loved him."

Jimmy lowered his P-74 and leaned against the wall. "I'd rather die fighting than fall victim to Rowlands' idea of a perfect world."

"Fight then and send yourself to an early grave. I want to go home to my father. Da will protect me and the baby. He's a good man. He fights his own war from the inside making law that will mold the world as the Accord intended."

Jimmy held his P-74 in the air like a declaration. "This ... is the only way to restore what's been taken from us. Words will never bring change. Do you really think your da can stop Rowlands? Governor Cavanaugh's a lone wolf in a pen of hunters. Did you know Rowlands has convened the governors at the Oceanic Retreat, and Governor Cavanaugh was not invited? Constable Becker's there as well. My sources say President Schumann will pay a visit too. Rowlands is certain to be Schumann's successor, and he'll stop at nothing to pass his precious Preservation Act. Your da will be no protection for you."

His words pulled her like the ocean tides. She returned to Ian's deathbed and spoke a question she knew he could not answer. "What should I do?"

Jimmy snickered. "You'll have to make your own decision, lassie."

"Jimmy, I need my da. Please. Take me to him."

"Stubborn as always. I'll do what I can. Let's go."

"Wait, I need to bury Ian first."

"No time. Savakis probably knows where I am. You're not safe here. This chamber will have to be Ian's tomb."

"I won't leave him to rot like fruit rind."

"You have no choice."

"You're heartless, Jimmy Kinnear. No wonder Angelina turned you in."

He yanked her arm and pulled her closer to him. "If you weren't pining after Ian, I'd show you how heartless I can be. Don't mention Angelina again." He retrieved a set of filthy pantaloons. "Put these on. I took them off Felicia."

"Turn around. I won't go into that privy again."

Bridget stripped off her privileged silk pantaloons and donned trappings as rank as the privy she avoided.

"March in front of me. I'll say you're a meme gone amuck, and I'm taking you in for maintenance."

"This will never work, Jimmy."

"It'll have to or we'll join Ian in the hereafter before we see another day. I'm going straight to hell, you know. At least, you'll have a heaven to look forward to."

Bridget glanced at her belly. Life was inside her, and Da needed her too. She blew a kiss toward Ian's body as she wiped away her last tear. "I'll make sure your son knows what a fine da you would have been."

Jimmy slipped restraints around her wrists. "Part of the act."

As they surfaced from Felicia's flat, the City's artificial light gave way to the sun's dominion, a ray of hope that by the morrow she'd find forgiveness in her father's arms.

CHAPTER NINE
Oceanic Retreat/Australian Province

Edwin Rowlands stretched—his poolside recliner as cushiony as his hotel suite bed. The late morning sun warmed his skin, a respite from the artificial glows of bubbled America Prime. Wonderful how natural sun, though blistering, relaxed a body taut from duty. He lathered skin lotion on his legs, arms, neck, and face, injected another hypo of radiation blocker then leaned back to sip his Coriander Mix, a spicy blend of tropical fruit and herbs. Normally, he added expensive, rare elixir to his fruit mixture. Not this time. Today required a clear head.

Everyone of importance had arrived including Constable Becker, the IEA Director—the real power behind Congress, and a man as easily managed as a cape. The remaining decisive votes now had become a mere formality once Becker strong-armed the undecided blocs. Only those loyal to Devereux and Cavanaugh openly resisted. Devereux was dead and Cavanaugh's time would come soon enough.

Edwin blinked his eyes and waved at a persistent bug, probably a mutated gnat. If so, their bite sometimes produced a life-threatening fever. He delt with the pest as he did all inconveniences—offense before defense. He squished the pest between his forefinger and thumb then trained his thoughts to his future and the implementation of his star legislation. His vision for a fifteenth article to the Constitution was within grasp, except for Cavanaugh's resistance. He'd be dealt with in due time—like the gnat. First, however, secure Schumann's nomination, win the governors' approval, then have his bid approved by Congress. He took another sip of his Coriander Mix, set his tumbler on his lounge table then bathed his spirits in the sun. Once Cavanaugh was out of the way, he'd vaporize the Revolutionary Army, Kinnear's militia, their stronghold too close to New Edinburgh and an affront to all the Constitutional Government stood for.

Cavanaugh feared a civil war if he stormed Kinnear's stronghold at Dunfermline Abbey, the last standing old-world church, a revered Highland landmark. The man argued Kinnear had too many friends within both the Reformation and the Humanitarian parties. Hogwash. Not even Kinnear was a match for the full weight of the IEA.

Schumann had realized the time had come to cleanse ethnic pride, complete uniformity the only certainty against civil war. The vanity of the Highland Province fed the Reformation factions like corn chowder to a Nomad. If the cause is burned, the Resistance vanishes. Once rid of Cavanaugh, Edwin would declare a state of emergency, install IEA control and wipe out both the Reformation Party and Kinnear's army.

His plan made him tingle like a playmate's massage.

He exhaled—his enthusiasm a breath shy of a whistle. He must exercise patience, woo the Humanitarians, show token concern for the starving Nomads and other outworld inhabitants and ease the suffering of those poor souls stuffed into every city's Sector Ten. His ways might seem harsh to some. Ultimately, he would do the world much good.

His plan pleasured him, more potent than a dream drug. If he held the Festival in conjunction with his Inauguration, every faction leader would be present within America Prime. He would arrange for an emergency session of Congress to pass legislation of the Preservation Act, round up the dissenters, and preempt any further civil disobedience.

Fared needn't know his governor's true motivation for agreeing to a Festival. Keep him deluded with the belief negotiations would heal the breech between America Prime and the Network. Unlike Schumann, sentimentality would not engineer Rowlands' administration—why he'd coerce this necessary amendment. With the rebel element eradicated, the world would be a new Camelot. He, Edwin Milton Rowlands, would be its Arthur.

His arm twitched when he remembered Michael. What to do about her, his beautiful Guinevere, Excelsior Media the Lancelot by which she betrayed him. His union with her had been the worst miscalculation of his political career—her refusal to sell the company, a blight on his backside. With a brat to manage, she'd be occupied. Dissolutions involving a child were much more difficult to obtain. Indeed, a child for Michael would be the apple he needed to bring her into submission.

"Will you have another Coriander Mix, Governor Rowlands?" The husky voice intrigued him. He opened his eyes and handed the ebony-skinned meme his empty vial. "Yes, of course."

As she left, he followed her sway, the uniqueness of her total attractiveness, and how her black locks fell wantonly over bare shoulders. Should he request of her owner a night of diversion with this beauty? Michael would be livid. Did he want to risk her disproval at so delicate an impasse in their contract? Though she owned memes, she abhorred their use for sexual pleasure. Let her live by her antiquated morality. A man had the right to use his property however he chose.

The meme returned and Edwin rethought his temptation.

"What is your name?"

"Lynette … Lynette Deschamps, after my designer, Jean Deschamps."

"Is this your first assignment?"

"I was commissioned yesterday from the factory in the Congo Province. Governor Cudrow brought me here as a demonstration model. Anything else, Governor Rowlands?"

"No, Lynette."

A hearty laugh made him turn. "Governor Rowlands, your flirtations will be your downfall, you know."

She left, and Edwin rose to shake hands with President Schumann. "My apologies. I didn't realize you were standing so near."

"Obviously not." He smiled. "I don't blame you, though. Who could resist such a beauty?"

He'd have to until he could figure out how to settle Michael's rebellion. "I see we are men of like tastes, Mr. President."

"Come join me for a short walk."

Once inside the hotel, Schumann led Edwin to an isolated corner. "Well, Rowlands, you've hosted a splendid party, as usual. You and Cudrow. Pity Cavanaugh couldn't be here. Please relay my disappointment."

"I will, Mr. President."

"I suppose you should be the first to know," Schumann said, a slight waver in his voice. "I plan on making the announcement before the governors discuss your proposed Preservation Act. I've scheduled my euthanasia two weeks from today. Cancer has spread to the liver and pancreas, beyond help, I'm afraid. I plan to formalize your succession. I'm certain the governors will approve, and your installment can be guaranteed at the Congressional Caucus next week."

"I am truly sorry to hear your health has forced this decision, Mr. President. The Constitutional Government is losing a valiant leader."

Edwin swallowed his delight, unable to digest his run of good fortune. In his younger days, this first President of the Constitutional Government gave the failed Accord its final blow and reshaped the world. Though once a great man, Schumann had served long beyond his usefulness. If cancer had not forced him to the Euthanasia Chamber, he would have been retired by assassination.

At the drafting of the Articles of Constitution, lifetime appointments seemed a good idea. The founders believed the fewer elections held the less likelihood of corruption by lobbyists. Unfortunately, the practice allowed the weak to remain in power far beyond their former genius, and leaders like Cavanaugh and Devereux refused to let the Accord die, thus the formation of special interests and multiple party platforms. The time had come for one party to assure one government for all continued.

"I am honored you have selected me as your elect, and if the governors uphold your recommendation, I will look forward to our change of command sessions."

"One more thing, Rowlands. My Second, Lemuel Sampson, has formerly requested resignation to private life the moment my death is confirmed. You will be free to appoint your own Second. I understand Ahmed Fared has remained as Second Governor. His loyalty to Devereux is a common fact. Do you think he can be trusted?"

Schumann sensed Fared's duplicity as well? "Mr. President,

Fared has a large following in every major political party, and his influence with the Network cannot be ignored. Better to have him in my corner than a cancer on my perimeter. His connections are too valuable to encourage their use against me. Wouldn't you agree?"

President Schumann raised an eyebrow in agreement. "The reason I recommended you, Rowlands. You are decisive, something I fear I've lost since I stopped soldiering and became a politician."

"Thank you for your confidence."

"I'll leave you to enjoy your Coriander and Lynette. Most of the governors are catching the night shuttle back to their home provinces. If you are confirmed, and I fully expect you will be, I would like to meet for breakfast."

Edwin waited until Schumann went into the pavilion before he grabbed the transponder. He should tell Michael the news. He hit her code then deactivated the hail. No. Better wait until after his meeting with President Schumann. Instead, he should buy Michael a gift to show his intent to give her a child.

Using the exterior lift to his suite, Edwin took short sips from his Coriander Mix while entertained by the play of light on the lift's protective frame. He whistled as he changed into his caped jumpsuit, rode the interior lift to the lobby and walked to the attached mall, a shopping service for retreat guests. He despised the chore of selection, though the managers walked the customer through the process via a micro-feed. He usually cajoled a staff member to buy Michael's gifts. However, he'd come to Oceania without his usual security detail.

Edwin approached the store counter, and a middle-aged, bronze-skinned meme greeted him. "Good day, Governor Rowlands. May I be of assistance?"

"I need a gift for my intimate. Something delicate, I suppose."

"I understand completely, Governor. Why don't I divert the scanner and allow you to peruse the merchandise in privacy? If you find an item you wish to purchase, I will retrieve your selection myself. Will that be satisfactory?"

The meme drifted into the back room while Edwin clicked the viewer and EVE projected. "Please state your desired merchandise category."

"Lingerie ... correction ... infant merchandise."

Babies were unlovely things. They spit up, wet, drooled, and cried for inordinate periods of time throughout the day. He would make sure his absences were frequent until the child reached school age. And he'd insist on a daughter—girls favored their mothers. His presence would only be required at special events, for propriety's sake and publicity opportunities.

EVE offered more instructions. "Select the sub-department you wish to peruse."

He scrolled the list of categories. Food, blankets, clothing. There ... tiny Jade earrings. Perfect. Jade covered nearly every inch of Michael's shelves. Edwin heated with the idea—brilliant—certain to convince Michael of his sincerity beyond any doubt. They would name their daughter Jade.

The sheer sentimentality of the gesture grabbed even his calloused heart.

CHAPTER TEN
The Denver Hub/Western America

Amber glows mingled with red skies as the sun gradually set against the horizon. Jacob never tired of the view, one blessing he'd miss if he repatriated. This evening, he contemplated both the troubles and the blessings the day had brought. He rested comfortably in his familiar trappings while Amelia finished her cleanup ritual, a chore she would not allow anyone to do. "There's a craft in it," she'd say any time he offered assistance.

She brought in a tray of her wild berry pie. Memories of his mother's desserts filled his senses. Joyful childhood sounds and smells before the tsunamis changed the world forever. Jacob's mind flitted back to a time when, at age five, his father had taken the family to a carnival. He remembered standing before the Ferris wheel, crying, afraid to get on.

"The reward is at the top," Father had said. He'd been right. Once Jacob made the first circle and caught the mountain sunset, he never feared the wheel again. Perhaps at the top of life's adventure, from the Maker's perspective, life will prove to have been worth the struggles.

One thing for certain, his wife finally had reason to be proud of her man, and snickers prompted by the meager Goodayle hut would be forever silenced.

Amelia wiped her hands on her apron and sat next to him as the last flickers of light faded. "So, my dear wife, Thomas Muldoon says the new manse will have ten bedrooms, each with its own privy including toilets and sonic showers. He plans on three kitchens."

"Three? Foolishness. What would a woman do with three kitchens and barely enough food to fill one?"

"One of the kitchens will serve the attached meeting house."

"Do you think a meeting house is wise? The IEA will be on our doorstep with the first plank laid."

Ahmed joined them as he swallowed a large bite of pie. "You're right, Amelia. A meeting house is certain to cause more than suspicion. Jacob, your Network must be more cautious. Wait until after the Festival before delving into controversial matters. The manse is one thing. A meeting house is certain to tempt fate."

"A festival, you call it? More like the fiery furnace, if you ask me."

"You're too paranoid. Governor Rowlands wants peace, not war. He's promised to listen to the Network's proposals. If you flaunt your defiance, you'll force the governor's hand."

Rowlands was a tricky devil indeed if he had fooled Ahmed into believing the breach could be healed through negotiations. One didn't negotiate with a rattlesnake. "And you, brother, are too trusting. From what our hacked feeds tell us, Rowlands will be President within a few weeks. Then what? With absolute power, will he still be interested in negotiations? He only has to say the word, and our homes, our hopes, and dreams will be leveled. I don't see this Festival of yours solving anything."

"You'll go?"

"I'll go. Only to please you." He squeezed Amelia's hand. "Besides, my wife insists."

The three retreated indoors to the hut's kitchen where Benjamin paced—his gait agitated, like a man possessed. What ails that boy? "Enough of this doomsday thinking. Son, get your zither. Amelia, hail the neighbors and let's have some music to celebrate our son's return."

Amelia hauled out the portable communicator from its protective case and hailed the five families who lived near the Goodayle hut while Benjamin found his zither and plucked a few strings then reset the player chip.

Amelia closed the communicator. "Done. Everyone will be here in twenty minutes. Sam Nottingham is bringing his piccolo, and Isaac Morris will bring his new water keyboard."

Ahmed laughed. "Never heard of a water keyboard."

Jacob laughed in sync with Ahmed. "Isaac's invention. Operates like the old pipe organ in Great Grandpa Goodayle's church, and it's portable."

Ahmed laughed. "The ingenuity of you people never ceases to amaze me."

Amelia brought out extra stick chairs from storage. "Jacob, take these outdoors while I get the repellent candles. I told everyone to bring their own lanterns."

Isaac, his wife, and their six children arrived first, and Ahmed hurried to examine the keyboard. "You know, you'd be a rich man if you sold these in America Prime."

"Don't care nothing about being rich, Ahmed. If you can think of a trade arrangement without going through Davu, I'd be content."

"I'll see what I can do."

Soon piccolo, keyboard, and zither sounds mingled as children broke into various groups to dance, play baseball, or ring toss. The grownups sang the songs of old, once-treasured hymns now nearly forgotten—hymns Jacob learned at Grandpa Goodayle's knee. He found comfort in their symphony of reassurance—the Maker had not abandoned his creation. As the last embers of the campfire died, the guests offered their host congratulations on his promotion to Chairman then made their way back to their rovers.

When the last guest had left, Jacob went back inside the hut and gazed at Benjamin who solemnly stroked his zither, as if a pet about to be euthanized. "Son, you've been far too quiet. Anything wrong?"

"Not at all."

Something troubled him. What? Perhaps he worried about his occupation. "What now, Benjamin?"

"What do you mean?"

"You'll be twenty-one on Friday. Time to choose your path. I hoped you'd be my assistant. You'd be a fine politician, son."

"I'd really like to. I can't."

"A teacher then? We need more teachers."

"No, Pops. I can't be a teacher either."

"Why not?"

Benjamin glanced toward Ahmed.

"Go on, boy. Tell your father the truth."

He paced the length of the hut before he sat, his aura weighted as if under a heavy burden. "I can't do those things because I won't be here."

"What do you mean, you won't be here. Where are you going? Oh? Well, if it's another community you want to help ... by all means. The Border Community is the worst off for teachers. Enrique Morales would be glad to assign students for you to tutor."

Benjamin dropped his hands to his side, leaned back, and sighed. "There's no easy way to tell you."

"Then out with it."

"I want to repatriate."

A pain shot through Jacob's chest, and he slumped into a chair across from Benjamin.

"Say something, Pops."

"Are you certain of this?"

"Yes. Uncle Ahmed understands."

Benjamin's leaded news, the worst a father could hear, had been topped with yet another sour dollop. Apparently, Ahmed had influenced Benjamin's decision. Jacob glared at Ahmed as he slammed a fist against the table. This emblem built to celebrate his son's birth now become a symbol of betrayal. "Et tu, Bruté?"

"Hear the boy out, Jacob."

"No. Benjamin, you cannot repatriate. I forbid it."

"You can't forbid me. I'm not a child."

True, Benjamin was a man, and therein rested Jacob's frustration. How did the father expect a son to do a man's job and not treat him as such? "Ahmed, what do you know of this?"

Ahmed took another sip of goat's milk then cleared his throat. "Benjamin mentioned his plans to me, and I did try to convince him to stay here. Unsuccessfully. You know how young people are these days."

Jacob's balled fists tightened with Amelia's commanding scowl. Was he surrounded by traitors? First his son, then his brother, and now his wife?

She grabbed a small, clean rag and dabbed her eyes. "Husband, I don't want this for Benjamin any more than you do. But, I beg you.

Don't draw a line in the sand that neither one of you can cross. We'll lose him for sure."

Her wisdom, meant to assuage a philosopher's soul, served only to stoke his rage. "Why, Benjamin? Why would you dishonor our family like this? What will the Network think of their newly elected Chairman, now? Huh? They will ask for my resignation before I hold my first meeting." He paced—the thing he did when his heart and mind waged war. After three laps through the hut, he faced his son. "Look me in the eyes, and tell me the truth. Why are you determined to do this?"

Benjamin thrust back his shoulders, a statue of defiance. "In December, at the Holiday Hunt, I met a girl."

Of course, a girl, the usual reason an otherwise intelligent lad favors stupidity.

"She's beautiful, Pops. We talked for a while. I managed to sneak into America Prime to see her. The last time, I was caught. I told the IEA I was looking for food. Of course, they didn't believe me and thought I was a spy. I didn't want to get her in trouble. What else could I do? I want to share my life with her. She was all I thought about while in prison."

"All? You gave no thought to your mother?"

"Of course, I thought about you and Mother."

"And the name of this harlot who has possessed you?"

Benjamin jumped and shoved his chair to the floor. "You'll not disrespect Christine. You, of all people. She is as honorable as she is beautiful, a Humanitarian like her father."

Like her father? "Christine Devereux, daughter of the late governor? You are leaving your home and family for her?"

Jacob had never laid a hand to his son and rarely raised his voice to the lad. Yet, there was no way he could sanction a decision that would take him away from home and a mother's arms.

"We would prefer to be married like you and Mother. At least, we will make our vows before the Maker and hold those more precious than a familial contract."

"Benjamin, you are so young. Christine is even younger; nineteen, I believe. Can't you convince her to defect, to come back here to live? Surely, if she loves you, she would see this is for the best."

Benjamin uncrossed his emaciated arms, a reminder of his prison ordeal. Jacob's rage softened. Instead of a rampage, he should give thanks to the Maker that his son survived imprisonment and ask for the grace to love him, if only from afar.

Benjamin's glare begged for understanding. "Pops, you know Christine cannot defect."

"I'm well aware the government does not allow civil servants or their families to defect, the very reason Ahmed cannot be a permanent part of our communities."

Ahmed leaned over the table. "You must realize, Benjamin, Christine is suspected of holding religious meetings in her home under the guise of politics. The IEA has targeted her for surveillance. If you repatriate and join with her in a familial contract, the surveillance will be tightened."

Jacob feared a worse fate—that Benjamin would lose his faith. "At least here, except for assembly, we are free to worship."

"Don't worry. I will not forsake my beliefs. Where there is a will, there's a way. You've taught me that."

He uttered the hope in vain. "Maybe Ahmed could help Christine escape."

Ahmed leaned back. "No, Jacob. You don't know what you ask of me. If Christine defected, the IEA would raid every hub in the Colorado Community or even the entire Network. Rowlands will use any excuse to terminate every defector in every outworld, especially the Network."

"He couldn't terminate us all. The Humanitarians would never stand for it."

"Pops, what Rowlands would do or not do, doesn't matter. Christine refuses to put anyone at risk … especially you and Mother."

Jacob punched the sod wall, and a large clump fell to the floor.

"Perhaps I should leave now." Benjamin headed toward the door.

Amelia threw her apron into the middle of the table. "Enough. Can't you see how much this boy, our son, loves this girl? Jacob, has your manhood grown so cold, you've forgotten what love means? There is nothing that can stand between two young people committed to each other."

Benjamin hustled to his mother's side and enveloped her into a hug. "I knew you would understand, Mother, even if no one else did."

Jacob had never won an argument against Amelia, and he'd likely not win this one either. Still, one more attempt to reason with Benjamin, if only for pride's sake. "This isn't about us. We're talking about our son."

Amelia teased with a seductive grin. "Remember how my parents argued against our defection? My father wanted to take a laser pistol and kill you on the spot when we told him. We chose this life. Now it's Benjamin's turn to decide for himself."

He'd lost. Best go down with a smile. "You never told me your father had murder in his heart toward me. I know he never liked me, called me a good-for-nothing dreamer and predicted I'd never amount to anything. Murder? Why haven't you mentioned this before?"

Amelia placed her hands on her hips. "It was only a threat."

Jacob pulled her into him as he glanced toward his son. "May your Christine be half the woman your mother is."

"I believe she is Mother's equal."

"Then you'll be a blessed man, son."

Benjamin turned toward Ahmed. "Uncle Ahmed, do you think you could smuggle me back to the outworld sometimes so I can see my parents?"

Far too much for Ahmed to risk. "No, Benjamin. We can't ask your uncle to do something so dangerous. Your uncle is right. Rowlands will use any excuse to raid the Network."

Ahmed stood. "Let me worry about Rowlands. Benjamin, I will do whatever I can to protect you. However, I won't have as much autonomy as I did with Governor Devereux. Rowlands will watch my every move."

Rover engines hummed in the distance. "Someone's coming. Open the door."

Benjamin slid the panel open with ease, and Amelia peered outside. "Now who would be foolish enough to wander through the outworld at this hour?"

Benjamin peered into the moonlit night. "They're in an awful hurry."

The two rovers halted nearly simultaneously, and the helmeted men disembarked. Jacob recognized Enrique Morales' decals. "Enrique? What are you doing here? And at this hour?"

"Not even a hello, before the inquisition?" Enrique put an arm around the other driver. "This is my son, Juan. My Second, too."

At least someone's son followed in his father's footsteps. So be it. Benjamin needed to follow his own path.

Enrique shook Ahmed's hand. "Juan, this man is amigo to our Community as well as the entire Network."

Juan removed his helmet. "It is an honor, Ambassador Fared."

Whatever prompted Enrique's visit had to be for some other purpose than to introduce his son to Ahmed. "Come in, gentlemen. It's getting too cold to chat outside. Amelia, could you make more coffee? I know they would rather drink yours than mine."

She busied herself in the kitchen while Jacob led the men to the table. "It's always good to see you, Enrique, although something tells me this is not a social call."

"Juan and I were camping by the river, not far from here when we heard the news. We're curious regarding your reaction."

News? "I'm afraid you have me at a loss. We've been busy, and I haven't checked the feeds or the relays either."

"Understandable, and we regret barging in on this time with your son. I knew you must hear this news, Mr. Chairman—"

"Enrique, you've called me Jacob for the past twenty years. No need to change. I am still your friend."

"Very well—Jacob. President Schuman has scheduled his euthanasia for two weeks from now, and the Board of Governors has elected Edwin Rowlands to succeed. He'll be officially confirmed at next week's Congressional Caucus, a mere formality. ¿Verdad?" Horror housed in Enrique's eyes as he turned his gaze toward Ahmed. "Most believe that you will be his Second. Tell me, what is to become of us?"

Jacob removed his son's rebellion from the forefront of his fears. As Chairman, he'd been thrust into a race against time, ill-prepared and untrained.

CHAPTER ELEVEN
The Grafton Family Cabin/America Prime Sub-city

Michael swallowed the pink conception pills Edwin had ordered and put her thumbprint onto the government approval disk kept in the safe these past five years. At long last, she'd be a mother. She returned the disk to the safe and donned the red silk chemise, then set the interior light to one-third brilliance. She inserted the vintage wine into the filled ice-bucket.to chill, then sequenced the home theater for mixed romantic classics. An orchestra projected onto the veranda, and soft violin music filled the cabin, her inheritance from Grandfather Grafton.

She peered out the window at the surrounding wilderness, grateful Sean, a distant cousin and her only living relative, graciously signed off any claim to the estate. Thoughts of Sean brought a sense of connectedness, and she mused over their chance encounter. When Mother died, Edwin had insisted Michael search for any lost family to prevent a later claim against Grandfather's wealth. Probably good advice. She'd thought herself the last of the Graftons. Grandfather never mentioned he'd had a brother, that there had been another family line. How comforting to know she had relatives. So what if he was a social worker. At least Eternal Pathways was the most advanced of the euthanasia facilities.

Since then, she'd managed a few contacts with Sean apart from Edwin's knowledge since he wouldn't have approved of her association with a social worker, whether family or not. The last time they met, she'd hinted at Edwin's increased paranoia. Sean cautioned her not to visit his office again. "Of course, if you ever need anything," he'd said, "anything at all, don't hesitate to seek me out." He'd handed her a disk with an encrypted escape plan. She tucked the disk away in her office and did not visit him again. Would she truly need to escape? Wouldn't fatherhood soften Edwin's darker moods?

Michael scanned the North Ridge where ten officers dotted the landscape. Why so many when she had none before? As she picked up a cushion from the couch, sudden rage filled her. She sat—a blob of resentment.

Get a grip, Michael.

She shook her head with new resolve. She must find a way to make their familial union work. Once she conceived, dissolution would become extremely difficult. If she and Edwin failed to reconcile, at least a child would be compensation for her unhappiness.

She blew out her resentment—anger did little for ambiance.

She returned to the window and gazed at the Rockies. The mountains Grandfather described were luscious green hillsides, snow-capped heights of grandeur, not these gray crags coated with moldy moss. At least, the sunset hues still sprinkled a rainbow against the azure sky from time to time. She especially enjoyed the occasional dew-spotted morning.

Though the Himalayas might be higher and more mysterious, in this cabin, she sensed Grandfather's presence—an echo of past family gatherings. She remembered how he sat on the sofa as he recited stories of Pike's Peak and the westward movement, a culture defined by rugged individualism. He thrilled her with tales of Wyatt Earp, the Gold Rush, and the outlaw Jesse James. At first, she thought Grandfather made up the names. They weren't in any of her school history disks. One day, he pulled out his books from his illegal home library. "Men will always try to rewrite history, Michael. Preserve the truth at all costs."

"I've failed you miserably, Grandfather."

She took out two steaks from the cooler then set the speed cooker for medium rare. In a separate cooker, she placed dehydrated mashed potatoes and a vegetable medley, grateful for the variety of foods her wealthier status afforded—the mainstay of the poor, fifth-generation cloned mutton was her least favorite food.

After dinner, she and Edwin would sit on the veranda and sip wine while the sun descended behind the mountains. She placed extra hypos in case they decided to linger outdoors. She thought about the many privileges she'd known since birth and the additional benefits she received as Edwin's intimate, including her hold of sub-city property. Since Grandfather had been branded a dissenter, if not for Edwin, the Constitutional Government would have seized her land for mining or as an animal reserve.

A set of strong arms encircled her, and hot, minty hops breath steamed her neck. "You are a sight for a starving man's eyes, my love."

"Edwin, I didn't even hear you come in."

"I hated to break your concentration. You seemed far away as if part of you lived in these mountains."

"I suppose in some way a part of me does. Grandfather Grafton spent a great deal of his childhood in the Rockies."

He pulled her in tighter. "Let's not dwell on the past, Michael. After all, tonight is for our future." Edwin kissed her shoulders.

"Don't you want to eat first? I've prepared an old-fashioned steak dinner."

"I suppose there's no rush. The pills have twenty-four-hour viability." He whirled her around and kissed her, his passion evident, so much like the Edwin of their youth before politics consumed him. When he released her, he held her hands as he spoke. "I suppose we shouldn't let your meal go to waste."

She placed the platter on the table by the picture window that overlooked a man-made pond. "I saw a frog jump out earlier. A good sign, isn't it? Life returning to the water?"

"I'll see about buying a few ducks."

"Since when did you become a nature lover?"

He reached into his pocket and pulled out a tiny black box. "Since I bought these. I can't explain it, Michael. Somehow the future seems more important to me now. For our baby girl. I want to name her Jade."

Her eyes misted as she fingered the tiny earrings. "Oh, Edwin!" There was hope after all. She took his hand and led him to her bedroom, dinner forgotten.

Edwin eased himself from Michael's arms, taking care not to wake her as he slipped from her bed. The earrings had worked like a potion—never before had she shown so much gratitude.

He paced the living room in the gray of pre-dawn, enamored by the moon's battle against the sun's emerging dominance, a natural sight few in the City were privileged to witness. Perhaps now would be the time to convince Michael to donate the cabin to the Conservation Department. Positive press, to be sure. He could use all he could muster.

He mused in his success. He'd climbed from a junior delegate to President-elect of Unified Earth in the space of fifteen years. Father's formulas worked. His number one principle—opportunity is made, not found.

Now that Edwin would be a father, he should plan accordingly. When he took over for Schumann, he must convince Michael to give up her private residences. Excelsior Media owned offices in ten provinces. He'd need a private militia to monitor all her activities. He'd prefer she be more in tune with his expectations of the First Lady of United Earth, a role he doubted she'd willingly embrace. How then to keep her in one place where she could be watched?

Then, there was Jade to consider. Perhaps he should rethink his earlier concept of absentee fatherhood. If he adopted a more parental persona, he might win over the Humanitarians who pushed child protective legislation. Even better. If he kept Jade by his side, he could prime her as his successor. Michael would object, of course. He'd have to find a way to keep her separated from Jade, to minimize Michael's poisonous opinions.

Interesting how soon a life changes in a matter of a few days. When he woke Sunday morning, his only thought had been how to manage his troublesome Second. The sun crept higher between the mountain ledges, and a soft glow filled the room. A pleasurable sight if he could afford the time required to drink its view. Right now, the world pulsed through his veins.

He switched on his micro and hailed Fared, who he hoped was back from his excursion, shaven and dressed in a regulation white suit. Only a fool risked death for a piece of cloth.

"Fared, here."

"Ah, good, you're back and appropriately attired, I see. Said your prayers yet?"

"You know I'm not a religious man, Governor Rowlands. Why do you ask? Do you need prayers said for you?"

Not even Fared's sarcasm could diminish Edwin's joy. "You amuse me, Fared. Maybe another reason I keep you alive. How was your trip to the outworld?"

"I have news. Benjamin Goodayle wishes to repatriate as does Kyle Skinner. They each have sponsors and are waiting in my office, under guard, until I complete their temporary paperwork later this morning."

"Chairman Skinner? Interesting. Who will take his place?"

"My brother, Jacob."

As a mayor, Goodayle posed little threat. However, as Chairman, his political views might head the Network toward a collision course with the Constitutional Government. Father warned against a man who veiled bravery behind humility. "Easy to see the two of you are not blood relatives. Goodayle is an honorable man, and one who is the antithesis of a career politician."

"Good leaders come in all types, Governor. As for the fire, the Network plans to rebuild the manse. Better than before."

"Indeed."

"Both Benjamin Goodayle and Kyle Skinner's repatriation will take place on Friday. With your permission, I have agreed to preside over both. Something else, I think you should know. Benjamin Goodayle and Christine Devereux plan to enter into a familial contract."

Should he be concerned? Probably in the long run. For now, he'd let them have their time together. "They're just a couple of kids. Let them sign. If they are busy in the bedroom, she will ignore those so-called Humanitarian meetings. I'd hate to arrest a dead governor's daughter."

Fared cleared his throat. "I'd like to make Benjamin my assistant. He's a bright lad with a good political future."

Jacob Goodayle was a Christ follower, as was his son. Did he want one involved in government? However, probably best to keep Benjamin under a watchful eye. "Granted. I understand young Goodayle's draw to America Prime. Christine is a beautiful woman. However, Kyle Skinner's repatriation surprises me. He's a native-born outworlder, isn't he?"

"His son has leukemia."

An unaccustomed sympathy pricked Edwin's conscience, an emotion he quickly eradicated. He must not allow impending fatherhood to turn him into a sappy sentimentalist. "I see. So, tell me, Fared, have you heard the news?"

"Yes. Congratulations, Mr. President."

"Not yet. Soon enough, I suppose. There should be no obstacle in gaining congressional approval at next week's caucus. I still want you as my Second."

"I am at your service, Mr. President."

Insincerity undercoated Fared's tones. No matter. Constable Becker already strengthened his detail on Fared, and Edwin would order one for Benjamin Goodayle as well. "Now I need you to speed up the Festival plans. Here's what I want …"

CHAPTER TWELVE
Sector Four/America Prime

Ahmed yawned as he placed his breakfast plate into the dish tumbler. He had tossed the entire night at Jacob's home. The next day, he'd helped his brother and nephew reconstruct the chicken coop, then tossed the night again, rising early to escort the three potential repatriates to America Prime. The transport of so many required four more ewes to add to Davu's expanding herds. Fortunately, the gouger accepted Ahmed's mark as pre-payment. At this rate, Davu would own every ewe in Western America within the year. Ahmed scratched his scalp. Four ewes would drastically drain his bank accounts. Maybe he could find a shepherd with family members needing relocation—a favor for a favor.

Hopefully, the outworlders were comfortably cared for by the guards. If not, he'd see their careers came to a quick end. He'd have stayed at his office with his charges if not for an intense craving for egg-dipped fried bread, what his adoptive mother called French toast until the Uniformity Act banned ethnic names. What nonsense. Tenderized beef would never taste as good as Swiss Steak.

He removed his thoughts from food to his future. How would an old-fashioned Arab fit into this new world climate? Though he regarded Rowlands with less esteem than a swamp toad, honor required a man serve a superior to the best of one's ability.

Poor Michael—a gazelle mated to a crocodile. The old folks said opposites were attracted to one another. Michael and Rowlands were more than polar anomalies, they were Mercury and Pluto. How much stranger could a union get?

Ahmed put on his government cape, pinned on his transponder, stuffed his micro into his satchel then programmed the security scanner for his workday absence. As he glimpsed his apartment, he realized Rowlands would most likely require his Second to live closer to government facilities. Ahmed sighed, resigned to his flavorless future.

Devereux once asked why Ahmed didn't want to move to Sector One, why he remained in substandard housing for a man in his position. "I'm a simple man with simple wants," he'd said. The truth? This had been his home with Anna. Memories were a poor substitute for flesh and blood. Yet, memories were all he had left of her.

Lemuel Sampson's apartment, six times Ahmed's current residence, was attached to the Presidential Palace. Sampson had five daughters and made good use of the space. What would a single man do in such large quarters?

No doubt his royal pain-in-the-rear-end would require the same senseless control over Michael. They'd both be prisoners of protocol. Devereux had respected Ahmed's waiver of a security detail and agreed insights could be gained through the mundane of normal city life. The public transport from Sector Four to Sector One allowed time to mingle with constituents and observe the masses.

Gain hedged on every loss. If he resided near Michael, he could protect her, and honor his promise to Hiram Grafton as he died in his mentee's arms. Hope pressed on the hearts of young politicians in those days. Ahmed had agreed to spearhead Grafton's campaign for the first delegate seat in the newly formed Constitutional Government. They had staged an outdoor rally at the air dock when the blast came from above and severed Hiram's shoulder from his torso. He bled out in seconds, his last words, "Ahmed, watch over Michael."

From afar, Ahmed had honored his request. He watched as she sprouted wings, helpless to prevent her union with evil. Perhaps he could save her when she inevitably fell from the sky.

He waived his implant to lock the door, then reprogrammed the exterior scanner.

Esther Feinmann approached him, still spry despite her terminal condition and an age of one hundred and ten. "Good morning, Ahmed."

"Good morning, Esther. And how are you today?"

"Today is a great day, Ahmed, though, sadly, my last."

For twenty years, Esther greeted him like a sunrise with her stories of life in Old Israel. "I don't understand. I thought your euthanasia wasn't for two weeks yet. I'm still trying to contact your daughter. She could care for you."

"President Schumann chose the day I originally planned. And of course, there are no others permitted on the President's Day."

"Why not later?"

"Eternal Pathways is booked solid for months afterward. Seems like euthanasia's getting to be more popular than living."

He thought he'd have more time to glean a few more stories. Mornings would never be the same without them. "Must you? You're still vital and strong. Certainly, you can wait a few more months."

"I know how much you despise the practice. I do, too. In my case, however, I'm left with no option."

The same desperation he'd heard from far too many these days. "There are always options."

"Not for me, Ahmed, not with a tumor in my heart the size of a handball. The doctor says in another month, I'll be bed-bound. I won't buy flesh for a heart transplant, and I won't buy a meme nurse to care for me even if I could afford one."

"Do you have a witness?"

Esther's dancing eyes dimmed in answer to his question. "No."

"Would you like me to witness?"

The sparkle returned, and she crushed him in a hug. "The Second President-elect to be my witness? Jehovah is mighty indeed."

Ahmed skewered a warning glance in Esther's direction.

"Don't worry so, Ahmed. By the time they come to arrest me, my ashes will be cold on the ground." She tugged on his cape. "Come back to my apartment. There's something I want you to have. Don't argue. It's customary to give the witness a gift, isn't it?"

He followed her into her apartment where columns of outlawed books marked a pathway from the door to the other side of her living room. Ahmed stayed near the entrance while Esther hurried toward the fireplace and retrieved a silver teapot from the mantle.

An odd gift—he didn't drink tea.

"This was the first present my Albert and I received on our wedding day, long before the Accord. My husband died during the Muslim assault on Tel Aviv."

"The war ushering in the Schism."

"Most of Tel Aviv was leveled. I sifted through our demolished home and found this teapot. It's the only possession I have left from those days."

Ahmed admired the intricate design and long spout like a swan's neck. "What are these markings on the molding?"

"Eggs, shells, and scrolls. It's an original Thomas Fletcher." She emphasized the name, perhaps an artist of importance.

"I don't know much about art. I'm sorry."

"That so?"

"Truth."

"What about the Renoir in your office?"

"A gift."

"If you're curious, Thomas Fletcher was one of the most important silversmiths in the 1800s. From what I've read, his collections in the Metropolitan Museum of Art were lost after the tsunamis. Most of the rest were destroyed by ignorant men during the Schism. I believe this might be one of a few that remain."

Given Esther's explanation, a useless teapot transformed into a priceless treasure before his eyes. "You could sell this and have enough to buy memes to care for you."

"How can I exchange one evil to avoid another?"

"You should not have to choose."

She thrust the teapot into his hands. "I want you to have this. You will appreciate its significance, I know."

"You mean beyond its material worth?"

Esther winked. "If you remember, I was born during much unrest in the Gaza Strip, a Jew among Palestinians, my life was threatened even when I walked down the street. I never understood the hate … we were neighbors."

"The Uniformity Act hoped to rid the world of such prejudice."

Did her smile mean she'd read his satire? "There is no legislation that can change a hateful heart."

How he'd miss her wisdom as much as her stories—stories more embellished than the surface of her teapot, yet, he never tired of them. Most he had heard dozens of times, except how she came by this treasure. Why today? Most likely, this tale had special significance. He would not brush her off, not on this last full day of her life. "Go on, Esther. You have my attention."

"When a mortar leveled our home, my family moved back to Tel Aviv. I went to the University to become a lawyer where I met Albert." She glimpsed heavenward. "Never was there a heart stealer as my handsome Albert. Matter of fact, he looked a lot like you. Well, if you were a hundred pounds thinner of course."

Ahmed shrugged. Should he be insulted she had called him fat or insinuated he looked like a Jew? "I'll take that as a compliment."

"Oh, my. That didn't come out as I hoped. And I'm taking too much of your precious time."

True, the morning whittled away. "Not to worry. Please, go on."

"My Albert and I experienced much turmoil in our years together. The ice-caps melted and the world changed almost overnight. Yet, humanity is still here, isn't it?"

Ahmed looked at his watch. "And the teapot?"

"Don't you see, Ahmed? This teapot survived a host of wars before being given to me: economic disaster, climatic upheaval, war as never seen before, the atrocities in Tel Aviv, the erosion of the coastal plains, the Schism, the Pandemic, the end of the Accord, and even the Constitutional Government's failure to put the world back together again. I have been relocated thirty times. And yet, this teapot survived. Every time I look at it, I am filled with new hope." Esther rubbed the pot like Aladdin's Lamp. "And that is why I chose this gift for you."

Who would have thought an ancient Jewess would remind him of his humanity on a day he feared most he might lose it? "I don't deserve this trust, Esther." Ahmed bowed and returned to his apartment. He would be late beyond excuse. However, some things exceeded the need for punctuality. He placed the teapot on the mantle next to his birth mother's favorite vase and Devereux's box. Though its content had been safely stored, he had kept the satin receptacle as a reminder of his pledge. Esther's gift must rest alongside all he esteemed most precious.

CHAPTER THIRTEEN
Grafton Family Cabin/America Prime Sub-city

Michael awoke and rolled over to the empty side of the bed. No use looking for Edwin. Most often, he satisfied himself, then roamed the house. A man who rarely slept, he'd nap in a chair or rest his head on his desk. Edwin ate, slept, and made love in snatches, like a bird picks at its food, never truly enveloped, except for politics—a vial of frenzied activity, he zigged and zagged through the portals of time. Permanency eluded him. No wonder she couldn't out think him. When he spent the night, less and less over the years, he'd wake hours earlier, bouncing from chair to sofa to micro to window, pacing, sitting, gulping coffee, and muttering at the air.

Most often, he was gone before she opened her eyes. If not for a hint of his aftershave, she'd suppose their time together had been a delusion, not even a dirty dish to prove he'd been there the night before.

Sometimes, however, she stumbled out of her bedroom to find him blasting away at his day. Given the solemnity of this visit, she hoped he would stay for longer than a peck on the cheek, longer than a hasty, "Love you, Michael," as the door shut him out of her life until Edwin Milton Rowlands decided he needed her again. The wall clock read the ninth hour of the morning. She should hail Barry and retrieve her messages.

She went into the common room where Edwin sat engrossed in whatever crisis occupied his mind. "Good morning, Edwin. I see you've drained the pot already. I'll make more coffee." He disconnected his micro at the sound of her voice.

"Not for me." He stood and pulled at his suit waistband. "I'm leaving in a few minutes. I waited for you to get up." He kissed her on the cheek and with no warning pulled her into a dip and covered her neck and arms with kisses. "I'm tempted to stay the day."

She returned a simple soft kiss to his lips. Would he? Not likely. Edwin had the world to orchestrate. How could she compete? "I should be going myself. I'm late getting into the office, and I don't want Barry to malfunction with worry."

Edwin's pout and little boy tempers riddled his too-practiced veneer. "Michael, I've told you at least a dozen times to trade up. Barry passed his peak years ago."

"Not so, Edwin. The earlier models live much longer."

"You're too attached to Barry. When Citizens start treating memes like equals, we're in for trouble. They're created to serve. Like a tram car. Nothing more." Edwin stuck his micro into his satchel, adjusted his transponder and summoned his security detail. "I'll call later to let you know the Festival plans. I didn't forget I promised to give you an exclusive on the event. We've decided to hold the Festival simultaneously with my Inauguration to include every city, province, and even the outworlds across United Earth."

"America Prime can't possibly hold them all. It'll be chaos."

"Except for the Western America outworld, I limited the invitations to one thousand from each province. The governors will send their requests to Ahmed for primary approval, then on to Constable Becker for finalization. Non-citizens will be housed in guarded tents in Sector Ten."

Like a warrior on his way to battle, he swept her into his arms, his face a mask of sincerity—pity his soul was so transparent. "I know I've been selfish. I don't expect I'll change very much, especially considering my new status. I do love you, you know. I can only promise I'll try to be a better father than I've been your intimate."

The vapor of a man left as thinly as he loved.

She stretched her arms across her abdomen. Part of her prayed she had conceived at long last ... though she doubted a prayer to an imagined god would take hold. If only she could believe in Jacob Goodayle's God, one who cared for His creation.

Funny she should think about Jacob Goodayle now after all these years. Memories of that day filtered in against her will. Grandfather Grafton had taken her to a defection ritual, what the newly formed Constitutional Government called the Rite of Expulsion, an inherited resolution from the Accord and tweaked to fit the new government's requirements. A so-called humane management of dissidents—humane in that those who argued against the established government were not quartered, hung, or executed by plasma burst. There were two insurgents that day—Jacob and Amelia Goodayle. The crowd assembled at the loading dock in Sector One and watched as medics stripped them of their clothing and plucked out their implants. Then, they were harnessed to a platform to be paraded to the Defector's Gate while paid spectators threw garbage and screamed words like traitor and malcontent.

Horrified, Michael closed her eyes and begged Grandfather to take her home. He handed her a handkerchief to dry her tears. "Remember this day, Michael, when ignorance triumphed over reason." He raised a dramatic fist into the air. "This is why I resist, why I fight for change." He bent down and lifted her chin. "These two are soldiers, Michael. While some soldiers fight with weapons, Jacob and Amelia Goodayle fight with words."

Michael dared look again in time to see a bloodied brick at Amelia's feet, a trickle of blood on her face. She swooned against Jacob's chest. He stood, a proud and defiant man clothed with dignity despite his nakedness. "This woman is my wife. If you must throw bricks, throw them at me."

Grandfather explained how only a few years ago, Citizens still held weddings where a man and a woman would make a pledge before a member of the clergy, much like he and Grandmother's ceremony. "It is a beautiful thing when a man pledges his life to a woman. I hope you will find a man worthy of you someday, Michael—a man who will love you enough to protect you from an angry crowd."

How could she have buried so vivid a memory?

Grandfather was assassinated three weeks later. The IEA swept his murder away like dirt from the floor, a cursory and unproductive investigation. Michael cried for days, and her mother offered no condolence. "Your father's father asked for trouble, Michael. He wrote those seditious articles even after the media closed his feed to the Mainframe. Then he ran for office. What was he thinking?"

Michael wiped away the fresh tears memory induced. She rubbed her stomach again as she made her way to the bedroom to dress. Her head swam, most likely a reaction to the conception drugs. When the dizziness subsided, she forced her mind toward pleasant things and reburied the memories deeper than they had ever been. "I'm sorry, Grandfather. It's too late. I have a child to consider."

Edwin had insisted on a girl, and she had happily agreed. Strange. Most men preferred sons. She retrieved the earrings from the drawer and clutched them to her chest. "For you, my darling Jade. A beautiful name, don't you think? The one your father selected himself."

Michael cramped from a sudden sense of doom. Of course, Edwin picked out the name, just as he had manipulated every part of this decision. Why? Why take interest in a child now, when he refused to consider fatherhood from the day they signed their familial contract?

What have I done?

Edwin didn't want a daughter. Rather, he wanted a loophole, a way to exact Excelsior from Michael or to use Jade to further his ambitions. She should purge the conception. To do so meant she would purge a part of herself.

Tears flowed.

"Oh, Jade. I wanted you so badly, I lulled myself into thinking your father would change. I've sentenced the both of us to the dictates of a madman."

For the second time in a few hours, she thought of Sean Grafton.

CHAPTER FOURTEEN
New Edinburgh/Highland Province

Bridget halted her steps. "I can't go on, Jimmy. I've got to rest. We've snaked our way through these tenements for the better part of two days. No sleep and no water and nothing to eat. Is your plan to march me to death?"

Jimmy scowled as he rested his P-74 against a pile of bricks. "City lassies are all the same. Soft. You can't do the hardships."

"A legless man could've crossed New Edinburgh by now, and we're still in Sector Four. What kind of chase are you taking me on? A fine way to treat a pregnant woman." Bridget inched down a wall and sat, grateful for even a rubble cushion.

"The closer we get to Sector One, the fewer tenements there'll be and the harder to avoid the scanners. By now Savakis has alerted the IEA. They'll be looking for us in full force unless your da can convince Savakis to ease up."

She wiped the sweat from her forehead. How she longed for a

bath, one where she slipped into gallons of perfumed water. Jimmy Kinnear could go to blazes. What had Angelina seen in him besides long, muscular legs, and a smile like moonbeams? Would she change heaven for hell—the shame of such thoughts about another man with Ian so newly ushered into glory. "My baby will die if I don't get something to eat soon. How much further?"

"Don't waste your dramatics on me. To answer your question, only a few hours more."

"I don't know why we didn't take a rover. Rumor is you have dozens at your disposal as well as a fleet of hovercrafts."

Jimmy's frown brought a speck of ugly to his otherwise handsome face. "An exaggeration, of course. Besides, IEA will be expecting us to utilize transport. The newer tunnels, private and public, are heavily monitored, and the old tunnels are too dilapidated for safe passage."

Bridget stood, unsteadied by a sudden rush of dizziness. She leaned against a wall. "I can't go another foot, not without food or at the least a drop of water."

Jimmy removed the satchel from his shoulder and fished inside. "Maybe the dead officer packed a lunch." He pulled out a small, white cube the width of his thumb. "No food. Only this."

"That's an emergency transponder."

"I know what this is, woman. I'm no fool. I can use one of our hacked codes. I'll only have a few minutes before IEA locks onto us. They'll be watching for any new activation."

Jimmy punched in a series of codes then ADAM projected. "Access accepted, Officer Bartelli, you may now proceed."

"You used Angelina's codes?"

"She's so transparent … she always uses a variation of her birthday."

Bridget laughed. "Make sure whoever you're hailing brings a stick of cheese and a water canteen."

A smile flickered across Jimmy's face. The man could charm the devil if he'd lose the chip on his shoulder. He whispered in ancient Gaelic then disconnected the hail. "Now we wait."

"You're crazy."

The transponder buzzed. "Falan? Are you in safe mode? Good … Aye, I've got Bridget. We're four hours from Checkpoint 90."

Bridget tugged on Jimmy's sleeve. "Oh. And bring a cheese stick and a water canteen."

He disconnected then pulverized the transponder with a plasma burst. "I had to disconnect—permanently. Someone already locked on to my hail."

"A foolish mistake Jimmy. The device might come in handy later."

"You really think I'm as daft as a beheaded chicken, don't you? There's a wee click when a transponder is locked onto by the monitors. Hard to detect unless you know what to listen for."

"What now? Or do we stay here and starve?"

"We'll need to backtrack before going on to Checkpoint 90. Don't worry. Falan will take you the rest of the way. You'll be in your da's arms before nightfall."

"And what will you do, Jimmy?"

"I'll take half of the cheese stick and go back to Dunfermline Abbey. If Rowlands intends to be President, I'll be very busy the next few weeks with all the folks looking to escape to the Northern provinces."

Bridget blew her disgust. How could anyone as vile as Edwin Rowlands be elected to the highest office of United Earth? "And there'll be fewer places to hide, too."

Jimmy straightened—his face stern with purpose. "The reason we fight. In the space of a couple of decades, the Constitutional

Government has spawned its first dictator, and he'll terminate a dissenter quicker than an afterthought."

Jimmy guided Bridget through an abandoned underground tunnel that led to Checkpoint 90, an access controlled by the Revolutionary Army. A few more hours and his package would be delivered, and Governor Cavanaugh would make the promised drop over the abbey in exchange for Bridget's safety: food, blankets, and weapons to restock his armory. Bridget needn't know the role she played to obtain the windfall. A stroke of luck the governor thought General Kinnear too hardened to help a hero's widow. Cavanaugh expected the worse from an outlaw like Jimmy Kinnear. Might as well milk the governor's distrust.

He'd rather enjoyed the subterfuge, and his target could not have been more beautiful, despite the stench the dungeon left on her.

Her pout softened. "I'm sorry, Jimmy."

"For what?"

"For acting like a wee brat."

"A wee brat, you say? More like a barracuda."

He rather admired her unconquerable spirit, a woman so far above Jimmy Kinnear, he'd have to climb to heaven to reach her—a heaven that wanted nothing to do with the likes of him. Nor would Bridget ever speak to him again once she learned he'd used her like a pawn.

He gazed at her form. A right beautiful lass. Jimmy had wanted her once, years ago, before Angelina, when Bridget had been assigned to his squad. Her hands were soft, the softest he had ever seen on any woman, let alone an officer. He thought then maybe she joined the IEA to prove something to her da. Blimey. Why would a beauty like her want to round up murderers and thugs? She fooled the lot of them, became the most capable officer in the squad, and positioned herself for promotion to provincial chief if she hadn't joined forces with Ian McCormick.

If he'd pursued Bridget all those years ago, would their lives be any different? No. She'd have scorned him then as she did now. So, he chose Angelina, available and willing. A choice he soon regretted, their affair like a global catastrophe. Let hell have Angelina. Maybe they'd reunite in the afterlife, a fitting eternal punishment. He heard she'd teamed up with Carlos Perez, a man too stupid to wipe his own nose without an order.

Bridget stared toward the horizon, unable to hide her tears, her sorrow not as spent as she pretended. Ian McCormick had been a lucky man to be grieved so. Seemed the privilege of grief ended with the tsunamis. Jimmy recalled the words Great-Grandmother Kinnear wrote in her journal. Before the calamity, the living still outnumbered the dead. They celebrated death with a festivity called a wake. The first wave killed millions. The aftermath—famine, disease, and lawlessness—killed millions more. Death trucks lined the streets to collect the dead, at first once a day until their presence became so prevalent the masses turned deaf to the engines' hums. With no one left to operate the crematoriums, those whose strength had not yet ebbed threw the corpses into the sea. Religions blamed each other for the madness. Schism survivors envied the dead and cursed the Maker for their sufferings while Earth heaved in imminent collapse.

Yet, through the decades of insanity, Great-Grandmother believed God had not abandoned His creation. Before she closed her eyes to eternity, she'd handed her journal to Jimmy. "Keep it, lad."

Though he read them often, he never took them into his heart. Jimmy Kinnear bowed to no man or god, nor would he waste tears on the dead. The living needed his help.

Jimmy gazed once more toward Bridget just as she stared at him. Could she possibly feel the same attraction to him as he felt toward her? Aye, the fire still burned in her. He put himself to shame for his want of a woman who carried another man's child, a man newly ushered into heaven. He was a rogue without honor. He must surrender her to the Maker she worshiped, let her mourn a great man in peace and comfort. His path to damnation was best walked alone.

All else aside, Bridget was a Christ follower—a strange lot, those people. Even Ian, a thinker and motivator, the father of New Edinburgh's Reformation Party, yet hardly a warrior. Jimmy recalled the rebuttals. He himself would trust no power beyond his arsenal. Even so, he would gladly die for any man's religion. Live and let live, each man true to his own code. That's the world he fought for, a cause worth every drop of blood in his veins and any scheme to accomplish.

Bridget stretched and yawned. "Thanks for the respite, Jimmy. Did you rest any?"

"Merely my legs. My many thoughts went adrift, knocked into each other and kept me awake."

"Hungry?"

"Aye. Pregnant women are not the only creatures in need of nourishment."

"I'm sorry, Jimmy. I've been testy and selfish. You've risked so much to bring me back to Da. We've planned a son, you know, Ian and me. I'd like to add your name to his progeny. How does Ian Bryan James Cavanaugh sound? I can't legally call him McCormick. I didn't get the final approval before I conceived. I pray to the Maker the government won't make me abort."

"Name the child whatever you wish, Bridget. I'm sure your da will find a way to satisfy the government."

He warmed to think a woman like her would hurl honor at a scoundrel. A boy would bear his name, granted a minor position in a row of names, yet his none the less.

They didn't speak again until they neared Checkpoint 90. "You're safe now. I can hear Falan's whistle, faint and off tune. He'll see you home."

"Are you sure we can trust this Falan?"

"Besides the fact, he's your da's new bodyguard, Falan is my brother. Same mum—different das. I trust him."

She gifted him a soft kiss on his cheek. "Will I see you again?"

His eyes rested on her dry, blistered lips. "Probably not."

"I'll pray for you."

If she did, hers would be the only ones lifted for his blackened soul.

CHAPTER FIFTEEN
Sector One/America Prime

Ahmed glanced once more at Benjamin's projected citizenship application. His prison record had been successfully expunged, a minor infraction and no formal indictment, and Ahmed had vouched for his nephew's conduct. What else? He clicked his tongue as he reviewed the plethora of line items. Normally he'd have one of the meme workers do this. Benjamin's processing required too many tweaks not in the realm of meme expertise. "Last chance to change your mind, Benjamin. You realize once you've affixed your thumbprint, there is no turning back."

"I've never been surer of anything in my whole life."

His whole life ... a breath shy of twenty-one ... an infant.

Ahmed handed Benjamin a programmed transponder. "All government workers are required to wear one at all times. I'll hail you with final arrangements."

"My father would have been pleased that you've gone so far out of your way to help us," Christine said. "I can't thank you enough."

"Your father was a good man. This is the least I can do to return his kindness to me."

And of course, Ahmed always had a soft spot for a pretty face. Benjamin, too, apparently. Christine's ruby lips and yellow hair reminded Ahmed of a younger Anna. Had she ever truly loved him? Perhaps for a short while. How could he compete with Romala Maslow, a man who could buy Unified Earth twice over?

Christine had far more heart, like Amelia. No wonder Benjamin fell head over heels in love with her.

Ahmed studied his protégé, the exact image of a once brazen Jacob Goodayle, a reckless upstart who never once considered how his theological passion impacted others. He preached from his professor's podium and raised every eyebrow in the Western America delegation as well as Congress. If Jacob had not been a prolific writer, the University would have sacked him at the first indiscretion. He should have heeded the warnings, been satisfied with the University's generosity. Instead, the fool organized a banned history curriculum at the same time the Constitutional Government took over.

Jacob didn't listen to Ahmed any better than he heeded the University's pleas. He railed even more against President Schumann and the fledgling Constitutional Government. A smarter man would have sealed his lips. Not Jacob, who cranked his rhetoric, stood on street corners and shouted his message to anyone who would listen. No one blamed the University for expelling a ranting lunatic.

Jacob took no accountability for being sacked, rather he saw himself a martyr until Ahmed finally touched a chord of reason. "Better to live in the outworld, brother, than force your wife to raise your child alone." Not to mention that his brother's seditious rhetoric did little to help Ahmed's political career. After much debate, Jacob finally allowed Ahmed to arrange the defection.

And now, he'd risen to become Second President-elect of United Earth. He would use his influence once again, not for defection, but rather repatriation of a boy he loved like a son. No sacrifice too small for Benjamin's happiness. Ahmed lowered his head and raised both eyebrows. "You understand the law requires a three-year waiting period before you and Christine can apply to have a child?"

Benjamin's scowl could mean only one thing, the boy was dangerously recalcitrant. Remember the scanners, my boy. "Yes. Christine explained everything to me. I don't have to like it, though. Do I?"

"I must remind you of your responsibility to protect Christine from motherhood until legally able. Unapproved pregnancies most often result in forced abortions, the tissues donated to the factories for meme production. You also must realize once you and Christine are joined, you cannot defect. Christine's status as a former governor's daughter will give you some protection, but if you are branded a dissenter, you'll be hunted down and executed without a trial, assuming successful passage of Governor Rowlands' proposed Preservation Act."

"Uncle Ahmed, I'm ready for this." Benjamin clutched Christine's hand. "I would gladly die for this woman."

And he very well might.

Ahmed tapped his desk. Had he forgotten anything? "Looks like we're all set. Give me a minute to go over the protocols one more time to be certain."

He scrolled the items, nodded with each completed task until he came to the section for job placement. "Now for the matter of your profession. Would you like to be assigned to my office? All these

Festival and Inauguration plans will have me running in circles. I could use someone like you to assist me."

"I trust your judgment, Uncle Ahmed. Any profession you pick for me is fine. I learn quickly, though my skills are limited."

Limited indeed. However, Benjamin's knowledge of the Mainframe would prove valuable in the uncertain days ahead. Better to pay him to work for the government than let him fall prey to a militia group's bribes. As his assistant, he could better watch his nephew's activities.

If the Festival proved successful, many would request repatriation. The mass relocation within a short period would likely cause economic strain on the government's already stretched resources. Outworlders had few skills adaptable to city life since employers favored memes for menial labor to keep costs at a minimum. No matter how willing the repatriated Citizens were to work, there would be few jobs available to them.

Thanks to the then delegate Rowlands and his Uniformity Act proposal, passed in the Constitutional Government's infancy, every city's Sector Ten bulged with relocated refugees from all corners of United Earth, left to forage on their own, with infrequent food drops and clothing provided by the Humanitarians. Although Christine's wealth would provide Benjamin with a home, food, clothing and privileges, he'd need his own financial resources to buy and sell.

"I almost forgot to tell you, an intimate cannot bank on the resources of another familial group member. I'm setting up a temporary account with your government stipend until you become a Citizen. Once you receive your implant, my authorization of your purchases will no longer be required."

"Christine and I would also like to sign our familial contract on Friday."

"Agreed. All will happen on Friday afternoon. Even though marriage is outlawed, contract celebrations are a common practice. I tell you what. In the absence of both your parents, I'll host a party in your honor. Where would you like the affair to be held?"

"The Partridge Oasis would be nice," Christine said. "The Fountain Room, if it's available."

"I'll do my best to fill the gala hall to capacity."

Christine's glow was worth every expense the affair would cost.

"This is so kind of you, Ahmed. My father would be pleased." She turned to Benjamin. "You don't mind me speaking for us, do you?"

Benjamin blushed. "Whatever makes you happy."

Ahmed winked. "Get used to saying that if you want this familial contract to work."

Christine bit her lower lip. "Benjamin, don't let your uncle confuse you. Each intimate must bear equal responsibility in the contract."

Ahmed laughed. "My dear, the law is one thing. Human nature is quite another." He handed Benjamin a micro card attached to a jeweled chain. "You'll receive your implant on Friday when you pledge allegiance to the Constitutional Government. This disk is your temporary identification. Wear this around your neck at all times. If you're caught without the ID, you could be sent back to prison or worse. Now, I need both your thumbprints on the familial contract projection." When they had sealed the document, Ahmed projected the Repatriation Application. "Benjamin, put your thumbprint by your name."

He scowled as he clumsily rested his thumb on the wafer-thin holographic image.

"I'll hail you when I've made all the final arrangements for your celebration. We're done. You're free to go."

"Christine and I thought we'd stroll through the park near the amphitheater."

"You have a lifetime to explore America Prime—no need to see the entire City in one day. Savor the experience like one of your mother's potato pies. Now, on behalf of Governor Rowlands, I welcome you to America Prime." Ahmed shook Benjamin's hand and slipped him a miniature disk containing codes and other data the boy would need for Mainframe manipulation. Be discreet, Benjamin. He tucked the disk underneath the sleeve of his peasant shirt.

That's what he forgot!

"Hold on, Benjamin. You will need to purchase uniforms and a micro from the account I set up. Of course, I'll have to approve your expenditures until you receive your implant."

"Can't I wear what I have? I promise you I'll make sure they're laundered and won't smell like the outworld when I report."

Ahmed laughed. "No use trying to break the fashion mode, son. It's not worth dying for. Each occupation has its own protocol. For us government types, it's plain white. Rank is identified by lapel pins."

"That's why you shaved your beard?"

Scanners. Always the scanners.

"Consider the funds a gift. Christine will show you how to make purchases."

"Thanks, Uncle Ahmed." Benjamin kissed Christine's hand, the two lovers as sappy as Benjamin's parents. "On your way out, would you send in Kyle Skinner?"

Christine and Benjamin walked out hand in hand, and a few minutes later, Skinner hesitated at the doorway.

"Ah, Kyle. I'm sorry to have kept you cooped up for so long. I didn't want you wandering the streets without your temporary identification, and there are only certain hours I'm able to access the repatriation protocols."

"Thanks again for all your help. The gate officers didn't believe even you at first. I shudder to think of what might have happened if Caroline and I tried to repatriate on our own."

Likely they would have been ushered into prison under suspicion, and left to rot while agents verified his story. "Where are Caroline and Peter?"

"Caroline's afraid of the scanners, so she hasn't budged from the lobby. She's been staring at your peculiar painting."

"The Blue River?"

"At least, she's occupied." Skinner eyed Devereux's Renoir behind Ahmed's desk. "Must be you have a special fondness for this artist."

"This one is a gift from the late governor. Not many Renoirs left in the world." Ahmed smiled broadly so there'd be no mistaking his intended humor. "Even the President-elect is jealous."

"As for the other painting, Caroline can't figure out what the lady on the water means.

"I'd like to know myself. I never studied art, though I'm fascinated by it. So few great works left. What the tsunamis didn't destroy the Schism tried to." May the Maker forgive his pride. Only the privileged owned art of any kind. Like Esther's precious teapot, Ahmed treasured the Renoirs, pieces of priceless history.

"Maybe you and Caroline can take in the museum next to the Opera House in Sector One. There is a showroom of approved modern artwork. These two buildings were the last cultural improvements under Devereux's administration. President-elect Rowlands has yet to reveal his plan for expansion of the arts, although he himself is quite fond of nineteenth-century statues and paintings."

Skinner wisely kept his opinion on the matter to himself. A true politician.

Ahmed rebooted his micro, and EVE took up the larger portion of the room. Her sultry voice commanded, "Enter your access code and nature of your inquiry."

Ahmed swiped his implant.

"Access accepted." EVE minimized, always near to escort the user through the maze of the Mainframe.

Ahmed gave Skinner one last chance to avoid the whole unpleasantness. "And you are certain you wish to become a Citizen?"

His eyes bulged and sweat beaded on his brow as if waking from a nightmare. How desperate he must be. A man should not be forced to choose between his honor and his child. This was not the government Devereux had envisioned.

"Tell Caroline to come in, assuming she's willing to unglue her eyes from the Renoir."

Skinner nodded, opened the office door and crooked his index finger. "Caroline, would you come in, please." Skinner turned toward Ahmed. "What about Peter?"

"Bring him in. I only need Peter's thumbprint for the Mainframe. Children aren't required to obtain an implant until the age of accountability when they choose to become Citizens and are assigned a vocation."

Caroline towed the frightened youngster who snuggled in the folds of her garments. Ahmed glanced at her coarse pantaloons and tunic. Her garments might be elegant enough for the Network. Unfortunately, she'd be vulnerable to ridicule by City socialites who favored silk pantaloons and transparent over-blouses. Caroline's heavy stockings and long boots, upscale and posh for an outworlder, would be considered out of style. He might ask some of the women in his circles to help Caroline find suitable clothing. Though she and Kyle would be assigned to the lowest of professions, she was still a dignitary's intimate.

Ahmed ached for Caroline's sacrifices. Her former home a veritable palace in comparison to the small quarters she'd now live in for the rest of her life. In the Network, Caroline was revered. In America Prime, she'd have little more status than a factory meme.

Her face froze in white panic. Skinner patted the chair next to him and Caroline sat—her back rigid and her eyes fixed on his Renoir. Ahmed guided Peter to a prized chair by the window. When Eve reappeared, Peter's eyes bulged.

Kyle might as well know now, he'd not be able to shield Peter from the sexual freedom of the City. Like a food staple, erotica was everywhere.

Ahmed ran through the list of identifiers and reasons for the application then turned the micro toward the repatriation seekers. "I'll need each of you to say your name into the voice recognition program and place your thumbprints on the document projections for Mainframe identification. Your processing is nearly complete."

Skinner and Caroline complied with no hesitation. If required, they would have severed an appendage to spare Peter's life. "You and Caroline will receive your implants ahead of Benjamin. He and Christine want to finalize their familial contract immediately after Benjamin's Rite of Accountability."

Kyle nodded.

The first protocols were relatively simple. However, approving their residence might pose a challenge. "Caroline, you have a relative willing to sponsor you?"

Kyle spoke for Caroline who remained frozen. "Yes, Bernard Merry. His name was changed from St. Mary after passage of the Uniformity Act. Caroline and her mother lived with him before her mother defected."

"How old was Caroline when she left America Prime?"

"Ten."

"As long as she was under twenty-one, her repatriation shouldn't be a problem."

"Of course, we'll want to obtain our own housing as soon as possible. Caroline believes his apartment is quite small."

Kyle apparently didn't know that most City dwellers crammed into small flats comprised of layered sleeping quarters; only the very wealthy could purchase apartments with two or more bedrooms. Best not to dump too much reality on them at the outset. They'd learn soon enough.

Ahmed projected Caroline's old records into the middle of the room. "I can't find much on Caroline's father other than he was born in the Northern Province. Apparently, he went to work for Bernard St. Mary's construction company, was highly instrumental in the rebuilding of America Prime when the Accord formed."

Caroline finally spoke. "Bernard is my father's uncle. My father was killed in a construction accident here in America Prime. Afterward, Mother and I lived with Uncle Bernard. Mother became disenchanted with the bubbled City and decided to defect. We lived among the Nomads for a few years. Mother died when I was still a young girl, and a Nomad chief adopted me. I met Kyle during one of his expeditions to the Nomadic camps in the Northern Province, and he took me to be his mate."

Caroline's story was typical during the early days of the Accord, where boundaries were redefined and cities rose in haste, one sector at a time; first governmental centers, then business faculties and residential areas, tearing down the damaged urban areas, brick by brick.

"I see your great uncle had no family of his own."

"My father said that Uncle Bernard's wife died in childbirth. That's when he left the Northern Province, then known as Canada, to find opportunity in construction. He believed the Accord would end world strife and wanted to be part of something great."

Ahmed stroked his chin. "Yes. It's all here."

Skinner raised an eyebrow. "I hadn't realized the government kept so much information on every individual. There will be much we'll have to get used to. No matter. Scripture tells us to render unto government what government is due."

The man had not incriminated himself, and government benefited from Christ followers submission to the scriptural mandate. Still, Skinner should be warned. "I must remind you not to promote any individual ideology. It's considered a crime. Understood?"

"Understood."

Ahmed highlighted tidbits on Caroline's family history. Her verbal accounts matched the data stream, and he could find no impediment to her repatriation. However, Bernard Merry had been branded a dissenter and required periodic surveillance by the IEA. Ahmed would have to juggle the record to clear the Skinners' assignment to Merry's flat. Housing a suspicious person like Skinner in the home of an identified dissenter would bring the IEA down on all of them.

"Let me make a few entries before we proceed."

Ahmed engaged EVE's projection and requested data correction protocols.

He made the necessary adjustments and put his thumbprint next to reason #10—clerical error.

Done.

Bernard Merry, aka Bernard St. Mary, as far as the Mainframe was concerned, was now clear of all suspicion. Before the Mainframe monitors figured out Ahmed's two-step, Skinner and Caroline would be declared Citizens.

"I see your uncle has a registered micro. I'm hailing him now to confirm his willingness to sponsor you and your family."

Merry's image projected into the office, an ancient, like Esther, born before the world disintegrated—a human history book. "Mr. Fared? This is indeed an honor."

"Your niece and her intimate are in my office. They have applied for repatriation, and Caroline has requested to be placed under your sponsorship. I have vouched for them; however, I need to verify your willingness to house them until they receive their implants."

"If I'm cleared to do so, of course."

"I see nothing in the data stream to nullify you as a sponsor."

"Then by all means. Do they know where my flat is?"

Ahmed projected Merry's vital statistics. "Do you still reside at the Condor Apartments in Sector Four?" Not far from Ahmed's flat and three blocks from Eternal Pathways.

"Yes."

"I'm very familiar with the area. I'll give Kyle and Caroline directions as well as a temporary identification card. I've set them up with a stipend and a provisional account until they receive their implants and begin their work assignments. Of course, until then, all their purchases must be approved by me. You can expect them in about an hour. I'll check in on them tomorrow."

"I look forward to becoming reacquainted with my niece. May I see my family?"

Ahmed turned the micro toward Skinner and Caroline and motioned for Peter to join his parents.

Merry smiled, his eyes filled with tears. "Thank you, Mr. Fared. You've made an old man very happy today."

Ahmed sighed and almost prayed.

CHAPTER SIXTEEN
Denver Hub/Western America Outworld

Davu Obote sat to face the thirty-six delegates and mayors from six communities. The assembly had convened under a canopy he'd provided for the occasion, since Goodayle's hut was far too small to manage so many. A few of the delegates fidgeted in their seats and twisted their necks, anxious to hear their new Chairman's first speech. Davu examined the mood—a mixed aura of expectation and fear—a court awaiting a speech from their king. Only, Goodayle was the antithesis of royalty, yet a peasant who stood tall among his peers.

Jacob extended his arms symbolically enfolding his flock—an ironic image since he was perhaps the worst farmer in the Network. If not for Amelia's knowledge, the family would have starved.

"My fellow leaders, though we are one world, let us not take away our individuality, the precious part of us that makes each and every soul unique to the Maker. His creation is so vast, every flower presses a singular stamp upon the Earth. How much more has the Maker endowed the creation into whom he breathed the breath of life? We must not let men take away from us what the Maker has given."

Davu trembled as Goodayle neared the end of his speech. No crystal ball, divinations, incantations, sorcery, or trickery, yet he outlined his vision for the Network's future as if he held the wisdom of the ages. His constituents gobbled his rhetoric like starving children.

Davu contemplated his strategy. Like Goodayle, he must appeal to this delegation as he would a child. Fortunately, children could be easily swayed. He merely needed to sour Goodayle's message, create division among the Network, do the job the IEA paid him to do and disrupt the illegal government. Goodayle's ideas came dangerously close to secession. If these hubs did the unthinkable, became officially autonomous, more outworld encampments would follow their example. A new era, a reversal of sorts, would return Earth to chaos as nations once again warred with one another.

The Constitutional Government, however unjust, provided United Earth with peace and prosperity. From what Davu knew of history, idealism destroyed cultures. Indeed, if no one points out the flaws in a garment, the wearer remains content. Reformers, those who sowed disenchantment, revealed the uneven hem in the fabric of mankind.

Goodayle's and Rowlands' ideologies would inevitably clash—each man unorthodox in his vision and dogged in his pursuits. They had different tractors, and each plowed through his own field. Better to follow the certainty of Rowlands' regime, the most likely path to continued wealth, than remain in the shadow of the Network's tenuous future.

The delegation applauded Goodayle's arguments. Fools.

Time to negotiate a quick disappearance, a cover so close to the top could not be held indefinitely. Rowlands' offer was too sweet a deal to pass over, a delegate seat and repatriation, possibly advancement to a governorship, although the seat not officially vacant until Rowlands became President. With repatriation, he could transfer his illicit assets to legal bank accounts. If he could bank, he'd become a greater economic force than even Romala Maslow, perhaps buy out Maslow's meme factories.

In Davu's mind, there was no conflict over the if. Only the how. How to bring Goodayle down, a man most considered a saint. Every man born of woman had an Achilles heel. The righteous Goodayle's vision would be both his glory and undoing. Zeal stirred the pot. Fear would slow his reforms, at least until Rowlands' Inauguration. Then the fertile Network cooperative farms would go on the auction block, and Davu would be first to make a bid.

Goodayle rambled on. "A Charter, my friends, would set us apart. As we stand now, we exist solely at the pleasure of the walled fortress, nothing more than memes born through the natural means of a mother and father …"

Goodayle's agenda—sheer madness. The Council of Mayors had not yet come to an agreement on whether they should build a formal meeting house—dangerous enough. Goodayle's proposition went too far. A Charter—a declaration that would formalize the Network's autonomy—was certain to bring about an IEA sweep and annihilate the entire Network.

As any gifted orator would do, Goodayle appealed to all facets of his audience, both the idealists and the conservatives. "I do not propose we become a new nation, separate and apart from United Earth."

Where else would a Charter take them?

"The Constitutional Government has lost her way. The Accord was beautiful—at last, humankind turned their weapons into plowshares and lived harmoniously as free people. Sadly, evil men—men who sought domination—seduced our leaders, and their cruel intent blemished the dreams of our founding fathers. These evil ones trampled what was good in the wake of their greed. The Network can be as arms of reason for eyes that can no longer see."

A noble concept. Yet, nobility crippled a mind, and those who followed were doomed to fall into the same pit.

So far, Davu had managed to dissuade the Network's governmental advancements through manipulation. Given the mayors' receptiveness to their new leader, perhaps the situation required an infusion of panic. Saint Jacob would not risk a rift among the leadership and would retract his proposal.

Every Caesar feared a messiah, and Rowlands was no different—Goodayle's threat reached beyond mere political competition. The man pushed a passion, one fostered by his outmoded religion. This Rowlands feared above all else.

Jacob cleared his throat. "Finally, my dear friends—let us not coil in cowardice, rather, we should progress as a people with purpose. A Charter is not tantamount to seceding from the Constitutional Government. Such a document is merely stating our desire to continue the peaceful coexistence we have enjoyed, but as equals, not servants."

Goodayle paused, and Davu stole the delegation's ear. "Chairman Goodayle, what you propose is contradictory. When the system of defection was devised, few expected the outcasts would ban together. When they did, even fewer expected these bands to thrive. Yet, we have. Nomads joined defectors and purified the land. When the Marauders threatened us, we circled our determination like the wagon trains of old and kept intruders at bay. Jews, Christians, Buddhists, Muslims, and those who hold no religious connection proved a diverse world can live harmoniously. Our engineers discovered ways to reclaim the poisoned land. Death rates declined, and healthier children were born. Crops yielded record harvests, more than we needed to feed our own. And the government allowed us to continue as long as we tithed our bounty. In a few years, we will have no need for the hunts. Life is good inside our Network. What Chairman Goodayle suggests would cause us to lose what we have strived so hard to build."

The assembly hummed. Davu continued. "Western America, under Devereux's leadership, became the model for other provinces, America Prime a paradigm by which all cities would rebuild. Crime is nearly non-existent, except in Sector Ten. With Congress firmly rooted within our hallowed province, America Prime is unparalleled. The ingenuity of the Resolution provides a peaceful solution for dissidents. Why upset the balance between both heavens? Forgive me, Chairman Goodayle. Your proposal would jam a stick in the cogs. I, for one, will not support it."

Davu's Second, as planned, stood in his mayor's defense. "Chairman Goodayle, I agree with Mayor Obote. What you propose is too dangerous. What is to keep the government from overpowering us? Since we line the pockets of the bankers, Congress looks the other way. A meeting house, Chairman, one that doubles as a school, is risky enough. A Charter? A manifesto? Would be the end of us all."

Goodayle's face furrowed. "Mayor Obote, your concerns are justified. However, we risk our way of life even more if we believe the status quo will continue."

A voice within the rear section of the delegation squeaked the question on many minds. "What does Ahmed say we should do?"

Ahmed Fared would never condone a near separatist action like a Charter. Why not use the revered ambassador's influence as a wedge? Davu stood again. "Excellent question, Delegate Lightfoot. Mr. Fared is our friend, as well as our ambassador. His opinions are highly regarded."

An avalanche of discussion rocked the tent. Chairman Goodayle raised his hands to quiet the brewing storm. "Is Ahmed your Chairman, or am I? Did you elect Fared to guide you? However, the ambassador is concerned for our Network. No, he would not favor a Charter and believes he can negotiate a continued peace with the Constitutional Government. There are many in the government who oppose our way of life. Unless we become stronger, we will be repatriated or annihilated regardless of my brother's good efforts on our behalf. Those of us who survive will be displaced or forced into servitude. We will be like memes and will till our lands for an indifferent population."

Davu glanced toward Mayor Mai Katakoa of the Wyoming Community who pursed her lips at Goodayle's words. Not surprising. Mai's experience with resistance cost her intimate his life. Rub salt into the fresh wound and gain her disapproval. Davu gazed over the crowd as an errant breeze whipped through the tent, a fortuitous, unplanned prop that puffed his garments like sails. "Mayor Katakoa knows better than any of us how intolerant the government can be. Tell them, Mai, how your man was terminated simply for teaching students in an abandoned building. Then ask yourselves if a school would be a wise venture."

Tears streaked Mai's dark cheeks. She stood next to Davu. "Mayor Morales and Mayor Obote speak for many of us. Perhaps this is not the time to cross a bridge from which we cannot return. I vote we defer building a meeting house, at least until after the Festival negotiations. I don't think President-elect Rowlands wants to destroy us. He must understand how much the Network benefits all of United Earth, not only America Prime."

Ripples of dissent billowed to a crescendo, and Davu nodded in self-adulation. If Goodayle truly considered himself a man of the people, he'd rescind his proposal against this great outcry ... one that would lead to an unwinnable civil war.

Jacob surveyed the group while delegations formed caucuses. The murmur rose to a near riot. He had expected this outcome as much as he'd anticipated Davu's opposition, a man who'd play both sides until he determined which would win. Jacob's suspicions as to Davu's loyalties reached its bitter conclusion: he'd hedged his bets with Rowlands, and as Mayor of the Nevada Community and Second Chairman, his arguments influenced many. Time to end the turmoil.

As was his duty, Davu stood to call for a vote. "The time is at hand to decide these three matters. I personally would like to see work continue on the new manse. I believe most of you share my opinion—in light of Chairman Goodayle's current humble situation, any negotiations with America Prime would be better received from a man who appears prosperous."

A respectful snicker circulated the canopy, and Jacob joined in their laughter. The former manse had been the pride of the Network, a testament to the engineering genius that bolstered the hubs. Thomas Muldoon's estate was even bigger than the manse. Yet, no other Network home compared to Davu's opulent mansion. The Gothic imitation with etched ceilings within and marbled statues without surpassed the Governor's mansion and rivaled the Presidential Palace.

Self-deluded emperors often displayed themselves in splendor. Perhaps Davu thought himself an Alexander the Great of economics, a man who accumulated many possessions and a brilliant financier who prospered even through the Network's antiquated system of bartering.

Davu rushed the vote. "Signify your approval by a show of hands. All those in favor of the Charter …"

A vote now would be ludicrous. Jacob raised his hand. "Mayor Obote, no need for a vote. I rescind all matters from the table. Let us consider this first meeting merely a discussion. We will reconvene after the Festival."

Davu offered a respectful nod. "We should, at least, formalize our desire to rebuild the manse. As is my right as Second, I will call for a vote. All in favor signify by your raised hand."

The assembly rose with loud applause to Davu's proposal. While their desire had been expected, Jacob wept at the overwhelming show of support. Amelia would be pleased. "Mere words cannot express my gratitude to all of you. I urge you to weigh what has been discussed today. We cannot risk the temptation to merely stagnate. We must move forward and grow, or we will die. Mayor Obote, please set the date and time for our next meeting."

"One week following the Festival. At the tenth hour."

Thomas Muldoon rose. "Chairman Goodayle, I'd like to offer my home for any future meetings until a new manse is built. I have plenty of room so we won't be choked by these desert winds. We should return the canopy to Mayor Obote as soon as possible."

Davu waved his hand to end discussion on Thomas' generosity. "The matter is settled then. Three weeks at the home of Thomas Muldoon. If there is no objection, I declare this meeting adjourned."

The delegations rose, then offered one another friendly farewells. Davu left first, followed by Enrique Morales and Mai Katakoa.

Thomas Muldoon held back after everyone else had departed.

"I liked your ideas, Jacob, and I agree. We've been too complacent. Our current symbiotic existence with United Earth cannot continue indefinitely. I grow beans in my private garden. They're hearty, and tend to take over whatever else used to grow there. I suppose our two cultures are like that. One will eventually sprout into the other's territory. We have a good life now, a life built from years of hard work. I, for one, don't want to see all our hopes vanish simply because we refused to stand up to paranoid maniacs like Edwin Rowlands. I'm not afraid to take up arms, if necessary."

"Thank you, Thomas. Your support means a great deal." Jacob liked the burly red-headed defector of a relocated Highlander, a man of integrity, his promotion to Mayor of the Colorado Community, fortuitous. The Council of Mayors needed his strong leadership, even if he claimed to be more a farmer than a politician. In America Prime, engineers were as revered as scientists, and Thomas might have been a wealthy man if his family had stayed in the City. Yet, he defected in search of freedom. Thomas added his vast knowledge to develop a sewer system and a power grid. Even the most remote hubs could now access solar energy and sanitation improvements—things Citizens took for granted, even those in Sector Ten. If only Thomas Muldoon were his Second.

Jacob retreated to the hut. As he entered, Amelia came in from tending the hens and kissed his cheek. "So how did the meeting go?" Did the Council approve your agenda?"

Jacob forced a grin to cover his worries. "As predicted. Most opposed my ideas, some at least listened. Next month you can pack up our belongings. We'll have a new home. Didn't I promise you a fine house some day?"

"So, they formalized the new manse? See how much the people admire you?"

"As much as I dream of a Charter, Amelia, I know my vision is merely fantasy. Davu is right. To declare autonomy will draw a line in the sand. If we declare war, we are not strong enough to win."

"Then why pursue the Charter?"

"To awaken the mayors to our desperate situation. In that, I may have succeeded. There will be tough decisions ahead, Amelia. We are destined to lose even the few freedoms we have gained. Now as for the manse, I suspect this will give them a purpose for the dark days ahead."

A series of barks followed her laugh. The bluish tint to her lips prompted Jacob's worst fears.

"And what does Ahmed say will happen if the Network formalizes their autonomy?"

He wished Ahmed would move to the Network to lead these people. Even his own wife looked for guidance from their Ambassador before their Chairman.

Amelia's coarse coughs deepened. He knew his wishful thinking could not stay off the inevitable any more than a Charter would make a difference where the Network was concerned. There'd never be a separate and free Network, and likely Chairman Jacob Goodayle would move into the manse alone.

He opened his micro. "Benjamin sent me an encrypted message from Ahmed before the meeting convened. Rowlands wants the Festival to coincide with the Inauguration. Ahmed says the invitation will extend to one thousand representatives from all the other provinces to include the outworld leaders. Since America Prime is the host, the Network will be amply represented to include a minor contingency from the Nomadic tribes."

"Will you go, Jacob?"

"I will, although I suspect there will be no positive outcome."

"And will you see Benjamin and meet his lovely intimate?"

Must she be burdened with still more dire circumstances? "My dear wife, there is additional news."

She sat on a stick chair and scowled. "Jacob, do not use my mind as a game board."

"No games, my dear. This news is both a blessing and a concern. We will have the privilege of frequent visits from Benjamin."

Hope brought a faint rose to her cheeks. As realization struck, her smile vanished. "Benjamin has been assigned as Ahmed's assistant, hasn't he? That's how Ahmed managed the message. He will use Benjamin's ability to hack the Mainframe."

Jacob nodded. "Ahmed is hopeful Benjamin will take over as ambassador to the Network when Ahmed assumes his duties as Second President."

Amelia's eyes bugged.

"Try not to worry. Benjamin's a smart boy, and Christine knows how the government works. Though her home is under continuous surveillance, Benjamin will be safe under Ahmed's watchful eye. In fact, Ahmed and Benjamin will both be here tomorrow to discuss the Festival plans."

"Then I best make my potato pie."

She saw through his pretense. She knew as well as he did that disaster loomed. She searched his face for comfort. He had none to offer. "What will become of us, Jacob?"

He tugged her to him, and he felt her weakness. "I don't know for sure. We will face whatever comes together, as we have always done since the good cleric pronounced us husband and wife."

"And what will you do when the Maker calls me home?"

"Then I'll shake a fist at him for taking you from me far too soon."

She looked up at him and challenged him with a scowl. "Promise me you'll finish the manse, continue the negotiations, and reach a palatable agreement with the Constitutional Government. There's no other course for you to take ... with or without me."

CHAPTER SEVENTEEN
Sector Three/Highland Province

Angelina Bartelli bolted upright, the transponder's squawk like nails scraping glass. Carlos stretched beside her, a clueless log, yet, so desirable, and their familial contract only a few hours old. She checked the ID. Who wanted to speak to her from IEA High Command? She answered the transponder's hail with as much professionalism as she could muster. "Officer Bartelli."

"Officer, you failed to answer your micro."

She strained to recognize the unidentified caller—masculine, unfamiliar, the accent more reminiscent of old Mediterranean cultures than Highland born, though not an anomaly. Thanks to the Uniformity Act, every province had been ethnically blended, relocations had become the standard in her parents' day. Papa often mourned for Old Italy.

"My micro is off-line. I'm on familial leave with my new intimate. Who is this?"

"Agent Nemo Savakis."

"I've heard the name. You head up the badlands unit. Found Jimmy Kinnear yet?"

"Jimmy Kinnear is not the object of this investigation."

"Investigation? Who are you investigating?"

"You."

Unbelievable. Why would IEA investigate her, a dedicated officer? "For what?"

"An emergency activation of an unauthorized micro appeared on your account while on leave. Highly irregular."

"I didn't activate a micro. Someone must have stolen my access code. I think I know who. I'm on it. Wire me the log entry. I suspect the activation occurred somewhere near Checkpoint 90?"

"Correct. I must remind you, in cases of unauthorized activation, you will be placed under suspension until the matter is cleared."

She'd served the law faithfully, and now the law deemed her a target? That prissy Scottish princess was behind this somehow. Angelina blew an errant curl from her forehead. She should have sent Bridget to her Maker, governor's daughter or not. Most likely, Jimmy Kinnear had a hand in the matter as well. Besides Carlos, only Jimmy and Bridget knew her code patterns.

Savakis droned protocols, a human ADAM. "Get your micro. I'll wait until you've linked into the Mainframe on a secure channel."

"Fine, hold on." She threw on a robe and clicked on her micro. EVE projected. "State menu choice."

"ADAM, clear channel, authorization Ba02rt15el40li."

"That encryption is no longer valid."

Angelina screamed into the transponder. "Hey, you, Agent What's-your-name."

"Nemo Savakis."

"How do you expect me to get on a safe channel if you've already erased my codes?" The so-called efficiency of the IEA.

"Apologies. My mistake." A click and a clack and then, "Now try it."

EVE projected. "You are now able to access IEA procedures." Angelina reentered her code and ADAM appeared. "I'm in. Maybe someday some hacker will do the world a favor by obliterating that obnoxious icon."

Savakis cleared his throat as his projection appeared. His face wore disdain.

That was a joke, Nemo."

"Agent Savakis to you, and I must warn you this conversation is monitored."

Heat surged. She'd been reckless yet again and ridiculed the President-elect's Mainframe invention, perhaps crossed a line of no return. In addition, she'd been insubordinate to a superior. A rookie had better sense. "Yes, sir."

"Of course, any Citizen, including an IEA officer, has a right to free speech as long as their words do not encroach upon the right of another Citizen not to hear said speech and said speech is not given in association with any group not sanctioned by the Constitutional Government."

A law this convoluted trapped even the brightest Citizen—and had now caught her. Nonetheless, a garbled law she had pledged to support and uphold. "My distaste for the icon stems from a humanitarian concern." Another irony. She despised the Humanitarians as much as the Reformists—Humanitarians were nothing more than self-satisfied do-gooders motivated more by image than true compassion. When she was orphaned as a teenager, the Humanitarians had forced her into a group home where she was raped and beaten in every dead spot.

Papa believed a person's past shaped one's present. Maybe those hard years turned her into the crusted officer she'd become. And now the very law she'd served condemned her. She had every right to vent.

Get a grip, Angelina. Don't fall prey to your anger again.

"Officer Bartelli, I'm relaying the log entry now. I'm not permitted to send you anything else."

"Understood." Angelina relayed the feed to her personal micro she'd established under a false identity. While she upheld the law, she'd never trusted it.

"I see you've copied this transaction. No matter. You'll have no access to any micro after this conversation is terminated."

That's what you think, Nemo. Do you take me for a complete idiot? Jimmy Kinnear was not the only former agent who knew how to forge Mainframe access.

"Now, I need your thumbprint to verify this conversation. You know the consequence if you don't comply."

"Understood." Angelina placed her thumb on the projection. She'd turn a P-74 on herself before she'd let anyone make her a former target's cellmate.

ADAM reappeared. "Receipt confirmed."

"Wish I could shoot that crazy icon."

Savakis' image scowled. "Excuse me?"

"I wasn't talking to you, Nemo."

"Agent Savakis."

"Yeah. Yeah. Agent Nemo Savakis. So, tell me, what is a nice guy like you doing with an outfit like the IEA?"

"My personal choices are not the issue here, Officer Bartelli."

Too late to retract. Might as well prepare for a duel of wits, the outcome wouldn't change regardless of her compliance. Apparently, Savakis was a stickler for protocols, not to mention conceited beyond the intention of the word. While she still had Mainframe capability, she copied his voice onto a disk and risked one more relay to her personal micro.

"You thinned, Officer Bartelli. What did you copy?"

"Your pretty face, Agent Nemo Savakis."

He smiled again. "A waste of time."

"Thanks for the heads up." She mimicked a playmate quality. "You have an honest face, Agent Nemo Savakis. I trust you will conclude this investigation soon?"

Carlos swaggered into the room. "Something wrong?"

She waved him back to bed. "Anything else, Agent Savakis?"

"No. I have deleted your access code ... as well as Officer Perez's."

Of course, he followed protocols to the letter. Carlos would be furious. She stared at the blank view screen while she attempted access. EVE reappeared. "That code is no longer in use."

Angelina shoved the IEA micro off the table, then disintegrated the offensive device with a blast from her P-74.

She sat and drew her weapon across her knees. She'd have to tell Carlos he was suspended along with his intimate. She'd have precious little time to figure out some plausible explanation before the surveillance routines kicked in.

She leaned her P-74 against the bedroom wall. She hadn't moved into Carlos' flat yet, although they had discussed the possibilities, unable to decide whose apartment to sublet. Hers was the bigger of the two, though his was closer to Headquarters. Moot debate. They'd be fugitives soon enough. Even if Savakis reported her innocent of unauthorized transponder activation, this current transgression would trigger an in-depth investigation into all her log entries. Any competent investigator would eventually uncover the Mainframe tampering connected to her botched arrest of two Reformists.

Carlos sat on the edge of the bed. "What's up?"

She whispered the horrid truth in his ear—their IEA careers were over, and most likely they'd be arrested. She loved Carlos, just not as much as she once loved Jimmy. At least, Carlos was pliable—most of the time. The one thing she did not expect was for him to take charge.

He pulled out two civilian jumpsuits from his closet and handed one to her. They dressed in silence then blasted their transponders. Carlos grabbed his scanner locator off his bureau, tossed the device into a satchel then pulled her into an embrace as he whispered, "Let's run. Ready?"

She hoisted her weapon and mouthed her answer. "Ready. I promise you, Bridget Cavanaugh will pay for this."

CHAPTER EIGHTEEN
Sector One/Highland Province

Bridget followed Falan into the mansion and straight to Da's den where she sat in the antique winged chair. "Wait here for your da," He left her alone with her thoughts.

So many memories. Mostly how she'd romped through the halls as she hummed an old Scottish lullaby Mum used to sing:

You take the high road

And I'll take the low road

And I'll be in Scotland afore ye

Da had explained the lilt's origins, how Old Scotland fought to retain its identity though geographically bound to the English throne. After the tsunamis changed the British Isles forever, all island subjects became Highlanders: English, Welsh, Irish, and Scots, and the masses of relocations—a forced uniformity. Through all of it, Da, as Scottish as a Highlander can be, hoped Old Scotland's heritage would be preserved.

Da had lectured her countless times, in this very office, especially when she ran around like a rugby player. "Watch your step, lassie," Da scolded. "My heart would break if you were harmed."

Perhaps she'd always been rebellious. Yet, Da never stopped loving her. Once during their daily walks in the garden, she wriggled from his hand and chased a ferret, and its bite induced a deadly fever. Da left the affairs of state to his Second and never left her bedside until she recovered.

An older Bridget still refused to listen. Mum had been dead only a few weeks when Bridget sat in this same chair and told Da she had joined the IEA. "You were born into the life of politics," he pleaded. "Be a delegate's intimate or campaign in your own right. Please don't join the IEA—most of them my enemies. Are you looking to get yourself killed and break your da's heart?"

She badgered him, and her stubbornness whittled away his defenses until he approved her admission to the academy. Later she learned how Da bribed her commander to assign her light duties. Bridget balked at his interference and stormed through his den, a defiant wind. Bridget recalled how he let her vent before he offered counsel. "Me darlin' Bridget, you are more than life to me. I'd gladly die to keep you safe."

He wept when she told him she would become Ian McCormick's intimate, for she had gone beyond her father's reach. "What have you done, lassie? You've put a stake into me heart, this time. How can I be your da now? You've joined with a Reformist. Something I canna condone. Nor can I look the other way. Go if you must. Know this. You'll have me love always even if you are not in my sight."

Would he scorn her now as he did then? Bridget fidgeted in the chair. What kept Da so long? She pulled at her rags, sniffed her hands and gagged. Three days with no sonic shower, lotion, or amenities of any kind. Da would want nothing to do with her even if she were scrubbed as clean as a vine-picked tomato. She deserved to be tossed back into Sector Ten or the badlands. Da had been a good father, she an errant daughter who scorned the one who loved her most.

The door opened, and Da entered. Bridget gasped at how much he'd aged, his once brown hair now completely silver, and his robust cheeks whitened with worry, no longer the man who chased her through the rose beds of her childhood.

"Da?"

At first, he stared at her as if she were something not real. Then he extended his arms, and Bridget rushed into them. "Oh, me darlin' girl! How your da has missed you." His wet tears rubbed against her cheek. "I had no intention of sending you to prison. I dinna order the raid. President Schumann authorized the arrest and used me signature. His right, of course. I had no knowledge of his plan 'til Falan discovered you were wanted by the IEA. Then Jimmy Kinnear wired he had kidnapped you. We traded supplies for your safe deliverance."

"Why that scoundrel." The heat singed whatever soft spot she'd found for the likes of Jimmy Kinnear. "He tricked you, Da. I wasn't kidnapped."

"You're home. That's all that matters now, lassie."

Da held her hands, his gaze sincere. "I be truly sorry your man is dead. I admired Ian, though I canna partner with his ideals."

"Oh, Da, can you ever forgive me?"

He twirled her around, and joy filled her as they wept together.

He tucked her soiled tresses behind her ear. "Nothing to forgive, darlin' girl. You acted by your conscience—the way I raised you. The important thing is you are here now. We won't wallow in regret—we'll only look forward. I'll do everything in me power to seek a full pardon. President Schumann has granted a waiver of judgment while he considers my pleas."

She rubbed her belly. "Da. There is a baby to consider, also."

He jigged around the room as if the Lord Himself had descended. "Has the Maker so blessed me, then? I'll soon be holding a wee grandchild in me arms? You make me proud, Bridget, even when you make me angry. A boyo, is it?"

"That's what I planned. I haven't taken the test to be certain. He'll be named Ian, after his da. First name only. I can't give him the name McCormick because I became pregnant before the final authorization. I hoped to give him our family name."

"Of course." His voice caught as he eyed the scanner.

"We'll celebrate as soon as you've had a chance to tidy up a bit." Da summoned the housemaid, Hazel, a custom meme patterned after the comic strip character found in the archives. "Take Mistress Bridget upstairs to her room and help her freshen up for dinner."

Hazel looked every bit as Bridget remembered—brown hair and a saucy disposition. Crowned with a maid's tiara, Hazel paraded through the house in a white house dress and a frilly apron.

Da embraced Bridget once again then gave her an affectionate push. "Your room is the same as when you left. I knew this day would come. You be medicine to an old man's heart, child."

Bridget wiped the last of her tears and followed Hazel upstairs. She bristled with energetic good humor. "Put those rags in a heap somewhere and I'll burn 'em. I'll draw your bath for ya. And while you're relaxin', I'll set out some clothes. You'll be needin' new ones soon. The ones you've left behind are so outdated they ain't fit for a rag doll. At least, they're clean."

When the bath was ready, Bridget sank into the soapy water and closed her eyes. How decadent. Most Citizens, even the wealthy, took sonic showers to preserve precious water supplies. She ducked underneath the foamy water and sat back up, feeling different, like a meme in wait for its final identity stamp. Who would she be now?

The water cooled and Hazel returned. "There're pantaloons and an over-blouse on yer bed." She handed Bridget a robe, and then, with hands on her hips, she stomped impatient feet. "Cook needs my help in the kitchen. I'll send Priscilla up to help you finish dressin'."

"Priscilla?"

"The new maid yer da bought last week. An odd creature, she is. She's a worker, though. Can do the job of three memes. Puttin' my kind right out of work, she is. We Hazels are ... obso ... what's the word?"

"Obsolete?"

Hazel winked. "That's it." The privy door thudded behind her.

Though Da and Ian both despised the practice of manufactured flesh, they differed in their approach. Ian fought toward abolition of the meme trade. Da, however, treated his memes like household members. He bought more than he needed, paid them well, and arranged for their eventual liberation. He never returned an errant meme for dispatch or forced an ill meme into the Euthanasia Chamber. And when a Cavanaugh meme aged, Da bought other memes to care for them and paid for cremations. He constructed a private crypt to store the meme's ashes, each cubicle marked with the meme's date of installation and death. "If I canna change what is, Bridget, I can make life more tolerable for those underneath its load."

Bridget left the privy and went to her bedroom and dressed.

A rap so loud she thought the door might burst. "Come in."

A petite maid handed her a small cloth bag. "Yer da told me to be givin' you this, Mistress Bridget."

"You must be Priscilla."

"I am."

She seemed young, even for a meme. Consumers demanded younger models, and the newer generations had a shorter life expectancy. The earlier models took five to seven years to mature in the factory and lived about thirty years. With improved processing, cost decreased, but longevity diminished. "Planned obsolescence," Ian had said, "to guarantee a continued market."

Bridget opened the bag and gasped at Mum's antique emerald hairpins. If ever she doubted she had been forgiven, she had only to fondle this precious gift. She would wear them proudly for Da's sake.

"Governor Cavanaugh expects you in the sitting room afore supper."

Odd auditory patterns … her voice stilted, as was her whole demeanor. No personality. Not like Hazel, who laughed at funny things and hummed through her work day. "That will be all, Priscilla."

"Yes, Mistress Bridget." Priscilla performed a militaristic one-eighty, then rushed out the door.

Bridget tucked Mum's pins into clean, curly hair, and moved her head from side to side to admire their sparkle. She sniffed the sleeve of her over-blouse—a hint of lilac. Hazel must have kept her closets fresh even though Da had no certainty his daughter would ever return.

She leaned forward and studied her profile as she rubbed her abdomen. Would her illegal pregnancy result in abortion, Ian's child given over to create memes? If she were ordered to abort, she'd swallow her pride and ask for Jimmy's help. Her baby would not become raw material to produce factory workers.

Nor would Da give up his grandson without a battle. Although Da's support base had diminished, he was still the Highland's governor, with the authority the title gave him. Dread flailed its hoofs at her momentary security. Even if cleared of the pregnancy charges and absolved of her smuggling crimes, she was a Reformist's intimate—the party most hated by the ruling congressional ideology. Death might find her at any time. What if her presence put Da in further danger?

She drummed helpless fingers against her dresser. If death found her, at least she would leave this world knowing Da's forgiveness.

She glanced at the timepiece on the mantle. She had kept Da waiting for over an hour. She smiled as she sashayed down the steps. The crinkle of pantaloons prompted memories with each step. Ian had refused to live off his parents' inheritance. Though meager compared to their prospective families' wealth, his delegate salary had been sufficient for their needs and a few extravagances. Until now, she'd pleasured in her sacrifice. Was it a sin to desire fine things again?

Da and Falan stood as he entered the parlor. "There's me darlin' girl. Now I ask you, Falan, isn't she a picture of loveliness? How much she looks like her mum."

"'She walks in beauty' the poet said." Falan took her hand and they followed Da into the dining room. For a former outworlder, Falan seemed genteel enough and could even spout poetry. Well mannered. Refined. Tall, like his brother, with a shadow of Jimmy's smile. Falan's demeanor seemed gentler, and certainly not what Bridget expected from a bodyguard.

Meme servants brought mounds of steaming vegetables, meats, chilled fruits, and desserts while Da prepared a carafe for the wine. "I have saved this bottle for a special occasion. I think this qualifies as one. Vintage 2020, one of the last from the old distilleries."

Da eyed the scanner, hesitated, and removed the cork to let the wine breathe. Then he took Bridget's hands into his. "They be watchin' us, Bridget. I dinna care. I want them to know I am a da afore I be anthin' else in this world. When I thought you lost to me forever, I prayed. I believed in the Accord. I have honored the Constitutional Government. Yet, I be humbled before me Maker who has granted these poor eyes to look upon me precious Bridget once more."

Da heaved leaded sighs. Bridget feared his speech gave Rowlands' spies more ammunition. Da had shown his weakness, this tower of strength Bridget had once rejected yet loved. She joined Da in a symphony of sobs as they fell into an embrace of complete reconciliation.

Once their sobs subsided, they allowed merriment to capture the remains of the day. Falan told tales he learned at his grandmother's knees, stories about fairies and leprechauns. Bridget couldn't remember when she'd laughed so hard.

Da lifted the bottle. "More wine, Bridget?"

She nodded as she recognized Da's glint, the prelude to his favorite ruse to pass along a secret message.

Da played the klutz and knocked the cork into her peripheral vision, and the encryption roused her curiosity. She wiped the corners of her mouth, then nudged the cork toward the edge of the table.

"Only a smidgeon more … the baby, you know."

Da held the bottle up as a question. "Falan?"

"Yes, Governor. I would like a wee bit more. A very fine wine, indeed, sir."

Da poured a scant amount into her goblet and set the vial in front of her. She feigned clumsiness, and spilled a red river across the table then leaped in pretense to rescue the goblet. "Oh, dear. Look what I've done. These crystals belonged to Mum's grandmother."

Bridget stood as she righted the goblet while she stealthily pushed the cork underneath the table. A meme servant rushed to her aide. "No, I'll get it. Here, please take these crystal goblets for safekeeping."

Bridget slid to her knees under the table out of scanner range. Though details were lacking, she understood. She and Da would attend Rowlands' Inauguration. From there, they'd escape to the Northern Province.

CHAPTER NINETEEN
Eternal Pathways/America Prime

Ahmed hesitated. How he despised these events. However, he'd promised Esther he'd be her witness—a promise he must keep.

Esther blushed like a virgin intimate. "So good of you to come, Ahmed. And right on time, too. These people like to keep to schedule, you know."

She took the arm of her escort, a young man in his thirties. Ahmed supposed women would find the young man attractive, creamy white skin and chestnut brown hair. Or perhaps they'd be captivated by his kind blue eyes. At any rate, Esther apparently pleasured in his company.

"Ahmed, this is my social worker, Sean Grafton."

No matter what these professionals chose to call themselves, much profit was to be made with little effort. Yet, euthanasia laws were so complex, to wade through the micro files without counsel proved far beyond the capability of most Citizens, and the reason Ahmed agreed to legislation that required social services for any euthanasia, regardless of class standing.

As expected, Grafton waited for Ahmed to offer the first handshake—a firm grip, the young man quite amiable, and his resemblance to Michael prompted the question. "Forgive my forwardness. Are you a relative of Michael Grafton? Not a common name in America Prime."

Grafton gave no response, and he gazed toward the scanners. Discretion dictated not to pursue the matter. The answer would have to wait until he researched Michael's genealogy. Right now, Esther's final moments deserved full attention.

Grafton clasped Esther's hand. "Mrs. Feinmann's affairs are in good order, except for one detail. She wants you to accompany her dispersal."

"Is this a common practice?"

"Sometimes. In matters of out-of-city dispersal, escorts are customary. We do need government approval. We can bypass the extra paperwork if you agree to ride along. She made this decision not more than an hour ago. We hoped you'd do her this last favor."

"Of course."

"Mr. Ives has obtained flight-plan approval." Grafton handed Ahmed a travel verification disk. "I'll need you to thumbprint this as a government official."

Ahmed projected the document then verified.

Inexplicable joy shimmered in Esther's eyes. "I've spent my last dollar on this occasion. Sean has agreed to the dispersal at no extra cost so I could afford music."

Grafton squeezed her hand. "The pleasure is entirely mine, Mrs. Feinmann."

"At least for the remainder of this event, you'll please address me as Esther."

Ahmed took Esther's hand. "Mr. Grafton, see that Esther gets anything she desires and charge any extra services to my account."

Her usually jovial face squished into a disapproving scowl. "You'll do no such thing. I'm quite content with the arrangements."

"As you wish." Grafton smiled and revealed a perfect row of ivory teeth—too perfect to be his own. If Grafton could afford expensive plastic surgery, then he certainly could afford to give Esther an unreimbursed hour of travel.

Ahmed met Grafton's gaze, honest eyes … compassionate … similar to those he'd witnessed from Christ followers, gleams of peace from a soul no longer at war with the Maker. An enviable tranquility.

"Mrs. Feinmann … excuse me … Esther … would like her ashes dispersed across the Negev Region." Grafton's tones softened with an undercurrent of sentimentality, a quality most social workers lacked, especially in light of the fact Grafton's normal estate percentage fee would be minimal.

Esther beamed like a child in anticipation of a birthday gift. "I want my ashes dispersed near where my Albert and I married. The Israel I knew no longer exists—occupied by Nomadic goat herders now. Most of the population has been relocated to more hospitable environments. I've lived in many places, Ahmed. My happiest years were spent near the Negev. I want to rest there."

"I understand, and I'll do my best to honor your wishes."

Esther winked. "I knew you wouldn't let me down."

A whisper of a man approached. Caretaker Ives' blue-sequined robe glimmered in the theater's dim lights. "It is time." He pointed toward the witness box. "If you would take your seat, Mr. Fared, Mr. Grafton will escort Mrs. Feinmann to the ready area. When preparations are complete, I will open the curtain. You'll find a transponder on your seat, linked directly to the viewing room. Feel free to converse. You've witnessed before, so I assume these procedures are familiar to you."

Far too many. "Yes."

"Any questions?"

"No."

Ahmed kissed Esther on each cheek. "And you are sure you want this?"

She nodded.

"I will miss you."

"Ahmed, my dear boy. I know this pains you. Sometimes we must choose what seems to be the lesser of two evils."

He accepted Esther's kiss of appreciation, as a mother to a son.

"Goodbye, Ahmed. Don't weep for me. I sense my Albert is nearby and will accompany me to my eternal rest."

Grafton escorted her behind a black curtain, and Ahmed took his place in the witness box and loosened the top button on his jumpsuit. A dishdasha would be far more comfortable—these latest government fashions were designed for much slimmer men. Silly thoughts. Perhaps one leaned toward the mundane to escape the horrific.

Ives bowed then exited to manage the production.

Ahmed took his assigned seat and gazed at his timepiece. Five before the mid-hour. He must deter his thoughts … focus on something else. While the morning brought sadness, the afternoon promised a joyful time. He'd planned to visit Bernard Merry's flat, honor his invitation to lunch. Perhaps his last happy duty as ambassador would be to bring Kyle and Caroline good news. Not only had Peter's operation been approved, they would be assigned to the hospital for their career placements. The pay would be abysmal, barely enough for them to survive. A start, at least. More advantages than the poor souls left to fend for themselves in the tenement squalors of Sector Ten.

And there was Christine and Benjamin's celebration to plan this afternoon. The governors, of course, would be invited, although doubtful they would attend. He expected their regrets since Rowlands would more than likely call an emergency meeting to cover their absence. Christine might be disappointed if the room didn't swell with guests. Time to call in a few favors.

His musings ended as the curtain drew. He'd promised to smile brightly for Esther, though he despised the ritual. No one pushed for alternatives to euthanasia, especially where the poor and elderly were concerned, those whom society would consider a burden. Not even the most liberal Humanitarians offered a viable solution. As Second President, Ahmed might be in a position to persuade Rowlands to establish care facilities, staffed by Sector Ten residents, for those unable to care for themselves, a double solution. Ahmed had leverage. Should he cash in his one trump card to curb euthanasia?

He marveled at Esther's brave confrontation with mortality. If brought to the same deplorable crossroad, what would he choose? Would he break his principles, buy a personal care meme to gain a few extra days of life?

Esther smiled—her face, a portrait of serenity. She waved to Ahmed as Ives spread a purple velvet sheet across her body then tilted the bed for optimum viewing. Ahmed pressed his hand against the view screen in farewell.

Ives handed Esther a white pill and a silver chalice. The viewing room dimmed while a kaleidoscope of dancing lights displayed throughout the chamber and music from Esther's youth echoed off the walls. Fifteen minutes later, Ives drew the curtain to signal Esther was no more.

Ives and Grafton came from the chamber and handed Ahmed a micro for his signature.

"What time will the dispersal take place?"

For all his staged tenderness, Ives might as well have been a prompt icon. "The shuttle leaves tomorrow at midday. Mr. Grafton happens to be a licensed pilot, and he agreed to operate the craft to alleviate some of Mrs. Feinmann's final expenses. Irregular, I know. Seems he has developed a fondness for this particular patient."

"Esther was my friend as well as my neighbor. I will be there at the appointed time." He'd always wanted to see the ancient land, the seeds of his Arabian ancestry as well as the Jews. He might not have another opportunity—the next euthanasia might be his own.

CHAPTER TWENTY
Sector Four/America Prime

Ahmed tucked his beret under his arm and accepted Kyle's handshake. The hat wasn't as comfortable as the shermagh. At least, it covered some of his thinning hair.

Clad in a blue muslin jumpsuit, the vestment of a meme administrator, Merry knelt before his guest. "So good of you to stop by. I am honored that the Second to the President-elect graces my domicile."

Ahmed brought him to a stand. "I allow no one to kneel in my presence. My former intimate will attest to my imperfections."

Merry blushed.

"Kyle is a good friend, and I appreciate your hospitality." Ahmed scanned the rectangular flat, barely the size of Rowlands' office closet. Appliances lined the far wall with portable bedding straddled against the opposite side, barely enough room for chairs and a table.

Ahmed assumed the one door hid a privy. The cramped quarters made Ahmed's three-room flat seem palatial.

He offered Merry a firm handshake. "I'll make Kyle and Caroline's housing permits a priority. I see you're a bit crowded."

Kyle laughed. "I suppose Caroline's uncle should move in with us. I understand the housing grants are sized according to the number of the family unit."

"Three-room flats are rare, Kyle. I'll try to find you a flat with two rooms."

Merry waved Ahmed's concern aside. "No rush. I'm away a great deal. I managed to finagle a day off since you were coming. Hard put to replace me, though. Not like folks are beggin' to take my job."

True. Meme supervisors were paid very little, and the turnover was significant. Those with any length of service quickly rose to high ranks. Probably why this labeled dissenter advanced to an administrator status.

"At least there ain't much stress. Most I have to do is complete a few files at the end of the day to verify I've returned the same numbers of memes that were transported. Don't want any meme to escape on my watch. Once in a while, I'll find me an errant meme and have to call the IEA to take 'em down. For the most part, my memes are well behaved. I've got me a good team of supervisors too. I do my job as good as I can."

Merry motioned to the small round table set with common pewter—for Merry's class, the equivalent of fine china, and adorned with a rainbow selection of artificial chrysanthemums.

Except for the occasional state gala, most nights Ahmed dined alone whether in his apartment or at an eatery. He had looked forward to this luncheon, as much a respite as his trips to the Network.

Merry retreated to a makeshift stove and returned with a platter of meat and vegetables.

Kyle gasped. "Bernard, I wasn't aware that the average Citizen could afford meat. How did you come by this feast?"

"This here's cloned food."

Ahmed offered Kyle an explanation. "To preserve livestock and vegetation, most consumers eat food cloned to several generations. Only the wealthy can afford first cloned meat, and fresh meat is only available on the black market."

Merry chuckled. "Even cloned hogget is scarce for us common folk, and cloned lamb is unheard of. Not to worry, though. I learned how to tenderize fifth-generation mutton so's you'd swear the meat was straight off the critter. I thought you folks would like a change from all them berries you raise."

Merry pointed to a chair at the head of the table. "Please, have a seat, Mr. Fared."

As they dined, Merry regaled the group with his tales of life before the tidal waves washed away civilizations, how he and Caroline's grandfather forged their way from the eroded western coastlines to the Sierra Mountains, how they enlisted in the Christian Militia during the Schism, and how their regiment was decimated by disease. The men returned to the mountains and raised sheep. Bernard left for the City shortly after his wife died in childbirth. "In those days, a cry went out for young men to come back to the cities and help rebuild. Hope whispered in the breezes that dissipated radiation clouds."

Ahmed and Jacob's youth had been so different than Merry's. Though Colorado Springs was spared the effects of the tsunamis, war destroyed what famine and disease had left unscathed. The Goodayles' survived the devestations. Jacob's father, an ambassador, worked with Jacques Fountaine, to build the Accord. Though orphaned, his youth was one of privilege.

Would his boyhood have been any different if his parents had survived? Young Ahmed would still have been influenced by his Christian mother's prayers, similar to those the Goodayles offered every sunset.

When conversation abated, Ahmed took the opportunity to leave. "Thank you for the meal, Bernard. You missed your calling. You should have applied to be a chef, although I'm amazed you still work every day. Have you considered retirement?"

Merry's laugh rested on Ahmed's ear like a lullaby. "I don't work for the money, Mr. Fared. I have enough. I wouldn't know what to do with my time if I retired. Besides, the memes like me. I make sure my team treats 'em right. Some of the other teams can be downright nasty, especially to the female memes, if you know what I mean."

Peter, who hadn't made so much as a grunt, piped up. "What does he mean, Papa?"

Ahmed covered his smile while Kyle peered toward his son. "Never mind, Peter, you're too young to be worried about things like memes. Say goodbye to Mr. Fared, then go play with the Matchbox cars Uncle Bernard gave you."

Surprising that a man of humble means such as Bernard Merry would own a priceless collection like Matchbox cars.

"To answer the question you politely did not ask, Mr. Fared, I found them in an abandoned house in Sector Ten a few years ago. Reminded me of the ones I had as a lad."

"They are irreplaceable, Bernard."

"Toys are meant to be played with, not kept in storage."

Most Citizens with connections to outworlds fell under suspicion, perhaps why Merry had been tagged a dissenter. Yet, he served the City as well as any Citizen.

Merry continued as he glanced toward the scanners. "As a youth, I was what my parents' generation termed a hellion. As I grew up,

I predicted where the world was headed and tried to warn folks. Few listened. No stopping the waves. Nope. Or the wars either. The louder we yelled, the deafer folks became. One day, I stopped screamin' and tried to live my life as best I could. I became a Citizen, not because I agree with the government; I figured if I wuz goin' to make life better, I should become a man of peace."

Ahmed stood and offered a handshake to both Merry and Skinner. "It has been a pleasure; however, I must take my leave. Oh, Kyle, I almost forgot. I have arranged for you and Caroline to begin employment at the hospital tomorrow morning." Ahmed pulled out two small micro cards. "Here are your career assignment verifications. Bring these when you report. And another thing, Peter's operation has been approved, contingent upon your repatriation. As soon as your implants are in, we can schedule his surgery."

Gratitude spread across Skinner's face. "Thank you, Ahmed. We are forever in your debt."

"No thanks, needed, Kyle. Be certain you give back to the government what the government has invested in you as any good Citizen would do. And shave the beard."

"I hope I can remember how to shave."

They laughed. Ahmed put his hands on the table, ready to rise. "Duty calls. I need to wire Benjamin Goodayle and make plans for his and Christine's celebration at the Partridge Oasis. You and Caroline are invited, of course. Since most guests will be government officials, the affair will be very formal. Bernard, would you help Kyle and Caroline acquire appropriate clothing?"

Kyle raised his chin. "Should I bring a gift? When a couple is joined in the Network, we bring food, linens, and household equipment to give the young people a good start in their new life together."

"No. A gift would be considered an insult."

"Thank you, Ahmed. We'll see you at the celebration, then. When will the governor return to his public offices?"

"Tomorrow morning."

Yes, tomorrow the storm fronts would arrive—clouds of change darkened the horizon, and Ahmed Fared didn't much like the forecast.

CHAPTER TWENTY-ONE
Sector One/America Prime

Benjamin Goodayle rose to greet the dawn as he anticipated the good things the day would bring. At the top of the list, he'd see Pops in this his first official day as Uncle Ahmed's assistant. If only his parents could meet Christine. Then they'd understand the decision he made.

He jumped at the loud buzz.

Christine had warned him about the noisy transponders. Against impossibilities, the hum intensified and the transponder shook. At least these modern devices flashed the hailer's identification … this one from the governor's office, most likely Uncle Ahmed. A quick response seemed appropriate no matter who had hailed him.

What a life. Though he found the City's technology fascinating, he preferred the practical communication alternatives in the Network, freedom from Mainframe monitors and less vulnerable to hacks, impenetrable even by IEA, thanks to engineers like Thomas Muldoon.

Benjamin picked up the transponder. Drat this contraption. Not even a mute button. There had to be an acknowledgment switch ... somewhere. The hail was so loud now, his ears ached. He could dismantle and reassemble a micro in twenty minutes. These transponders surpassed the most complex devices he'd encountered.

Why so many gadgets? In the City, devices seemed to outnumber people. No wonder the City used implants—no need to remember passwords and access codes for a gazillion different machines.

Benjamin turned the cube-like pin around, the squeal loud enough to make him deaf for life. He fumbled the device again, clicked a minuscule switch, and the buzz stopped. Was he online now? Just in case, he lowered his voice to sound more official. "Goodayle."

"Ah, Benjamin. I was beginning to think you were otherwise occupied," Uncle Ahmed's bellow was as loud as the transponder buzzer on full alert. "In the future, don't delay your response. Protocol requires notifying the IEA when a government official's hail goes unanswered after five minutes. I would not want to report you derelict on your first day."

"Sorry. Couldn't figure out how to operate this thing."

"Don't worry. You're a smart boy. You'll have all these gizmos figured out before day's end, I'm sure. Isn't this a glorious day?"

"Wouldn't know. I just woke up."

"Did you sleep well?"

"The night glows kept me awake."

"You'll get used to them. Though I must say, one of the things I most enjoy about the outworld is the calm of darkness."

Benjamin peered behind the lacy curtain toward the horizon. The sun peeked above the Governor's mansion, a castle-like fortress, partially obscured by the dome's subdivisions. He missed the outworld views where morning painted the Rockies like a rainbow. Citizens and outworlders looked at the same sun yet from completely different worlds.

"We have a lot to accomplish today, Benjamin. Meet me at the air dock in one hour. We'll need to return earlier than expected. I have another flight to catch at noon."

"I'll be there."

"Fared out."

"Goodayle out."

He hoped he had used proper protocol. Now, to figure out how to turn the transponder off. He slipped the slide switch to its original position and the slight hum stopped. The thing was either off or broken. Time would tell.

Benjamin hopped into the sonic shower, then put on his official white jumpsuit. In the Network, clothing was merely a means to keep warm. No one heeded personal tastes. Men and boys usually wore long hemp pants, leather boots, and sleeved hemp shirts. The older women preferred hemp pantaloons, while younger women wore shorter pants than the men. Their tunics were modest, unlike the over-blouses of the City.

He tugged on his official jumpsuit. How did anybody keep track of all the classes of uniforms? White for judicial and legislative branches—black for IEA and Mainframe monitors—red for medical—blue for meme control, and the list went on. As if the colors weren't enough to remember, every government man, woman, and meme wore an insignia-badged beret and lapel pin to identify rank. He'd have to wait for his implant before he received his identifiers.

Benjamin hitched a desperate breath. He must accept the complications City life brought or die.

He hurriedly combed his hair, anxious to meet Christine on the veranda for breakfast before he rushed off to report to Uncle Ahmed. He counted the minutes until they would no longer sleep in separate rooms. They'd agreed to abstain from sex until they signed their familial contract. However, the promise had proven difficult to keep. Why wait if they could not be married like his parents?

In the Network, a man and woman simply joined hands and said their own vows, found a hut and moved in together. Sometimes, the girl took the man's name as her own, like Caroline Skinner. Christine said City familial contracts are less and less popular … pursued only when a couple wanted to have a child.

Perhaps children were not popular, either.

During the tour of the City, he noticed very few children on the streets or in the parks. Christine said that as soon as a child was weaned, they were sent to specialized schools dependent upon their classification and testing scores where they would be trained for their professions. They were reunited with their parents during intermittent respite holidays.

At least he'd had the benefit of day-to-day education from his father. He missed the sounds of children as they played hide and seek, his favorite childhood pastime. He ached for the children of the City, whose life guides were impersonal holographic educators.

He filled with sudden desire. Soon, he and Christine would be one. He'd never bedded with a girl, and Christine said she'd never been with a man. He squared his shoulders at the prideful thought they had saved that special part of themselves for the one they knew would share their life, though most of his friends thought chastity as antiquated as knights and the round table.

"Sex is like food," his friends teased. "When you're hungry, you eat."

Most boys his age had coupled dozens of times by age twenty-one. When he met Christine, he suddenly wanted to do all the things his friends talked about, only with her. She occupied his thoughts day and night, and when she wasn't paying attention, he liked to watch her walk across the room.

He'd almost coupled once … with Madeline Muldoon. She'd let him fondle her long hair as he kissed her. Most of the farm girls cropped their hair or wore their locks high on their heads. Madeline's fell over her shoulders like a silk shawl. Some of the boys in the hub claimed Madeline liked to introduce them to sex. Something about Madeline made Benjamin want to be her student. As they danced, she pressed against him, and he thought he might like to go into the Muldoon shed and get a diploma. Instead, he suppressed the urge. He wanted the first experience to be with someone he loved.

When Benjamin met Christine, saw her at work during the hunts, he knew he loved her even before she spoke. The other women threw the hunt commodities into heaps. Not Christine. She stacked the bricks and folded the clothes with great care. Her hair was long like Madeline's and braided to lie obediently over her right shoulder. When he saw her, even from a distance, his heart jumped as if something eternal had rooted.

Benjamin pulled on his boots, checked his attire in the antique beveled mirror and raced down the stairwell. Christine sat on the veranda, an angel of the morning, her lace over-blouse billowing in the man-made funnel breezes. Non-meme servants scurried from one corner of the house to another as they polished, scrubbed, served, and cooked.

He'd worried that he'd become accustomed to meme labor and turn aside from his aversion to the practice. Thankfully, Christine hired servants from Sector Ten. She claimed most of those she employed were so grateful they served her well, content with their stipends, holidays, and board. Christine's system proved non-meme flesh could be managed as economically as memes. Her brave stance against the tide of public opinion made Benjamin love her all the more.

He pulled her to her feet and pressed against her, glad she didn't resist his heated kisses. "Are you still sure we should wait? I have thirty minutes before I have to leave."

She smiled and sighed simultaneously. Maybe the wait was equally hard for her. "Only a few days more, Benjamin."

A maid poured his coffee while he filled his plate. A Network feast was not as abundant as this breakfast offering. "Do you eat like this every morning?"

"This is light fare today."

He lifted his head to acknowledge the maid. "Thank you."

She blushed and Christine giggled. "It's not customary to show verbal courtesies to servants. I think it's sweet you do."

Benjamin's cheeks heated. "I've never been compared to a dessert before."

"Sorry. Guess I'm in a maternal state of mind, today. I've been imagining three little boys running through the house, and they all look like you."

He smiled. "Funny. I picture three girls."

"We'll have to wait, though, according to law."

"In the Network, we don't worry about babies. They just happen."

"No contraceptives?"

"Young people are told their duty is to populate. Network births and deaths must be registered. I'm afraid the death column is the longest."

Christine's lips quivered. "Then how is the Network's population growing?"

"Defections. More and more every year."

Christine's eyes filled with tears. What had he said to upset her? "Your people have endured so much for their freedoms."

"Pops says the current birth statistics are actually a huge improvement since the days he and Mother came to the outworld. He says if the trend continues, eventually most mothers will carry babies to term, and more healthy babies will outnumber frail and sick ones." He brought Christine into an embrace. "Maybe one day, the Network will be as civilized as America Prime."

Christine glanced at the veranda scanner. Had they said too much? She took a sip of her coffee, then smiled at him. "Did you sleep well, Benjamin?"

Apparently, Christine had sent a signal to change the subject. "The night glows bothered me. I'm used to total darkness when I sleep. I'm also used to a lumpy mattress, not these tempered ones. Maybe I was too comfortable."

He'd been in America Prime a little over a day, yet he longed for home. He'd not anticipated how a simple word or object would make him yearn for the freedoms he'd given up. "Since my earliest memories, Pops promised to find better mattresses in the next hunt. Truth is, he deliberately falls back to let the ancients and sick glean first. By the time he has a chance to scavenge, the best has been taken."

Christine squeezed Benjamin's hand. "I didn't think your father's poverty was due to incompetence. I've always suspected more noble reasons."

He liked the way Christine talked, the way she got inside people and felt what they felt. Not many people understood Pops' nature, how he sloughed off the taunts, and that his low estate was more by design than failure.

"Please give my kindest regards to your parents when you see them today. I have a gift for them."

She left the veranda and returned holding two storage containers full of silverware. "Tell your father there is no worm or mite in all of creation able to bore through these storage bins."

He kissed her again. "Mother will be even more pleased than Pops."

A servant girl brought in a wash bowl and towels. "I don't even have to get up and wash my hands?" He glanced up at the girl, a child really, probably no more than thirteen. "Thank …"

Christine shook her head, and Benjamin smiled his appreciation. He listed his many blessings—among the most precious, a future with Christine. He'd managed to escape the horrid corridor of Sector Ten where an assignment as a houseboy or a meme escort was considered good fortune.

"I've gotta hurry, or I'll be late." He stole one last passionate kiss then headed toward his future.

Benjamin bit his lower lip as his heart rate accelerated. He didn't dare be late this first day on the job. He hadn't anticipated the difficulties he might have with public transportation, how the trams whizzed by at speeds too fast to calculate or how crowded they would be in the morning. He should have hired a private transport as Christine suggested. How does one get a tram to stop?

Benjamin slapped his forehead. "Oh, shoot! I forgot. I have to punch in a stupid code to grab one."

What was his code, anyway? For the first time since he signed his intent for repatriation, fear pricked him like radiated raindrops against exposed skin. How could he possibly adjust to a life where every step required a code and every breath vulnerable to a monitor's analysis?

He checked the micro card. There were at least five different sequences—the first showing an icon of a tram next to it. He entered the sequence and the public transport slowed to a stop. "Yippy!" The scanners! Best he internalize his exuberance.

The hinged door opened and Benjamin entered a cubicle already occupied by a woman three times as large as Caroline Skinner and a boy, probably about Peter's age. When Benjamin keyed the close command, EVE projected. "Re-enter your temporary verification and destination."

Too many sequences to remember. He pulled out his card again, then re-entered the series of letters and numbers. EVE didn't budge.

"Please enter your destination."

Benjamin found the alpha keys and entered air dock.

"That information does not match any authorized destination. Please provide an exact location." Did this infernal prompt want an address? There was only one air dock in America Prime. He clicked on his transponder and checked his card. Now, how did he make a hail? He spoke into the device, "Fared, Ahmed. Authorization, Goodayle, 057NB96."

A monotone voice rebuked him. "That information is incomplete."

Benjamin flipped the card over again. "Temporary code 957211."

For the first time, he actually looked forward to the implant and the convenience the device afforded.

"Benjamin? Is something wrong?"

Embarrassment burned his cheeks. "The tram I'm in is stuck. I have to enter an address for the air dock."

"There should be a shortcut icon at the right panel by your cubicle."

Benjamin veered his gaze as directed. "Oh. I see the display now."

"I'll give you a map with exit codes when we meet up. I should have given you one yesterday. Although, perhaps Christine will accompany you until you learn how to navigate the City. Or at the least, arrange for private transport."

The young boy pulled at Benjamin's sleeve. "Hey, mister, you going to be all day? My holiday is over, and I need to get back to school."

Benjamin touched the air dock icon then sat. The woman's glare, like Mother's paring knife, peeled his ignorance with her disdain. "First time on a tram?"

"First day on the job. Sorry."

The Mainframe monitors probably would have a good laugh at his expense; however, the woman and boy showed no amusement. Benjamin mourned the loss of friendly faces so prevalent in the Network. There, neighbors rushed to assist a newcomer, interdependence the cornerstone of survival.

Sometimes Benjamin liked to walk about in other hubs, even hubs in other communities. Pops sometimes fumed when Benjamin told him he was late returning from the Nevada Community because Mayor Obote asked so many questions. Some hub members nodded when Benjamin strolled by. A few asked, "How are you today, Benjamin." After he met Christine some said, "You've got a new spring in your step, young Goodayle."

Life sure takes on twists. He felt more alien on this tram than he had in prison. After he'd met Christine, he longed to leave the Network. Now, he hungered for all things familiar. He must throw off these useless feelings and commit to his new life. His decision to leave was irreversible. Focus on the good things the City had in store … first and foremost, he and Christine would be together for the rest of their lives. Thanks to Uncle Ahmed, Benjamin had a great profession—assistant to the second most powerful man in

United Earth. Perhaps at Uncle Ahmed's side, he could bridge the outworlds and the cities—fight for the rights of memes as well as the forgotten in Sector Ten. He and Uncle Ahmed would honor Charles Devereux's vision for Western America as well as United Earth and restore the Accord's ideals.

The young boy glared. "Something funny, mister?"

Maybe he should have suppressed his smile. So what? Let the Mainframe monitors wonder. For the time being, his thoughts were still his own.

CHAPTER TWENTY-TWO
Sector Two/America Prime

Michael projected Excelsior Media's schedule for the upcoming month. Heat burned her cheeks. Government censors had canceled her prized program—a series on life in the outworld. In all likelihood, Brockway Media would be given the coveted time slots to promote their erotica programs.

Blast Edwin.

Focus, Michael. Channel your energy toward something productive. She scanned the revisions. Grandfather Grafton was heralded for his passionate portrayal of the real world, not the government's propagandized version. How she wanted to fill his shoes. If only Edwin would stop his interference.

She'd spent months on this outworld project, her most trusted reporter sent to live among the Nomads. And now large portions of his documentary had been deleted. Since most Citizens believed Nomadic outworlders were brutal and ignorant, Michael sought to show the truth—how the tribes were in some ways more civilized than Citizens. Her sources indicated that one of the Montana tribes intended to form another community within the Network.

There seemed to be enough data to fit in one of the educational slots still open. Not as lucrative. Far more suitable for children than the risqué cartoons Brockway produced. Michael had donated large sums to the Humanitarian lobbyists who fought to prevent the rapid infiltration of pornography into children's programs. Edwin continued to fund Brockway, and scorned the Humanitarian efforts to block overtly sexual images on the grounds moral decency was not the government's concern.

"Since the Constitutional Government, however imperfect, accomplished what the Accord could not and has returned order from chaos," Michael reasoned, "in time, the government will benefit if Citizens return to a moral code."

Her insight had been lost on Edwin who laughed at the length of her sentences.

"All in good time," he said. "Perhaps after I've spearheaded a movement to restore the space exploration programs, I'll suggest the development of an ethics council and expand the Uniformity Act to develop standardized conduct."

Another empty promise.

Grandfather spoke of an old medium called television where journalists promoted the public interest twenty-four hours a day. Unfortunately, the news channels then become more entertainment than a public service. The truth was skewered to fit what would attract advertisers. She'd vowed that Excelsior Media would hold to the highest standards of journalism and be a bell ringer for social progress.

Barry's buzz brought welcomed respite from her introspection. "Yes?"

"President-elect Rowlands has hailed you."

"Put him through." Michael hit project and cropped the image to fit on her desk. He appeared as a man whose plunge into insanity's abyss was almost a certainty. She'd need every gram of integrity to fight his manipulations. Sean had crafted her escape, should she go through with his plans?

"How are you feeling, my dear? One week and we'll know for sure."

"You never call to chat or even inquire as to my welfare. What do you really want, Edwin?"

"How well you know me, my dear. I'm sending officers to escort you to the Governor's mansion until we move into the Presidential Palace. I need you by my side. You're too distracted with this drivel you choose to broadcast."

He hadn't asked, rather commanded. She glimpsed her future—reduced to privileged captivity, chained to the whims of a fascist.

"What about my work? Do you really expect me to rearrange my whole existence to look the part of your devoted intimate?"

Edwin's smile vanished, replaced by a sneer. "Michael. There is no room for argument, not with opposition at every turn. Our lives are threatened and that of our child. I'm doing this for your sake as well as Jade's."

"No one wants to hurt me or our child."

"You may continue your broadcasts from the estate. We'll install what you need for off-site management. You can even bring Barry with you. When Jade is born, we'll discuss the sale of Excelsior. You'll no longer need the diversion. Motherhood will keep you sufficiently occupied."

This was his true motive for her imprisonment. Not her safety. Not even her child's safety. He would use motherhood to silence her. Edwin had pushed too far. She refused to sacrifice her independence, her integrity, or her identity. She could never sell Excelsior—Grandfather's gift to her—not for Edwin, not for anyone. If she gave her child nothing else, she hoped to pass on a sense of connectedness from Grandfather's generation to hers. She would not allow Edwin to rob Jade of her heritage.

"No. Edwin. I will not."

"You refuse me?" Enmity frosted his words.

"If you kill me, you murder our child. Not even you would stoop so low."

"I want you where you'll be safe."

"Controlled, you mean."

His image wobbled like a winded runner. "Either come willingly, or I'll authorize the officers to take you by force. I will not allow your continual public opposition to cause me any further embarrassment. If you won't do this for your intimate, then you will do this for your President."

Edwin leaned forward, propping his hands on his desk, his miniature likeness like that of a buffoon. One did not fear a fool.

"No."

"Michael, I'm serious."

"No."

"You have left me no choice."

"I'll defect."

"Don't be ridiculous. If you try to escape, you'll be caught and thrown into prison. Is that what you want for Jade? This conversation is over."

"Yes, it is." She disconnected, a thunderclap, the last blow to all deliberation.

CHAPTER TWENTY-THREE
Sector One/America Prime

Edwin fumed. How dare she discontinue a transmission from the future President?

Perhaps he should have used the transponder to hail her or blocked her ability to view him. While he disliked others viewing him, he used others' images as insights into contradictions. The body often betrayed the mind.

Father taught him well. "Focus on the hands, Edwin. Posture can reveal much about a person's true intentions, boy. Always watch the hands. The feet, too. Be wary of shufflers. Deceit makes one restless." Father said people often disguised their voices to sound sincere or even calm whereas the hands and feet rarely lied, except for Edwin. Thanks to his father's instructions, he'd learned the value of deception and mastered the art of emotive suppression, able to confound even Father.

Never, Michael. She read him like a mirror.

If Edwin were going to harness Michael, he would have to retract his dictates, crawl through the dust—offer promises instead of threats. Yet, her bristly determination called to him. She was indomitable, a mountain of resistance that must be conquered. He would propose a truce, a candlelight dinner at the cabin, and this time he'd prepare the meal himself. No meme servants. Only a few discreet guards at the perimeters.

He positioned his transponder. "Michael Grafton, authorization Rowlands G06O09V38."

He waited. No response. Was she refusing his hail?

He switched back to the micro and Barry's stuck smile. "Governor Rowlands, how may I assist you?"

"Put Mistress Grafton online."

"I'm sorry, Governor Rowlands. She left."

"Did she say where?"

"No. She said nothing. I assume she'll be back. She forgot her transponder."

Edwin paused, his heart faint like a hamster too long on the wheel. Michael might forget an item at the market but not her transponder. She only removed the cube when they made time for one another. Would she really try to leave America Prime? He ran trembling fingers through his hair—amused at the desperation she brought him to—the most powerful man in the world as frightened as a lost boy.

She alone touched his stony soul, stirred his sense of vulnerability, and reminded him he was only a man. She alone raised his conscience, stoked the moral embers long forgotten. He'd survive without her if he must, though as half a man, the better part lost to him forever. Edwin regained his composure and returned to the view screen. "Did she seem upset or angry when she left?"

"I don't know, Governor Rowlands. After all, I'm only a meme. I'm not engineered to notice such things."

More flesh beyond his power to control. If only the law would let him strangle this creepy assistant. "Track her on the Mainframe."

"Sir, memes don't have access to the Mainframe. Of course, you knew that. Is this a test?"

"Never mind."

"I'll let Mistress Grafton know you would like her to hail you as soon as she returns."

"Absolutely." Edwin disconnected. No time for meme tricks. He tracked the surveillance disk he'd installed to enhance scanner range. She couldn't have gone far. He thought he caught her image near a Sector Two tram, then zoomed in and highlighted it. "Verify."

ADAM projected. "Michael Grafton."

The viewer went blank. Solar hiccup or sabotage? How convenient for Michael. Might be minutes—precious minutes before the Mainframe came back online.

Edwin shook with anger. He reverted to self-talk, Father's panacea when emotion threatened judgment. "You are the President-elect. No one dares defy you. Not even Michael Grafton."

Edwin accessed his direct link to Constable Becker.

Interminable silence.

When Becker's image finally appeared, dark chocolate oozed from the corners of his mouth. Caught in self-indulgence, Becker offered a lopsided smile.

"Really, Constable. Chocolate so early in the morning?"

"Chocolate is good any time of day, Sir."

"Especially when laced with strong elixir."

Becker swallowed his delicacy and placed both hands on the edge of his desk.

"I assume this call is of utmost importance, Mr. President?"

"I'm not your President yet. Soon enough."

"President Schumann has instructed me to serve you as I would him."

A double-edged sword. One could never be certain where Becker's loyalty rested beyond his own political advantage.

"Becker, I need your top agent. A personal matter."

"Best agent? That would be Nemo Savakis. Very clever man. I'm afraid he's on a high priority case in the Highland Province." The constable snickered as his shoulders heaved in gross amusement. "He's enlisted a couple of unwitting IEA officers to help bring down Kinnear, once and for all."

"Good work, Becker. Right now, I have a higher priority. Michael has disappeared."

"Surveillance is in temporary shutdown. Hackers I suspect."

"I suspect so, as well. Before I hailed you, I located her near Sector Two tram."

Becker tightened his grip on the desk and his knuckles turned a ghostly white. "And you think she will try to leave America Prime? Over a lover's quarrel?"

"You need not concern yourself over the why. If you value your position, you'll find her as soon as possible. When you do, bring her to me."

CHAPTER TWENTY-FOUR
Sector Ten/Highland Province

Angelina leaned against the Revolutionary Army's tunnel that bridged Sectors Nine and Ten while Carlos paced in front of her. "We need to keep moving. If we stay here, we'll be dead before morning, either by suffocation from this awful stench or a P-74 blast."

Carlos scowled. "You're such a comfort."

Heat burned reason. She'd trusted the law, defended the law, and jeopardized her life at times to do so. Now, the defender became the hunted. Maybe she and Carlos had run in haste. She should have given Savakis time to clear her.

Maybe he purged her from the IEA because of her association with Carlos, a maverick, except with her. Funny how Carlos proved to be an able partner both on the beat and in their moments of intimacy. At least, his knowledge of Sector Ten might very well save their hides from a charred death.

When one cannot go backward, the only option is to move forward.

Carlos released the safety on his P-74 and spoke in near whispers, his tone tantalizingly authoritative. "The Revolutionary Army controls most of this tunnel. There's an aperture ahead that connects IEA service routes. Not heavily guarded, and generally, they leave Kinnear alone. They'll be on the lookout for us." Carlos peered into her eyes. "Are you sure you want to go underground?"

Foolish or not, their course was set. "Too late to change our minds."

"It's only too late if you're dead. I say we forget Kinnear. We might be able to access the defector's portal and make our way to the Arctic Province."

Carlos had limited insight, but he did have strong arms. "Jimmy Kinnear is our ticket back. Leave him to me—you concentrate on getting us to Rendezvous Point. Then I'll take over."

He hedged. "Listen. Haven't you wondered how we've made it this far without any sign of trouble?"

Carlos was right. They should have encountered some IEA resistance by now, even though they had removed their implants. What was Savakis up to?

He turned to face her. This time, his sensuous smile brought on an unexplained passion, not the usual physical desire, something more indefinable. She pulled Carlos into an embrace. Some say anger is an aphrodisiac. Probably true where Jimmy Kinnear was concerned. They argued far more than embraced. They were like an axle and wheel. Only, who turned who? She didn't love him in the way she once loved Jimmy, yet, Carlos reduced her anxiety, like cornstarch on an itch.

A man who ticked when he should have tocked, Carlos was unexplored country, fiercely violent yet putty in her hands. Not because she dominated. He surrendered his masculinity as a love offering, a gesture that both unnerved and aroused. Maybe this was the essence of love, what Bridget tried to explain when she left the IEA to become McCormick's intimate. If so, then Angelina Bartelli did indeed love Carlos Perez.

Carlos returned her passion then pulled back, his face contorted into a question mark. "What?"

"If we're going to die, I thought you should know I love you."

He laughed. "I don't expect to die today. And, for the record, I love you, too." He positioned his P-74 and readied for action. "I spotted only one officer at the aperture. It's now or never. Ready?"

She nodded. They ran the length of the abutment, P-74s ablaze, and the officer fell. For the moment, Angelina believed the situation dictated the kill. What if Carlos had been right—the IEA had let them escape? If so, she'd killed unnecessarily. She shrugged off her momentary regret … remorse a useless emotion.

They cleared the aperture and resumed their trek through tunnels, now thick into Jimmy's territory. A few miles later, they emerged near Rendezvous Point. Here, those who had been denied defection hired militia escorts into the badlands or joined the Resistance at Dunfermline Abbey.

"What now, Carlos?"

He pointed to the dusty street tiles. "We sit and wait."

"For what?"

"For help or death."

The nightglows softened as the first flicker of morning flitted across the square. They'd waited four hours while they sat together in silence, barely daring to breathe, with P-74s prepped and ready.

They were still an open target for Revolutionary militia or IEA, whoever came first.

Ire heightened as her thoughts turned to Bridget. The Scottish princess probably sat on her royal cushions eating her royal curds and whey, attended to by royal memes and adored by her royal da. She caused these woes. The hours ticked in rhythm with Angelina's fantasies, visions of a dead empress and revenge exacted.

Carlos brooded. What thoughts tossed in his simple mind?

She glanced at his thick stubble. She hated beards. Papa grew one after the Uniformity Act outlawed them as religious entrapments. His motive had not been spiritual—merely rebellious. "Government has no right to tell a man he must shave or not shave. A beard is a personal matter, like a person's faith. I am also a man of peace and would never fire a weapon. So, I'll fight through resistance—fight for a man's right to grow a beard."

Papa had done just that … fought to his death.

Angelina suspected his fight went deeper than man hair. He still fumed over his family's forced relocation during the roundups … evacuated merely because the government sought to infuse the Highlands with non-Celtic blood.

Papa died in prison. For what? Mama said he forfeited his life for a stupid cause. What sane man dies over a beard? "Causes rob a person of common sense," Mama said when the warden hailed her about Papa's death. "Promise me, Angelina, you'll never join a cause. Obey the law, no matter how unfair regulations seem. Government exists for our own good. Don't ever forget it."

Mama died soon after. Her words stuck.

Carlos grabbed his P-74. "Someone's coming."

A lanky figure shouted from the shadows. She recognized the long legs and broad shoulders. The army had sent its general. Jimmy fired a warning shot over their heads from what appeared to be a

P-94—an experimental, streamlined plasma issue—rapid-sequence-firing with deadly accuracy. Five times the firing power of a P-74. If Jimmy had brought reinforcements, she and Carlos would be outmanned and outgunned.

Carlos dropped his weapon and raised his hands. "Better do as he says, Angelina."

She hurled a dictionary of obscenities as she surrendered.

Jimmy rested his weapon across his shoulder. "Well, well, well, look at what the devil has brought us." He'd laugh until his sides hurt if he could afford the time to pleasure in Angelina's plight. "Get their weapons. Be careful. Never met an officer I trusted."

Angelina had to be up to something. His tracers caught Savakis' communiqué. Unfortunately, the intercept shorted out before they caught the entire message. The question was not if Angelina had come as a setup, rather, did she herself know she was being used? The more likely reason for Angelina's presence was a thirst to kill him and be reinstated as a hero. Still, he'd risk her rescue. She and Carlos might prove useful to the cause.

Brown eyes speared him. "We're at your mercy, Jimmy. We're here to join your Revolutionary Army."

"Tell me one I can believe, Angelina."

"It's the truth. Someone activated a transponder using my emergency code. We're being investigated by the IEA."

He knew she knew that he and Bridget had used her code, and she knew that he knew that she knew, like an old-time, convoluted mystery novel. Why not tell the truth, for once? "I was the one who used your code to activate a transponder. I thought you would be reinstated once your innocence is proven." Unless Savakis set her up.

"There's more."

Jimmy laughed, then leaned against a pole. "This should be good."

"We let Bridget Cavanaugh and Ian McCormick escape. I felt sorry for her. I mean, after all, she was my former partner. I always liked Bridget. Any competent investigator will be able to trace the botched arrest back to me and Carlos. So, you see? We're in a bit of a bind."

"Always liked Bridget? More blarney than I've heard in a decade. The fact is you've never had a good thing to say about Bridget. So, why don't you tell me the real reason you're here." The truth lay buried in her deceit. "Last time we spoke, you vowed to blast me to a pile of pulp. Give me one good reason why I should trust you."

Her eyes widened and her hands shook. Hunger, fear, or exhaustion? "I'm happy with Carlos. Why would I still want revenge?"

Jimmy motioned to his sub-generals to put hoods over his captives. "Kristin, you and Angus lead the way. I'll take up the rear. Best to keep a few extra set of eyes on these two."

As soon as the hood was removed, Angelina assessed her exact location. The sight jogged happy memories of excursions with Papa to this once cherished landmark before the Revolutionary Army made the compound their headquarters.

"Keep them restrained," Jimmy bellowed. "Give them food, water, and clean clothes."

Angelina scanned their prison. A single, spacious room. No furniture except two mattresses on the stone floor and a privy attached to the west side of their room. A woman dressed in old-world fatigues entered carrying two bowls of gruel.

Carlos gobbled his portion like a sweet dessert. Angelina threw hers across the room. "You won't break me, Kinnear. You hear me."

CHAPTER TWENTY-FIVE
Denver Hub/Western America

Jacob stopped his search for fresh eggs and ran toward the hovercraft—no time to change, let alone wash off the stench. He should have sent Davu's service to pick up Benjamin and Ahmed or asked one of the mayors. This was not merely his brother and son paying a visit, rather they were here as dignitaries on official business. Benjamin's old race craft would have been faster but only sat two. The Chairman should have a reliable transport ... fast, too, like a Series 456. At the next mayor's meeting, he'd requisition one.

Amelia had taken to her bed this morning and left the chores to him. How could he possibly tend to the animals and still care for her? Alice McGivney was a competent nurse, and she complained her children were too ignorant. Maybe he could trade extra school lessons in exchange for Amelia's care.

He should resign from this foolish position as Chairman and nurse his wife like a loving husband. She should not have made him promise to do otherwise. "Jacob, the communities need you more than I do. We'll manage."

Dread sat on his shoulders. In all their years together, illness never had driven her back to bed, even on her worst days. Not until today.

Jacob parked the hovercraft and huffed his way to the pad as the government shuttle landed. Benjamin disembarked first, then turned to help Ahmed squeeze himself free of the narrow hatch. As his son handed Jacob two canisters, he pondered Benjamin's sad aura. One would expect a young man on the verge of a familial union to bounce with every step.

"Be sure to thank Christine on our behalf. Such a thoughtful gift. I knew you'd choose a woman with as much perceptiveness as your mother."

"How is she, Pops?"

How could a father be honest and not transfer a burden onto shoulders too young to carry its weight? "She's resting."

"You don't have to protect me, Pops. I know she's dying."

How could he help Benjamin confront the graveness of Amelia's condition without confronting the truth himself? "All we can do now is pray."

For the moment, Jacob's spirit lifted ... a chance to spend time with the son he feared forever lost. "We'll stop at the hut for a quick repast before the meeting, so I can change into something more befitting a Chairman. I'll brew fresh coffee. I traded a chicken for one of Davu's special blends."

Ahmed laughed. "Brother, I'm afraid your coffee does not improve with an elevated price tag."

Their conversation turned to unimportant matters—the increasing humidity and the planting season ahead. Jacob let Benjamin and Ahmed off in front of the hut, then parked the hovercraft behind the shed. His guests, a strange way to think of them, waited at the stoop while Ahmed examined the new door.

"When did this happen?"

"Thomas sent a crew over yesterday. Tomorrow, they'll build a temporary foam addition. I'm afraid the mayors are spoiling me. They thought I'd need extra room for Amelia's care."

Ahmed stroked the stone railings. "Nice masonry. I can think of at least a half dozen people in America Prime who'd envy you. Now there's a reversal of fortune."

Jacob glanced at Benjamin who remained disturbingly quiet. "Your mother's in our room. She won't rest until she sees you, so you might as well go in now."

Benjamin pulled back the pressed hemp curtain and knelt by his mother's side. While low tones buzzed from the bedroom, Jacob set the percolator on the hearth and motioned for Ahmed to sit in one of the stick chairs.

"Thomas Muldoon has a powered oven, pre-programmed for all sorts of meal preparations." Jacob filled the air with anything except what pierced him. "He installed some kind of gizmo that brews the coffee right on top of the stove—a ready supply of freshly brewed at his fingertips all day long. Hit a button and there you have it. The man's a genius. In the ten years he's been in Denver, more than half the hub has an internal power source. He's taking full charge of building the manse ..."

Ahmed pulled at Jacob's sleeve. "Jacob, you're rambling. Let your grief out. A man can cry, you know."

Jacob banged a fist on the table, the force so hard a piece of wood fell off the corner. "Speak for yourself, Ahmed. You never let yourself in on your own pain."

"We're not talking about me."

Jacob spilled his grief with leaded sobs while Ahmed listened. "How much Amelia would have loved the new house. She'll not see the Festival either."

Benjamin joined them at the table, his eyes moist. "Mother wants to talk to you, Pops. I'll keep Uncle Ahmed occupied."

Jacob nodded. "Coffee's ready. Help yourself."

He scanned their bedroom as he knelt by Amelia's side, the place of their most private moments now a death watch.

"Did you think I couldn't hear you and Ahmed? I told you not to grieve me." Holding a weak hand to his cheek, she wiped his forbidden tears.

"I love you. How can I let you leave?"

"You have to face the truth. My time is near."

She coughed.

"No need to talk. Save your strength."

"You mustn't silence me. Remember, you promised you'd continue as Chairman. Do not go back on that promise."

"Have I ever broken my word?"

"Good. Now bathe, then face the delegation with dignity."

Jacob hurried his bath. What he wouldn't give for a sonic shower as Citizens enjoyed. A short burst and done. He threw on his best garments then returned to the kitchen. Ahmed rose from his chair, his cup nearly drained. "Much, better, Jacob. Now, I can breathe when next to you. Benjamin, your father and I should leave. If you'd like, you may stay behind and attend your mother until we return."

"I don't want to shirk my duties on the first day."

"Your absence might prove advantageous. If my notes are incomplete, I'll have the excuse my assistant could not be there."

A funnel cloud sped across their paths, and Jacob gazed at a threatening cloud. "If my suspicions are correct, this storm will be nothing compared to what lies ahead."

★ ★ ★

Ahmed pocketed his micro as he approached Thomas Muldoon's complex. Even Davu would be envious of Muldoon's ingenuity—three sheds, a carpentry shop, and a studio big enough to house an assembly of delegates. Ahmed admired the Highlander, a gentle sort, with intelligence to match his frame, massive shoulders and a head above any other man in the Network.

Thomas greeted them with a firm handshake.

"I hear congratulations are in order, Mayor Muldoon."

"Thank you, Ahmed."

"You'll make a good mayor. Of course, family loyalty requires me to say you won't do quite as well as Jacob. As good a replacement as the Colorado Community has to offer."

Thomas laughed. "This way, gentlemen."

He led them to a spacious open area. "This is what I call a social room. I suppose I should hold a dance or two once I finish installing the solar lights." He pointed to the micro Ahmed carried. "Must you record this meeting? We never have before."

The entire Network would soon learn that nothing would be the same as before Rowlands' election. However, Network residents would be alive, free to buy and sell, and to access medical care. Better to be alive and infringed upon than dead. What good came from a right to assemble if none were left to attend?

"The President-elect requested a formal record. I'll send the feed to my private micro in my office so that Benjamin will have a chance to adjust the record before I pass the transcript on to the Mainframe archives. The best I can do."

He scanned his audience. Most he knew by name and counted them as friends. His chest heaved from the burden he must transfer to them this day.

Davu Obote rose. "Ambassador Fared, Chairman Goodayle, honored mayors, and distinguished delegates, the purpose of today's meeting is to discuss the President's Festival and his Inauguration. Chairman Goodayle?" Davu fluffed the tails of his gold-threaded suit coat as he sat.

Jacob stood, his stance slightly off balance. "Thank you, Davu. Honored mayors and delegates. Ambassador Fared has taken time out of his increasingly busy schedule to address this assembly on how the proposed Preservation Act will impact us. Let's hear what he has to say. Ambassador…"

Inhaling deeply, Ahmed took the stage. So much at stake if they failed to listen. Disillusioned by the failed Accord, most of these present had defected to pursue once-treasured freedoms. Now, he must ask them to give up everything they had gained or face inevitable destruction.

"Friends, as you know, the President-elect has requested we meet before the Festival to discuss the proposed tenets of his historic Preservation Act. The President-elect, as well as every member of Congress, admires your accomplishments—how you brought order from chaos, reclaimed the land and added your signature lifestyles to the heartbeat of America Prime."

Nods of agreement circled the table.

"Only a few decades ago, a hostile world dropped their arms and sought peace. And so the Accord was born, an unprecedented union of diverse peoples."

Obote clapped. Thomas Muldoon sat back in his chair and stared as one resigned to change. Some of the mayors leaned forward. If only Rowlands had agreed to resell the land to those who repatriate … a nugget of appeasement.

A peaceful change would be in everyone's best interest, wouldn't it? "In response to your great achievements, the President-elect would like to offer an olive branch. During the time of celebration, he intends to convene an assembly from the Network, as well as other outworld groups, for peaceful negotiations. He will listen to your visions and seek to continue a parallel prosperity in exchange for repatriation. He is prepared to offer amnesty to all previous defectors."

Thomas stroked his chin then stood. "Pardon me, Ahmed. No disrespect. You have proven to be a true friend to the Network. We are not fools. Sounds to me if we accept repatriation, then we will again be under the dictates of the Articles of Constitution. What will happen to our land?"

The room filled with an aura of both anxiety and resistance. "Remember, legally, the land is not yours. You live here only by the grace of United Earth."

Thomas snorted. "The truth, Ahmed. What does the President-elect want in exchange for our repatriation?"

"He envisions a parallel prosperity. He will extend the quality of life found in the cities to the outworlds. As Citizens, you will have the right to buy and sell. Unfortunately, there is no guarantee you'll be able to purchase the land you now occupy. Properties will be auctioned to the highest bidder."

A loud roar erupted, and Thomas motioned for quiet. "How can we buy our land if we have no money?"

"Your skills will be needed to maintain prosperity in the outworlds, not only for Western America. For all of United Earth."

Thomas raised his voice to a near shout. "What you're trying hard not to say, Ahmed, is that we'll be forced to farm our land as laborers with no say. We'll be told what to plant and how to plant it. We'll receive no direct benefit from our efforts." Thomas sat. "Suppose we refuse this negotiation? And we want the truth. Don't use your lathered speech or tell us what you think we want to hear.

We don't question your loyalty to us or to the President-elect. We understand you're trying to help. If we refuse to repatriate, will we be terminated as our Chairman believes?"

Ahmed cleared his throat. The moment he most dreaded arrived … to present the horror of these times. "My brother is right. The President-elect is determined to gain control of the outworlds—one way or another. He has the support to pass the Preservation Act. Once he does, defection, past and present, will be considered treason. If you refuse what he feels is a generous offer of repatriation, you'll be imprisoned or terminated by a simple presidential edict and without right of trial."

All eyes widened at his bluntness.

Thomas rose again. "What you're saying is, we either become Citizens or the IEA will swoop in and kill us all."

Ahmed offered his one kernel of hope. "Who knows what the negotiations will bring? I urge patience. Leaders will rise among you. Perhaps some will run for delegate positions, and together with the Humanitarians and Reformists, reshape the Constitutional Government."

Thomas Muldoon addressed the assembly. "If what Ahmed proposes is true, we have few options. None of us wants civil war. None of us wants to be pulverized by the IEA, either. And none of us want to lose what we have worked so hard to gain."

On this one issue, Ahmed agreed with Rowlands. The Network residents were connected to the soil that sustained them, an ideology for which some would be willing to die. Did they truly believe they were strong enough to fight a global military? If the Network were to be saved, the Preservation Act would have to be defeated. How?

Was there a third alternative?"

CHAPTER TWENTY-SIX
Sector One/America Prime

Edwin engaged his micro and projected Becker's image. Soft, rainbow glows indicated the hail came within the corridors of Eternal Pathways. "I'm sorry, sir. We were too late."

"Explain."

"Her implant has flat-lined. I had no idea she had brain cancer. I am truly sorry for your loss."

Edwin sat to hide his shaking knees. "Michael did not have cancer. You have one minute to tell me you've made a horrible mistake."

"I've viewed the feeds, Governor Rowlands. Mistress Grafton was most definitely here. While there are some irregularities, I find nothing illegal. The euthanasia was pre-paid and all the required authorizations are in accordance with regulations, including the physician's certificate."

"You idiot. It's all forged. Michael was pregnant, not terminal."

"Her implant registered her death on the Mainframe at the same time Eternal Pathway recorded it. If Mistress Grafton was not ill, we'll have to label this a suicide."

Saliva thickened in Edwin's mouth. Had he driven her to the extreme, forced her to take her life … and that of their child? "Suicide seems highly unlikely. When I last saw her, she was happy with the prospect of motherhood and very grateful to me, if you know what I mean."

Becker offered a lopsided grin.

"You'll treat this as a missing person's case."

"Everything checks out, Governor. If you wish …"

If Michael had indeed committed suicide, someone must have helped her. Who plans a suicide a year in advance?

Becker hemmed. "We haven't questioned the social worker yet. He escorted Mistress Grafton's body to the crematorium."

"Hold delivery and examine the remains."

"Too late, sir. Mr. Ives explained they were overbooked today. Everyone wants to get in ahead of President Schumann, so the euthanasia was rushed. We have sent her implant to forensics for examination. There is the possibility she ingested the Macabre drug."

"It's illegal."

"But available on the black market. The drug is potent and can be dangerous if taken without medical supervision. If Michael did use it, forensics will find trace elements on her implant."

Edwin burned the air with expletives. Michael wasn't dead. No matter how despondent, she'd never take Jade's life along with her own. A plan pushed his rage aside. Possibly, he could use Michael's indiscretion to his benefit. He'd let Unified Earth believe she'd affronted him with her suicide and murdered her unborn. After he filed her death certificate, he'd contest her will and vie for rights to Excelsior Media.

"How long before you get the results?"

"A few days, sir. We'll expedite the process, of course."

"Give me the results. Regardless of your findings, I want the official report labeled as an illegal suicide."

"Because of the pregnancy?"

"Exactly. If you can prove the social worker had foreknowledge of Michael's pregnancy, arrest the lot of them."

"Won't this be an embarrassment, sir? You don't need a scandal so close to your Inauguration."

"On the contrary. We will milk the sympathy to my advantage."

Becker lowered his glance. "As you wish, sir. The social worker's plane departs in ten minutes. I can dispatch the IEA to intercept on your order. According to Mistress Grafton's agreement, she requested dispersal over the Denver cabin. However, the manifest lists a subsequent flight to the Negev immediately after Mistress Grafton's dispersal."

"Unusual for a social worker to serve as pilot. Any passengers?"

"One. Second Governor Ahmed Fared is scheduled to attend the Negev dispersal."

"Why?"

"The remains are those of Esther Feinmann, a close friend to Mr. Fared."

Edwin heaved the micro across the room. Of all Michael's rash behaviors, this abandonment bruised him the most. Her inclusion of Fared in her scheme was salt on the proverbial wound.

The transponder's hail could only be Becker. Best to answer before a security team breached his private quarters. "I'm fine, Becker. The micro met with a minor accident."

"We'll arrange a replacement immediately. Sir, Mr. Grafton's flight?"

If they intercepted, they'd pulverize the shuttle with Fared aboard, a move certain to alienate both the Reformation and Humanitarian Parties. He'd lose the necessary votes to pass the Preservation Act. What if Michael were still alive? Better to live with the theory she had fled than to make her death a certainty. There was Jade to consider, some compensation for Michael's desertion. He'd find her, then after he took everything from her, confine her until her pregnancy came to term, then execute her for treason. "Arrest the social worker as soon as he returns. He and Ives will regret their haste. You will keep me apprised of this investigation?"

"Yes, Governor."

"Find out if Mr. Fared had any knowledge of the double dispersal, and run a trace on the social worker."

Becker's prideful squeal raked Edwin's ear. "We ran the social worker's name, sir."

"And?"

"My great-great-grandmother would call the relationship between your intimate and the social worker shirt-tail cousins."

"Meaning?"

"Sean Grafton is a distant relative to Michael—their grandfathers were brothers."

"I see."

Whatever course he took from here on out, Michael was lost to him. Sorrow simmered. Did she think him incapable of love? Of course, and she was right. The cold stone that should be a heart was Father's fault. Michael's embrace had been the first since Mother's death he hadn't bought, stolen, or forced. Sometimes when they slept together, tremors woke him and Michael wrapped him in tenderness.

"Arrest Ives, too."

"Mr. Fared?"

"And torch Eternal Pathways."

"On what grounds, sir?"

"Make one up."

Becker cleared his throat. "Sir, President Schumann intends to use Eternal Pathways for his euthanasia. Retaliation will not be viewed favorably."

"You're right, of course. Perhaps leniency is the best option for now. Rather than arresting the two, put a tail on them until further notice."

"Anything else, sir?"

"No. Rowlands out." Edwin clicked off his transponder. He'd bide his time, and when he did find her, she'd suffer a worse fate than death. Jade would be his and his alone.

CHAPTER TWENTY-SEVEN
Air dock/America Prime

Ahmed Fared paced the air dock while he waited to complete his next unpleasant task. Grafton was late. Had he been detained for some reason?

Wobbly knees brought on by fatigue prompted him to sit. He looked forward to a nap on the flight to the Negev. And he could scratch if needed. No scanners on dispersal flights as they interfered with refrigeration.

Sometimes the incongruity of technology proved to be advantageous. Such was the price of progress, complication upon complication, a constant realignment of incompatibility. Today, this incongruity afforded a busy man a nap.

At any rate, for the next several hours, no one could require anything of him. Unless of course, Ives came along for the ride, the man so thin he made projections look three-dimensional. Instead of a nap, perhaps he should sit in the co-pilot's chair and engage the social worker in conversation. Curious as to why an amiable sort like him chose such a distasteful career.

A slim figure dressed in a blue-sequined robe approached. Drat. Ives did decide to come. Probably to steal his Second Governor's ear for his proposal to reform current euthanasia laws. So much for a nap. Or maybe he came to squeeze money for last minute expenses. Strange. The natural light cut at least four inches off Ives' height. He appeared much taller in the shadows of Eternal Pathways.

Ahmed offered a handshake … Ives grip much weaker than remembered. "Is there a problem, Mr. Ives?"

He shook his head.

"Or are you coming along for a chat?"

"Yes. Yes, indeed."

The voice far too sultry, not at all like his nasal whines. This figure before him was definitely an imposter. The question was, why? Ahmed gazed more intently into cobalt eyes … Michael.

If she'd developed so complicated a ruse, she must desperately need his help.

"I'll enjoy the company, then. Lead the way, Mr. Ives. I've never done this part before. I hope you'll give me a full explanation."

The group boarded, and Sean hastened to the cockpit. Ahmed strapped in while Michael removed the robe and wig, only to reveal yet another costume … that of a Nomadic woman. She sat and secured the harness. "I'm sorry to deceive you, Ahmed."

"I'm sure you have a good reason."

Her eyes clouded with tears. "Last year, when Edwin started to show signs of mental instability, Sean and I discussed an escape plan similar to this. I've hemmed around the whole idea, but the morning after I conceived, I knew the time had come to put the plan into play. Edwin is no longer teetering on insanity. He has fallen headlong into an abyss, and there is no saving him. Ahmed, I don't know who he is anymore. I tried to turn him around. I loved him once, you know."

"I share your fears where your intimate is concerned. Why go to this extreme?"

Ahmed listened intently as Michael explained how Sean obtained the Macabre drug, substituted a stored meme cadaver, and forged DNA confirmation. "I've not heard any reports of your untimely death, so I imagine this took place during my absence to the Network?"

"Less than an hour ago."

"The drug is dangerous and traceable."

"Sean has used the drug before and has minimized my risks through counteracting medication. Hopefully, by the time the IEA confirms I'm still alive, I'll be out of America Prime."

Ahmed shouted toward the cockpit. "Sounds like Michael isn't the only one you've helped escape through Eternal Pathways?"

"The less you know, the better, Mr. Fared."

True. If he were a betting man, however, he'd wager Grafton's detestable career choice had been a cover for the Resistance.

The dome opened, and the shuttle ascended.

Ahmed shook his head. "Michael, you are every bit as brave and foolish as your grandfather."

"You pay me too high a compliment."

"Not intended as a compliment. What now?"

Michael's lips spread into a half smile. "My will stipulates my dispersal be made over Grandfather's camp. I'll jump when we reach the coordinates, outside of Mainframe range."

"You'll still be in the sub-city. They'll find you. Most likely, Edwin has already ordered Constable Becker to initiate a Unified Earth manhunt. And what about Sean? He'll be arrested as soon as he lands back in America Prime."

Sean shouted back from his pilot's chair. "Won't be the first time." He engaged the autopilot and joined them in the passenger hold. "We're nearly to the sub-city. Ready?"

Michael dabbed her eyes with her sleeve. "Sean … Ahmed's right. I should never have involved you. You'll be arrested. I can't have your termination on my conscience. Take me back."

Sean squeezed Michael's hand. "You're forgetting I'm an attorney. Granted, not a highly respected one. I know the law. I'll get out of this. And I'm well connected with members of Congress. Did you know you coerced me with a concealed weapon? I have a disk to prove you threatened me."

Michael faced Ahmed. "And I'm putting you at odds with Edwin as well."

Ahmed embraced Michael in a fatherly hug. "You happen to have the Second Governor and soon-to-be Second President as your passenger, and I do have some authority." He scribbled instructions on a slip of paper and handed them to Sean. "Reprogram the flight manifest to these coordinates and use the codes I listed."

"Are you certain you want me to drop Michael in the middle of the desert?"

He glanced toward Michael. "Trust me?"

"With my life, Ahmed."

While Sean entered the flight alterations, Ahmed drew Michael a rudimentary map of the drop zone. "The Christ followers call this place the Sacred Rock because the boulders resemble the shape of a cross. The drop zone is not far from there, in the southern sections of the Front Range, near the Border Community."

Sean returned. "I know where this place is. I've made drops there before."

"As I suspected. Michael, help may not come for a day or two. There is a shallow cave underneath the Sacred Rock where you can hide until help arrives. Where are the emergency rations stored?"

"In the rear near the hatch. Not many. Ashes don't require food."

Ahmed released his harness, opened the container and stuffed a medicinal kit, rations, and a water canteen into a satchel. "Are you sure you're up to it, Michael?"

She nodded.

"Sean, in the hustle, I hope you did actually bring Esther's ashes."

"Loaded right after her cremation."

Ahmed smiled. No doubt Esther would have enjoyed this caper. "Sean and I will complete Esther's dispersal, and I'll explain the change in flight plan as official business, perhaps do an aerial inspection relative to the President-elect's Preservation Act. Sean, do you have the ashes from the fake cremation we can disperse over the cabin?"

"Right here." He held up an urn. "The meme's name was Yvonne."

Humility was an emotion foreign to Ahmed's psyche. Of course, there was another soul in this event who required remembrance.

"I've been in and out of the hubs for the past several days, so a detour is not highly suspicious. I'll send help as quickly as I can."

Michael's face drooped. "Be careful, Ahmed. Edwin is a man obsessed. I'm pregnant, at least I assume so. I expect I will be a mother to a beautiful girl."

"If she grows to look like you, she will take every man's breath away."

Michael rubbed her abdomen. "I don't want my child to grow up in the world Edwin is determined to make."

The shuttle re-entered the atmosphere and slowly descended. Grafton turned to face them. "We're at the coordinates for the drop."

"What about sky monitors."

Grafton smiled. "Already disabled. You must hurry before they come back online."

Ahmed took his micro and sent Benjamin a public message: Must change the plan … will meet with Mayor Morales of Border Community then resume course to the Negev… saddened to learn of Michael Grafton's passing … will disperse her ashes over Grafton cabin on way to Border Community. He closed his micro. "That should buy us a day or two before we're discovered. By then, Michael should be safe."

She kissed Ahmed on the cheek and with a determined click secured her parachute. "Ready."

CHAPTER TWENTY-EIGHT
Sector One/ Highland Province

Bridget pulled on her cocoa-colored, silk pantaloons, already snug from baby bulge. A few seconds more and the blood prick would confirm the sex.

"Can I come in yet, Bridget?" Da squeaked the question like an overanxious schoolboy. Of course, he'd be excited.

She made a quick check in the mirror. Not exactly fashionable. During these next few days of preparation, she preferred comfort over style. "Come in, Da."

"Do we know yet?"

"Any second now."

"A grandfather has the right to know if he should be buyin' his grandchild trucks or pink pantaloons."

"Da, girls like trucks, and boys wear pink."

"I'll not have me grandson wearin' pantaloons. Equality only goes so far, Bridget."

She squeezed her father's hand. "There are some boys, real men, who like to wear lace and frills, Da. I'll not have you put my child into a predetermined lifestyle. What if he likes to read books and dream like his father?"

Da's smile disappeared. "I regret I did not know Ian better."

Bridget wove the sandal strap through the last loop then pulled back the test strip. After a quick glance, she hummed Danny Boy and rubbed her stomach. "Ian Bryan James McCormick Cavanaugh, I'd like to introduce you to your grandfather, Bryan Devon Cavanaugh, Governor of the Highland Province, former delegate to the Accord, and the most honorable man left on this planet."

Da smiled as his eyes grew misty. "A boyo, is it?"

"What we'd hoped for."

Da picked up the telltale strip. "This test amazes me. Your mum had to wait until much later in the pregnancy before the bairn's sex could be confirmed. Now all a lass has to do is prick her pinkie, drop a wee bit of blood on a yellow stick and all is revealed in seconds."

Da's tilted head meant a somber thought would soon be uttered.

"Something to be said for a stable government, Bridget. Progress. Scientific advancement." He waved the stick in the air like a conductor's baton. "Can't develop these wonders when the human race is near extinction. We'd gone so far backward, progress had to wait for us to catch up before we could go forward again."

Bridget studied Da's face, serious now, the twinkle almost gone. "'Tis me humble hope Ian Bryan James McCormick Cavanaugh is born into a world where he can play with trucks, wear garments of his choosing, and not be criticized for his tastes." Da pulled himself to his full height. "I better file me grandson's paperwork."

"Be certain you register all his names."

"Aye, lassie, I promise, providing the micro screen is large enough."

She laughed. "You're sweet to register him."

"And dinna be forgettin' we have to pick up the Gregory model tomorrow."

Bridget played her part for the scanners. "Da, do you really think I need a pleasure meme? I'm not really in need."

Da took her hands into his. "I understand, Bridget. I dinna worry about your loneliness for a man. You'll be needin' protection. I'll rest knowin' there be an extra set of eyes on ye, in places Falan is too much of a gentleman to go."

"Sounds more like a guard dog than a playmate. Besides, Ian would—"

"Bridget, I'll have me way on this one."

She kissed him on the cheek to complete the ruse. "Only until the baby is born. Then we will emancipate the Gregory. Understood?"

"We'll see." He danced a jig toward the door.

Da had promised he'd find a way to exempt her from the unlawful pregnancy. There'd been no chance to ask him how he planned to manage a pardon.. He stood by the door, one hand on the knob. "There still be the matter of a substitute guardian, Bridget, in case somethin' happens to me before young Ian reaches the age of accountability. What about Falan?"

"Falan is a good man."

"He's willing, Bridget. He likes you. You should be kinder to him."

Da kissed her on the cheek and left. Worry pervaded her thoughts. Da's purchase of two new memes should throw off suspicions. Falan was certain no one suspected their plan to slip away to the northern Rockies the morning of the Inauguration. He'd arranged for a pilot to masquerade as a Gregory, why Da chose the playmate venue. She'd allow the meme into her sleeping quarters if need be. There the script would have to end.

Bridget glanced at the timepiece on her mantle. Falan would arrive soon. She looked forward to their strolls in the garden. She hadn't left Da's estate since she arrived, and Falan brought news of the outside world. On their last walk, he shared how Angelina and her intimate joined Jimmy's band. "I doubt she truly swallowed her pride. More like she's plotted revenge against my brother."

Bridget's growing concern for Jimmy puzzled her, especially after he forged her kidnapping to bribe Da. The less time spent with him the better, yet, he unnerved her as much as Falan's presence calmed her. Hard to believe the two men came from the same womb, even if Falan were a decade older. He had a comfortable look about him, not handsome as some might judge, yet, a pleasant face. Educated at the University, too, like Ian. If she were to choose another intimate, she would want a man like Falan, not one bent on revolution, like Jimmy. A moot consideration for she had no need to love again. All she wanted in a man was a good role model for young Ian, and Da's influence would be sufficient.

The loud rap startled her. "Come in."

Priscilla entered, curtsied, and stood in statuesque patience for Bridget's response. Those eyes … expressionless, placid features … an odd trait in a meme. Da said the Priscillas were engineered without facial nerves. Eerie. Like looking at a moving photograph.

Priscilla's features were daintier than any meme Bridget had seen, yet she could carry five sets of bedding at one time; her generation, diminutive for style, strong for efficiency.

Da's memes were an eclectic mix, purchased from varying factories and provinces. He collected brands like Great-Grandmother saved antique salt and pepper shakers. "I abhor the practice, Bridget. At least my memes will ne'er be euthanized or mistreated." Da had proposed a Bill of Rights for memes. The measure fell upon deaf ears, defeated before the bill came to deliberation.

"Well, Bridget," Da said when his proposal failed, "if the government won't listen, we'll teach by example." Da gave every meme in his household a stipend, rest day, and vacation passes. A few Humanitarians followed suit. No wonder Rowlands despised Da. If memes lost their status as property, the whole economy of United Earth might fail.

Priscilla stared at the back wall as she waited for a prompt—like EVE to a micro. "What is it, Priscilla?"

"Would Mistress Bridgett be taking a stroll in the garden soon? Mr. Riley is wantin' to know."

"You may tell Mr. Riley I'll be ready in thirty minutes. He can accompany me if he desires."

"Very good." Priscilla turned a precise one hundred and eighty degrees then left the room.

A shame Da felt his only recourse was an escape. The world had become a better place because of Da's hard work, and now Rowlands pushed her father into obscurity. As a youth, her biggest decision of the day had been which sandals to wear. IEA service purged the spoiled brat, and Ian had taught her compassion. Perhaps a more mature Bridget Cavanaugh was ready to join the heat of reform after all. She prayed for a rake of truth and a shovel of determination. She snatched her cloak from the wardrobe then descended the stairs to where Falan waited.

"I thought we'd stroll in the gardens today, Bridget."

She nodded her agreement. Falan must have weighty news if he sought the most private spot afforded on the estate. Shrubs of every variety encapsulated the nineteenth-century reflection pool, the envy of every governor. The fountain disrupted scanner feeds. They sat together on a concrete bench overlooking the western gardens.

Falan held her hand as he often did these past few days. "We'll leave in the morning."

"So soon?"

"The governor has accepted Ahmed Fared's invitation to attend a celebration he is giving in honor of Christine Devereux and her intended intimate, Benjamin Goodayle."

"Jacob Goodayle's son?"

"Aye. One and the same." This event and the Inauguration have given us the perfect cover for our plans, and your da feels we might as well enjoy ourselves for a few days and ward off suspicion. Our itinerary includes a sight-seeing trip over Western America on the morning of the Inauguration. The Mainframe monitors will believe our shuttle went down in the desert and there were no survivors."

"The plan scares me, Falan. Too complicated. Something is sure to go wrong."

"Nothing will go wrong. We'll make it, Bridget."

She fought the tears. "The same words Ian spoke moments before the IEA burst through our doors."

Falan squeezed her hand as if to comfort. "You must trust the plan, Bridget. Granted, spies are everywhere. Thankfully for us, greedy men are still easily bought."

"You sound like your brother."

"I suppose in some ways we are a lot alike, different in our root motivations. However, Jimmy is driven more by revenge than passion, angry about so many things."

"And you have adopted a different perspective?"

"I no longer hate." Falan started to say more. Instead, he put a hand to her lips. He leaned in as if to kiss her and whispered in her ear. "Keep talking as if I'm next to you." Then he darted into the shrubs.

While Falan twined his way through the bushes, Bridget spilled an account of how she met Ian. A scream … bustling feet. Falan returned with a feisty Priscilla in tow. He reached behind her back, made a move as if turning a knob, and she humped forward.

"She's not a meme," Falan said. "She's an automaton. Very cleverly designed. She even fooled me."

"Why would Da buy an automaton and disguise the model as a meme maid?"

Falan took out a knife from his satchel and pried open Priscilla's scalp, revealing a mass of wires. "I think I see the factory signature. These automatons are used for surveillance, their sensors feed into the Mainframe. They can go places scanners can't. I don't think your father had the slightest suspicion."

"How did you know Priscilla wasn't a meme?"

"The scream wasn't human nor that of a meme. More like the squeal of a stuck gear."

Bridget sighed. "Then our plans have been discovered?"

"Maybe not."

Falan switched on Priscilla's micro. Snatches of conversation projected. "She recorded enough to warn her owners of our desire to escape. No details as to how. Her feed has already been dumped. We'll be watched closer than ever."

"The question is, Falan, who planted her?"

CHAPTER TWENTY-NINE
Outer Perimeter/the Border Community/
Western America

Michael hobbled to a large boulder and leaned against its hot surface. She should have added some sort of hat to her disguise.

What day was it? Hard to tell how long she'd been here. She supposed at least a day and a half, long enough to confuse hunger and thirst. She must not wander too far from these coordinates—the cave her only shelter.

She'd been careless, tripped and cut her leg. Infection had already set in, and she'd used the last of the salve with no effect. She'd wasted most of her water ration to cleanse the wound and thrown her food to stave off a pack of wolves. Hunger prompted her toward the revulsive. She pummeled rocks and ruts in search of vermin or insects. Useless effort. The undersides were as arid as the ground around her.

A light, flat rock she'd discovered next to the cave made a makeshift head covering and blocked the sun sufficiently so she could scan the horizon. Desert sameness in all directions. Where was the promised help? Should she start walking toward a hub? Which direction? Dehydration began to take its toll. She slumped to a sitting position and rested her rock bonnet within ready reach. Might come in handy as a weapon.

Pain shot through her leg. She'd used the last of the pain salve as well. Nothing to do now Might as well wait to die of hunger, thirst, or fever. She laughed. "Well, Michael, at least you have a cool crypt in which to breath your last."

A scrawny mouse nibbled at her sandal. Brazen critter. Food! She pounded the rodent with the rock then sunk her teeth into the carcass. Ugh. The things desperation made people do.

A sound like sand against sand echoed in the distance. Wolves? Did they want her mouse, too? She crawled inside the small crevice behind the Sacred Rock for shelter then peered into the glaring sun. Not wolves, human shapes and they rapidly approached.

One of them, a man, spoke. "I don't see her. Ahmed said she'd be near the Sacred Rock."

Michael snaked from the crevice then pulled her body to a stand, the figures blurred. "Are you angels?" As the question left her lips, the ground rushed up to meet her face.

She roused from unconsciousness. Four men leaned over her—three of them, Hispanic. She recognized Jacob Goodayle, though slightly heavier than the man who so lovingly guarded his wife at their defection. He placed something like a pillow under her neck. "How do you feel?"

"I've seen better days."

A near-toothless man handed her a canteen. "Aqui, Señora Grafton, agua."

Michael would have gulped the entire contents if Jacob had not pulled the canteen away.

"Easy. We have plenty. You'll make yourself ill if you drink too much at once."

Jacob introduced her Spanish angel. "Michael, this is Enrique Morales, Mayor of the Border Community. These two are his sons, Juan and Rafael."

"Yes, I heard the Border Community is comprised mostly of Nomadic Hispanic cultures. Do you all speak Old Spanish?"

Enrique smiled. "Among ourselves, we do."

"A very beautiful language."

"Five generations ago, my ancestors came from Old Mexico to the northern reaches of the Sierra Province, then known as Texas. Our community straddles both the Sierra Province and Western America. Hence our name."

With Jacob's help, Michael rose to a stand then slumped as another sharp pain shot through her leg.

Jacob caught her before she fell. "Your wound needs the attention of Enrique's wife, an herb specialist. She'll have you fixed up in no time. Can you walk?"

"I'll manage."

"The hovercraft is not far from here."

"Next time you talk with Ahmed, please find a way to let him know I owe him my life."

"We all do, Michael."

CHAPTER THIRTY
Border Community/Western America

A vaguely familiar scent mingled with yeast. Honey? Since the commodity was limited to black market availability, only the wealthiest could afford the delicacy. How then did these peasant-type outworlders come by such a treat? She sat up as a Hispanic woman placed a tray of delicacies in front of Michael. "You are hungry, no?"

"An understatement."

The woman's smile radiated peace, and her eyes seemed kind enough. "My name is Lucia, Enrique's wife."

"Wife?"

"A priest married us days before the Uniformity Act outlawed religious ceremonies. How is your leg, Señora Grafton?

"Call me Michael, please."

Lucia set down the tray. The woman gleamed with simple beauty: milky brown skin, dark hair, rosy cheeks, and chocolate eyes that danced with her smile. "I bring clean clothes." Her head tilted to the side as she measured Michael with her glance. "My size bigger than you."

"We'll make do. Thank you, Lucia. You and your family have been more than kind." She bit into the honey-coated biscuit. "Um. Delicious. You know, I don't think I've ever had honey on a biscuit before. Only in tea and in secret."

"We grow sometheeng …como se dice…similar. Would you like?"

"Please, don't go to any bother." Michael lifted the vial on the table next to her cot. "I have water and these delicious biscuits coated with a delicacy many would kill for in the city. I am spoiled already. So much tastier than the mouse I had earlier."

When Lucia left, Michael brought herself to a stand to examine her wound, now covered with a thick, green paste. She swiped a finger through the balm and sniffed it. Camphor, mint, and a familiar scent from her childhood. Aloe? Rare in the both the City and sub-city.

Whatever this concoction, these people should market the product in the City, certain to make them a small fortune, enough in trade to keep them independent of the hunts for many years. Some in Congress, in addition to the Humanitarians, believed outworlders' right to buy and sell would benefit both the City and The Network. Edwin thwarted the movement at every turn.

Her eyelids drooped, and a yawn escaped. She lay back down on the cot and pulled the woven blanket to her chin. Soon blessed sleep ruled.

CHAPTER THIRTY-ONE
Morales Hut/Western America

Jacob shook Enrique's hand. Hopefully, a few days rest would have Michael back on her feet. She would need her strength for the uncertainty ahead—uncertainty he had come to share with her. "Ahmed is grateful for your kindness to Michael. How is the patient doing this morning?"

"She is resting, and her wound is well healed."

"And her child?"

Enrique smiled. "She is only a few days along. That much we can confirm. Too soon to say if she will have a boy or girl. She took pills in hopes of a girl. They're not foolproof. She is as well as can be expected after such an ordeal as she experienced by the Sacred Rock."

"Risky business that Macabre drug."

"This boy, Grafton, knows his medicine. Dangerous to give to a pregnant woman."

Jacob nodded. "Ahmed said Michael was either very brave or very foolish. I opt for brave, myself. If I may, I need to speak with her."

Enrique turned to his wife. "Por favor—Lucia, see if Señora Grafton is dressed."

Lucia nodded and disappeared behind a curtained alcove.

Enrique sat like a plank in a chair, rigid and immobile. Granted this was Jacob's first official visit as Chairman. He and Enrique had been friends for years, his sons among Jacob's first outworld students—formality never an issue until fortune elevated Jacob to a height he'd rather not have achieved.

The Border Nomads had formed their own community decades before there was a Network. Only through Enrique's tireless work did his bands agree to join forces with the other communities. Their contributions to the Network had been a boost for all. However, these times might bring a rift beyond repair.

Enrique's question ended the awkward silence. "More coffee, Chairman Goodayle?"

"Enrique. I told you before. My name is Jacob. Though I am your Chairman, I am first and foremost your friend. To answer your question, yes, more coffee would be much appreciated."

Enrique sauntered into the kitchen and soon a flavorful aroma wafted through the air. He re-entered with a pot and two cups.

"That was fast, Enrique."

"Thomas' invention. Fresh coffee all day."

"I've thought of trading for one myself. What did this invention cost you?"

Enrique laughed. "My best cow."

"Are you sure you got the better end of the deal?"

"A happy wife is worth any price, no?"

Jacob sighed. "Yes, indeed."

"How thoughtless of me, Jacob. I chat on about Lucia when Amelia is so ill. How is she today?"

Jacob lifted a hand. "She grows weaker by the hour." Best to thin this uncomfortable air. "While I'm here, I'd like to visit your hubs and talk to your delegates regarding the Festival. I know I can count on you to tell me what your constituents truly think. Tell me as my friend, not as Chairman."

Enrique rose from his seat and gazed out a portal. "What I think maybe is not what is best, verdad? I am the son of an outworlder who was the son of an outworlder. I am of this land as are my children. Juan's woman expects her first child next month. Jacob, you are a child of America Prime ... as is your wife. And your son has known both now. He claims the City is La Vida bonita ... the beautiful life."

"Yes. Benjamin believes the City offers many good things."

"So, you see? Reason to stay. Reasons to repatriate. I am not a learned man such as you are, Jacob. I have read books on history. Some say Old America fought hard for freedom. We have made this Network as our ancestors made the colonies. And those colonies yearned to be free—King George would not allow freedom, so they revolted. They were few, yet, they persevered. I think they win because the idea inside them was so powerful they want nothing else. They risked everything to own their land—not to be slaves to King George."

Simple words ... strong truth.

Enrique leaned forward. "Tell me. Was Old America good?"

"My parents said Old America was a shining example of freedom, a time when people worshiped the god of their choice without fear ... a time when books were plentiful and art hung in the museums for all to see ... a government for the people and by the people."

Enrique nodded. "And so I believe. Yes, Unified Earth has a Constitution and a President. However, if what you say is true, something is lost. In the quest to be equal, we've lost the right to be different."

Lucia helped Michael into a chair, and the men ceased their conversation. Jacob felt his chest constrict. How could he tell Michael the worst of her ordeal was yet ahead?

She met his gaze. "Lucia said you wanted to see me?"

Jacob rose and paced. The woman needed rest, not what his father had called the third degree. "I hate to disturb you so soon. Unfortunately, time won't allow me to be more considerate."

Michael's ashen face highlighted sunken eyes. "You want an explanation for my actions?"

"Not so much an explanation as to understand how committed you are to your escape."

"I don't understand."

"I'll be brief. Our Network is at a crossroads. We must make hard decisions in the days ahead. You left your intimate for good reason. Now, I must ask you how much you know about his intentions for the Network. Do you think he would annihilate us if we refuse his proposals?"

Tears spilled from her eyes. "He is capable of that. He is like a boy who pulls off an insect's legs for sport. Though I carry his child, he is no longer in my heart. I thought about asking Lucia to find medicine for me to end this embarrassment—"

"No, Michael. Life is never an embarrassment. Who can tell what the Maker has in store? You are sure you will have a girl?"

"I took medicine to be sure. Mr. Chairman—"

"Jacob will do."

"Jacob, I still want this child, and I will still call her Jade. Is this all too foolish?"

"Not at all." To think one could assure conception and choose the sex were wonders beyond his simple mind. Outworlders would benefit from these miracles. Perhaps forced repatriation would be a hidden blessing rather than the curse so many believed.

Jacob refocused on the hard news he'd come to bring. Michael would have to leave Enrique's care to live underground—where children's faces hid behind muslin clothes—where sand choked the uncovered—and where not even the brightest sunlight penetrated the dust clouds.

She studied his face. "You need to tell me I can't stay here? I agree. These people have been kind. I do not want to put them at further risk. I'll go wherever you think best."

She'd unburdened him with her insight. Still, she most likely had no concept of the hardships she would yet face. "Enrique will take you to the Sierra Province through the cavern system. The tunnels are heavily guarded by the Western America branch of the Revolutionary Army."

"I understand. Edwin cannot touch me there until he is officially President."

"Ahmed said you were perceptive."

Michael smiled. "Don't look so worried, Jacob. I shall look charming in a face scarf."

CHAPTER THIRTY-TWO
Revolutionary Army Headquarters/Highland Province

Angelina tugged against her restraints and attempted a seductive pout. Time was she could seduce Jimmy with a simple tilt of her head. Apparently, those days had passed. She'd have to find a new approach. Perhaps he'd respond to a vulnerable ex-lover? "What must I do to convince you of my sincerity?"

He dodged her ploy yet again. "Do you think I'm so easily fooled? You're being used, Angelina."

"By whom?"

"Savakis. He let you escape so you'd come to me. Now my question is, did you two have a prior agreement, or are you being duped? I know you. You think if you capture me, the IEA will reinstate both you and Carlos. Forgive my cynicism. There is no way you came here to join my army. Although, I hope I can convince you you're better off with us than against us."

"You're wrong, Jimmy. I no longer care about the IEA. Tell him, Carlos."

Carlos waved his tied hands into the air. "Jimmy, regardless of the reason we may have fled, you know we aren't going anywhere. Untie us."

She blew frustration at a wanton, soiled curl. "Come on, Jimmy. We've got nothing more to say. If I told you I had a burning desire to rid the world of all its wrongs, you'd know I was lying."

Jimmy circled them, his jaw taut and his brow wrinkled. "Fine. I still don't trust you. Angus, you're on their detail." He took out a multi-bladed knife—more sophisticated than IEA issue—and cut the heavy cords that bound them. "Tomorrow, I'll be headed to America Prime on a special mission. Angus will be in charge until I get back. If I get back."

A twinge of regret notched a corner of her heart. Shame if a man like Jimmy met an early death. She'd hoped to be the instrument of betrayal. Yet, these past few days served only to confuse her. Jimmy had changed. Or perhaps the change occurred before he escaped into the badlands. He found a cause … the thing Mama warned her against. Would he convince her to join in spirit what she had joined in pretense? For now, she'd move forward with her first plan and try not to fall into Savakis' trap.

She rubbed her freed wrists. Too wobbly to walk, she sat back down. "I feel like a newbie sailor trying to find his sea legs. Carlos and I need a good stretch, Jimmy. Your hound can tag along."

Jimmy nodded. "Angus, take them into the garden."

She stood again, then rubbed her legs to induce better circulation.

Angus motioned them to follow then led them through a portal into a long, dark passageway void of light except for the laser on the weapon he held and ready for use.

Angelina soaked in the sounds and smells of the former landmark. Mildew lined the interior passageways, and water lapped at her feet. Finally, the balmy night breeze swooshed through her loosened hair as she gulped clean air and the scent of heather. The crescent moon hung at about the tenth hour.

No need for a guard. Even if she did manage to elude Jimmy's soldiers, where would she go? She had no officer's manual to guide her, no ADAM for Mainframe information. Nor could she depend on Carlos who seemed to admire Jimmy and his cause. She examined Carlos' prideful gait. He'd changed like Jimmy had changed. She'd lost yet another lover to a cause greater than Angelina Bartelli.

She stopped. "I need a rest, Angus."

"Aye." He pointed to a bench a few yards up the path where they sat, his smile as prickly as a taunt. His perfect teeth glowed in the moonlight. Either they were cloned implants or ...

He met her gaze. "The lass has an inquisitive stare."

"I'd like a private word with my intimate."

"I need to stay close. Jimmy's orders. I swear to you, I won't breathe a word of anything I hear."

Angelina nodded agreement then turned toward Carlos. "What's with you? You don't buy into Jimmy's world, do you?"

Carlos kissed her, not with desire, rather as one filled with compassion. "The way I see it? I agree. Savakis figured out we let Bridget escape, and now he has set us up so we'll bring down Jimmy's army. Who better than you? Everyone in the Highland Precinct knows how much you hate him. Only, Savakis didn't plan on us becoming converts."

"I'm not. Are you?"

"Maybe. Jimmy makes a lot of sense. Do you know Rowlands' plans?"

"I know he's a scumbag. So what?"

"So what? He's going to make defection a crime, punishable by death. No trial. A person can be convicted on mere suspicion. They'll be lined up and executed like cloned cattle for slaughter, or mowed down in the streets. Guess who'll be doing his dirty work?"

Rebellious military shoots sprouted in every province. If something drastic wasn't done, civil war would be a certainty. A strong government would guarantee peace, wouldn't it? Still, mass murder of defectors based solely on suspicion seemed beyond the scope of reason.

Carlos' gaze bore into her like a judge's guilty verdict. "Is this the kind of government you want to serve?"

"We've killed before … in the line of duty. How would this be any different?"

"Defectors are not criminals. They're ordinary people like me and you who have different viewpoints about how life should be lived."

Was this the man who shared her bed, the malleable Carlos who romanced her all the way to a familial contract? This man who held her hand now believed in something larger than the IEA, larger than the two of them—so much so, he dared to challenge her. This new Carlos drew her, and she had never wanted him more than at this moment. Yet, the very passion she felt might be the sword to divide them. She asked him a question she had never asked another soul. "What do you think I should do?"

He embraced her, as a father comforts a child. "You follow your own conscience, Angelina. I won't speak your mind for you."

She shouted down the path at their guard. "Hey you, Angus."

He joined them, his nostrils steaming like a bull at charge speed. "My name is Angus O'Doul. If you need something, you will address me as Mr. O'Doul, not 'Hey You, Angus.'"

"Whaddya know? They've sent sassafras to shadow us."

He drew his lips into a thin smile. "What do you want?"

"Are you allowed to answer questions?"

"Depends on the question."

"So, your army likes to disrupt things—ignite a bomb here and there, make a few heists and give the money to the wretched populace of Sector Ten, or maybe help a dissenter or two escape. That sort of thing. Right?"

"We're an army, of sorts, and every bit as organized as the IEA. We fight for freedom."

She laughed. "By the looks of your weapons, I don't doubt you are a significant force. What I want to know is what happens if you win?"

"Win?"

"Yeah. Say you manage to disrupt things enough, and the government falls apart. What then? What system will take its place?" Angus looked at her as if she'd asked him to calculate the square root of ten billion. "Come on, now, a simple question. What will the new government look like?"

"We don't want to take over. We want the government to change."

She giggled. "Change, in what way? Except for the people in Sector Ten, life is good in New Edinburgh. Personally, I don't see any sense to what you're trying to do. Although, getting rid of a few scanners here and there might be a good thing. I think surveillance ought to require a judge's order, too. I could live with changes like that. How would you make the world a better place?"

"Choice."

"And what would you choose?"

Angus rested his weapon across his knees and stared toward New Edinburgh. "See, Officer Bartelli, some in our society are created for a singular purpose."

"You mean memes?"

"Yes, memes. And if they fail to perform that function, they are tossed aside or destroyed, like a broken toy."

Now acclimated to the darkness, she studied Angus' too-perfect features—flawlessly handsome with exquisite blue eyes. "You're a playmate."

"Yes, I am. Only, I wasn't supposed to have emotions. I was designed simply to please."

"Are you saying you developed feelings for your mistress?"

"Yes. And she loved me, too."

"Impossible." Angelina laughed. "You do tell an amusing story."

"My owner bought me to keep his intimate company. He traveled for long periods at a time and thought my presence would keep her faithful to him and ease her loneliness."

"Nothing wrong with that. Quite acceptable."

"Only, my mistress didn't want a playmate. She wanted companionship. She asked questions, and we talked for hours at a time. We discovered an attraction for one another beyond the bedroom. When my owner returned, my mistress confessed her love for me and asked to put me into the familial contract mix. Outraged, my owner claimed me as defective and sent me back to the factory, then admitted my mistress to a psychiatric facility."

All too ridiculous. "Let me guess. You were scheduled for euthanasia."

"Yes. I managed to escape with the help of Jimmy's operative at the Euthanasia Chamber. So, I joined his army."

Something stirred Angelina's soul—something she had forgotten after Papa died, the emotion as unsavory as pork left too long in the sun—compassion the bane of the feeble-minded. Memes were property, like a chair. At the most, a pet. One might be especially fond of a dog, but to join in a familial relationship seemed somehow immoral. If memes were adjudicated as capable of basic human relationships, they'd deserve the same rights as Citizens. To render such rights would throw United Earth into absolute chaos.

As if he read her confusion, Carlos squeezed her hand. "See what I mean, Angelina? I can't look at the world the same way any longer. Congress has perpetuated all these lies for the sole purpose of subjugation and economic advantage. Meme production is nothing more than slavery. We were brought up to believe life should be only one way. Why can't there be another? Truth doesn't have a side you know."

What was truth? Maybe … just maybe … for once in her life … she should digest an unselfish thought.

Jimmy Kinnear smiled as Angelina and Carlos made their way back from their stroll. Carlos joined the rest of the band while Angelina slumped into a chair and pouted. So, she discovered Angus was a meme. Poor Angelina. Left with no one she could control. Not her former lover, not Angus, and not even Carlos.

The micro hail brought Jimmy from speculation to reality. He projected the encrypted image. "Falan? How long do we have?"

Falan seemed out of breath as urgency hemmed his words. "Not long. You need to know we found a mole in Cavanaugh's household. An automaton disguised as a Priscilla maid."

"A plant?"

"Aye. She's been deactivated. We're uncertain how much she divulged to the Mainframe. We must alter our plans. I'll hail you when the channel's secure again. Falan out."

Most likely Priscilla was Rowlands' mischief. He wouldn't rest until Governor Cavanaugh was as silent as Devereux. The madman had to be stopped, once and for all. The Festival provided the opportunity, and Jimmy had the military knowledge and means. The deed must be done—the act his and his alone

Rowlands must die.

CHAPTER THIRTY-THREE
Sector One/America Prime

Benjamin changed into his civilian suit and pulled on leather boots, his thoughts more on Christine than on the anticipated ceremonies. He took the stairwell three steps at a time and found her at the breakfast nook on the veranda. The morning couldn't start until he held her in his arms. She kissed him far too passionately, tempting him to forget his promise to wait for his pleasure of her. From the passion in her return kiss, perhaps she'd like to forget their pledge as well since their contract was only hours away. He kissed her neck hungrily, drew her breath from her lips and drank her perfume.

They found the strength to resist and drew back from one another.

"Only a few more hours," he said. How could he take advantage of her weakness?

She squeezed his hand as if in gratitude.

"Think, Benjamin. The Partridge Oasis for our party."

He'd have been happy with any venue. "Uncle Ahmed said he liked the challenge … parties his favorite thing to plan. He said your father took advantage of this talent on many occasions."

Her enthusiasm curbed. "I remember those affairs. We'll set a chair for my father in his honor. He'll be there in spirit."

She shouldn't feel sad on this their special day. "Uncle Ahmed hired a large orchestra. You love music."

Instead of a smile, her face contorted with horror. She tugged Benjamin's sleeve and pulled him into her. "And do they dance in the Network?"

"Of course." He swelled with pride. "I won the jig contest four years in a row."

"Orchestras do not play jigs. And we'll be expected to do the first dance."

"Then you'll have to teach me what I need to know."

She played with his cape. "You look handsome in these clothes, Benjamin."

A pair of hemp pants, sturdy boots, and a leather vest were the only vestments a man needed in the Network. "I like the government jumpsuits, loose and comfortable. Can't say I'm a fan of these civilian formals." He flounced the flaps on his shirt. "I feel like a flying squirrel."

Her laughter washed him with anticipation. Would he and Christine be as happy as his parents? The thought occurred how much Pops would lose when Mother passed from this world to the next. Hard enough to lose a mother. How did one accept the loss of a mate? If Christine died, he would not want to take another breath.

She cupped his chin and turned his head toward her. "You're deep in thought."

"I wish my parents could be here."

"I want your father to stay with us during the Festival. He is a dignitary, of sorts, even if the Constitutional Government refuses to acknowledge his status as such."

Christine squeezed his hand, and her touch brought wonderful sensations he must wait to act upon. "Pops said he'd watch our ceremony on the micro ... Thomas Muldoon thought he could hack a feed from the Mainframe. I didn't realize these events were broadcast."

"Repatriation and familial contract ceremonies bring in large crowds, especially when political figures or celebrities are involved. That's why they're held in the arena."

"I wasn't nervous until now. I hope I don't embarrass you."

"You could never embarrass me, Benjamin. I love you."

He brought her hand to his lips. "I don't know if I can be as good an intimate to you as my father has been a husband. I pray the Maker makes me so." He rubbed her arm as he kissed her hand. "I needn't tell you what I'd rather be doing right this minute. A shame we need to leave. We're supposed to meet Kyle and Caroline at Uncle Ahmed's office. From there, we'll be escorted to the Sector One amphitheater. Kyle and Caroline will declare first. Then our familial contract ceremony will follow my repatriation."

Christine clutched her satchel and took his arm. "Let's not keep Uncle Ahmed waiting."

Benjamin checked his timepiece. "Four more hours. The minutes tick by slower than sap from a maple."

Christine squished her eyebrows together like Caroline Skinner looked at Peter when he said something outrageously funny. "You do say some strange things, Benjamin. What is sap? What is a maple for that matter?"

Would he have to leave behind every stitch of familiarity? Language and expressions so integral in his everyday life, understood by every outworlder, now made him an ignorant misfit. He'd have to listen more and talk less if he hoped to fit in with Christine's friends.

"A maple is a tree, extinct now. Outworlders from the Northeastern badlands tell stories about them, how they used to put buckets on the trees in early spring to collect the sap. They processed the sap into what they called syrup ..."

Christine's eyes widened as if hearing something miraculous. "City trees are manufactured in factories, like memes.

"It's all history now." His heart sagged with so many losses United Earth experienced within a single generation. Pops was only a small boy when the tsunamis hit and changed the world as he knew it. Maybe why he studied history. Perhaps the best way to plan for the future was to understand the past.

Christine rested her head on his shoulder. "I know the adjustment to so many changes has been difficult for you." She led him to the front portal. "Before we go, let's say our vows before the Maker. Here."

Benjamin nodded, and they clasped hands as they knelt.

"You first, Benjamin."

"Maker of all things ... I thank you for this woman you have given me. We are here now to pledge our love for each other. I willingly forsake all others and will cling only to her until death parts us."

Christine looked in his eyes. "Maker of all things, thank you for this man you have brought into my life. Make me a woman worthy of his love. I forsake all others and will cling only to him until death parts us."

Benjamin rose, then brought Christine to her feet. As they embraced, their hearts beat in synchronized rhythm. Would they be as happy tomorrow as they were at this moment?

CHAPTER THIRTY-FOUR
Sector One/America Prime

Ahmed Fared raised his hand to still the crowd gathered in the amphitheater. When quiet returned, he called Kyle to the center platform then uploaded the Repatriation Ceremony. Hopefully, Thomas Muldoon would perform his magic from the Network's end and hack the feed Ahmed had engaged on the Mainframe.

He explained the custom for Kyle's sake. "Both Repatriation and Familial Contract Ceremonies are considered mandatory viewing. When I uploaded the ceremony protocols, every receiver in every sector, as well as all domiciles except for Sector Ten, automatically turned on."

Kyle's eyes bulged. "I never much liked to be the center of attention."

When he received the green light to begin, Ahmed motioned Kyle to step forward. "Kyle Skinner, you are here today to join our beautiful City as one of its Citizens. And you do so willingly?"

"I do."

"Raise your right hand. Do you, Kyle Skinner, solemnly swear to uphold the Constitutional Government and the purpose for which it stands: one people, one world, one government until the end of time?"

Kyle gulped then proceeded. "I do so solemnly swear."

"Then signify your allegiance by placing your thumbprint to this document."

Kyle pressed his thumb against the micro as dutifully as any dedicated Citizen.

EVE projected to thunderous applause. "Congratulations, Citizen Kyle Eugene Skinner."

Ahmed signaled the attendant to bring out the scarlet cloth containing Kyle's implant, the sapphire class—a step up from the Sector Ten repatriate. After receiving the implant case, Ahmed approved its content.

The crowd cheered again, "Kyle … Kyle … Kyle …"

Ahmed raised his hand for silence. When the din simmered, he held the case above his head as an offering to the people. "Having duly promised allegiance and having verified the same by the rendering of your thumbprint, receive now this symbol of your citizenship."

Kyle's pallor whitened. Ahmed regretted his failure to reassure him the procedure was both simple and painless. He swiped Kyle's hand with an anesthetic then whispered in his ear. "This is the worst of it, my friend, although you may develop a slight rash that will disappear in a few days."

Color returned to Kyle's face.

"Extend your right hand, palm up."

The attendant retrieved the sterilized inserter from the case, slid the implant into the device, and then injected the pre-coded jeweled chip. Ahmed shook Kyle's hand. "The symbol of your allegiance has now been implanted. You are free to transact business as a duly recognized Citizen."

The crowd stood and applauded.

Kyle's eyes bugged. "That's it?"

"That's it."

He stepped back and Ahmed repeated the pledge and ceremonious implant for Caroline, her obvious lack of enthusiasm close to sedition. When Ahmed shook her hand, the implant shifted and lodged in a tender spot on her palm, the pain likely only temporary, rare in these situations. She scowled as she muttered, "I'd hoped this wouldn't hurt." She huffed as she took her place next to Kyle and surrendered a faint smile for the crowd.

And now for Benjamin—both a pleasure and a dread. "Come, my nephew." Ahmed allowed himself one breach of protocol and hugged the boy like a father would a son. "Are you ready?"

Standing tall and proud, Benjamin's melodic affirmation resonated with the crowd, not a mechanical declaration like Kyle Skinner or with the disdain of the newly named Caroline Evangeline Merry.

EVE projected. "Congratulations, Citizen Benjamin Jacob Goodayle."

Benjamin beamed. Did the boy understand the finality of this pledge? How long before he came to realize his religion would be a stumbling block, a hurdle he must inevitably leap in days to come? Let the boy bask in the moment for reality would bite soon enough.

Next, he called Christine to stand at Benjamin's side and projected the familial contract document while supporters screamed their enthusiasm.

Benjamin swallowed as he and Christine held hands.

Ahmed consoled his nephew in low tones. "Nearly, done,

Benjamin. You were expecting a ten-page legal brief instead of a paragraph?"

"Something more substantial. Seems an event this important should—oh, I don't know—be meaningful?"

Ahmed rattled off the familial expectations and legal requirements regarding fidelity and property ownership within the circle. "Do you so pledge?"

"We do."

Benjamin and Christine affixed their thumbprints and then Ahmed added his.

EVE projected. "Congratulations, Citizen Benjamin Jacob Goodayle and Citizen Christine Francesca Devereux. The Constitutional Government declares you intimates under the law. May the days ahead bring you both happiness."

The crowd jumped to their feet again. When the thunder abated, attendees rushed to the trams.

Ahmed wrapped an arm around Christine's waist. "Come, my children. A party awaits."

Benjamin held back. "Can you make a disk of this, Uncle Ahmed, for a keepsake?"

"I'll see to it, my boy. Now, you should arrive ahead of your guests. I hired a private transport, a Series 456 limousine."

Benjamin beamed. "This is great. Pops will be jealous. Costly, I imagine."

"Benjamin, don't worry. Diamond Transport Company owes me more than a few favors."

They boarded, snapped their harnesses into place, and the platform descended into the underground tunnel system. Within minutes the transport screeched to a halt, ascended to the street level, then rolled until they reached the Partridge Oasis.

Ahmed laughed as he disembarked. "I think the best feature of this transport, besides its speed, is the spacious hatch."

The whoosh of another transport filled the air. Benjamin stepped back and gawked. A luxury limousine rolled to a stop in front of the restaurant.

Christine scowled. "Governor Rowlands' transport."

An IEA officer opened a larger hatch. First out were hordes of bodyguards who formed a line of protection. Rowlands emerged and exchanged salutes with each guard.

Ahmed's stomach roiled. He'd hoped to escape the political world for at least this night.

By now, Rowlands must know Michael was alive and in hiding from his jurisdiction. Yet, he continued to let Unified Earth believe he'd been bereaved. One thing was certain. He had not ordered the governors' attendance out of courtesy to his Second. Christine's celebration provided a platform where he could play the bereft intimate, a means to promote his precious Preservation Act.

Yet, there were signs Michael's defection had touched the core of the man most thought unreachable. Servants reported the President-elect stormed from room to room on a rampage of destruction for hours at a time. And on three separate occasions, security details were called to his den when he failed to acknowledge Becker's hail. Since Michael left, Rowlands barely managed a speech without rambling like tumbleweed in a storm. If the reports held so much as an iota of truth, Ahmed worried for the affairs of state. The pulse of United Earth would soon be at the mercy of a man in the throes of a psychotic episode.

Ahmed lowered his head in expected reverence. "Governor Rowlands, so good of you to come, given your current circumstances."

"The world has not stopped spinning because its future President grieves." Rowlands shook Benjamin's hand and shot Christine a lascivious glance. "Congratulations, my boy, to corner such a beauty."

Like a trained diplomat, Christine dismissed the affront with grace, her aplomb under pressure admirable. No wonder Benjamin abdicated his freedoms to be near her. How often had humanity's course been altered by a woman's charm?

Benjamin's short political experience served him well. "President-elect Rowlands, you do us a great honor. Of course, we did reserve a spot with the hope you'd send an emissary. Joyously, here you are in person."

"I look forward to an evening of diversion. In fact, my doctor has ordered it. Mr. Fared, lead the way."

As they entered the Partridge Oasis, Rowlands' security team encircled the facility, ready for irregularities, though none were expected. The guest list was comprised of the governors and their pre-approved contingents, selected delegates, elite businessmen, prominent artisans, and Christine's Humanitarian friends—a respectable crowd—attracted more by Presidential Mandate than by allegiance to a deceased governor's daughter.

Rowlands surveyed the room. "You've outdone yourself, Fared. I've heard you throw a good party. If this is any indication, my Inauguration should be unparalleled."

"Thank you, sir. Yes, this pales compared to your feasts. I arranged for a succession of anticipatory events to be held at the Governor's mansion and in the finest clubs America Prime has to offer. Of course, the After Ball will be held at the Presidential Palace."

Rowlands raised a hand. "We'll talk about my plans later. This night belongs to Benjamin and Christine. One item of business, however. Consider yourself informed as the law requires. I have arranged for a mandated congressional session immediately following the oath of office."

Rowlands sneered, perhaps indicative of what to expect during his reign. He'd dance around the rules, or change them, to suit his purposes. Ahmed's heart constricted with sudden awareness. He'd been duped. Rowlands never truly intended reform—his so-called olive branch had been a ruse to sucker his Second's cooperation. As for the Network? Their ambassador, not their emperor, had fed the Christians to the lions. With the faction leaders gathered for the Inauguration, the massacre would be simplified. Those who did not repatriate would be dead within hours of his climb to power.

Ahmed offered Rowlands his expected seat on the right of the happy couple and took the seat reserved at Christine's left. Rowlands nodded to his detail to allow the guests to enter, and meme servants escorted each to their assigned tables. Although most likely mandated, every governor had accepted the invitation, even Cavanaugh.

Ahmed pointed out the Highland leader to Benjamin. "Governor Cavanaugh has requested an extended visit to enjoy the beauty of the sub-city."

"Should I be concerned?"

"Perhaps not, however, a closer watch would be advisable."

When all had been seated, the wait staff brought out champagne for each table and filled the guests' vials for the toast. Ahmed prompted the crowd to rise. "First, to our President-elect, Edwin Milton Rowlands. Long health and prosperity be yours."

The guests clinked vials. "Here! Here!"

Rowlands nodded his acknowledgment then stood while Christine and Benjamin sat. "If I may do the honors, Mr. Fared?"

"By all means."

Rowlands lifted his vial. "And now to the happy couple, Benjamin Goodayle, and Christine Devereux. May your years together be filled with joy."

More clinks and murmurs.

Ahmed spread his hands in the way of invitation. "Let the festivities begin!"

For most celebratory occasions, music consisted of a pre-programed projection from the Mainframe entertainment feeds. Ahmed cashed in a sizable amount of credits to obtain a thirty-piece live orchestra. The guests stood to applaud the musicians as they paraded into the pit. Soon classical music filled the room while submerged fountain lights shimmered with the vibrations. Ahmed poked Benjamin's arm. "The guests will not take the dance floor until you and Christine perform a waltz."

Benjamin's eyes widened. Christine took him by the hand. "You'll be fine. Three minutes. Then you won't have to dance again. I promise."

As the young couple skated across the floor with sufficient grace to earn the guests' approval, Ahmed marveled at Benjamin's accomplishments in so short a time. A shame the event wasn't postponed until his father arrived for the Festival. A moot regret. Apart from Christine and Benjamin's party, all festivities had been canceled until after the Inauguration. Rowlands wanted nothing to compete for United Earth's attention. No surprise he allowed Ahmed to proceed with this familial celebration. What better venue to showcase the President-elect's resilience in the face of horrific loss.

Rowlands stretched across the table and whispered in Ahmed's ear. "You did submit my request for Schumann's pardon of Bridget Cavanaugh?"

"Yes, sir. President Schumann signed the paperwork this morning. Everything is in order. I have forwarded the document to your official files."

"Good."

As soon as Benjamin's dance ended, Rowlands circled the room. He lingered at Cavanaugh's tables and monopolized his daughter's attention. What game was Rowlands up to now? Did his improved temperament have anything to do with the undocumented meetings he'd held over the past few days? Highly irregular, though technically not illegal, since he was not yet President and the meetings did not involve specific Western America interests. Official notification to the Second Governor was not required. However, Ahmed's exclusion from these meetings indicated Rowlands intended to minimize Ahmed's influence as much as the Constitution would allow.

Perhaps he should pose a formal objection. To what end? Rowlands had not violated any regulation, merely bent the law in his favor. If Ahmed resisted, he'd put himself in the same political hot seat as Cavanaugh.

When the last dance finished, Ahmed rose. "Thank you all for making my nephew and Christine's special day more memorable. Go now in peace and safety."

Each guest came to the head table to offer Benjamin and Christine congratulations and to shake the President-elect's hand. As Bridget Cavanaugh took the arm of her bodyguard, Ahmed gazed her way. A beauty to be certain. No surprise the lascivious Rowlands found her irresistible. As for Cavanaugh, known for his jovial nature, the man had not cracked so much as a pretentious smile the whole evening.

Bridget accepted Falan's arm as he helped her into their transport. She clicked her harness, leaned back and mentally replayed the night's events like an entertainment feed. Not as grand as some of Da's galas. At least, she had danced her apprehensions away. Had her enjoyment been disrespectful to Ian's memory? She had loved Ian with every ounce of her being. He could never dance with her again, nor could he hold her in his arms. She stared at Falan—so handsome in his caped evening suit. Was he the explanation for her lighter moods?

She pondered the President-elect's attentions toward her. Perhaps he didn't mourn as deeply as one might think. When he twirled her during their waltz, the crowd's eyes pressed on her as if she were a wayward projection.

Da stared out the transport window, his demeanor like one in deep concentration. "Did you enjoy the party, Bridget?"

"I did."

"Good."

"Da, you're too somber tonight. What's wrong?"

"Dinna worry, Bridget. The trip has fatigued me. Nothing more."

"Rowlands' attention confused me. I loathe him."

"Accept his interest, Bridget. This public acknowledgment legitimizes you, me girl, and silences the rumors about your pregnancy. And dinna forget he arranged for your pardon, and Ian's, too, postmortem. You owe him gratitude, if only for that."

Must she? She'd do so for Da. No one else.

The hired transport ascended in front of their hotel. As they walked toward the main portal, Bridget inhaled the night wonders of America Prime, twice the size of New Edinburgh, a city of dual importance, Western America's capital as well as headquarters for United Earth. The artificial breezes fluffed her blue taffeta gown. She had fancier but hadn't wanted to outshine Christine. Not to worry, the girl would have glowed in rags, content as Benjamin Goodayle's intimate. Bridget remembered the day she and Ian made their vows in secret as well as the public declaration of their familial contract. They'd been filled with incomparable joy, though subdued by Da's absence.

The large crowd on the elevator blocked the spectacular views of the Presidential Palace and Governor's mansion. She checked her timepiece, a little early yet to retire. Perhaps later she and Falan could take in the sights from the roof-top's vantage point. Thankfully, there were no scanners in the hotels, only voice recorders. Pretense required Jimmy stay in her room unless instructed otherwise. He played his part well, perhaps too well. He'd rendered an extra bow here and there, and not one smirk or scowl at her silly orders for attention.

Da and Falan entered the shared sitting room attached to their suites. "I've asked Gregory to attend our meeting as we discuss our plans for the next few days."

Jimmy passed notepads around while Falan prepared the drinks. Da slipped a message to Falan, then waved his arms to signal the meeting would begin. Falan took over for Da.

"Governor Rowlands has invited Bridget to a tea Sunday afternoon. Governor Cavanaugh accepted on her behalf, so long as I escort her. Tomorrow morning the governors will be shuttled to a catered brunch at President-elect Rowlands' cabin in the sub-city. Tomorrow evening we'll attend the opera, followed by a gala at the Governor's mansion."

Jimmy passed a note around. Best to keep up appearances. The gates will open in a few days providing sufficient chaos for us to make good our escape. All is going according to plan. He winked at her, and rebirthed anger jarred her senses. She clasped Falan's hand in rebellion against her attraction to a rebel.

CHAPTER THIRTY-FIVE
Denver Hub/Western America

Jacob sighed as Amelia's incoherent mumbles rattled with each labored breath. Occasionally she spoke with chilling clarity through blue lips. "There. See? He's here to bring me home."

"Stay. Please. A little longer."

As quietly as dusk turns to night, she slipped away.

Davu Obote checked Amelia's pulse, closed her eyes and grasped Jacob's shoulder. "I'm sorry, Chairman. She's gone."

Jacob had known great pain in his life—the boring of a nail through his foot, flesh ripped by a wolf, and near death from a parasitic infection. None left him hollow like this. He rested his head where Amelia's heart once beat. He wanted to summon all nature to share his loss, to rend his clothes like Jacob of old when he thought his son lost—forget the promise made to mourn her privately.

"Chairman Goodayle," Davu said, "we must prepare the body quickly ... the humidity."

"Give me a few minutes. Please, Davu."

Jacob kissed Amelia's dead cheek. "I trust the Maker is as joyful to see you as I am crushed by your absence." With a sigh, he turned to Davu. "Do what you must."

Benjamin rushed into the bedroom and fell to his mother's unresponsive side as Davu slipped a shroud over Amelia's face. "I'm too late. I wanted to say goodbye."

Jacob hugged the boy inside the man. "Say what's in your heart, son. She'll still hear you from another realm. She's probably already telling Gabriel how proud she is of you. Heaven has become much richer today, my son, while we are poorer for her leaving."

Benjamin prayed for a moment, rose and sobbed unashamedly, enough for both father and son. He led Benjamin to where Ahmed's paid mourners groaned."

Prayers and chants of all faiths filled the hut. Jacob recalled the days when there were no ceremonies, when corpses outnumbered those left alive. He thanked the Maker for these few minutes to grieve.

Davu's crematory pilots, dressed in black tunics, transferred Amelia's body to a stretcher for transport. "Chairman Goodayle, what instruction as to her ashes?"

"She requested to have them dispersed by the river. She wanted me to plant a rose bush in her honor."

"Consider the matter taken care of."

"Thank you, Davu." His assurances generally came with a padded bill. He could have what few chickens Jacob had left in the coop.

Ahmed scrunched a suspicious brow. "Jacob, do you want me to oversee these arrangements? To assure all is done as she wished?"

Sobs broke through Jacob's veil of feigned strength. I'm sorry, Amelia. I tried. Even the strongest dams give way from time to time.

Ahmed turned toward Benjamin. "Stay here with your father until I return?"

"Thank you, Uncle Ahmed."

"We'll be back in about two hours."

Jacob put his arm around his son. "Walk with me, Benjamin." Best to get the lad out of the hut—no need for either of them to witness what would follow. As a politician, Jacob understood the expediency—as a husband, he balked.

They strolled to the river, the place where he and Amelia recommitted their lives to the Maker after joining Kyle's hub. Here, Jacob would plant Amelia's rose bush.

He pointed to a mound of wood and stone about forty-yards down river. "As you see, they've already laid the foundation for the manse. Your mother loved this stretch. We often strolled along these banks."

"I remember."

"I want you to take your mother's Bible ... her greatest treasure ... for Christine."

"She'll be pleased. I'll find a way to get around the monitors."

"Perhaps, one day, Bibles will no longer be considered contraband."

A small sprout grew on the river's bend and swayed in the wind, confident and strong; eerie, yet beautiful, defiant, oblivious to its slim chance of survival. "Look at this sapling, Benjamin."

"Amazing, Pops. The only trees I've ever seen are stunted pines on the mountain peaks and the factory ones in America Prime."

They moved to examine the sprout. "I can't explain how this sprig rooted here. I saw a large willow once when I was a sapling myself. An old man told me there weren't many left because of the droughts and the wildfires."

"Funny, isn't it, how a father and son can be born into the same world yet their experiences, nowhere near the same. I suppose if I have a son, his world will be far different than mine."

Jacob swelled with pride for the man his boy had become, full of wisdom and empty of hate. "Yes, I'm afraid you're right. Unfortunately, our legacy from one generation to the next seems to be more about change than heritage."

"Pops, are you still angry at my decision to repatriate?"

"I think I understand why you made that choice. I know your mother did."

"I can make more of a difference in America Prime than if I stayed here to farm."

Jacob gestured toward the barren mountains. "I met an ancient Nomad who told me the Rockies were once the most beautiful mountain range in the hemisphere. Now their nakedness pokes the clouds. Look, Benjamin. Can you see the specks of vegetation here and there on the horizon? Hope, boy, a sign the Maker has not given up on us."

Benjamin skipped a stone across the water. "Rowlands' agenda will stall progress, not promote it."

"On that, we both agree." They stopped at the construction site, and Jacob scooped up a handful of dirt. "I have no heart for a new house, Benjamin. The people insist, however."

"One thing I've learned from you, Pops, is the power of a common goal. I say let them build."

"The Council of Mayors hoped to have the meeting room completed by the next regular session."

"When will that be?"

Jacob sighed. Should he vocalize his fear the council would never meet in regular session again? "Following the Festival."

"Christine wants you to stay with us. Uncle Ahmed said he could arrange your clearance to do so. I hate to think of you stuck in the tents of Sector Ten."

Jacob smiled through his grief. "I can feel your mother's push against my back. She'd want me to go, although, I have great fears."

"Why? The Network has much to offer—for all United Earth, not just America Prime. Rowlands is too savvy a politician to destroy what we've built. Such action would hurt the economy, and he'd have to shoulder the blame."

"You learn quickly, Benjamin. The world of politics suits you." Perhaps his son was more like his uncle than his father. And Benjamin would find it equally as difficult to balance his integrity with the demands Rowlands' politics placed upon men of conscience.

The shuttle's whir brought both their attentions heavenward. "Come, Benjamin, we'll walk some more while you tell me about this woman of yours."

As the crowd surrounding Jacob Goodayle's hut dispersed, Davu Obote totaled his trade profit from Amelia's deathwatch—the net hardly worth acknowledgment, his best for a dilapidated hen house, one rooster, and twenty hens. However, both his father and grandfather taught him this truth: established good will was just as valuable as commodities. There was a time to exploit and a time to demonstrate compassion. Jacob had shown his gratefulness in front of a thousand potential customers.

In a land where death occurred more regularly than birth, Obote Dispersal Services had proven to be more lucrative than his transportation business. He served Nomads and defectors alike, and his profits far exceeded expectations. Not to mention each haul into America Prime provided an opportunity to bankroll his hidden assets as an operative with the IEA.

He basked in the hope Rowlands would soon be able to fulfill his promise of repatriation. Once he received his implant, he could enjoy the benefits of legal financial gain.

Davu walked behind the coop and pulled out his two-way micro. He hesitated as the thought struck. What if Network hackers intercepted his transmission? There were no prisons in the outworld—revenge could be swift and terrible. Perhaps he should have asked Becker to encrypt this transmission as he had done all the others.

No matter, this whole charade would end in a matter of days, and he'd slip into temporary obscurity as Becker promised. After the passage of the Preservation Act, he'd be given the newly created post of Minister of the Exterior, his primary assignment to parcel the Network's developed land to be farmed by memes—a prize worth the masquerade.

Still, better to hedge all his bets. If the worst transpired and the Festival resulted in civil war, he could always start over among the Nomads.

Perspiration beaded on his brow while regret spiked his conscience. Jacob Goodayle had proven to be a capable leader ... though a pauper, a man of much integrity. Davu considered many outworlders as personal friends—friends he must betray if he were to restore the Obote empire in America Prime. Before the Schism, before the end of civilization, Obote Industries ruled the world of commerce. Fashionable women frequented Obote boutiques ... athletes flocked to Obote Sporting Goods Stores ... Obote Novelties offered toys to satisfy the child in everyone.

When earthquakes leveled empires, the Obote fortune vanished. A grieving woman cared nothing for fashion, a man with an empty cupboard had little time for recreation, and hungry children cried for bread not toys. Given the challenges, he had managed to become the wealthiest man in the Network and its Second Chairman.

Now, however, fortune teetered on the brink of change, and Rowlands' succession brought an ill wind. To stay would be suicide. Constable Becker's offer brought immediate rewards—the only cost one's self-respect, a poor substitute for a cash enterprise. Davu wiped the sweat from his forehead, the debate in his soul finished. No matter how imperfect the Constitutional Government, America Prime held the most promise. Whether he escaped to the northern tundra or served the new President, Obote Industries would rise like the phoenix.

He transmitted the hail with vigorous determination then minimized Becker's projection in case an outworlder wandered by. "Constable Becker."

"Greetings, Obote. What news?"

"Amelia Goodayle has expired."

"Whatever our intent toward the outworlds, Jacob Goodayle has our sympathy. He's a good man."

Davu fumed. Was there a man alive who did not admire Saint Jacob?

Becker's voice quavered. "I have an additional assignment. Of course, you know Michael Grafton is still missing."

"She's alive, then?"

"Forensics ran the toxicology on her implant—"

"Let me guess, the Macabre drug?

"Our sources indicate you're quite familiar with it, Mr. Obote."

Would Becker now turn on his informant? "Are you making an accusation, Constable?"

"Let's say, I believe you're well connected with those who market the drug. The President-elect wants to shut down the trade. I'll need names … you'll be exempted from prosecution, of course."

"Anything else, Constable?"

"We have brought Grafton and Ives in for questioning. Both plead ignorance as to Mistress Grafton's whereabouts. We do know Sean Grafton shuttled Ahmed Fared for dispersal of a Jewess over the Negev and requested a flight deviation for a quick side trip to the outworld. I suspect Michael Grafton's disappearance and this flight are connected." Becker stated the obvious as if he'd uncovered the lost Hope Diamond.

"I believe you're right. I assume you've questioned Second Governor Fared."

"He claims he deviated to the Border Community perimeter to drop food and medicine at the request of the Humanitarians."

"Judging from your tone, you don't believe him."

"Not for a minute. Fared's a sly one … almost as slippery as you, Obote. Savakis thinks Michael is hiding in the Network. Find her. I don't need to tell you the President-elect will be very grateful when you do. He has more important issues to tend to than the impulsive nonsense of a disgruntled intimate."

If found, she'd be executed, and her properties would be up for auction. If he supplied Rowlands with satisfactory information, he might be grateful enough to bestow a land grant of the acquired farm hubs. "If I were President-elect Rowlands, I'd begin my search in the Border Community. I'll see what additional information I can glean. Obote out."

CHAPTER THIRTY-SIX
Revolutionary Army Headquarters/Highland Province

Angelina woke with a start. Where was she? With the stampede of footsteps, she instinctively reached for her weapon. Not there. Then she remembered. She was essentially a prisoner, though Jimmy now considered her part of his team.

Angus and three others broke into her quarters. "Time to move." He threw a P-94 at her and Carlos. "Angelina, your lover boy says you handled explosives in the IEA."

"Yes, during my stint with the relocation unit. Some roundups resulted in standoffs and we smoked the natives out with a few well-placed detonations."

"Then, you'll be on my team. Carlos, I need you to lead the other squad. We're taking out the air dock."

Angelina gulped. "You can't be serious. There are at least fifty security officers. You expect our group of seven to outman them?

How do you plan to dodge the scanners? No dead spots for a radius of two miles and they are tamper proof."

Carlos smiled. Had they already briefed him? Why keep her in the dark until now?

Angus threw Carlos a container of forged implants. "I'm sorry, we left you out of the plan until now. We weren't sure you could be trusted. I've watched you the last few days. Jimmy thinks you should be included, though I'm still not convinced. Carlos agrees. This will give you a chance to prove your worth to us."

Angelina pulled Carlos in for a kiss. "The surprises keep coming, don't they? Count me in, Angus."

He handed her a rocket halter. "Ever use one? These are from a weapons development firm. They're not on the market yet."

"Rocket halters have been in use since my great-grandmother's day."

"Not these babies … they can zoom as fast as a Series 456."

"Seems the gangs are always better armed than the good guys."

Angus snorted. "We're the good guys, Angelina, and don't forget it."

"I suppose good depends on which side of the fence you're on."

Angus showed her how to put on the halter and explained the various buttons and levers. "This switch serves like a transponder. The other buttons are color coded: green for launch, yellow for forward, brown for reverse, and red for descent. So simple even a meme can do it."

"Ouch."

"The helmets are equipped with transponders. Make sure it's on before you launch. This stick steers the device once you're airborne: left for left, right for right, up for up and down for down. Think you can handle it?"

"Try me."

Angus laughed and turned toward Carlos. "I'll take her up for a spin."

She slid on the halter and engaged the green button. At fifty feet, she catapulted a few times then jerked to level her flight.

Angus zoomed beside her. "I probably should have warned you to go easy on the levers—touch sensitive."

"Now you tell me."

When they descended, he slipped on a backpack and handed another one to Angelina. "Charges are in here. We'll take the large hovercraft to the security circumference where Carlos' squad will disable the air dock utility feed. Then you and I will fly in under cover of darkness. We'll have two minutes before the Mainframe self-corrects and scanners are back online."

A new admiration surfaced—Jimmy's army was more sophisticated than any rebel factions she'd heard of, able to infiltrate even the tightest security. No doubt Jimmy's experience with the IEA gave him a leg up. He knew the Mainframe like a mistress. Counterfeit implants, though no small challenge, would not be difficult for a criminal mastermind like Jimmy Kinnear.

Angus took charge. "Let's move it. Time is critical. Remember. No civilian casualties unless absolutely necessary."

"Why the caution, Angus? I say we blast anyone who gets in our way."

"Jimmy has no stomach for killing."

He had only fired his weapon once during his IEA career. Yet, as a rebel, the whole of the Highland Province feared him, and his name struck terror even among officers. "Jimmy Kinnear is a coward?"

"No, Angelina. The man's no coward. He happens to think life is non-disposable. Any man's death, even that of the enemy, tears him up inside. Not too long ago, one of his operatives killed an officer. Mourned him like a brother. In some respects, I suppose he was—

the dead man Jimmy's one-time IEA partner. No, lassie. Jimmy will kill if need be, but he takes no pleasure in the deed."

Angus signaled the rest to board the hovercraft. "Carlos will rig a fire alarm to clear out the air dock. Then we'll set the charges to detonate in thirty seconds. Should give us enough time to rocket free of the blast."

Angelina sensed she had changed, at least from the officer whose sole focus had been Jimmy Kinnear's end. "Have you heard from Jimmy yet?"

A woman soldier laughed so loud Angus swiped his hand across his throat, a signal to tone down. Older, more callous than most of the others, she held her P-94 like a trophy. "What do you care, Bartelli?"

"I don't, really. I still haven't figured out why he would risk his life for a snob like Bridgett Cavanaugh."

The woman snorted. "You don't have a clue, do you?"

"Clue? About what? What's going on, Angus? If I'm putting my life on the line, then I want to know why."

Angus looked over at Carlos, who gave a short nod, unlocked his harness and sat next to Angelina. "You want to know why we're wasting the air dock?"

"Yeah, Carlos. I do."

"Jimmy doesn't want the IEA swarming the Highlands."

"Why?"

Truth, like hail, hit hard. "He intends to assassinate Rowlands."

The woman soldier spat, her stare hateful. "He tried to keep his plan from us. We figured out what he was really up to. If Jimmy has a mind that's what's needed, ain't one of us with a mind to stop him."

CHAPTER THIRTY-SEVEN
Denver Hub/Western America

Jacob hesitated, the murmur so loud Thomas' social room rattled. Except for Davu Obote, every mayor was in attendance. When the delegation hushed, Jacob addressed them. "We have called this meeting to discuss Ahmed Fared's encrypted feed. Rowlands has betrayed him. There will be no negotiations—this so-called Festival is merely a ruse. Unless we repatriate, we will be annihilated. Ahmed warned the President-elect has slated a congressional session immediately after the Inauguration. Passage of his Preservation Act is expected at that time, and he will implement his new powers within hours. Since the majority of Network leaders will be present, we'll be easy targets.

"I address you as your friend, not merely your Chairman. My heart breaks for our future loss … a way of life United Earth will obliterate no matter how we vote today. This is the reality of our circumstance. One I have prayed would never be."

Thomas Muldoon now occupied the chair as Second Chairman in view of Davu's absence—presumably a permanent vacancy as he had already repatriated. Thomas stood. "Why can't we simply refuse to attend? You've always recommended a Charter. Perhaps the time has come for us to declare ourselves a sovereign nation, independent of United Earth, fight to make this land our own."

Jacob gripped the table for support. "Most of you know my convictions as a Christ follower, and many of you share similar views. Our Holy Word urges one to count the cost before waging war. We have the spirit to fight, and we have much to fight for. Unfortunately, this is a fight we cannot win. We have no weapons. No military. No fortress. No treasury. No allies. We are corralled on every side. To resist in view of a madman's unstoppable determination is suicidal."

Echoes of fear bounced from the rafters. Thomas Muldoon raised his hand, and the delegation quieted. "As instructed, each community has held their own referendum on this matter. We will call for each independent vote in a few minutes."

Was there no sun within this gloomy forecast? "There is always hope, Thomas. Perhaps, that hope lies within America Prime. Ahmed believes since the government is dependent upon the food we produce, most of us will return to our homes after we repatriate. True, our hubs will lose their distinctiveness and will become as moons to the City's sun. At least, we'll be alive. We will find other ways to follow our hearts and worship the Maker according to individual conscience. There is a time to stand and a time to surrender. This … this, my dear children, … is the time for the later."

Thomas stood. "Jacob, this is a turn-about for you. Why do you advocate submission now?"

"I still believe in the cause of independence. There will come a day to revolt, to declare our sovereignty. Now is not that time."

Jacob nodded to Thomas to take the vote.

"Given the solemnity of this session, I will address each mayor to declare their community's intention. In Davu's absence, I call upon Second Mayor Ron Lightfoot of the Las Vegas hub, to cast the vote for the Nevada Community. What say you?"

"The Nevada Community will repatriate."

"Mai Katakoa of the Wyoming Community. What say you?"

She bowed her head and stood. "The Wyoming Community will repatriate."

"Jonas Smith of the Utah Community. What say you?"

"The Utah Community will repatriate."

Thomas' declaration came next. "The Colorado Community will repatriate."

All eyes focused on Enrique Morales. Jacob sensed his answer even before Thomas called his name, and all the rhetoric in the world would not persuade one Border hub otherwise. Thomas gulped. "Enrique Morales of the Border Community. What say you?"

He stood the full of his six and a half feet. "No. The Border Community will not repatriate. We choose to fight."

"So be it. Know that you must stand alone."

Enrique nodded as he and his sons put on their hats and left the room.

Jacob's eyes moistened for the finality of this day. "We are adjourned. Return to your communities and prepare your hubs for evacuation. I will wire Ahmed of our decision. May the Maker have mercy on us."

CHAPTER THIRTY-EIGHT
Sector One/America Prime

Bridget gawked at the improvements in the Governor's mansion. She'd visited this estate during her childhood when Devereux took office and remembered the Neo-Greek figurines scattered about the gala rooms as well as the former governor's Impressionist artwork that hung along stairwells and in his private quarters. Rowlands had replaced the age-old masterpieces with pornographic faux cubism—a popular art form that grotesquely rearranged the female anatomy.

Da had arrived a little earlier, stating the President-elect requested a special audience with the Highland governor, perhaps to offer him a seat on the expanded Repatriation Committee. Thankfully, Ahmed Fared graciously stepped in as her escort for today's event, at least until Da joined them later. Falan trailed behind as she and Ahmed entered the gala room. "What would you like to drink, Mistress Cavanaugh?"

"Something delicious, Ahmed." She looked down at her abdomen. "No elixir for young Ian, though."

Ahmed excused himself, leaving Bridget to be amused by the latest fashion, surprised that even the older women preferred sheer over-blouses. She'd been advised each event would be more formal than the previous. She'd shopped at America Prime's most exclusive shops and found the selection for the more modest taste nearly non-existent.

Marta Hanson of the Alpine Province galvanized the room in a brown, gold-speckled crepe suit. Then again, a woman of her stature, the owner of four fabric mills, and the governor's most outspoken advocate would be forgiven a little glitz. She entered on the arm of her intimate, Lorenzo Avalone, the operatic baritone who enthralled last night's audience.

Bridget pulled at her single-drop diamond necklace in nervous anticipation. She'd despised these events as a teenager. Whenever Da insisted she attend one, she had voiced her rebellion with the declaration, "These affairs are the epitome of hypocrisy."

After Ian won the delegate seat, she had looked forward to the party life his position might have afforded. Disappointingly, few invitations were extended to the head of the Reformation Party. If she and Da made good their escape, galas of this magnitude would be non-existent. She might as well enjoy the extravagance while she still had the opportunity.

A meme butler offered her a chocolate-covered strawberry, and she heartily accepted. She gazed at the rainbow-clothed tables filled with every imaginable delicacy, strategically placed to create pockets for small group gatherings—a recognized political maneuver.

Though Ian's family was considered wealthy, they chose to follow the common man's diet of dehydrated cloned meats and vegetables, first generation foods a commodity for the elite. The signs of recovery were everywhere, but at what cost? What had humankind lost so that the rich could enjoy a chocolate-covered strawberry? As the butler made his way back to her, she put the untouched delicacy back on the tray.

President Schumann seemed content to stay in Marta Hanson's company. He paraded through the room and waltzed away his dwindling time on earth.

Da had finally arrived and stopped by President Schumann's table to chat. Unable to hear their conversation, she sensed her father's final plea for reform. The world of politics had always spun around polite exchanges over exotic foods and beverages.

Ahmed brought her a tomato-based garden medley cocktail. "No elixir, my dear, as you requested."

"Thank you."

He sipped his drink of squeezed Passion Fruit. "I hope you are enjoying your stay, Mistress Cavanaugh."

"Very much so. Western America has much to offer. Thank you for approving our sight-seeing flight the morning of the Inauguration. Da wants to catch a view of your famous Pike's Peak."

"Your flight plan is over dangerous outworld territory. With all the flights in and out due to the Network's repatriation, we cannot supplement your guard contingency, and we cannot guarantee your safety. I tried to dissuade your father, but he is adamant you would be most unhappy to return to the Highland Province without the full exposure to all Western America has to offer. Do you think the tour wise, given your condition?"

Did Ahmed suspect their true purpose?

"Da is quite right. I would pout for the entire trip home if I missed the natural beauty of Western America. I'm sure you greatly exaggerate the risks." Falan sidled next to her, and she took his extended arm. "As you see, Ahmed, Da's guards are very capable."

He offered a handshake. "Now that you have a better escort, Mistress Cavanaugh, I must beg your leave for matters of state. We expect the first transport of outworlders within the next hour."

"Where will you house them all?"

"We've built a tent city in Sector Ten next to the designated camp of outworld delegations. Most will be housed there. A few have been cleared to live with sponsors in the other Sectors. How are the relocation negotiations progressing in the Highlands outworld?"

Falan snickered. "You will have to ask Governor Cavanaugh that question. My duties are limited to the protection of the Highlands' first family."

"Mr. Riley, my instincts tell me you are well informed but too discreet to reveal the depth of your knowledge. Perhaps you should be a politician."

"Who's to say what the future may bring."

CHAPTER THIRTY-NINE
Sector One/America Prime

"Rise before your enemies, Edwin," Father often said as he shook Edwin from a sound sleep in the early morning hours. Neither the darkness nor the ghostly memories held terror any longer, and he became one with the night. In the stillness before dawn, strategies excited him the moment his eyes opened.

He jumped from his bed to start his calisthenics. Three more days before United Earth would be his to command. The Goodayle boy's celebration could not have been given at a better time. The governors' early arrivals provided a relaxed venue to assure swift passage of the Preservation Act on Inauguration Day. Ahmed's Festival topped off all his good fortune—and the fact Cavanaugh would no longer oppose him, the crowning jewel of all his joys.

Edwin allowed the vivid fantasies of what his administration would look like. Schumann was a warrior before becoming a politician, his presidency a soldier's reign. He lived a Nomadic life, his palaces, a hodge-podge of décor from every walk of life, a display of gifts and conquests. Edwin planned to redefine the presidency. Opulence would shroud the kingdom he would inherit. He planned to fund the newly formed art societies and offer patronage to budding artisans, especially the neo-cubists.

After a round of stretches, Edwin headed for the water shower, a quick luxury he allowed himself despite the favored legislation to ban them due to the shortage of clean water. He lathered, rinsed and toweled in less than two minutes.

His thoughts veered toward the unfortunate Schumann. With no intimate or heirs, he was destined to die alone, his only legacy a list of achievements—a warrior king who became the first President of United Earth.

Edwin mused how governments evolved along with society. The Accord had brought a divided world together. As cities grew, the realization dawned among leaders that freedom was an illusion used to appease the masses. The Accord's concept of a benign Ruling Council comprised of nine elders had to give way to a more stable government, thus the birth of the Constitutional Government of United Earth. Schumann's appointment by the newly elected Congress was, of course, a wise choice—his popularity guaranteed the new government's ratification.

However, the man had outlived his genius, and current societal climates dictated a new order. Edwin Rowlands would unify the world once more—to preserve the holiest of tenets: one people, one world, one government for all time.

Yet, how would the world remember him in years to come? Followers of great men tended to rewrite history for their own glorification. Would his legacy read like a single paragraph in an encyclopedia? Edwin Milton Rowlands was the youngest delegate to Congress and the second President of United Earth. The only child of the Mainframe's inventor, he died … when? Would this be the scant summary of his existence?

If Michael had stayed, how differently his biography might read. Michael, whose touch brought him as close to a heaven as he would ever know, cracked his stoicism and proved he was more than an empty shell. She alone both vexed and challenged him. She alone filled the void left when Mother died. Despite her abandonment, he'd grovel at Satan's knee to have her back.

Loneliness is a bitter brine to drink.

As his custom, he dressed in the clothes Sidney placed on his bureau the night before. Unlike Schumann, Edwin allowed no one to assist in any aspect of his grooming—nakedness the worst of vulnerabilities, why he never completely exposed himself during his sexual encounters—except with Michael.

He donned his government suit, pinned his insignia on the shoulder and took the steps to his private den. Cook had already prepared his morning fare—two eggs, bread, and goats milk. He guzzled his drink then tucked his eggs into his wafer bread. He rang for Sidney who brought in a coffee urn, a hybrid roast engineered by Davu Obote.

Edwin sipped as he paced. Must he face the greatest dawn of his life alone? Of all the women he'd enjoyed, Michael was the only one he wanted to love. Was he as incapable of the emotion as she suggested? If so, he had Father to blame. "Never let a woman into your heart, Edwin," Father advised. "Passion has been the downfall of many kings. Satisfy your lust, but keep your heart protected."

Edwin laughed at the irony. Though he'd obtained vast knowledge from his tutors, not one of them taught him how to love.

His den provided the only spot in United Earth where he could be himself. No micros and no scanners. Constable Becker insisted the President-elect have a minimum-security plan of two escape routes behind the fireplace and a transponder with a direct link to IEA headquarters. Here, in this den, Edwin Milton Rowlands was free to be himself. Here he unleashed his sorrow, his sobs so loud he woke Father's ghost. "Never let your thoughts wander far from your business, Edwin, not even for the sake of pleasure, certainly not for sorrow."

Edwin forced his thoughts back to presidential matters, yet Michael's face shadowed every corner of his mind. Obote's latest report indicated she was in the Border Community. Reason dictated she must have had help from either Fared or Goodayle ... or both.

Edwin paced and contemplated the most advantageous time to demonstrate his power. "Discretion the better part of valor," so the adage went, but Edwin Milton Rowlands read from a different book. He might never gain the joy of love, but absolute power was easily in his grasp. Michael must be brought to justice as well as the community that sheltered her. Swift retaliation would prove his authority, and United Earth would cower at his feet.

He would not have to wait for the Inauguration to exact his revenge. The Border Community had committed treason when they harbored Michael—justification enough to order an attack. He'd find Michael, bring her back to America Prime, and stay her execution until Jade was born. He'd lost her love forever, but a daughter might revere him. He would smother the child with attention to compensate for his inability to love.

He shivered with a sudden chill. Not from the excitement of a world soon to be at his command. Rather from the sudden remembrance of Scripture: For what is a man advantaged, if he gain the whole world, and lose himself, or be cast away?" Mother quoted the verse just before she plunged a dagger into her heart.

Emotions killed her. Father was right to avoid them, and why his ghost still inhabited Edwin's psyche, his Holy Book of wisdom the nuggets that propelled the son. Morgan Rowlands' presence was never further than the next thought to pop into Edwin's mind.

He hailed Becker on the transponder.

"Governor Rowlands?"

"Constable, arrest Ahmed Fared for treason. Let's see how he likes the prison he built. First, escort him to my den. Arrest Benjamin Goodayle as well."

"On what charge?"

"Make one up."

Edwin hesitated. Not over his decision, but how best to ferret his own brand of justice. "Make a sweep of the Border Community. If you find Michael, bring her to me. If not, you know what to do."

"Yes, Governor. Anything else?"

"Bring Chairman Goodayle to me. Perhaps the arrests of his brother and son will loosen his tongue. If not, arrange for his public execution."

CHAPTER FORTY
Denver Hub/Western America

Jacob checked his timepiece while he paced the sod floor and let out a series of belches sure to make Ahmed jealous if he were present. He and Benjamin should have been here an hour ago. Jacob moved his suitcase next to the door and paced again. If Amelia were alive she'd know how to treat his upset stomach.

The floor vibrated with the whir of a hovercraft. The engine had a different purr than the many IEA transports that had flown in and out of the hubs since the evacuations began. He opened the door to investigate but stepped back when a sharp pain radiated down his left arm and across his chest.

Thomas Muldoon and Mai Katakoa stood on his new stoop.

"I gather from your grim faces you are not here to bring good news."

Thomas took off his hat. "No, Chairman. We're not."

A part of him wished his heart would stop altogether ... that the Maker would allow him to join Amelia and not have to endure these days ahead.

"Chairman Goodayle, have you seen the feeds in the last hour?"

"I've been busy. I expect Ahmed and Benjamin at any moment. I've been cleared to live with my son and his intimate. They should have been here hours ago. Why haven't you left yet? Or have you decided to live among the Northern Nomads?"

Mai's sobs echoed through the hut.

"Come, now, Mai. Repatriation won't be so bad. Will it?"

Thomas sighed. "Chairman, there have been developments."

"Enough with the Chairman. We're friends. Just tell me."

Thomas raked his beard, his eyes welled with tears. "The Border Community is decimated."

"Decimated? How?"

"An IEA sweep, this morning, before sunrise. Rafael Morales escaped in a hovercraft but was shot down over the Denver Hub. He lived long enough to come here and let us know about the raid. I wired Mai and she said to meet her here and we'd tell you together."

"And is no one left alive?"

Thomas' rage turned to groans. "The IEA carried off perhaps a dozen elderly as well as a few women and children. Some managed to slip into the Sierra Province, while others headed to the northern regions. The rest were slaughtered in their beds."

"We expected this to happen eventually, Thomas, but why now? This makes no sense."

"Apparently, they were looking for Michael Grafton. Of course, she wasn't there. When no one would divulge where she'd gone, Constable Becker ordered every hub in the Border Community leveled."

Jacob had known Thomas Muldoon for many years and recognized when the man held news too horrible to share. "There's more you don't want to tell me. I insist."

Mai's round, brown eyes mirrored her sorrow. "One of my hubs hacked a communication from Governor Rowlands. Ahmed and Benjamin have been arrested. Benjamin was incarcerated immediately, while Ahmed has been brought in for questioning. We expect he is also in prison by now."

Jacob clenched his fists and the pain returned. "Both of them? Why? Benjamin knows nothing. Ahmed and I deliberately kept him in the dark for his protection. Rowlands has no right to detain either one of them. Besides, Benjamin is a Citizen, now."

Mai and Thomas exchanged glances.

"What else?"

Thomas clenched his teeth. "Rowlands has ordered their executions to follow the passage of the Preservation Act."

Jacob collapsed into a stick chair. "There's still more you're not telling me. So long as I am on this soil, I am still your Chairman. Out with it."

"The governor will release them on the condition you tell him where Michael is. He has sent a security team to arrest you."

Whose life mattered more—Michael? Ahmed? Benjamin? If he told Rowlands where Michael was hidden, would he spare her life or exact retribution on still more innocent people?

"If I'm to be arrested, I cannot fulfill my final duties as Chairman. I need you to make certain the rest of the evacuations take place in an orderly fashion."

"I will not abandon our people."

"Good. Assign a delegation to represent us on the outside chance Rowlands will relent and offer some compromise so we can keep our lands."

Thomas nodded. "I'll find a way to contact you when I reach America Prime. Before his arrest, Ahmed obtained permission for me to stay with Kyle and Caroline. They have moved into their own apartment. It's small, but sufficient, according to Ahmed."

"Good. Now go, before you're arrested along with me."

When Thomas and Mai were out of sight, Jacob paced. Within minutes, two IEA officers stood in the doorway, P-74s aimed. The taller one shouted as one in command. "IEA. Jacob Goodayle. Come with us."

He turned and smiled. "Am I so dangerous? Two weapons for one man?"

The younger officer spoke in a near whisper. "I'm sorry about all this, Chairman Goodayle. Orders, you know."

The officer's vibrato rang familiar, but from where? Ah yes. One of his first students when he came to the Network, only a few years older than Jason, the boy repatriated four years ago. Was he now an IEA officer? "Are you Gil Renault?"

"Yes, Chairman Goodayle."

Jacob smiled. "Has the City done well for you, my boy?"

Gil kept silent. Jacob scoured the room. Should he ask? If they searched it, they'd find his Bible hidden in a scanner-proof pocket, an ingenious invention by Thomas Muldoon. "May I bring my satchel or will I be a guest of your fine prison?"

The higher-ranking officer took charge. "Our orders are to bring you to the governor's private office. After that, I don't know."

They made no move to search his hut. Jacob threw the satchel over his shoulder, and the effort brought on yet another sharp pain. He gasped with the finality of the moment. "I'm never coming back, am I, Gil?"

"No, sir. I expect not."

CHAPTER FORTY-ONE
Sierra Province

Michael cleaned the stone chair then tossed the dust catcher into the scrubber and met with Marietta's disapproval.

"Mademoiselle Grafton, you should not do such hard work. You must rest. You are not used to such conditions."

The coarse air, thick even to the naked eye, made breathing difficult. There must be some way to help. Marietta said the huts were ventilated via the underground airways. Three ceiling fans recycled the interior atmosphere. Even then, every inch of habitation had to be scrubbed four times a day.

"Will I ever adapt?"

"In time." She retreated to the glass-encased kitchenette consisting of a brick stove and a solitary cupboard. When the scrubber cycle completed, she put the cloths into a dryer. No wonder these Nomads preferred single-room dwellings. Large spaces required far too much maintenance.

The soft chime from the antique timepiece signaled the fourth hour. Marietta dropped to her knees as she did each time the chime rang. She stretched her arms outward as if her Maker were in the very same room. Prayers and household tasks took up so much of her day, when did she find time to simply be?

Michael stroked the granite table. Much of the furniture seemed made from the same crushed material, even the beds. Marietta said the sand eroded wood.

The Sierra Nomads worked constantly with only short sleep intervals. In the City, a Citizen's labor amounted to no more than six hours a day, their free time filled with leisure activities such as entertainment feeds, walks in the secure parks, concerts, or time with friends and associates. Here, bed linens had to be stripped at sunrise, scrubbed, dried and stored in plastic bedding until time for sleep. Specialized awnings were lowered to filter the increased silt at sunset. With the dawn, they were scrubbed and stored until the next nightfall.

Marietta had warned Michael about the dangerous sand storms that carried infected fleas. More than mere comfort measures, the scrupulous sanitation methods assured survival—an endless vigilance against a relentless enemy. Michael ached for their toil, yet admired their diligence.

Though work their only existence, the Sierra Nomads were the most generous people Michael had ever met. They accepted her, nursed and fed her, and they took from their few precious moments of leisure to serve her though she could do nothing in return, too taxed to wipe a chair.

Marietta embodied mystery. Older than Michael and of a slender build, her black hair glistened even in a land devoid of sunlight. Although attentive to her guest's needs, she spent little time in conversation. The questions swirled in Michael's mind, and she craved answers. What drove these Nomads to this wasteland? Why would they prefer this isolation over repatriation or even the Network?

The Sierra Province had no hub, no communities or prime city, and Governor Sanchez's mansion was little more than a walled fortress, a place he occupied for only twenty-six weeks out of the year, the minimum required by law. The conditions so severe, the census takers were unable to make a count, the population of the Sierra Province anyone's guess. Nor could the IEA enforce roundups for uniformity within the province.

The occasional IEA hovercraft circled high above, probably more to satisfy congressional mandates than a need to keep law and order. The Nomads kept to themselves, and there were no reports of violence. Nor did Marauders choose to live under these harsh conditions. No need for a police force, and according to Governor Sanchez, nothing much to govern.

At one time, Michael had studied the maps to determine viable entertainment feeds to the Sierras. Ultimately, Excelsior abandoned all telecommunication links to the inhospitable climate. Although the largest province, Sierra's outworlders consisted of only a few scattered tribes throughout Old America's southwest and the Grand Isles—what remained after the tsunamis wiped out most of Central America and joined the Atlantic and Pacific Oceans above the Southern America Province.

Pity that schools eliminated the study of history from their curriculums, legislation Edwin pushed through. When she objected, he laughed. "My dear, we must not let the evils of our past impair the progress of our future." The masses readily swallowed his political rhetoric. In truth, uneducated masses were far easier to control.

Marietta rose from her prayer. "Does Mademoiselle desire something to eat?"

Maybe this time, she would share more than a few words. "I'm not hungry for food, Marietta, but I'd love conversation. Please, sit awhile. And I insist you drop the Mademoiselle. My name is Michael."

Marietta sat and leaned forward. "Like the angel Michael."

"My father died before I was born. According to family legend, Grandfather, my father's father, chose the name against my mother's wishes. Grandfather said when I was born an angel visited him and told him I was destined to be an instrument of peace. Mother thought Grandfather had dipped into her wine. She appeased him, however, and agreed to the name. Funny, I should be named after an angel."

"How so, Michael? You do not believe in the Maker?"

"I prayed to any deity that would hear me while in the wilderness. I am alive and so is my child. I'd like to say thank you, but I'm not sure to whom I owe the thanks or if I was simply lucky."

Marietta opened a trunk containing an assortment of religious artifacts, crosses, plates and works of literature. She pulled out a worn leather book stored in a hermetic bag then joined Michael at the table.

"This, Michael, is the precious Word of God."

"But Bibles are forbidden."

"In the Sierra Province, no one bothers us. We are Treasure Keepers, clerics devoted to the study and preservation of these sacred texts as well as to all works of art and literature that give glory to the Maker."

So, this is where the Reformists smuggled antiquities for safe keeping? "The rumors are true? Your Treasure Keepers safeguard ancient religious artifacts in underground vaults?"

"Oui, Michael. The Sierra Nomads are the descendants of banished priests and clergy, most from the Mediterranean Province, the former France, Spain, and Italy. Some of my ancestors served in a land known as The Vatican. The great cathedrals were destroyed during the Schism. The priests, they do all they can, to save what is left, no? My aïeul—how you say—grandfather—roamed the provinces in search of treasures. One day, the Maker spoke to him in a vision and told him to colonize the Sierras. Many thought him mad to settle where no life survived, but we have flourished. Our numbers grow, but no one notices. Not even Governor Sanchez. You see … the sand storms, our greatest curse, are our greatest blessing."

These people felt safe in their Maker's hand, far from Edwin's temper tantrums. Michael recalled the many theories presented at City galas as to how the Sierra Nomads survived. When she asked Governor Sanchez, he had replied, "Now there's a mystery, Michael, how anyone can survive there. I fly in for a week and fly out. My Second and I hold office hours as the law requires, but no one ever comes. Mount Sanchez was built on the highest peak, the only place a shuttle can land and not be choked by the constant sand storms."

Marietta slid the Bible toward Michael. "I give you this treasure, Michael. The Maker does have a plan for you. I believe your aïeul named you well. After we have had nourishment, I will show you the treasures."

Marietta opened the partition and left Michael alone to peruse the gift. Michael held the Bible and sniffed its musty leather. The dank odor reminded her of the one Grandfather kept hidden between his mattresses. As a child, she honored his secret. Mama burned the treasure the day after Grandfather died. Useless to anyone in her weakened state, Michael reasoned she might as well pass the lonely hours with a forbidden book.

Where to begin? She once read Grandfather's banned novel, Treasure Island, also hidden under his mattress. He detested modern novels, mere pixels projected into a room. Michael, however, spent many hours journeying through virtual worlds.

She opened the book, and pen markings caught her immediate attention: Born to Samuel and Estelle Bouvier: Samuel Jr. born 1987 died 1989. Julia born June 1, 1988, died June 4, 1988 … only one of the ten names apparently lived to adulthood … Pierre Bouvier. Was this Marietta's aïeul ? Michael turned the page. The words resembled an ancient form of English. Though she knew Bibles were forbidden, she had no knowledge of how the revered work came about. As she read the information, she marveled how a king—a king of questionable moral conduct—had authorized the translation of ancient writings into the tongue of his subjects and earned the title, DEFENDER OF THE FAITH.

Most Old-World Literature had been destroyed or purged from the data streams. Surviving manuscripts, like the plays of William Shakespeare, had been edited and modernized. As she continued to read the accreditations, she was drawn to a particular paragraph, as if her namesake angel had pointed to the words with a holy finger:

But among all our joys, there was no one that more filled our hearts than the blessed continuance of the preaching of God's sacred Word among us, which is that inestimable treasure which excelleth all the riches of the earth …

This Word, then, was the thing for which the Network and Grandfather had risked death to protect. Not the ink on the page, but the message within its pages. She skipped the table of contents to read: In the beginning, God created the heaven and the earth. She remembered Grandfather's words as tears of joy filled her eyes. "All things begin and end with the Maker."

Michael jumped at Marietta's command. "I am pleased you find this so fascinating, but you must eat."

Michael put the Bible back into its protective case. "May I read it again?"

"Oui. But, I will put the treasure away so the sand does not destroy. Each day, you may open and read a little."

The women laughed while they ate as if long-time friends. When they finished, Marietta put the bowls into a dish scrubber. When she returned, she handed Michael a face cloth to put on. "I take you to the vaults. We must travel one mile. Difficult against the sand funnels. Do you wish to try?"

Michael nodded as she slipped the facecloth over her head, wrapped the scarf portion around her neck, and buttoned her over-blouse to the top. Marietta handed her a pair of thin gloves. "No skin can be exposed. The fleas are dangerous."

Marietta led the way through an airtight entryway, closed the granite door behind them, secured the seals, and then opened the portal to the outworld. Within seconds, a sand funnel pressed against them, and Michael struggled to breathe. Perhaps she'd been too eager to accept Marietta's invitation.

Michael felt for the guide rope as instructed, and soon Marietta disappeared into a pillar of dust. Had she been swept away by the sudden gale? Michael clasped the rope with all her might, not able to cry even if she dared. Her legs buckled, and she stumbled forward, certain she'd die in this very spot. Marietta returned and lifted Michael back to a stand. They continued forward, hand over hand on the guide rope until they came to a wall of rock.

Marietta led the way through a portal. "Do as I do," her voice barely audible against the deafening screech of the wind.

They descended a flight of stairs then entered a small chamber and undressed. Marietta pulled a lever, and soon the room filled with hot steam. After several more minutes, they stepped into yet another chamber and donned white robes and golden slippers.

Curiosity must be satisfied. "Why such preparation?"

Marietta smiled as she tied the satin belt on her robe. "This must all seem strange. No? We take great care to avoid contamination."

"I think I'm set. Unless there is something else?"

"No. We are ready."

She led the way through a hall of thick plastic curtains that led to a cavern. Hundreds of paintings hung in climate-controlled dens. Sculptures and historic implements, encased in glass, rested on velvet pedestals. Marietta punched a series of numbers into a keypad located near the entrance. "This adjusts the climate for our presence."

Michael had been to America Prime's rarely visited sole art museum curated by trained memes. Antiquity failed to draw Citizens like the technology fairs at the Oceanic Resorts.

"How did you come by all this?"

"Much of this we recovered from an exhibit in Old Denver. They were buried in an underground cave. The exhibit was a display borrowed from New York City Metropolitan Museum of Art during the time of the tsunamis."

"Yes, I've heard of the great losses when the coasts flooded."

"These visionaries brought to safety."

"In anticipation of the days ahead?"

"Oui. Many museums that were not flooded did the same."

"I assume much of what was left on the surface was destroyed by the elements if not ransacked or burned during the Schism. There are some in America Prime who tell stories about those dedicated to the preservation of art and literature. I see, now, these reports are true."

Marietta smiled. "We have ten of these secret places in the world. This place was once known as Carlsbad Caverns. These dens and chambers go for many miles."

A large painting took up most of the exterior wall, perhaps a late nineteenth-century scene. A young woman held a sheet of music. Underneath the painting was the title, The Organ Rehearsal. A legend gave the picture's description and history: This painting is attributed to Henry Lerolle. Popular history believes the woman singing is Lerolle's wife, and in the background is his brother-in-law, a composer.

Marietta pointed to a smaller painting displayed on the opposite wall.

"This one inspires me."

Robed men lined up behind a three-foot rail. A man dressed in fine robes, perhaps a priest, held a chalice into the air. One of the brown-robed men knelt in front of the altar. She viewed the title, The Choir of the Capuchin Church in Rome.

As Marietta scanned the work, her face mirrored a portrait of serenity. Michael read the legend: This work reminds us there will come a day when we who follow Christ will be able to worship him without government control. When Granet painted this picture, Pope Pius VII was greatly encouraged. A few years before, Napoleon Bonaparte had forced the Pope to reside at his coronation as Emperor. Napoleon persecuted the organized church. But the call of Christ beckons us to his feet despite the danger, just as these Monks sang to the Maker and knelt in His presence.

"Come, I have another room to show. We cannot stay long."

Marietta led the way into a sealed chamber. A single candle perched on a gold stand in the middle of the room. "Francesco and his brothers serve as Keepers of the Flame. The candle, is lit day and night and represents the hope we have in the Maker. These works tell of Christ on the Cross."

Michael wanted to look away, but something compelled her to study the ugly beauty found in the picture. A dead Christ hung on a cross beam of splintered wood, the dark sky broken by a background light. Underneath the painting was the inscription: The Crucifixion, by Bartolomé Esteban Murillo

Marietta pointed to the background images. "Jerusalem."

As Michael viewed mankind's tribute to the Maker's Son, a man called Jesus, a stirring, like that of the first recognized movement of a fetus, caught her breath. "Why is a dead Savior the central theme of this room?"

Her guide's eyes moistened. Through broken English, she explained a wondrous yet mystical plan—a plan of redemption designed from the very beginning of time. "We who worship the Maker's Son, Jesus, believe He is not dead … He is alive … this is our hope."

"Whew. You've described thousands of years of beliefs in a few simple sentences."

Marietta gently pushed Michael's shoulder and held her chin to view one more exhibit on the back wall. Michael read the caption: Allegory of the Church by Johanne Vermeer. Her glance leaped from image to image. A woman stared outwardly while a globe lay at her feet. Behind her was the Christian cross. To the left, underneath a heavy stone block, the artist depicted a gray snake that spewed blood. Michael's curious eyes searched for the legend underneath the inscription: The Woman symbolizes Faith, a faith that encompasses the whole world, not just for a few individuals. The bloody snake signifies the death of sin by Christ's death on the cross and His resurrection. The stone signifies Christ who is described in the Holy Bible as the Cornerstone.

Michael knelt in awe but rose quickly at the rap from the far end of the cavern den.

"That is Francesco." Marietta said as she opened the chamber door.

A stooped, smallish man entered. He hurriedly replaced the candle then spoke in English. "I did not wish to disturb your prayers, Marietta, but I must tell you the news Brother Simeon has brought us."

Marietta sighed, as if in anticipation of calamity. "Go on, Francesco."

"Enrique Morales is dead, as are his wife and sons. No one is left alive in the Border Community. The IEA brought a dozen or so into Sector Ten for repatriation. A few dozen more escaped into our tunnels. Perhaps a dozen found refuge with the Nomadic tribes in the Northern provinces. The others were slaughtered, and the IEA has burned every hub to the ground."

Michael sorrowed for the innocents. "This is my fault. If I hadn't come—"

"No. You are not to blame,"

Francesco clasped Michael's hands. "When Enrique brought you to us, he said his hub felt blessed to have helped you. The Border Community refused to repatriate with the others. The government would have acted sooner or later. Governor Rowlands used you as an excuse."

Michael weakened, and Marietta helped her to a bench. "I have been Edwin's intimate for fifteen years. I know he can be ruthless, yet, this act goes far beyond reason. I'm afraid the father of my child is insane. There's no telling what he might do next."

Marietta helped Michael to a stand. "We must return to make another plan. You will not be safe much longer."

CHAPTER FORTY-TWO
Sector One/America Prime

Edwin spun Bridget twice then dipped as he led her in a suggestive tango. This woman was indeed a marvel—intelligent, beautiful, as well as a graceful dancer. Though Ian McCormick lived a short life, he was indeed a lucky man to have had Bridget at his side. Bridget. Her name brought images of a warrior princess in an epic Celtic poem. Bridget Cavanaugh—a woman with spit and fire yet finesse enough to know when to squelch the blaze—born to be a politician's intimate.

Sidney stood in the back and held up four fingers, the signal for matters of state. Perhaps the package had arrived. "Excuse me, Miss Cavanaugh. I hope we will be able to finish this dance later?" Edwin escorted her to a table then joined his butler.

"Yes, Sidney?"

"Constable Becker has asked to meet you in your den as per your instructions."

"Yes, that's correct. Tell Constable Becker I'll be there shortly."

"Most irregular."

"It's alright, Sidney."

"Then I shall escort him there right away."

Edwin returned to Bridget's table. "I'm sorry for the interruption, my dear. Mr. Riley, I'll hold you personally responsible for seeing our fair Mistress Cavanaugh safely to her suite."

Bridget smiled. Not a light in the room matched the sparkle in her eyes. "Da excused himself about an hour ago, said he and Governor Sanchez had business to discuss. I'm afraid the two have absconded to some mischief or another. How kind of you to be concerned for my welfare, Governor Rowlands."

Riley stood—a dutiful sentinel, positioned as if he owned the woman. "If the President-elect permits, the hour is late. I should see Mistress Cavanaugh home now."

"By all means."

Edwin kissed Bridget's hand. Would his lingering lips betray his want of her? He must not rush, though. Too many would view his haste as improper though not illegal. He could dissolve the union with Michael on the grounds of desertion, then his acquisition of Bridget would not require Michael's agreement if his contract with her was nullified. "I hope you will do the honor of accompanying me to the Inauguration and After Ball? Boring affairs made pleasant if you are at my side."

"Da and Falan will join us, of course?"

No. Governor Cavanaugh would not be there if his current absence meant he fulfilled his end of their bargain. "By all means. Until then."

Edwin walked briskly from the ballroom, through his living quarters, up two flights, and waited a moment before entering his den—his solitary place where he conjured schemes—the place of secret meetings—the place where he met with Cavanaugh within hours of his arrival to America Prime. Man-to-man with no servants, bodyguards, micros, or scanners.

How fortunate Cavanaugh's attempt to register Bridget's pregnancy had been brought to Edwin's attention—the perfect hammer to drive the unarguable bargain. Father said every desire had a price tag, why Edwin agreed to provide for the fair Bridget even before he met her. He hadn't anticipated this need to possess her. She would be his next intimate, his queen, and they would rule their empire like Napoleon and Josephine. Bridget was the gravy—Cavanaugh's silence, the meat of the pact.

When he found Michael, he would order her confinement until his daughter's birth and have her terminated immediately after. Bridget's son and Jade would be raised together.

Edwin opened the door to yet another chess game.

Accompanied by a much greater security detail than required, Jacob Goodayle bowed his head in polite recognition.

"Gentlemen. Please, sit." Edwin pointed to his antique settee, a gift from Marta Hanson. "Chairman Goodayle, if you would."

Goodayle merely glanced at the furniture.

Edwin circled his prey then picked up one of the swan vases. "I thought the settee's wide stripes would set off these unusual pieces, a gift from Governor Sanchez. The IEA intercepted a Nomadic smuggler. After he terminated the poor devil, he brought the vases to me."

"Governor Rowlands, when will my son be released?"

Edwin sat in the matching upholstered chair and leaned forward. "I must insist you take a seat, Chairman. I'm sure all this unpleasantness has left you exhausted."

Goodayle remained fixed as if glued to the floor, his stare like a laser blast to Edwin's conscience, but with no effect.

"Never let your opponent get you riled," Father's ghost said. Edwin leaned back and crossed his legs. "Chairman Goodayle, your son will be executed for treason, as will Ahmed Fared."

"You know my son is innocent. You dance at his celebration, then have him arrested?"

Becker rose at Goodayle's angry tones. Edwin signaled him to stay at a distance. "Understand my position, Chairman. Your son is guilty by association. I'm afraid Mr. Fared's crimes cannot be ignored."

"I don't understand. Benjamin is a mere boy. As for Ahmed, whatever decisions he makes, he does for the good of the government. He is loyal in ways no one else is."

The man's last statement was perhaps the most ludicrous of all. Fared might have the interests of America Prime in his heart but certainly not those of his President-elect. "You amuse me, Goodayle, you and other Christ followers who forego common sense for the sake of your misguided tenets. Did you think my investigators are so stupid they would not find out you harbored a traitor?"

"I don't know any traitors."

Perhaps Becker underestimated Goodayle's political grit. "Michael … my intimate. You and Enrique Morales helped her when she fled America Prime. You cannot say you are unaware government officials and their families are not permitted to defect. Therefore, her temper tantrum has escalated into treason. If she had returned before this, I might have managed a pardon, argued her behavior merely a hormonal lapse of judgment. She is pregnant, I expect. However, the window of mercy is closing fast. I may have no recourse but to charge her for crimes against the state, along with anyone else involved."

Goodayle pitched forward, his face alarmingly ashen.

"Chairman Goodayle. Are you ill?"

"No." He shifted his stance and took a step closer, his fists balled. Would he strike his President-elect? Let him. Becker would end the matter once and for all. "What do want from me, Governor? You obviously are using my son as some kind of ploy."

Father's voice wafted on the air. "Keep your enemies on the defensive." He turned toward Becker and cocked a trigger finger, a signal for the constable to prepare for any hostility on Goodayle's part.

"I want your testimony against Fared. I will release Benjamin as soon as I have your signed affidavit. You'll be arrested, tried, and executed, of course. Benjamin will go free. Your life for his."

Goodayle stayed amazingly calm. "You think I would betray my brother to save my son? Benjamin is innocent. You have no proof against him. He is a Citizen now and has the right to a fair trial."

Edwin forced his ire inward. He would allow no Citizen, and certainly not this barely-washed outworlder, to speak to him with disrespect. "The law is very complex, Goodayle, and all of us are guilty of an infraction or two. Benjamin will remain in prison for as long as I wish it. Trials can be indefinitely postponed for any number of reasons. After the Preservation Act is passed, treason will be managed swiftly and without the onerous affair of judicial process."

Becker's frown threw Edwin off guard. He still needed the constable's support, at least until the presidency was secured.

"So you see, Mr. Chairman, I will win one way or another. However, I am willing to release Ahmed and Benjamin on one condition and pardon you in the process."

Goodayle sighed as he tilted his head—his profile tightened then sagged. "And what is that, Governor?"

"Tell me where Michael is."

"I ... honestly ... don't know. You ... killed ... the only ... man—"

Goodayle slumped to the floor in mid-sentence.

"Becker, attend him!"

He checked Goodayle's pulse. "He's alive. Looks like a stroke or heart attack. If you expect to use him at all, you'd better see he gets to a hospital."

"Very well. See to it immediately."

"And what explanation do I give the doctor?"

For a man in his position, Becker had no imagination. "Just say he collapsed on a tram. Surely, your staff can alter the feeds accordingly."

"As you wish, sir."

"I do need to extract information. See that he gets the best of care on my order. The public must think I've extended courtesy to a dignitary. No one must know he was here. The Humanitarians will try to say I stressed the man to death."

Becker's men carried the unconscious Goodayle through the secret passageway, his sudden illness a major interruption in a well-contrived plan. Had Goodayle's God declared war? Let Him. Edwin Rowlands, President-elect of United Earth, son of Milton Rowlands, was invincible.

CHAPTER FORTY-THREE
Sector Ten/America Prime

Jimmy Kinnear repeatedly struck his palm with his fist. Bridget was late. His heart wanted to tell her there'd be no escape to Western America, but she needn't be afraid. She and her da would be safe come morning. If he did, she'd be grateful and fall into his arms. The fantasies drove him to distraction.

No. She must believe the group plan was on course. Bridget and Falan were to feign a romantic interlude. As far as the audio surveillance would indicate, she ordered her playmate to vacate her suite and sleep elsewhere. As Falan and Bridget understood the plan, this dismissal would allow Jimmy to prepare for their escape in the morning. He must be careful to give no hint of his very different agenda.

Jimmy sighed at the rustle of Bridget's silk evening gown. Far more temptation than a man should endure. He'd forsake everything if she gave him the slightest hint she wanted him. Falan entered behind Bridget. They embraced as expected, yet their kiss seemed genuine.

Would Falan be her next intimate? Let them have one another. He deserved happiness, and Bridget needed a man to help raise Ian's son. A good match. Perhaps he'd endure hell a little better knowing Bridget was loved by someone he trusted. As if they suddenly remembered Jimmy was in the room, they faced him. Bridget slid into her role of a playmate's mistress. "As you can see, Gregory, I won't need you tonight. You may sleep in the hovercraft." Her dismissal, even a rehearsed one, whipped his heart.

"I understand, Mistress Cavanaugh." As he left, Falan and Bridget fell into another embrace.

Once outside the hotel, Jimmy sniffed the processed air, a hint of the putrid to those used to natural breezes. Citizens were the true outcasts, trapped inside an artificial sphere. He hurried his pace toward the platform. The Gregory implant would provide necessary freedom of transit within America Prime, a privilege afforded few memes.

He scanned the platform for other passengers. An African man stood nearby. He flipped his temporary identification card from side to side, his jaw taut, and his eyes fixed straight ahead. Was he a man or a meme? Perhaps he was a recent repatriate. Memes were not permitted to initiate conversation. Jimmy's curiosity bubbled—the man's face familiar.

He spoke. "Nice evening. Are you a Gregory?"

"Yes, I am."

"Seems the trams are running slow tonight."

Recognition dawned ... Tyrene Benedict of the Congo's outworld delegation. Had he recognized the famous general of the Highlands Badlands? Perhaps he said nothing as he was about his own mischief.

What business did he have in Sector One? He had no other status and should have been confined to the tents in Sector Ten.

A group of chatty Citizens crammed the platform just as a tram screeched to a halt. Jimmy made certain to be the last passenger to embark and took an unoccupied cube. He keyed in his destination, grateful for the few minutes of solitude.

Sometimes he wondered why a man was born into the times the Maker selected for him. A pity he did not know the world before upheaval upon upheaval scarred the face of Earth like a smallpox victim.

He remembered Grandmother Houlihan's scribbled words: millions lost with the first wave. Rowlands' assassination, though necessary, would bring political tsunamis—tidal waves that would reshape the world for the better, a vision for which he'd gladly die. If Rowlands' death caused the collapse of the Constitutional Government, so be it. The militias would rise, led by the Revolutionary Army and usher in a new era.

He had hoped for a better win. He'd wait until Ahmed was installed as Second. A good man, Fared would listen to the outworlds. His leadership would be just. He'd find a way to extend representation to the outworlds. Whatever fallout came, the result would have to be far better than a Rowlands' dictatorship—for surely the man would not rest until all of United Earth knelt at his feet.

The tram halted at the air dock, Jimmy's stop. If his unit had succeeded, all air docks would be in lock down. At least fifty men and women disembarked and formed a line. Good. The longer line would cause impatience. The guards would be distracted by the unrest and call for assistance from the other Sectors, including Sector Ten.

Jimmy checked his timepiece. Once again Grandmother Houlihan crossed his memory. She believed in an uncompromising morality. "The commandments, Jimmy, guide us," she'd said. She made him memorize all ten thou shalts and shalt nots. Why did they crash on him now?

Thou shalt not kill.

"Implant?" The officer's gruff command harbored him from useless self-incrimination.

The woman ahead of him, from her insignia, a pilot from the Alpine province, waved her hand over the micro as the next tram pulled onto the platform.

"I'll need to view your visual identification, too. The Highland Air Dock was sabotaged earlier. Security has been ordered to level four ... only Constable Becker can give clearance for any arrivals or departures."

Jimmy bristled with pride ... his band had succeeded.

He clicked on his fake transponder and in hushed, unintelligible tones, spoke to the officer who furiously clicked his way through upgraded security protocols. "I need to backtrack. My mistress has not relegated me to the hovercraft after all. Seems her bed is cold."

As Jimmy veered back to the tram, he caught the woman's exasperated squeal. "I assure you, officer, I have the highest security clearance."

If not for the scanners, Jimmy would permit a smile, the Alpine pilot's agitation opportune, though he probably could have returned to the tram without the diversion. A short ride would bring him to Sector Four platform near Eternal Pathways, closed and secluded until President Schumann arrived for his euthanasia. Gil Renault, Jimmy's most trusted operative in Western America, waited for him at the stop. They shook hands, and Jimmy examined the high-speed rover. "A beauty. America Prime Officers sure do ride in style."

Gil handed Jimmy a uniform and helmet. "Orders, General Kinnear?"

"The less you know, the safer you'll be. Do not veer from my instructions and do not ask questions."

Renault saluted and left. Jimmy rode alone into Sector Ten, like the proverbial moth to a flame, destined to die in the fire of his purpose.

CHAPTER FORTY-FOUR
Sector Two/America Prime

Angelina keyed in the shuttle's landing sequence and ignited the plasma shield to cloak her transport. She had six hours before the scanners would discover the craft. Once more she marveled at the Revolutionary Army's technological superiority over IEA inventors.

Before he dozed off, Angelina had told Carlos she volunteered for security duty. He'd held her, reluctant to let her go as if he sensed her lie. She figured when she left, the trip would be one way.

She checked her weapon charger, holstered her P-94, loaded her satchel with food rations and slipped a dagger into a sheath underneath her sleeve, an extra layer of protection never a poor choice. She tucked her hair under her cap. Hopefully, her black attire would be sufficient camouflage against the sub-city night. However, once inside Sector Ten, the nightglows would light her up like an ebony candle. She opened the hatch, took a deep breath and plunged into what might prove the worst mistake of her life.

She supposed every city's Sector Ten held the same risks to officers. Populated by forgotten repatriate candidates with no implants and illegal defectors who hoped to find escort into the outworld, the desperate masses proved to be unmanageable. Did America Prime house their factory memes in Sector Ten as well? She also supposed, as in the Highland Province, Sector Ten provided a good hideout for someone about to become a criminal. Instinct told her she'd find Jimmy there, why she'd agreed to partner with Savakis on this collar.

A tiny sliver of moonlight spread speckles of gray throughout the sub-city. Otherwise, the area remained pitch black, the dark spots as eerie as a horror movie feed. She'd be spooked if she believed in werewolves and vampires. She rubbed her dagger for reassurance.

What if Savakis had led her into a trap? She'd have to trust him. Rowlands might be a reptile, but he was still the President-elect. She'd not permit anyone, not even Jimmy Kinnear, to take the law into their own hands. Justice, though often slow, eventually triumphed.

She'd guessed most of Jimmy's plan except the when and how. Would he take the shot before or after the oath of office? Either way, an assassination would create chaos, what Jimmy counted on, the opportunity for his Revolutionary Army to take over. No secret Kinnear had treaties with every outworld militia in United Earth. An assassination would set the stage for global military takeover. No doubt he had the support of many in the IEA as well.

Rowlands' morals were not her concern. Though she despised the man, she respected the office. The Constitutional Government provided stability in a still shaken world. She'd not have Jimmy destroy what many gave their lives to build."

She should have listened to her gut where Savakis was concerned. Carlos would call her mistrust a "cop's instinct." If Savakis knew so much about the Revolutionary Army, why didn't he swarm them, wipe them out? Or maybe he only wanted the head. Cut off the head and the body will die, a tactic taught first-year cadets.

Hopefully, she would find Savakis before the sub-city scanners picked her up, their sweeps infrequent but none the less accurate. Given the increased protocols, the highest security would be centered near the Governor's mansion, the Presidential Palace, and tomorrow's potential parade routes. And of course, security would require the actual route not be divulged until the very last minute. Jimmy would need a cover until then, and given the influx of thousands of outworld repatriate candidates crammed into tent villages, Sector Ten would be the ideal spot to lay low.

What she knew, Savakis must know. With Jimmy's Mainframe expertise, he'd be able to hack privileged IEA security measures. If he were bent on assassination, he would succeed, unless stopped … permanently. Pity. Did she really want Jimmy dead?

She keyed an audio tone on her timepiece. Twenty-two hundred hours. Savakis should be here soon. She shrugged off the growing doubt. You are doing the right thing. Right does not always feel good. After all, Jimmy betrayed her first when he scorned the thing she most treasured—the law. Twice. First when he illegally defected, secondly, this planned assassination. Sadly, she would not betray a mere man, but a movement. One she had begun to understand, though beyond her ability to accept. Reform might be needed—however, not Jimmy's way.

She'd have stayed a little longer for Carlos' sake … and, if the truth were known, she enjoyed the rush of a mission edged with danger like the air dock raid, her boots charred by a close brush with fire. Foolish Angus pushed her away and positioned himself to take the full front of the blast. She scooped him up, and they escaped inches ahead of the fireball. Fortunately, they only sustained a few minor burns. As per Jimmy's order, no life had been lost except for a few mindless memes who ignored the sirens and refused to evacuate.

The hours-long celebration proved to be a perfect diversion. She'd slugged down equal amounts of ale—her resolve, however, sobered her. While the rest slept in a drunken slumber, she'd managed to contact Savakis.

A snap, and then a gray outline emerged from the shrub. She raised her P-94 in readiness. "Stay where you are or I'll fire."

"If I don't shoot first. You think I'd meet up with the infamous Angelina Bartelli unarmed?"

Angelina lowered her weapon. "Agent Nemo Savakis—a legend in the flesh."

"We have ten minutes before the sub-city scanners engage again. Let's save the pleasantries and tell me where I can find Kinnear. When we've apprehended him, I'll reinstate you as promised."

"I suspect he's disguised as a pilot of some kind. He's with Governor Cavanaugh's delegation."

"Then why did you think we'd find him in Sector Ten?"

"Copper instinct. Trust me, Nemo."

Savakis smiled. "I wondered why Bridget Cavanaugh would want to bring a playmate. Word is, she is the belle of the ball and has won the favor of the President-elect. Reportedly, she is in the frequent company of her father's bodyguard, Falan Riley. We've checked the genealogy reports. He's Kinnear's half-brother. Not hard to connect the dots. I expect Riley's an insider. They're all a bunch of hooligans."

"Nemo, you're wrong. These people are not criminals, thugs, or murderers. They consider themselves at war, armed, and ready for battle. If someone dies, it's considered collateral damage."

Savakis sneered. "Like my brother."

Had she teamed up with a man more interested in revenge than the prevention of an assassination?

"What is Jimmy's plan? Details, Bartelli, or I'll signal my team to arrest you right now. We're running out of time."

"Yes, we are."

Clarity descended at the speed of light. She'd been duped yet again. One more mistake to add to a lifetime of miscalculations. At least she could rid herself of this one. With swiftness learned from years of practice, she plunged the knife into Savakis' abdomen. He fell without a whimper. She removed his implant before the Mainframe registered his flat line. "Sorry, Nemo. Too many officers in this quest."

She tossed the implant aside, cleaned the knife, and stared at Savakis' body, unaccustomed to this strange aura of guilt. She had taken lives before, and never gave their deaths a second thought … all in the line of duty. Where did duty rest now? Savakis was driven by hatred, not justice. Besides, she and she alone owned the right to kill Jimmy Kinnear.

She rummaged through the agent's satchel for something useful. Ah … a miniature blaster and a micro. She didn't have Jimmy's skill to hack IEA protocols. She'd have to steal Savakis' codes. Think Angelina. IEA codes followed a logical pattern. Savakis would, too. She entered a series of numbers and letters.

Success. Too easy, Savakis had used his badge number.

She minimized the ADAM icon then accessed the latest IEA arrests and orders. A data stream projected. The President-elect's gala was officially over, and officers were instructed to be vigilant about all departures, strict adherence to the curfews expected. The Highland Air Dock disaster had prompted even tighter security for all United Earth air docks. No transports could leave unless they had been given clearance by Constable Becker.

What was Jimmy thinking? How could he escape if all shuttles were grounded? That's it! Jimmy hadn't meant to escape. Instead, he'd become the sacrificial lamb. He would only get one clear shot before quick and decisive retaliation. Where and how would he launch his murder-suicide?

Three minutes before the scanners kicked on. Now or never. Either forget this mission, go back to the shuttle, or proceed to certain death. She raised her weapon and ran toward the portal that led to Sector Ten.

CHAPTER FORTY-FIVE
America Prime Detention Center

Ahmed whisked a tiny worm off his prison-issue jumpsuit. He had lived alone, preferred to dine alone, and had remained alone in his bed these past two decades since Anna left him. Solitude, one of the few pleasures afforded him after a long day of two-stepping a madman's idiocies.

This prison solitude, however, was far too entrenched. Not a word, a smile, a touch, a micro, or a transponder. An inmate stared at gray concrete walls as cold as the air he breathed. Social deprivation of this magnitude seemed far too cruel. At least his sterile cot, more like a granite perch made of bacteria-resistant crushed stone was surprisingly comfortable, perhaps the only luxury an inmate would experience. Ironic—the designer now tasted the very essence of his creation. A hard way to learn its weaknesses.

Since the guards confiscated his time piece upon his arrest, he had no way to know the hour. What he wouldn't give for the darkness of the outworld about now. An encased ceiling crystal provided constant illumination—a blaring, blinding, unrelenting, bombarding beam. There were no windows, no openings of any kind save the vent holes, big enough for the worms to invade, but not big enough for a man to slip through. Meals were as unpredictable as everything else—an attempt to disorient. Confusion made one dependent, and a dependent prisoner proved to be more compliant. In theory, the whole concept seemed reasonable, until Ahmed found himself at the opposite end of the program.

Benjamin told Ahmed the prison had two systems, one for Citizens, and the harsher, for outworlders. Ahmed found small comfort to know this time around Benjamin would fare better than before.

Booted steps echoed near the cell door. A meal? Or—he laughed to think he actually hoped for it—an interrogation? Respite from the isolation. He turned toward the click-clack of sequential keying. As the door opened, he hauled his form to a stand. Constable Becker stepped into his cell accompanied by three agents. Did he think the obese Ahmed Fared a threat to a mature but still young athlete like Becker? A thinner, more muscular man would think twice before he picked a fight with the Constable, his only unhealthy habit an occasional deleteriously laced chocolate bar. Ahmed enjoyed a perverse pride in being considered a significant threat. "Constable Becker, am I so dire a menace you brought a squad to question me?"

"You men can wait down the corridor. I'll be fine. Mr. Fared and I are going to have a little confab."

Ahmed stretched his muscles to avoid atrophy. "I'm sure your visit is not motivated by a need for casual conversation."

"Hardly. I'll cut to the chase. Jacob Goodayle collapsed not more than twenty minutes ago."

Another ploy to make their prisoner talk?

"He lives. He's at the hospital, attended by our best medical staff. The President-elect will use every means at his disposal to assure your brother receives optimum care."

"You are not here merely to tell me news about my brother."

Constable Becker laughed. "We are not heartless, Mr. Fared."

"That remains to be seen."

"The President-elect wants to know where to find Michael Grafton. A general location is all we need. For the information, Governor Rowlands is willing to overlook your involvement in her treason. He understands Michael is like a daughter to you."

"Is Benjamin aware of his father's condition?"

"He will be told in due time."

"Benjamin is of no use to you. He was unaware of Michael Grafton's euthanasia."

Becker snorted. "You and I both know her so-called suicide was a ruse and that she is hiding. Grafton confessed. He dropped Michael over the Border Community perimeter at the coordinates you provided him."

A confession no doubt obtained through torture.

Becker stood, his stubby nose an inch from Ahmed's face, his leek-laced breath enough to suffocate a man. Might as well play Becker's game. How much more had they been able to piece together? "Sean Grafton? Didn't know the man very well, but our paths did cross at Esther Feinmann's euthanasia."

Becker rolled his fists. "I came here in the hopes we'd have an intelligent conversation. Why do you insist on games—games endangering Benjamin Goodayle's life as well as yours? Your executions are scheduled for tomorrow immediately after passage of the Preservation Act."

"Without trial? We are both Citizens."

"Under the new law, the President-elect has the power to waive the right of trial in matters of treason."

He had no fear of his own death—this world long ago ceased to charm him. Benjamin had barely had a chance to live. Perhaps the time had come to cash in on Devereux's gift. "Is this conversation being recorded?"

"The scanners are off at my request. Say what you will."

"I don't know where Michael is. If I did assist a defector, the Border Community would have provided the best cover. The pity is if Michael had managed to get there, and they, in turn, helped her to find some other hiding place, Governor Rowlands has massacred the only people who knew where to find her."

"Nice try, Mr. Fared. Something tells me you have a good hunch where they would have taken her next."

Ahmed turned and faced his accuser. "I'll tell you this, Constable Becker. Be certain our soon-to-be President hears this. I have evidence if made public might result in serious charges against him, and could lead to prison or worse. At a minimum, his political career will be over."

Becker rose and shrugged his shoulders. "Evidence, you say. About what? Where is this evidence?

"Safe. Even when I was young, moral conduct seemed old-fashioned. My father believed the ills of our world were like those of Noah. Mankind had lost any concept of morality. Yet, from where I stand, the rape of a minor is still considered a despicable crime. The Humanitarian Party will be outraged to learn an elected official committed such acts. They will demand he be punished to the full extent of the law, President or not."

"And you have proof?"

"Irrefutable."

"What kind of proof?"

Ahmed crossed his arms. "First, I want Benjamin released. Then I'll tell you and the President-elect all you want to know."

"I will advise President-elect Rowlands."

"By the way, what time is it, Constable Becker?"

"The dawn of a new day."

CHAPTER FORTY-SIX
Ambassador Suites/America Prime

Bridget awoke drenched in sweat. This dream was too real. "Da!"

She checked her timepiece—one in the morning. Inauguration Day and soon their party would be heading for the Northern Province. Falan stirred from his deep slumber. Too much the gentleman, he'd feigned a drunken state to fool the audio scanners.

He sat on the edge of the bed. "What's wrong, Bridget?"

She tweaked his cheek. "A bad dream. Go back to sleep."

How she despised these antics, though she understood the necessity. Political life, while intoxicating, would never be a substitute for freedom, to be one's true self, not limited to those times your bodyguard managed the occasional hack.

Bridget traced her lips as she remembered Falan's kiss. How could she desire another man so soon after Ian's passing? She craved for a man to hold her, to rub her face against a freshly shaven chin.

For now, she'd wait, not rush to give her love away like a moldy sandwich.

This present pretense cheapened her. Why had she agreed to it?

Falan rose, strutted toward the closet, grabbed a robe for himself and threw one to her. "Here, put this on. Then tell me about this dream."

She pointed toward the audio scanners.

Falan took the hint and managed a short blackout. "Done."

"Something's wrong, Falan. I sense it. Something's happened to Da."

He stroked her hair. "I'm sure he's fine. If you want, I'll check his room."

"I'll go with you. I have to see for myself."

"We have a few minutes before the interrupted feed corrects itself. We might as well get dressed. We're supposed to meet Jimmy at the air dock in two hours."

Bridget put on the travel pantaloons she had set on the chair the night before. When dressed, Falan holstered his P-74 and slipped his micro into his satchel. They accessed Da's suite through the common lounge. He waved the duplicate key to Da's room, and Bridget listened for his snores. Nothing. She nearly screamed the instruction. "Lights."

No sign of Da, and the bed had not been slept in. A white envelope stood propped against a desk lamp. "It's addressed to me."

"Perhaps this will explain his absence."

Anxiety flailed at her like an errant meme. "What does this mean? Where is my father?"

As Falan scanned the letter, his pallor grayed. "Bridget, I'm sorry."

Instinct told her Da was dead. The letter merely explained how. Rowlands had used her illegal pregnancy to push Da into the Euthanasia Chamber. She rubbed her abdomen. "Falan, Da sacrificed himself for me. My pardon came at too great a price."

CHAPTER FORTY-SEVEN
America Prime Detention Center

Benjamin fumed at the injustice. The IEA officer hadn't bothered with the arrest protocols afforded Citizens. No indictment. No appointed counsel. He rubbed his wrists, still sore from the grips thrust around them during his arrest. What charges had been filed against him this time? What happened to Ahmed? Where was Christine? Pops?

He tried to rest on the excuse of a bed. Useless. He stretched then did pushups against the wall. His stomach groaned from hunger. At least he would eat once a day instead of the rations outworlders received every third day.

Why hadn't he been interrogated yet? He closed his eyes, but the overhead crystal beam still burned his sockets.

Three clicks right, four clicks left, five more to the right, one to the left. Perhaps counsel had been appointed. Or, maybe Uncle Ahmed had negotiated his release. A squeak and a slide, then a man entered. Benjamin had never met Constable Becker but recognized him from his micro-projections. How should one act in the presence of United Earth's IEA's director? Bow, stand, or stay put?

He rose from anger, not respect. "Constable Becker, why have I been detained? I am a Citizen. I demand counsel."

A chair-carrying goon followed behind Becker. What kind of man couldn't carry his own chair? Becker sat and crossed one leg over the other. "As soon as the Preservation Act is passed, you'll be charged with treason and stripped of all your rights as a Citizen. Until then, we have the right to hold a Citizen on the grounds of suspicion ... with careful manipulation ... indefinitely."

"Treason? Ridiculous. I've done nothing wrong, except maybe pray in Christine's house, I thought praying was still legal in a private residence?"

"Yes, private domiciliary prayers are still legal, for now. Your uncle abetted a defector, Michael Grafton. You are guilty by association."

"I thought she was dead."

"Hardly. She faked her death and escaped. The defection of a government official or an intimate of a government official is considered treason. And anyone who assists in such defection is also guilty of treason."

"Will President Rowlands execute an innocent man?"

Becker rose and jabbed Benjamin to the shoulder. "I suppose you are innocent of intent. No matter. In cases of treason, under the Preservation Act, any known associate of the offender receives the same punishment."

"Where's Christine? My father?"

"Relax, Benjamin. Christine is safe at home. As for your father, I do have some unfortunate news."

Benjamin slumped. He had just lost his mother. What if Pops were dead, too?

"Chairman Goodayle has suffered a stroke."

Benjamin gulped.

"Apparently, a mild one. He is on the mend and expected to make a complete recovery. The President-elect will pay for all your father's medical expenses. So you see, we are not unsympathetic, and we wish Chairman Goodayle a speedy recovery. Would you like to see him, Benjamin?"

Did Becker think his prisoner a fool? "You already know I do. What do you want from me?"

Becker's sneer widened into a sickly, prideful grin. "Tell us where we can find Michael Grafton."

"I've never met Mistress Grafton. I only know of her through her editorial projections. Why would I know where she is? Can't the President-elect take better care of his intimate?" A stupid thing to say. If he found his way out of this current mess, maybe he should reconsider a political career. He'd never been good at chess games. "I'm telling you, Constable Becker, I don't know where she is. My uncle keeps me out of his personal business."

"Maybe so. However, you have made trips with him to the Network to see your father. Perhaps the business of Michael Grafton has arisen?"

"My job is to record meetings and enter data into the Mainframe as instructed by my uncle. Half the time, I don't understand what the notes mean. I'm a government aide, not a politician. A meme could do my job."

Becker snorted. "All that is true. However, as the Chairman's son, you know how defections work. Think hard, Benjamin. Let us say, hypothetically, your uncle did assist Michael. Where would he hide her?"

"I don't know."

Becker's smile disappeared. "That, my son, is a lie. I think you do know. You've helped your father hide many defectors. Where, Benjamin? Think of Christine. A pity if she's scheduled for termination, too."

"Christine is a loyal Citizen. You wouldn't dare risk having the whole Humanitarian Party convene at the Presidential Palace."

"The President-elect is not interested in bloodshed. He merely wants to find his intimate. He will exchange mercy for information."

Hate swelled like a river at flood-stage. Anger dispelled reason as he pushed Becker against the cell wall. "For the last time, I don't know where Michael Grafton is. Why won't you believe me? I've done nothing wrong."

Three guards opened the door. Two held Benjamin's arms back while a third injected a hypo. Every muscle quickly numbed. He fell to the floor, still conscious, but immobile.

"Now, why can't you be reasonable, boy? You want to see your father. I want to know where Michael Grafton is. Seems we should be able to help each other."

Might as well tell them. By now, Enrique had hidden Michael somewhere else. There would be no betrayal in that admission. Even IEA knew the Border Community was one of the first base of operations for defectors. "Fine. What do I care about Michael, anyway? I suspect they've taken her to the Border Community. Why not ask Enrique?"

"Benjamin, Benjamin, Benjamin. Do you think we are incompetent at our jobs? Of course, we suspected the Border Community. We already know she's no longer there."

So, they'd searched and found nothing.

Becker's loud snorts irritated more than a buzzing fly. "Unfortunately, Mayor Morales is deceased."

Becker helped Benjamin to his bed. "I should terminate you on the spot for your impulsive outburst. However, I like your father. Think long and hard. I'll be back."

CHAPTER FORTY-EIGHT
Medical Center/America Prime

Jacob tugged at the restraints. Where was he? Why couldn't he move his legs? He tried to speak but could only moan. What had happened to him?

A row of micros chirped a stream of vital signs. How did he end up in a hospital? A mistake, certainly. Only Citizens had access to medical care. He had no money, nor did he have any means to transact business.

He gazed at his palm. How had he received an implant without the benefit of ceremony or thumbprint? He had no possessions to barter in exchange for these extravagant services: a private room, a sterile bed, and a team of nurses in and out of his room. He'd have to sell his soul to pay for all this.

A micro-toting female meme dressed in medical reds entered. "You are awake, Chairman Goodayle. I am Monica One, the head nurse of this facility. The doctor will be in shortly to explain everything." She took his pulse and spoke terms into the micro he'd heard Amelia use when with a patient.

Another woman entered, more human than a meme. She too wore a starched, red uniform. The caped jacket indicated prestige. "I'm Dr. Newell. How are you feeling?"

Words perfectly formed in his mind, came out garbled like a hacked feed.

Dr. Newell found a cloth and wiped the spittle from the corners of Jacob's mouth. "Your speech impairment is temporary. You suffered a mild stroke. Apparently, the episode was preceded by an undiagnosed myocardial infarct, also mild. You are otherwise healthy and in good physical shape for a man your age, so I expect the residual damage to be minimal, some aphasia and short-term memory loss perhaps. Otherwise, your cognitive abilities are fully intact. We've scheduled your transfer to the rehab ward for tomorrow."

She examined his eyes, ears, and throat. "The bio scans indicate you have no contusions or blood clots."

She stroked his feet. "Feel anything?"

He nodded. His mind said, it tickles ... his words were incomprehensible.

"Try to move your leg."

His useless limb moved a quarter of an inch.

"Very good."

Good? Why didn't the Maker let him join Amelia? Why put him flat on his back, a useless lump of clay. How could he help Benjamin and Ahmed from a hospital bed? Before Jacob could toilet himself again, Benjamin and Ahmed would be executed.

Doctor Newell rattled off a series of medical terms to Monica One, who keyed them into the micro. "Don't worry, Chairman Goodayle. You are getting the best medical care money can buy. Courtesy of our President-elect. The Inauguration will begin in a few hours. Some of the patients will observe the ceremonies in the solarium. I would prefer you stay here. I'm sure a Monica will give you reports as events unfold."

Jacob pulled on the restraints and managed one intelligible word. "Remove."

"Of course." She released the clamps and held Jacob's hand in hers. "Try to squeeze my hand."

He managed a weak squeeze in return.

"Good. Don't worry. Your strength should return in a week or two. I'll ask a Monica to help you sit up. Would you like to try some liquid nourishment?"

Jacob mouthed his thanks. Dr. Newell appeared as attractive as she did kind. Gray streaks highlighted her black hair. Ebony skin suggested heritage from the Congo Province in contrast to her Germanic accent.

"I'll see that someone brings you a tray." With that, she left.

As for Rowlands' generosity, what did he expect to gain? Enrique might have taken Michael to any one of a dozen hideouts including the Arctic Province. The most likely place would have been the Sierras via the underground tunnels. No need to tell the government what they already knew, that the Sierras linked the Reformation and militia groups. Did Rowlands plan to invade the Sierras next?

Aha! Perhaps this was less about Michael and more about control. The Treasure Keepers, the last bastion of religious resistance, was a constant thorn to a Caesar-like Rowlands. The IEA's strength rested in its air power, useless in the Sierra winds—so harsh, an air dock could not be established. If IEA were to attack, the only access would be via the heavily guarded tunnels. Perhaps Rowlands wanted to know the schematics in order to invade.

If he told Rowlands what he wanted to know, Ahmed and Benjamin would be free. By now, the Treasure Keepers would have learned of the Border Community massacre, and Michael would have been safely transferred to one of the Northern Provinces. Why not divulge what he knew, which was very little, probably not enough to be of benefit. Besides, the treasures were mere things: paintings on canvases and scratches on paper. Something to consider. He sighed with resignation. His integrity, all he had left, demanded silence. Not hard for the moment since he couldn't talk.

He looked up as Kyle entered the room. "I'd hoped to see you under better circumstances, Jacob."

His mind said, "So good to see you, Kyle." Words failed him.

"Don't try to talk, old friend. I only have a few minutes anyway. I've been assigned as your orderly thanks to the kindness of my supervisor, Monica One." His eyes roamed the room—in search of scanners, perhaps. "I can't say much. Caroline's uncle has caught the news feeds. I'm so sorry for all your losses, Jacob. I share your worry for Ahmed and Benjamin."

"Carol …? Pe … ter?"

"They are well. Peter's operation was a success, and Caroline complains she is not as fashionable as City women. She finds solace in her job as Cafeteria Supervisor. She works the day shift, and I work nights. Bernard decided to retire so he can help with Peter's care since our shifts overlap. We have our own apartment in the same building as her uncle's place. It's small, especially compared to the manse, but comfortable. We have all we need and Peter is alive. Ahmed has worked tirelessly to help us settle. Most who repatriate rot in Sector Ten. We are very grateful."

Two Monicas entered. They were nearly identical to Monica One, except each had different hair texture and color. Jacob mused at the Maker's ingenuity. No amount of DNA manipulation could alter a meme's uniqueness … no two were exactly alike.

The Monicas helped him into a quasi-upright position. One pinched a straw and held a vial of water to his lips. The other lifted his hands and placed them around the vial. "Do you think you can hold this?"

He struggled to raise his arms. "No. Can't."

The Monicas both smiled. One said, "Don't worry, Chairman Goodayle. These symptoms are temporary."

Dr. Newell promised returned vigor as well. Was this good news? If the Maker were kind, death would find him before it claimed his son and brother.

CHAPTER FORTY-NINE
Sector Ten/America Prime

Angelina slipped behind a brick tenement to avoid the scanners. If she slithered from wall to wall and kept in the shadows away from the night glows, she might be able to navigate undetected. She gazed through the glass dome at the split sky. Daylight would soon filter through. Harder to hide.

By now, IEA had located Savakis' body and there would be a wide area search for his killer. The hunter now became the hunted. "The perpetrator of violent acts," Cavanaugh once spoke, "will die as they live." She suspected the words prophetic in her case.

If she found Jimmy before he sent the world into another cataclysmic spin, perhaps her last act on earth would count for something larger than herself. She pulled out the forged micro and risked a brief projection against the wall, hopefully sufficiently hidden from any passerby. "ADAM, tell me where I can find Jimmy Kinnear?"

He droned his pre-programmed response. "Insufficient data. Please restate your inquiry."

"Never mind." She flicked off the micro.

She gazed at the cracks of natural light on the horizon. She had wandered this sector for five hours. The shields would degrade soon, and the shuttle would be detected. She'd be found and shot. Her only redemption would be to kill Jimmy before he killed Rowlands.

She spotted a rover parked outside a tenement. IEA issue, top grade. No Sector Ten patrol would be provided with a transport of this classification. Not likely the officer's residence either, IEA pay scales were generous enough to afford housing in the better Sectors.

She reached into her satchel—three slices of wafer bread and a cloned orange. Could be enough for a bribe. Most Sector Ten residents would sell their mother for a piece of fruit.

A thin waif, perhaps nine or ten, came out from the suspected tenement. Angelina drew in a breath for courage and brought herself into the open. The child raised an accusatory finger. "You IEA?"

"No. I'm not IEA. I'm looking for a friend. A friend to you, too. He's a head taller than anybody you know with dark hair and a smile like moonlight. Seen him?"

"What you got to offer?"

"An orange and a slice of bread."

"I ain't eaten for three days."

Angelina tossed him the food.

"Yep. I seen him." He pointed toward the third level.

She located the apartment indicated by the kid, and hesitated at the portal. Should she blast her way in or coax Jimmy out?

At the click of the latch she ducked into an alcove. Jimmy, all right, dressed in IEA garb. The weapon wasn't standard … different from Jimmy's stash—yet familiar. A prototype?

Did Jimmy plan to pass himself off as security? She stepped into the open, weapon raised. "Sorry, Jimmy." She fired, and a piece of her heart burned as he fell to the ground.

CHAPTER FIFTY
Sector One/America Prime

Bridget had cried the better part of the pre-dawn hours, not concerned if scanners caught every loud sob. Da was dead. His letter a lie—that he was tired of life and he was going into the chamber, that Governor Rowlands had already given him a psychiatric override, that by the time she found this letter, his ashes would be scattered over the nearly deserted outworld.

Falan had not left her side, his presence some comfort. "Lies, Falan. All lies. Da was not depressed. He looked forward to being a grandfather."

She should have realized the trap herself, seen the signs. She was a diplomat's daughter and knew how politics worked—a favor for a favor, a life for a life. Had she been so naïve to think her pardon had been so easily obtained? And the President-elect's sudden interest in her could not be coincidental, probably more politically motivated than falling victim to her charms. How could she possibly join with a man as repugnant as a boa constrictor? She'd played this silly game for Da's sake. Now Da was dead.

She wiped the last of her tears and signaled Falan to disrupt the Mainframe. "I'd have gone to the chamber myself rather than let Da give up his life for mine."

"He loved you, Bridget. He believed this was the only way to assure your freedom and engineered the escape plan to throw you off track. None of us knew his real reason for the ruse. Not even Jimmy. Rowlands might be a scoundrel, but he is true to his word. You're safe now, fully pardoned and free. It's what Governor Cavanaugh wanted."

"Free for what? What will I do? I can't go back to the Highlands, can I? Da's Second will be the next one forced into the chamber. And Rowlands will be certain to appoint a puppet in Da's place."

Falan wrapped his arms around her, a buoy in her sea of grief. "The President-elect likes you."

She gave him a slight shove. "Do you think me empty enough to enter into a familial contract with a man like Rowlands, witness Michael's death, and be a surrogate mum to her child? No Falan. I'll not be Rowlands' intimate—no matter how luxurious the benefits. Take me from here. I don't care where or how."

"I will, Bridget, soon. Here's what I suggest. We'll attend the Inauguration, and you'll pretend to be interested in Rowlands' offer of a familial contract. Ask him to keep me on as your bodyguard."

"Why can't we still escape? Jimmy's waiting for us, isn't he?"

"I don't know where Jimmy is. We've lost contact."

Jimmy had either betrayed them or been discovered. Either way, she and Falan had been deserted. "You promise I'll not have to give myself to Rowlands? I'd rather be eaten alive by sandworms."

Falan smiled. How she wished she could love him with the same devotion he showed her. Why did the memory of a moonlight smile and long legs pull her from a saner choice? When she gazed into Falan's eyes, she only saw Jimmy's. She loved the wrong brother. There she'd admitted it. She loved Jimmy Kinnear. Perhaps she had always loved him. The shame of that truth drove her to near madness. Her love for a Reformist cost Da his life. She would never give herself to Jimmy, align herself with the Revolutionary Army, and throw away the freedom Da bought for her.

Rowlands couldn't terminate her if she refused him. She was a fully pardoned Citizen with rights, at least until the new President managed to have them rescinded one by one. She would campaign for a delegate position, make a life for herself and her child, and be dependent on no one. She gazed into Falan's sympathetic eyes. "By now, Da's Second has been promoted to governor, and, if Rowlands has his way, he'll insist on Paddington as the new Second. That leaves an empty delegate seat. What do you think? Would you be willing to campaign for me?"

"You'll be a fine delegate, Bridget." Falan pulled her in close, and his lips trembled in obvious want of her. "Would you let me campaign as your intimate, Bridget?" He held a hand to her abdomen. "The lad will need a da to raise him. I'm up for the job if you'll have me. I am after all, legally responsible as his surrogate guardian."

Da, no doubt, seeded the idea into Falan's mind before he went into the chamber. Shouldn't she honor her father's wishes? She'd learn to love Falan in time. She certainly admired him. Wouldn't that be enough? "You know any lass would be blessed to have you as her man—"

Falan put a finger to her lips. "Ssh, Bridget. I know you don't love me as you did Ian. I'd never expect you to. We would be good together, you and I. You're a smart lass, and we both know the government inside out. Can't you picture it, Bridget? Together we could turn the world back to the Accord—a bloodless coup."

He made perfect sense. Why then did she hesitate? "In the Maker's good time, Falan ... not now. First, I need to be more independent. I'll still need a good friend to counsel me now and again."

Falan embraced her once more. "I'll die a happy man simply to stand in your shadow."

"Do you think Rowlands will approve my run for delegate?"

"The man is lovesick for you. He would approve you for any position you ask. Granted he'll stoop to no end to manipulate your political passion to suit his agenda."

Falan's micro buzzed, and Gil Renault's form projected. "Go ahead, Gil. Be quick. This blackout is about to expire."

"We've received intelligence inside IEA that Rowlands is using Mistress Grafton's disappearance as an excuse to raid the Sierras. Constable Becker suspects she is hidden there."

Falan's face whitened. "Thanks for the information, Gil."

More deaths. More losses? Bridget wiped away a new wave of tears. "If Rowlands invades the Sierras, civil war will be a certainty. They are aligned with Jimmy. Maybe that's where he's disappeared to. To start a war."

"For the moment, Rowlands has no jurisdiction, and Schumann is disinterested in the province. Rowlands can take no action until he is officially declared President."

"He will destroy the treasures, too?"

"I honestly don't know. The man is beyond insane ... an avalanche of unpredictability. Sometimes I wish someone would take a P-74 and end this nightmare once and for all."

"Ssh, Falan. An assassination will solve nothing. There must be another way."

CHAPTER FIFTY-ONE
Sierra Province

Indecision conquered at last, Michael Grafton clenched her fists. She had paced for hours, the question repeated in her heart with each step. "What would Grandfather want me to do?"

Francesco advised she should wait the night before she decided. "Thanks to the funnel clouds, United Earth ignores us. Our tunnels are heavily guarded. We are impenetrable. However, for your safety, we can arrange your transport to the Andes Wilderness via hoverboat."

"What if I decide to return to America Prime?"

"Not a course we'd recommend, Mistress Grafton. If you insist, we will contact our operatives on Sanchez Mountain. The President-elect will certainly arrange for your safe passage home where you'll be arrested and most likely executed."

There was Jade to consider, the reasons she left America Prime in the first place. The Andes Wilderness was as humid as the Sierra was dry, the mildew deadly if ingested. On the plus side, the area, considered as inhabitable as the Sierras, was free from IEA patrols.

On the other hand, so long as Edwin lived, he'd not give up his search and would continue to spew his revenge on any who helped her. Was her freedom worth the sacrifice of millions? One assurance. He'd not harm Jade. He'd let her live until she was born.

As anticipated, Marietta was up and at work with the pre-dawn. She crooked her head to the side. "You will return to America Prime, no?"

"Yes."

CHAPTER FIFTY-TWO
Sector One/America Prime

Edwin checked his timepiece. Only a few hours more.

As was his custom, he ate little before or during a gala.

Sydney entered with his attire. Too bad his generation was scheduled for deletion. Edwin rather liked the way his Sidney strutted about like the valets of old, laid out his master's clothes, rubbed his shoulders and back, and possessed a genuine interest in the ritualistic review of his master's daily schedule. Funny, he hadn't thought of his Sidney as an antique, like his neoclassical statues.

Sidney's morning ritual was programmed as perfectly as his timepiece. Would a newer butler know his master's nuances as well as his Sidney?

Perhaps he should plan for Sidney's euthanasia before he wore out. He already showed tufts of gray at the temples. Planned obsolescence still pushed the markets—so much for modernization. Sidneys would be destroyed to make room for the next innovation, as would the next generation of butler memes. Such was the way of the world. One must adapt ... and embrace the new.

Sydney removed Edwin's empty tray. Alone again, he ruled his thoughts toward this morning's guest list while visions of Bridget tickled his desires. By now, she knew of his bargain with Cavanaugh and would most likely cringe at Edwin's advances. Let her. He'd manage a way to whittle her resistance.

Besides, Schumann technically gave the pardon. Edwin merely engineered the deal. Cavanaugh knew he had no other choice. Life for life. Once the Preservation Act was passed, a pardon would be far more difficult to impart. In time, Bridget would come to understand the necessity of Cavanaugh's agreement and hate Edwin less for his part.

He'd win Bridget by charm or by manipulation, one way or another; once he settled Michael's illegal defection, Bridget would become his next intimate. What would be the icing on her cake ... the lure to his den? Like most women, she enjoyed baubles and fashion. However, material things did not define her.

The idea struck him like a vein of gold. Ian had been the leader of the Reformation Party. They were too few to affect his agenda. Why not set up his widow as its new voice? Edwin would offer Bridget a seat in Congress ... give her opportunity to write new law. As the President's intimate, no one would vote against her, her election assured. Her desire for reform would be the magnet to his bed.

Sidney's rap at his door put an end to the delightful fantasies. "Enter."

He handed Edwin a micro.

"What is this? You know micros are not allowed in my den."

"Sir, you have a most unusual hail from the Sierra Province marked urgent."

Edwin examined the hail source. "How did a transmission get here from there with Governor Sanchez in America Prime?"

"I really don't know, sir. I am only a butler."

"Yes, yes, of course, Sidney. Carry on."

As Sidney left, Edwin logged on, and EVE projected. "Do you wish to accept the hail, Governor Rowlands?"

"Yes. Yes."

Transmissions from the Sierra Province required a special underground cable used only by the governor, an antiquated system from earlier in the century. Someone must have hacked into the governor's communications modem … a risky maneuver or one done in desperation. EVE projected a text with Michael's words: I want to come home. Respond immediately.

"Transfer to image projection."

Despite her bedraggled appearance, the sight of her pierced him. "Well, well, well. The prodigal returns. Does she want a pardon? Why would I grant you one now that I know where you are?"

Eyes of the purest blue misted. "I heard about the Border Community. Why? Those people only wanted to help me, they were not seditious."

"I offered everyone repatriation. The Border Community refused. They paid the ultimate price for their dissension … as you will."

"Your threats don't frighten me, Edwin."

"What do you want, Michael?"

A wretched desire for her drove him to near senselessness.

"I'll come back under these conditions: First, you release Ahmed Fared and Benjamin Goodayle—immediately. Ahmed is only guilty of being my friend. Benjamin is completely innocent. I want a full pardon for Sean Grafton, as well as Ives."

"Ives? Even I think he's a greedy infringement to society."

"Yes. Ives. Regardless of his lack of integrity, he is innocent in my faked euthanasia."

"The man is a clown."

"He's no threat."

"I know. Out of respect for President Schumann's euthanasia, both Grafton and Ives have already been released to resume their occupations. Under close scrutiny, of course."

"I'd hoped as much."

As cunning as she was beautiful, Edwin feared what else she might request "A first request usually signifies another is close behind. What else do you want?"

"There is to be no reprisal against the Sierra Province."

"I'll consider foregoing retaliation. Tell me, are you still pregnant? The Macabre drug did not cause you to abort?"

"Sean had medications to minimize the effect of the drug. The doctors here have confirmed all is well. Jade will be her name, one I've grown fond of."

A twang of pride at pending fatherhood unnerved him. He must check this emotion. "And you'll accept whatever punishment the law deems necessary?"

"You will let my pregnancy reach term?"

"Of course, what kind of monster do you take me for?"

"I don't know what you're capable of anymore."

Should he consider her terms? "Hypothetically, if I do agree to your requests—"

"I will surrender to whatever punishment you deem appropriate. If you dispatch a shuttle to Sanchez Mountain, I can be in your custody within the hour."

He didn't need to agree to anything. Constable Becker could manage a retaliating attack. Father's words echoed in his heart. "Haste, especially when angry, too often produces clumsy results."

Michael had been deep into Treasure Keeper's territory. Her knowledge would be invaluable, a workable excuse to stay her execution until Jade was born. "I'd like to know how you managed this transmission."

"Honestly, I don't understand the mechanics. These people are extremely resourceful. No more discussion. Do you agree to my terms of surrender or not?"

He traced her lips. How did a mere holographic image evoke his want for her? "I am almost convinced. However, there is the matter of Excelsior Media."

"What of it."

"I've already submitted a civil suit to examine your sanity since you willed Excelsior to Barry. I doubt the High Court will rule in your favor and grant a meme property. The legal ripples would bring down the Constitution. However, courts are burdensome and time-consuming. Now that I can prove you're alive and prove you are a traitor, your properties will be confiscated and put up for auction. I will have Excelsior one way or another."

"Let me guess. You don't want to wait for the courts?"

"If you agree to give me Excelsior, I'll commute your execution long enough to let you hold your child—"

"Our child, Edwin."

"Yes … our child. As I said, I'm willing to give you even more than you've asked for … if you turn over Excelsior Media to me."

"Only if Barry is emancipated. He must be granted a sizable allowance and live out his retirement as he chooses."

"First generation memes have a long expectancy—a very costly support."

"I will not allow him to be euthanized. Agree or this entire negotiation is over."

Michael's projection shimmered—an indicator of intense emotion, her determination unmistakable. He could back down and still own Excelsior in time—expediency, however, more prudent. The public would never know of this transmission. He'd make sure Becker erased all traces. He would present Michael's terms as his own, demonstrate his capacity for great mercy, a move certain to win more cooperation from the Humanitarian Party than he'd ever dreamed. "Done."

"I want an agreement drawn up immediately. Everything I've asked for. I expect you'll re-word my commands as your ideas … I'll still sign."

Michael's projection thickened with her resolve. Was there no love left between them? No matter. Edwin Rowlands had lived a loveless life before Michael. Intimacy was easily purchased. Love proved to be a tiresome emotion.

"Michael …" He loathed the weakness she evoked in him. "I wish there were some other way. If you hadn't run off. Or if you had come back sooner, I might have been able to manage a pardon. You have boxed me in, and I see no other course left to me."

"I know. Edwin, I … forgive you."

"You sound like a Christ follower."

"I am."

Her voice buoyed with conviction, a thing against which he had no armor. "I'll send Becker. I'll have him bring you to me, first, before he incarcerates you."

"What's the point?"

"I have to see you, Michael."

"You'll release Ahmed and Benjamin now?"

"Some say I'm cautious to a fault and slow to make a promise. That I'm unable to compromise, and that I'm ruthless. They're probably right. My one admirable trait is the ability, once given, to keep my word."

"Not your only virtue, Edwin, you are clever, too."

He worded the agreement to demonstrate his benevolence toward egregious actions against him, projected the document, placed his thumbprint, and then wired the amended version to Michael as well as a copy to Becker. "See? For now, the Sierras will remain as they are. Mark my words ... if I even suspect them of another treasonous act, I will level the province."

"I expected as much. As they do. You'll not succeed, Edwin. Unlike the Network, they have the means to resist."

He ended the transmission.

Somewhere, within the deepest part of his heart, what the Christ followers called the soul, he understood why Michael chose to become one of them. Let the Maker send him to Hades, if such a place existed. This wrong he would not forgive—Michael had surrendered to a power greater than Edwin Rowlands.

Why didn't she jump from province to province, become a global Nomad, enough places in United Earth for a determined defector to hide. She didn't need to force his hand, to be a martyr. He'd learned to manipulate the law, reshape legislation for his purposes. Ultimately, he was as subject to the Constitution as anyone else. A day would come, a day when a power beyond himself, benevolent or otherwise, a force he neither comprehended nor worshiped, would hold him accountable. Until then no man or woman, flesh or meme, would deter him from the course he had set.

CHAPTER FIFTY-THREE
Sector One/America Prime

Bridget took Falan's arm as security led them through the mansion entrance to the gala room where sixty handpicked guests waited to be seated.

Governor Rowlands met them within minutes of their arrival and fawned over her like a lovesick teenager. "My fair Highland maiden, my eyes are gladdened by the sight of you."

His affectations hedged the obscene.

"Governor."

He kissed her hand. "I'm truly sorry for your loss. Please rest in the knowledge this was your father's choice. I would have preferred he'd accepted my offer of retirement and lived a life of luxury in the Australian retreat."

A huge fabrication. Rowlands' alternative must have been too bitter a pill for Da to swallow, worse than death no matter how the deal was iced. "Da was never one for idleness. He did what he thought honor required. I won't cheapen his sacrifice by assigning blame."

Rowlands wrapped his arm around Bridget's waist. "Mr. Riley. I wish to speak to your mistress alone. I assure you, she'll be quite safe."

Reason assuaged fear—he didn't dare make a public scene, especially on this all-important day. She nodded to Falan, and Rowlands escorted her to the back of the room, more private indeed. Thankfully, not far from Falan's view. The governor took her hands in his. "I don't have much time, Bridget, as duty calls me away in a few minutes. I have a proposal. Please don't answer until I've thoroughly explained my intentions."

"Continue."

"Due to your father's untimely death, the Highland delegation has a vacancy for a junior delegate. Have you considered a political career?"

"As a matter of fact, I have."

"You will make an excellent candidate, Bridget. You have your father's integrity and passion. I do fear you may oppose me as he did."

His offer must be a trap, of course—his enticement, her one ambition. "What do you propose, Governor Rowlands?"

"You know I am very attracted to you. As your father requested, you have been fully pardoned of both your illegal pregnancy and your criminal activities. Although President Schumann signed the pardon, I managed the deal at your father's request. I'd rather hoped for your gratitude."

What kind of favor requires a da to be euthanized? How could a travesty be rationalized as anything good?

"I am proposing a familial contract. I need a voice in my ear, a conscience if you will. In our private moments, I welcome the challenge your opposing views bring. I only request you be discreet with your public opposition."

Privilege would be the sword by which he silenced her. He'd make her his puppet and negate her influence. "To become your intimate would bring an injustice to you, Governor. My heart belongs to another."

"I don't expect your love, Bridget, merely your loyalty."

"You have given me much to consider. I trust you'll not press me for an answer this very moment."

"Perhaps we'll discuss the matter again at the After Ball?"

"Until then, Governor. The next time we chat, I'll be able to call you Mr. President."

He smiled with presumed victory, no consideration of Schumann's impending death. At this moment, the unfortunate man was on his way to Eternal Pathways. A shame he'd pass into the next world uncelebrated. No media feeds. No parade. No gala. A servant as his witness. A sad end for a great man.

Rowlands took her arm then led her to a table and waited until Falan joined them. "Take good care of her, Mr. Riley. You know, I could use a good man like you."

Baited. Bridget determined not to nibble. She'd suffer through these few hours and figure out a way to refuse Rowlands.

Falan leaned in. "What was that about?"

"We'll talk later. For now, let's feast on sausages and omelets. Little Ian says he's hungry."

CHAPTER FIFTY-FOUR
Medical Center/America Prime

Benjamin Goodayle linked his fingers with Christine's as they stood in the entrance to his father's hospital room. Tubes and machines encircled his bed. Seemed he'd aged ten years in the space of a few days.

If Mother were here, she'd say to trust the Maker. "Worry drains the soul," she'd have said. "Can't look for solutions in the face of worry."

Benjamin moved a chair next to Pops' bed. Should he wake him? Dr. Newell said Pops needed rest. He stirred and opened his eyes, and his lips formed a lopsided smile. He gibbered something that sounded like "Glad to see you" as his eyes fixed on Christine. Before Benjamin could introduce her, a Monica entered and took command like an IEA captain. "Chairman Goodayle needs his rest. No visitors until the eleventh hour."

Pops waved his hand in objection. "M … my …s … son."

Another Monica entered, and the two raised Pops' bed and fluffed his pillows. Monica One glared at Benjamin. "Five minutes. No more."

Kyle Skinner entered with a tray. "Breakfast, Chairman Goodayle. Benjamin, Christine, it's good to see you."

Benjamin pulled Christine near the bed. "Pops, this is my intimate, Christine Devereux, the wife of my heart."

Christine's blush made her impossibly more beautiful. Pops patted her hand as he would a child's. "Pret … ty." Now Benjamin blushed. Not from embarrassment. Joy. His father finally gave his blessing.

Footsteps thudded down the corridor. He turned as Uncle Ahmed blocked the doorway. "So, are we having a reunion in the hospital room?"

Kyle set up Pops' tray. Before anyone noticed, he grabbed a spoon and tried to feed himself. No one scolded him for the mess he made. Kyle tried to assist, and Pops grit his teeth. On the second try, he managed to go from plate to mouth with one spill.

"Both Uncle Ahmed and I have been reinstated, all charges dropped, so our presence is required at the Inauguration. I'll be back to see you as soon as I'm able to shake loose from my duties."

Uncle Ahmed motioned to a Monica. "Would you bring in a patient micro for my brother?"

"I'll see what I can do. Normally they're only allowed in the solarium."

Pops grabbed Uncle Ahmed's arm. "How?"

"Long story. Someone apparently convinced our soon-to-be President of my innocence, Benjamin's too. Becker has apologized for the inconvenience."

Benjamin laughed. "Inconvenience, he says, as if—"

Uncle Ahmed's slap on the back, a reminder. Scanners were everywhere ... the constant surveillance enough to drive a man insane.

Christine kissed Pops on the cheek. "When we come back, we'll talk about moving you into our house. We'll see to your care."

With effort, Pops raised his hand as if to surrender to a more indomitable force.

The Monica set a miniature micro on a bedside table. "Is this sufficient, Chairman Goodayle?"

He raised his arm an inch and the Monica enlarged the view. "Good," Pops said.

The Monica pushed Uncle Ahmed toward the door. "Now, sir, you must leave. No more visitors until early evening. Understood?"

Only a Monica, engineered for complete focus on her patients, would dare bark orders at the next Second President.

Kyle picked up the tray then paused at the door. "Monica One assigned me to your room today."

Pops nodded approval.

"Jacob, we have found a good life here, Caroline, Peter, and me. Once you recover, you will too."

As Kyle left, Pops extended his hand toward Benjamin. "Love ... you ... son."

He glanced toward the feed and shook his head as if to object. "Excel ... feed?"

Benjamin adjusted the micro and EVE projected. "Please wait while your feed transfer is processed."

An automated text message appeared, and Benjamin read aloud. "We are pleased to announce the sale of Excelsior Media to Rowlands Industries."

Apprehension filled him as Pops spoke, "Michael ... not ... sell ... unless ... trouble. Tell Ahmed."

CHAPTER FIFTY-FIVE
Sector Ten/America Prime

Angelina checked Jimmy's pulse. He moaned and opened his eyes. "Looks like you'll live to aggravate me another day thanks to my bad aim."

"You don't miss, Angelina."

"Might have, still not used to these P-94s."

The nightglows surrendered to the dawn. She glanced at her timepiece.

Jimmy closed his eyes as he asked the question. "What time is it?"

"Too late for your plans, Jimmy."

He sat, grabbed his side and leaned forward as he emitted several deep breaths. "I think you hit my rib cage. Why didn't you kill me? You've wanted to long enough."

"More fun to make you wonder if I'm a poor shot or if I saved your sorry behind because I still love you." She kissed him. "Nope, the fire's gone."

"What are you after, if not revenge?"

She clicked her disdain. "I won't let you start a civil war. There's got to be another way."

"I planned to wait until after the oath of office. With no named successor, Fared would take over until Congress voted on a new President. He's well liked and a good man."

She checked the charge on her weapon. Almost out of juice. "You'll have gone too far. Just or not, Fared would be forced to order your execution, and your army would look for revenge as an excuse for bloodshed. It's how war starts, you know—blood for blood—religion against religion. Before you know it, there are more factions than causes."

Angelina helped Jimmy stand. He grunted, and clutched his side. "I suppose I should thank you I'm still alive."

"Don't make me sorry I missed." She engaged the micro.

"This isn't ours."

"Nemo's."

"He handed you his weapon just like that?"

"He didn't put up a fight."

Jimmy ripped a spiel of coughs. "Come again?"

"He's dead."

"Must be your aim was better for good old Nemo."

"Not funny. I stabbed him. We'd met in the sub-city."

"What now?"

"We wait. We'll both be killed. At least I won't die alone."

"Not if you take me back to the Highland Province. I'm assuming you got here with one of our shuttles."

"By now, the cloaks are degraded and the shuttle has been discovered. Afraid you're stuck here with me."

ADAM projected, and Angelina smacked her lips and whistled. "ADAM, what's new in the police world?"

The projection shifted as he minimized and popped back up. "Please restate your inquiry."

"Okay. ADAM, show news feed summary."

Projections rolled like an ancient movie reel. Angelina scrolled the data. She stopped at Excelsior's list of headlines. "I don't believe it."

Jimmy groaned as he rose to his full height. "What?"

"Says here Governor Cavanaugh's dead."

"How?"

"Euthanasia."

Jimmy raised an eyebrow. "Probably he and the President-elect struck up a deal for Bridget's pardon."

"From these reports, our Scottish princess has been the belle of the ball. I wouldn't be surprised if Rowlands has her primed to add to his family."

Jimmy groaned again.

"Let me look at your wound." She examined the gash. "You're oozing blood. The scent will draw wild dogs."

She ripped off a length of cloth from her jumpsuit and bandaged his wound. "Now you won't drip all over the place."

"You don't kill me but let me die of infection?"

"I probably didn't plan this well."

"There's the first truthful thing you've said since you shot me."

She placed the micro back in the satchel. "Any word from the Highlands?"

"I risked a communiqué before someone rudely blasted me. They're fine. The IEA is scrambling to reopen the air dock. You did a great job, by the way. Any loss of life?"

"Only a few memes."

Jimmy scowled. "They count, Bartelli."

Maybe so. She would mourn Angus if something happened to him.

"Why did you stop me? I came so close."

"Killing Rowlands is not the answer."

"Then what is?"

"I don't know for sure. I do know you don't bring order by causing chaos."

He rubbed his stomach. "I'm hungry. Got anything to eat?"

"I used the last of my rations as a bribe."

"Ssh. Do you hear that?"

"Hear what?" She gasped at the howls. "We've got to get out of here. I'd rather be vaporized than become breakfast for a pack of canines."

Jimmy hesitated, and Angelina aimed her weapon. "Move it, Kinnear. Or this time I won't be so generous."

"How am I supposed to defend myself against wild dogs."

She threw him his weapon, and stared at the labyrinth of crumbled walls. "Too late to outrun them. Sounds like a dozen or more." The lead mutt snarled, probably a mix of wolf and Rottweiler. A magnificent animal if he weren't bent on eating her. "On the count of …"

A wide white stream streaked the air—the beast exploded before her eyes. Jimmy sprayed a series of smaller blasts, and the rest of the pack littered the ground.

"Whew, now that's what I call a weapon."

"Neat, huh?"

"Let's get out of here. IEA is sure to spot us now. The shots can be heard a mile away."

"Follow me." Jimmy led them back through the building, down the hall, and out the back alley near the outside wall. He hoisted his weapon, adjusted a dial and shot pure energy into the perimeter. Cement flew every direction. When they had tunneled through, five officers met them on the other side.

Angelina fired first, and the return blast tore through her body. The winged forms that hovered over her, called her by name.

Jimmy threw his weapon to the ground and put his hands behind his head in surrender. "You're a fool, Angelina."

She'd sacrificed herself for him, the one thing he never thought her capable of. Or maybe she found her revenge at last. She robbed him of a hero's death. Prison would be his lot.

CHAPTER FIFTY-SIX
Sector One/America Prime

Ahmed grew impatient as an agent escorted him into Becker's office. He wasn't sure what irked him more—coerced to endure a security detail or this unscheduled stop. What did Becker want now? Maybe the President-elect had rethought his generosity and decided to arrest the whole of United Earth.

Foolishness to have revealed evidence against Rowlands to Becker. Benjamin had been released without the bribe. Becker would want to use the information for some other scheme.

They shook hands in feigned congeniality. "Constable Becker, I trust you have a good reason for this detour. I would think all the necessary extra security would keep you more than a little occupied."

"Mr. Fared. Good to see you looking so fit. I trust your confinement has had no ill consequences." Becker signaled his agent to leave. "Please have a seat, Mr. Fared. Soon, you will be my superior. I thought before then, we might have a little chat."

Refusal was not an option. "Go on, Constable."

His tiny eyes radiated, hot and red like a target finder on a P-74. "Look. I want to set the record straight. I've disengaged the scanners."

"I'm not sure this is appropriate—"

He raised a reassuring hand. "You probably already know your release was independent of your so-called evidence against the President-elect."

"Yes. I figured as much. Am I to assume, you do not plan to advise the President-elect of its existence?"

"Perhaps later … when the time seems right."

"Michael Grafton surrendered in exchange for our freedom, didn't she?"

"We have her full confession. She claims she coerced you, and to her knowledge Benjamin was innocent."

"I see."

"President Schumann issued a temporary stay of judgment until his successor is duly installed. The President-elect intends to write the execution order to be implemented after the child's birth. Until then, she will receive the best medical care available."

"How thoughtful." Ahmed's heart raced. Michael had given her life for his. He was the one charged to look after her. Was there nothing in his power to save her? "What will happen to Excelsior Media?"

"Michael transferred all her accounts to Rowlands Industries with the condition her meme Barry is emancipated, retired and given a lifelong stipend."

Answers this detailed weren't free. What did Becker expect in return? Ahmed risked another prompt. "Davu Obote?"

"Since his quiet repatriation, he is tending his coffee beans for the time being."

My brother?

"President-elect Rowlands wishes to avoid bloodshed and will offer one last call for repatriation for past defectors before he institutes the Preservation Act. As for Chairman Goodayle, the President-elect does not wish to cause him further stress, and his assistance to Mistress Grafton was after the fact. Therefore, the President-elect has chosen to drop collusion charges, including those against Mr. Ives and Sean Grafton."

Becker turned off his lamp, holstered his weapon, and pointed toward the door. He apparently had no intention of halting his jig. He merely waited for a slight change of tempo. "Duty calls, Mr. Fared."

"I agree."

Becker activated his transponder. "Agent Hobart, you may take Mr. Fared to his destination."

Ahmed stood.

"I've arranged for Benjamin's detail as well. He'll meet you at the Inauguration platform. He'll be seated on the lower risers, of course. His intimate will join him there. You'll be escorted to the podium by Agent Hobart's team. I've taken every precaution to give you and Benjamin Goodayle optimum security."

Security or surveillance? Becker's unspoken purpose, now crystal clear—he intended to keep his Second President under his thumb. He'd command the evidence as blackmail against Rowlands. For what purpose? To keep his job or secure more power?

Becker continued his spew. "At last report, Schumann has entered the Euthanasia Chamber. Agent Savakis was supposed to oversee the President-elect's detail. Unfortunately, he has died in the line of duty by the hand of a disgruntled officer, Angelina Bartelli. She was located in the company of General Kinnear and was killed. However, we have Kinnear in custody, a far more valuable asset to us alive than dead."

Ahmed emotionally steadied for the next tidbit. "Anything else, Constable Becker?"

"I think we understand one another well enough."

Becker planned to use Ahmed's information to move pieces around the chessboard. If Ahmed refused the constable's terms, he'd go to the President. As far as Becker was concerned, he'd reached checkmate on both boards, Rowlands' as well as Ahmed's.

Not so. Becker had grossly underestimated his opponent.

Ahmed coughed.

Becker signaled his agent. "Get Mr. Fared a vial of water."

The agent left, and Becker glared while Ahmed purposely stalled by taking several small sips of water. Rowlands might be a snake. So was Becker. At least, Rowlands' maneuvers were predictable. Better to stand next to a rattler than a cobra.

Ahmed set the vial on the table. "A very informative chat, Constable Becker. I look forward to future ones."

"A toast might be in order if other matters did not compete for our attention."

"I do have one request. I need to make an unscheduled stop at my office. I have a gift to present to the new President."

Becker raised an eyebrow. "A gift, you say?"

"Yes. He's always admired the Renoir on my wall. I'd like him to have it."

"Very well. Agent Hobart, make sure Mr. Fared has the opportunity to pick up his gift."

CHAPTER FIFTY-SEVEN
Sector One/America Prime

Guests awaited their assigned transports while Edwin, with Bridget on his arm, circulated around the room set for the gala. His lead security officer motioned for an audience. Edwin turned to Bridget. "Affairs of State again, my dear. I look forward to our first dance at the After Ball."

He quickened his pace toward the back curtain. "You have her?"

"In your private den."

Edwin hurried up the back stairwell—his thoughts raced as fast as his feet. No doubt Fared would campaign for her release. Let him. He might succeed. Either way, Edwin won. If Michael were spared, all well and good. If she must be executed, he would still have Bridget and Jade.

He gasped when he saw her. Thick, loose desert muslin could not hide her figure. "Leave us."

"But Governor—"

"Mistress Grafton will pose no threat. Besides, there is nowhere for her to go. If you insist, you may post a guard at the exit. See no one disturbs us."

"Yes, Governor."

At first, he stared at her. Words should not be this difficult to find. "I still can't believe you surrendered without a vicious fight. You could have eluded me indefinitely and kept your estate tied up in court battles for years. Of course, I'd have won eventually. Submission is unlike you, Michael. There is a deeper reason ... not Ahmed, Benjamin, or Barry. What's your game?"

"There is no game, Edwin. I have everything I want."

"In all likelihood, you'll be executed within hours of Jade's birth. Is that what you wanted?"

"What will be, will be."

"Do you think the Maker will swoop down and pluck you from my evil grasp?"

Michael's face gleamed with, dare he say, peace. He hoped she had not put her pregnancy at risk. He would make certain she had an army of physicians at her disposal. Jade would have the best of everything from this point on.

"Ahmed and Benjamin?"

"Fully pardoned, everything as you requested. You may view my public memo on Excelsior's feed. Barry is on his way to your Oceanic property to live out his days."

Her body relaxed, then tightened as tears filled her eyes. "I'm sorry, Edwin—sorry I caused you pain."

He thought of Bridget. "I shall recover, my dear."

"Where am I to be incarcerated?"

"Where not even clever Ahmed will find you."

She cast her eyes toward the carpet. "You are cruel, Edwin. Will I have no visitors at all?"

"Your medical team and me. No one else. I can't trust you."

Tears pooled in his eyes, and the sincerity of the emotion surprised him. "I'm sorry our journey together ends here, Michael. Your defection gave me little choice."

"There is always a choice to do the Maker's will."

"I don't believe in this Maker of yours."

"I wish you did."

"If I did believe, I would ask Him to find a way to save you. I think I will die a little at your execution."

"You are the one who will sign the order. You will be the one responsible for the death of your child's mother."

He hailed the guards. "Take her away."

He hadn't expected this much pain, and he turned to hide his sorrow until alone. He glared at Father's portrait. His ghost spoke the same advice he gave Edwin at Mother's death bed. "Successful men do not grieve, Edwin. Feed your ache, and you will grieve forever. Purge the pain, and grief will vanish." A squad of meme playmates, male and female, purged Father's pain. He sent some of them into Edwin's room. At the age of twelve, the boy became a man.

Sidney stood in his doorway.

"Yes, Sidney?"

"I noticed you are without both your micro and transponder, sir. You have a strange hail from Mr. Fared. The response requires a micro connection. I knew you would not want a security team to barge into your private quarters."

"No, of course not. Bring me my devices. I'll patch the hail through."

Sidney returned with a micro and handed Edwin the transponder.

"That will be all, Sidney."

Though images patched through transponders were not as clear as micro-to-micro, the call's location was crystal clear. Ahmed hailed him from his office privy. How crude.

"What do you want, Fared."

"I have a gift for you, Governor."

"You hail me from your privy to tell me you have a gift? I'm in no mood for your nonsense."

"Trust me. You will relish this gift. You recall the Renoir?"

"The sisters?"

"The very one."

Fared's expression could not be fully read from a patched transponder image. "Say what you have to say."

"I apologize for my environment. I had to shake my detail. I told them even global leaders succumb to nature's urges."

"Yes, yes."

"Kind of fitting, though."

"I don't understand the significance."

"You know I attended Devereux's euthanasia as his witness."

"What does that have to do with this charade?"

Ahmed leaned forward. "As his witness, Devereux presented me with an additional gift, besides the Renoir."

"Get to the point or this transmission is ended."

"Do you recall a certain delegate's minor daughter, a girl you met at Devereux's mansion? Why, the very room is a few yards down the hall from your den. Of course, you've redecorated the privy since then. The disk is dated and no one can dispute the place, time, and … activity."

Edwin minimized the projection, the whole incident still vivid in his memory, how Devereux had walked in on Edwin and a minor girl in the act. The girl had not willingly subjected to Edwin's advances. Devereux seemed to dismiss the matter. What politician did not bend laws to his favor? If one looked hard, Devereux most likely had a few indiscretions himself. The two political figures simply worked out a deal to let the matter drop, and the girl was duly compensated for her silence. She conveniently died soon after. With both Devereux and the girl dead, the matter should have been buried when their ashes were scattered. Edwin resumed the projection. "I see I have no choice but to accept your gift before the ceremony."

"I thought you'd see the urgency. Now here are my terms …"

CHAPTER FIFTY-EIGHT
Sector One/America Prime

Bridget held her breath as the transports lined up in front of the mansion. A few hours more, then she'd be on a shuttle back to the Highland Province. As what? Where would she live? Certainly not as Rowlands' intimate. There must be some way to sour his interest in her. He'd not relent otherwise. He had insisted she sit next to him on the podium like a wolf marks his territory.

Falan signaled for her attention. She pulled out Mum's necklace from her formal satchel and sucked in courage. More bad news? She handed the necklace to Falan. "Assist me."

He pulled back her hair, fit the bauble around her neck, and whispered in her ear. "Jimmy's been arrested and Angelina's dead."

Though Falan's report terse, if true, Jimmy's sufferings had only begun. He'd be tortured until he had no more information to give, then executed. King Edwin would have his public beheading after all.

Her costumed driver led her toward the specially designed transports, each detailed to resemble antique coaches complete with micro-projected horses. Falan assisted her into the coach before taking the seat next to her. His constant presence a balm to her troubled spirit.

A tedious day stretched before her, festivities from sunrise to sunset. Dignitaries would be required to appear joyful. How could she pretend any longer? Her heart ached for her losses—Ian, Da, and now, Jimmy.

Each event of the day would supposedly outshine the preceding, the last to be the ball of balls, more like a coronation. He'd planned for a one hundred-piece orchestra. Foods had been flown from the most exotic gardens in United Earth.

She fidgeted as she looked at her timepiece. Why the delay? Her transport was supposedly directly ahead of the President-elect's. Yet, he had still not been escorted to his transport. She glanced back at Falan who shrugged. Something was wrong. Rowlands prided himself on punctuality. Millions were glued to the overhead monitors and private micro feeds.

Nothing she could do but wait.

CHAPTER FIFTY-NINE
Obote Plantation/Congo Province

Davu Obote maximized the parade feed, still aflutter from the good fortune that had burst upon his day. His assignment as Secretary of the Interior had been promised … to be announced along with all the cabinet positions following the Inauguration. He basked in his appointment as CEO of Excelsior Media, a dream come true.

He reveled in projected improvements for the company. With the President's permission, he would install erotica feeds—the demand high and the returns lucrative. He'd need a staff. First, he'd replace the retiring Barry with a Clark model, designed for top efficiency. By the time Clark wore out, the automatons would be perfected and ready for implementation. He'd pocket the savings and boost his salary.

Davu placed himself in the middle of the projection as the transports stopped in front of the podium. He had hoped to be invited. However, Rowlands suggested seclusion until the Network evacuations were completed.

The transports at the rear emptied first—those who governed the untamed lands. When he became Minister of the Exterior, as the President-elect promised, he'd parcel the land and exact high prices rather than auction the properties to the highest bidder. In this way, land grabs would be controlled and exchanged for favors from the wealthy.

When the last of the groups disembarked, the feed zoomed in on Rowlands. Crowds roared as he stepped from his transport, walked to the podium, took his seat next to Bridget Cavanaugh, and kissed her hand, a public declaration of his intent toward her. Good. A romantic interest would distract the President. And the more he was distracted, the less he'd care how Davu administered the outworlds and Excelsior Media.

CHAPTER SIXTY
Medical Center/America Prime

Jacob thrashed in his hospital bed. Monica One said his restlessness was a good sign his strength was returning. Kyle Skinner brought him a vial of water, and Jacob managed the straw himself. Hope welled with every improvement. Now that Benjamin and Ahmed had been released, Jacob looked forward to rehabilitation. Most Network inhabitants had agreed to repatriation and other outworlds had followed their example. Civil war had been averted, at least for now. Yet, social change of this magnitude would ultimately sow a different unrest.

If Michael's exposé of the proposed Preservation Act had been accurate, Rowlands would enforce repatriation on the Nomads next. Had he thought through the potential hazards of hurried and numerous repatriations? United Earth could not possibly adjust to the influx. Nor could the economy endure massive dependency.

Starvation would no longer be limited to Sector Ten. Rowlands' inadequate preparations would sow seeds of war, not peace.

Jacob turned his attention to the Inauguration coverage, as one by one IEA officers assisted delegates to assigned places. Bridget Cavanaugh seemed a portrait of serenity in the face of her multiple losses. Speculation rippled through the hospital corridors as to whether she would accept a familial contract with Rowlands.

The feed zoomed in on Benjamin, and Jacob swelled with fatherly pride. One close up showed Ahmed and Rowlands engaged in an animated discussion, the President-elect's face pale while Ahmed beamed with confidence.

What have you been up to, Brother?

Jacob sighed. What function would he play in this Brave New World? He was no longer a chairman, merely one in a horde of nonessentials—displaced and ineffectual. He grieved the failure of his life. Whether he survived this stroke or not, he would never see the fulfillment of his dreams for an autonomous Network.

Jacob lifted the mute on the micro as Ahmed took the podium. He read from his personal tablet. Odd. Most government speakers used a prompter, their public speeches pre-approved by Mainframe monitors, written for entertainment value, with background fanfare and streamed visuals.

"Fellow Citizens. Our great President Schumann has passed from this life to the next. I will read to you his parting words: 'Friends and fellow Citizens. This world I leave today has journeyed from despair to hope. We are stronger now than in the days of our grandparents. We have learned hard and fast lessons from the ills of the early century. We have embarked on a new era, the creation of lasting peace through one unified government. Our Articles of Constitution will be tested time and time again, and I urge every Citizen to honor the rule of law. Congress has met and voted my replacement as the Articles require. Today marks the twenty-fifth anniversary of the Constitutional Government. Our world has thrived because of the security these Articles have given us. However, we dare not rest. There is still much more to be done. We must not let the desires of the few upset the will of the many. Work for the morrow. Work for the dream. When the Caretaker closes my eyes in my eternal sleep, I will rest in the knowledge I leave a better world than the one I came into.'"

The crowd broke into thunderous applause. Ahmed held up a hand to request silence, and the roar softened into murmurs. "And now, I present to you Edwin Milton Rowlands, The next President of United Earth."

Rowlands stood as the crowd cheered. Becker brought a bound manuscript to the podium and instructed the soon-to-be President to stand next to Ahmed. "Gentlemen, I will now offer the charge of office."

Ahmed and Rowlands shook hands … for show? Could these polar entities have reached some kind of agreement?

"Mr. Fared, if you will place your left hand on the Articles of Constitution. Raise your right hand and repeat after me."

Was that a smirk on Ahmed's face?

Becker continued. "Do you, Ahmed Mohammed Fared, solemnly swear allegiance to the Articles of Constitution, to uphold its law and to faithfully discharge the duties of Second President as herein stated?"

"I do."

Ahmed took his seat, then Rowlands came to the podium, a mask of solemnity, an odd countenance at this his triumphal entry. Caesar should glow. Rowlands placed his left hand on the Articles of Constitution and raised his right hand.

"Do you, Edwin Milton Rowlands, solemnly swear allegiance to the Articles of Constitution, to uphold its law and to faithfully discharge the duties of President as herein stated?"

Rowlands swallowed hard. "I do."

Cheers erupted and the music swelled to decimals beyond tolerable. Jacob muted the feed. Becker left the podium and took his assigned seat while all eyes fixed on the President. The broadcast commentators had predicted a short speech, shorter even than Schumann's farewell address. Perhaps the new President was anxious for his first congressional session.

"My Fellow Citizens," Rowlands' voice trembled. "I come before you a humbler man than even an hour earlier. A great man has closed his eyes for me to obtain this privilege to lead United Earth. You have grieved with me these past few days as personal troubles descended upon my household. After my closing remarks, we will honor our fallen hero. Then Congress will convene to consider my amended Preservation Act."

Amended?

"I now present the meat of these changes to you, the Citizenry, as they will be heard by Congress: First and foremost, I will request a redefinition of citizenship, no longer limited to the privileged and the few, but to all inhabitants, including Nomads, both within the walled cities and their surrounding territories, populated provinces and isolated as well. Let us build on what unites us, rather than splinter because of what divides us. Let us broaden government's definition to assure all the world's inhabitants receive fair representation.

"Secondly, I will instruct Congress to amend the current legislation to allow free trade between the cities and the outworlds. Many of our once barren wastelands now thrive. The free flow of goods to and from cities will only enhance the quality of life for all United Earth.

"Lastly, I am instructing Congress to write and ratify the Fifteenth Article of the Constitution to address the preservation of free speech without prejudice to religious preferences. In our paranoia, we wrongfully silenced the flow of ideas. We did so because we feared another Schism. As enlightened beings, we now realize we must not stifle imagination and inadvertently bolster a regressive society. Rather, government should foster ingenuity so all people prosper.

"And in this spirit, I am requesting a full pardon for Michael Grafton, whose courage has brought me to these conclusions ..."

All activity within the hospital corridors stopped as if frozen in this historic moment while Jacob raised grateful hands toward heaven.

EPILOGUE
Chapter One
One Year Later/America Prime Detention Center

Jimmy Kinnear rose from his bed and wobbled to greet his interrogator, this time the warden himself instead of a handpicked henchman. A good sign, or did this mean he'd finally be ushered from this earthly prison into eternity?

"Follow me, Kinnear. You have a visitor."

Jimmy merely nodded. Speaking taxed his strength.

Warden Barnes led him to a chamber constructed entirely of marble. "Sit here." He motioned for a guard. "Restrain his ankles and wrists—not too tightly, of course."

Jimmy shielded his eyes from the glare, brighter than the solitary light in his cell. At least, since Fared's prison reforms, they shut the beam off for eight hours at a time. Though the hours varied, each inmate was guaranteed a full eight hours of dimmed light in which to sleep. No amount of reform, however, lessened the sting of imprisonment.

Warden Barnes checked Jimmy's restraints. "That should hold you. You can thank Ahmed Fared for this visitation room—and three meals a day. Don't know how he expects the Citizenry to pay for all these reforms. Taxes are already higher than Citizens are willing to absorb." With that, Warden Barnes exited through the rear door.

Cut off since the first day of his arrest with not a single wire, news from the outside oozed thinly into Jimmy's world, dependent solely upon what his guards would share or what he gleaned from terse mandatory prison meetings. Otherwise, except for his daily interrogation, he'd been deprived of any other human contact.

Today he had a visitor. Who remembered him? Who had gained permission to break his sentence of isolation?

The lobby door opened, and Falan strode in like a summer breeze. Gray tufted his temples, a different brother than Jimmy remembered—much more confident.

He found the strength to stand. "Well, if I've been correctly informed by the guards, my first permitted visitor is a celebrity, the newly elected Governor of the Highlands Province. Let's have a look at you."

Falan clasped Jimmy's hand with all the tenderness of a father. "My heart pounds to see you, boyo. Acting-President Fared warned me you might be a mite weak, said prison life goes hard on a man. Most inmates don't survive more than a few months let alone a year."

Jimmy coughed.

"Are you ill?"

"Probably another bout of pneumonia coming on. I had hoped the first one would kill me. No such luck. Are you in America Prime for Fared's Inauguration?"

"Yes, Congress unanimously approved his succession. All the governors are expected, including Benjamin Goodayle of Western America Adjunct."

"Adjunct?"

"The new term for the outworlds, including the former Network."

"Benjamin Goodayle, is it? Why didn't the older Goodayle get the post?"

Falan's laugh soothed like a lullaby Mum used to sing. "Jacob prefers the role of grandfather. Benjamin and Christine are expecting their first wee one in about eight months. They wasted no time after the waiting period was nullified by Congress."

Jimmy attempted a deep breath, but the pain brought on yet another cough. Falan sat and motioned for Jimmy to do the same. "The world is changing by the hour, Jimmy, a fast road to peace and prosperity, a brighter future than any of us dreamed possible—managed without war."

To experience these changes, to glimpse the reality of a once-treasured vision would be all he'd want before death took him. Would he be like Moses—only able to witness the fulfillment of a mission alone upon a mountain top?

As another harsh cough erupted, concern etched Falan's glare.

"Not to worry, Falan. These bouts are far from fatal." Jimmy laughed. "Though, every day I ask the Maker to take me home."

"Perhaps the Maker delays because his plan for you remains unfinished."

Jimmy laughed. "What could the Maker want of me here?"

"I, for one, believe he's not finished with you, yet." Falan stroked his chin.

"The beard suits you, brother."

"Most men opt for one these days since Ahmed's bill to repeal the Uniformity Act passed Congress."

"So, tell me, if you can, what really happened to Rowlands? I don't believe the rumor he died of a cerebral hemorrhage."

"The late President rushed his shower and slipped on a bar of soap."

Jimmy allowed his amusement full reign. "Did he now? Seems like a fitting end for a dirty scoundrel."

"Don't rail the dead, Jimmy. Scoundrel he may have been. He did usher in a new world, thankfully not the one he thought he would. Of course, no one can say for sure. Most believe Ahmed Fared had something to do with the late President's about-face."

Pressure built in his chest, and Jimmy bent over with the pain. "For the life of me, I can't figure out why I'm still alive."

Falan looked him squarely in the eyes as if a question were to follow.

"What is it, brother? Am I finally to be terminated?"

"No, Jimmy. Actually, President Fared has commissioned me to offer you a pardon."

"A pardon, is it? By the look on your face, this pardon comes with conditions."

"Constable Becker has requested retirement immediately upon Fared's oath of office. Guess he figured he should retire before he was fired. Most expect Fared will completely rebuild the Cabinet of Ministries."

"What will Becker do now? He's too young to receive a government subsidy."

"He'll become an ordinary Citizen, find private employment."

Jimmy laughed. "I doubt he'll stay ordinary. He's as crafty as Davu Obote. Speaking of Obote, how is the conniver these days?"

"Fuming at his lot in life. Rowlands willed all his properties, including Excelsior Media, to Jade, naming her mother as manager until Jade reaches legal age. Michael gave Obote the heave-ho before Rowlands' ashes hit the ground."

Jimmy stretched as much as his shackles would allow. "He's like a cat and will always land on four paws no matter how high he's dropped."

They both laughed.

Jimmy turned his gaze full on Falan. "And this pardon you mention has to do with Becker's retirement?"

"Aye. President Fared wants you to be his replacement."

"IEA Director? Me? A felon?"

Falan stood and paced. "I know the offer is a strange one, Jimmy. As President Fared reminded me, we all have a past."

"But, why me, Falan? Why not you? Or Benjamin Goodayle?"

"I never had the heart of the warrior, Jimmy. Not even when we fought side by side in the Resistance. Under your leadership, the Revolutionary Army became a force to be reckoned with. United Earth has no need for a revolution. However, General Kinnear will always need an army to lead. Why not the IEA?"

An intriguing offer ... one Jimmy would not have believed if offered through anyone else. "You know, inmates are only allowed one vial of water a day, enough to prevent dying of thirst. Not enough to quench it. When I'm free, I'll want a pitcher of water at my side at all times."

"That means you'll take the job?"

The irony of ironies—the rebel becomes the enforcer. "I'm not sure which alternative is the worst—to take Becker's place or stay in this hell. I'd be a fool not to enjoy the sun again."

"I'll advise President Fared immediately. By this time tomorrow, you'll be a free man."

Jimmy recalled the moment he finally surrendered to the Maker—the day after his incarceration—the day he believed his life was over. Perhaps, instead of a Moses, the Maker had called him to be a Joshua. Were there battles to fight for the Maker's glory rather than those of Jimmy Kinnear?

"I have one more question before you go, Falan."

"Anything, boyo."

"Bridget?"

"I wondered when you'd ask after her."

"How is she?"

Falan smiled. "She's a delegate in the Highland Adjunct. The wee one's a sturdy lad, like his da."

"And has the lad a new da?"

"No, Jimmy. Bridget has refused me and at least a dozen others. She's a very determined woman."

The reason Jimmy loved her. "Will she attend the formalities?"

"Aye. She wants to see you."

Probably not nearly as much as he desired to see her.

EPILOGUE
Chapter Two
Sector One/America Prime

Acting-President Ahmed Fared paced the whole of his private quarters in the Presidential Palace. Time to put the past to rest. He took the Renoir off its perch, gripped the antique letter opener, sliced open the linen backing, removed a miniature micro disc from inside the frame, and tossed the device into the fireplace. Let fire consume fire. The late Edwin Milton Rowlands would now be required to give an account to a higher power.

Ahmed squeezed himself into the chair he'd brought over from his former office. He closed his eyes. Soon, he would make his first address as the duly elected President of United Earth. What should he say?

Sidney knocked. "Come in."

He was glad Sidney opted to stay on—with a stipend at Ahmed's insistence and a letter of emancipation. Poor meme wouldn't know what to do with retirement. He held a box in his large hands. "Sir, here is the package you requested from your old quarters."

"Thank you. You may put the box on the table. That will be all."

"Very good, sir."

Sidney deposited the container, turned and left. Ahmed removed Esther's teapot and placed her gift on the fireplace mantel then rehung the Renoir. He'd have the frame repaired and claim the back caught on a nail. In fact, he would have the whole den remodeled. Maybe design the room around both the Renoir and the teapot.

As he recalled Esther's stories of how both she and this timeless work of art endured so many uncertain days, inspiration filled him. He remembered a day long ago, the day he came to live as a member of Ambassador Goodayle's household. Even then the scholarly Jacob quoted Scripture, a boy's attempt to ease another child's grown-up pain. These were the words Ahmed would give a hopeful world …

While the earth remaineth, seedtime and harvest, and cold and heat, and summer and winter, and day and night shall not cease.

THE END

ABOUT THE AUTHOR

Award winning author, LINDA WOOD RONDEAU, writes to demonstrate that our worst past when surrendered to God, becomes our best future. A veteran social worker, Linda now resides in Hagerstown, Maryland. When not writing, she enjoys playing golf with her best friend in life, Steve, her husband of forty years. Readers may visit her website at www.lindarondeau.com. Contact the author on Facebook, Twitter, Pinterest, Google Plus and Goodreads.